STARDUST IN THEIR VEINS

LAURA SEBASTIAN

DELACORTE PRESS

Text copyright © 2023 by Laura Sebastian
Front cover portrait copyright © 2023 by Lilian Liu
Jacket frame used under license from Venimo/Shutterstock.com
Map art copyright © 2023 by Virginia Allyn

Visit us on the Web! GetUnderlined.com
Educators and librarians, for a variety of teaching tools, visit us at RHTeachersLibrarians.com

Library of Congress Cataloging-in-Publication Data is available upon request.
ISBN 978-0-593-11820-7 (trade) — ISBN 978-0-593-11821-4 (lib. bdg.) —
ISBN 978-0-593-11822-1 (ebook) — ISBN 978-0-593-65029-5 (int'l. ed.)

The text of this book is set in 11.6 point Sabon MT Pro.
Interior design by Jen Valero

Printed in the United States of America
1st Printing
First Edition

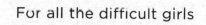

For all the difficult girls

WALDER MOUNTAINS

ESTER RIVER

CHANCELLY LAKE

GARINE FOREST

FRIV

THE
SILVAN ISLES

TEMARIN

Vixania Ocean

VELLINA RIVER

LAKE BELISTA

AMIVEL WOODS

ILLIVEN RIVER

KAVELLE

MERIN RIVER

TENIN RIVER

CALIMA LAKE

ALDER MOUNTAINS

VESTERIA

Avelene
Sea

The Royal Families of Vesteria

Bessemia
House of Soluné

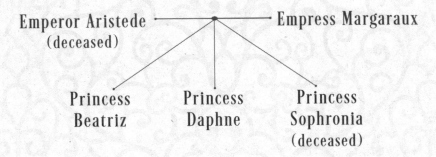

Emperor Aristede (deceased) — Empress Margaraux

Princess Beatriz · Princess Daphne · Princess Sophronia (deceased)

Friv
House of Deasún

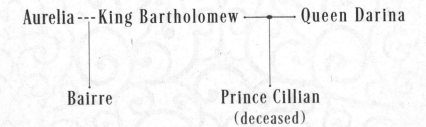

Aurelia --- King Bartholomew — Queen Darina

Bairre · Prince Cillian (deceased)

Cellaria

House of Noctelli

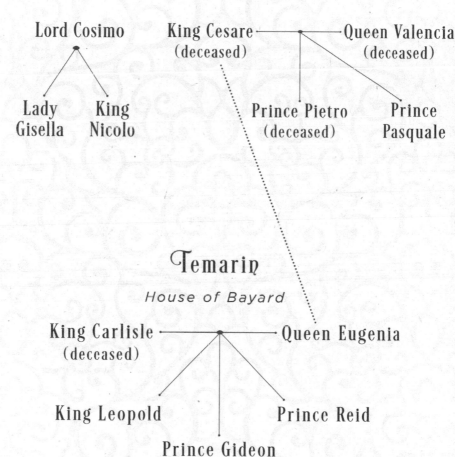

Lord Cosimo

Lady Gisella
King Nicolo

King Cesare
(deceased)

Queen Valencia
(deceased)

Prince Pietro
(deceased)

Prince Pasquale

Temarin

House of Bayard

King Carlisle
(deceased)

Queen Eugenia

King Leopold

Prince Gideon

Prince Reid

Beatriz

Beatriz paces her cell at the Cellarian Sororia nestled in the Alder Mountains, ten steps from wall to wall. It has been five days since she was brought here, sealed away in this sparse chamber with only a narrow bed, a threadbare blanket, and a pitcher of water set on a small wooden stool. It has been five days since she heard her sisters' voices in her head, as clearly as if they were standing in the room beside her. Five days since she heard Sophronia die.

No. No, she doesn't know that, not really. There were a dozen explanations for it, a dozen ways Beatriz could make herself believe that her sister was still out there, still alive. Whenever Beatriz closes her eyes, she sees Sophronia. In the silence of her room, she hears her laughter. Whenever she manages to sleep for a few hours, her nightmares are haunted by the last words she spoke.

They're cheering for my execution. . . . There is so much more at play than we realized. I still don't understand all of it, but please be careful. I love you both so much. I love you all the way to the stars. And I—

And that had been all.

Beatriz doesn't understand the magic that made the communication possible—that was Daphne, who'd done it once before to speak with Beatriz alone. The magic had cut out then, too, but it was different the second time, like she could still feel Daphne's presence a few seconds longer, her stunned silence echoing in Beatriz's mind before she too cut out.

But Sophronia can't be dead. The thought is unfathomable. They came into the world together: Beatriz, Daphne, then Sophronia. Surely none of them could leave it alone.

No matter how many times Beatriz tells herself that, though, she never fully believes it. She *felt* it, after all, like a heart clawed out of her chest. Like something vital lost.

The sound of the lock scraping open echoes in Beatriz's cell and she turns toward the door, expecting one of the Sisters to bring her next meal, but the woman who enters is empty-handed.

"Mother Ellaria," Beatriz says, her voice rough after so little use these past days.

Mother Ellaria is the Sister who greeted Beatriz upon her arrival, leading her to her cell and giving her a change of clothes that look identical to what the older woman wears herself. Of those clothes, Beatriz has only put on the gray wool dress. The headdress still sits at the foot of her bed.

In Bessemia, it was a great honor for Sisters to don their headdresses. There were ceremonies for them—Beatriz herself had attended several. It was a celebration to honor a woman's choice to devote herself to the stars above all else.

But Beatriz has chosen nothing, so the headdress remains off.

Mother Ellaria notes this, her eyes moving from Beatriz's messily braided red hair to the headdress sitting on the bed. She frowns before looking at Beatriz once more.

"You have a visitor," she says, disapproval filling every syllable.

"Who?" Beatriz asks, but Mother Ellaria doesn't answer, instead turning and walking out of the room, leaving Beatriz no choice but to follow her down the dark hallway, her imagination running wild.

For an instant, Beatriz imagines it is Sophronia—that her sister has traveled from Temarin to assure her that she's alive and well. But it's far more likely to be her onetime friend Gisella, come to gloat again, or Gisella's twin brother, Nico, here to see if a few days in the Sororia have changed her mind about his proposal.

If that's the case, he'll leave disappointed. Much as she hates it here, she prefers it to returning to the Cellarian palace while Pasquale lives out the rest of his life in the Fraternia on the other side of the Azina River.

Her chest tightens at the thought of Pasquale—disinherited and imprisoned because she convinced him to trust the wrong people.

They haven't seen the last of us, Pasquale said after their sentence for treason had been handed down. *And soon enough, they'll wish they'd killed us when they had a chance.*

She lets the words echo in her mind as she follows Mother Ellaria down the dimly lit hallway, running through a mental list of all the ways she could overtake the frail older woman and escape . . . but escape where? The Alder Mountains are treacherous terrain even for those who are prepared to scale them. If Beatriz were to escape, alone, with nothing more than a dress and cotton slippers, she wouldn't stand a chance of living through the night.

Her mother always cautioned patience, and while it has never been Beatriz's strength, she knows it's necessary now. So she keeps her hands at her sides and trails after Mother Ellaria as she rounds a corner, then another before stopping at a tall wooden door and fixing Beatriz with a withering look, like she's caught the scent of something rotten. Though Beatriz knows the woman dislikes her, she doesn't think she's responsible for that particular look.

"Due to the . . . status of your guest, I've allowed the use of my own office for your meeting, but I will return in ten minutes, not a second more."

Beatriz nods, even more certain that it will be Gisella or Nicolo awaiting her—Nicolo, after all, is King of Cellaria now, and as his sister, Gisella's status has been elevated as well, though Mother Ellaria might disapprove of them every bit as much as she disapproves of Beatriz.

Ignoring those thoughts, Beatriz steels herself and pushes the door open, stepping inside. She immediately stops short, blinking as if the figure before her might disappear.

But no matter how many times she blinks, Nigellus remains. Her mother's empyrea has made himself at home in Mother Ellaria's chair and watches her over steepled fingers as she enters. Her cell has no windows, and Beatriz lost track of the time of day soon after she arrived, but now she can see that it's nighttime, the full moon shining through the window behind Nigellus, the stars brighter and bolder than usual.

It is the first time she has seen them in five days, the first time she has felt their light dance upon her skin. She feels dizzy with it, gripping her hands into fists at her sides. Magic, she thinks, though she still can't quite believe it, even though she's used her power twice now, accidentally, to call on the stars.

Nigellus notices the white-knuckled flex of her hands, but he doesn't say anything. The door closes behind Beatriz, leaving them alone, but for a moment they only look at each other, silence stretching between them.

"Sophronia's dead, isn't she?" Beatriz asks, breaking the silence first.

Nigellus doesn't answer right away, but after what feels like an eternity, he nods.

"Queen Sophronia was executed five days ago," he says, his voice level and without any kind of inflection. "Along with most of the Temarinian nobility. Your mother had armies waiting at the border and amid the chaos, they seized the capital. With no ruler to surrender, she's simply claimed it as her own."

Beatriz sinks into the chair opposite the desk, all of the life leaving her in that moment. Sophronia is dead. She should have been prepared, should have expected that. Didn't their mother always tell them never to ask a question they didn't know the answer to? But hearing her biggest fear confirmed saps everything from her. Beatriz feels like a husk of a person.

"Sophie's dead," she says again, not caring about the rest of it. Not caring about her mother or her armies or the new crown she's added to her collection.

"It is by pure luck that you and Daphne are not," Nigellus says, drawing her out of her thoughts.

She looks up at him, wondering what he would do if she were to launch herself across the desk and pummel him. Before she can, though, he continues.

"It isn't a coincidence, Beatriz," he says. "The rebellions, the plots, the dead kings. The chaos."

"Of course not," Beatriz says, lifting her chin. "Mother raised us to create chaos, to plot, to stoke fires of rebellion."

"She raised you to die," Nigellus corrects.

The breath leaves Beatriz's lungs, but after a moment, she nods. "Yes, I suppose she did," she says, because it makes sense. "She must be terribly disappointed to have only gotten one out of three."

"Your mother is playing a long game," Nigellus says, shaking his head. "She's waited seventeen years. She can wait a little longer."

Beatriz swallows. "Why are you telling me this? To taunt me? I'm locked away in this miserable place. Isn't that enough?"

Nigellus considers his next words carefully. "Do you know how I've lived this long, Beatriz?" he asks. He doesn't give her a chance to answer. "By not underestimating anyone. I'm not about to start with you."

Beatriz laughs. "I might not be dead, but I can assure you, my mother's beaten me quite soundly."

Even as she says the words, Beatriz doesn't believe them. She promised Pasquale they would find a way out of this, and she knows that is the truth. But it is far better that

Nigellus—and by extension the empress—believe her to be hopelessly broken.

Nigellus surprises her by shaking his head, a wry smile curling his lips. "You aren't beaten, Beatriz. I think we both know that. You're waiting to strike out, picking your moment." Beatriz purses her lips but doesn't deny it. He continues. "I'd like to help you."

Beatriz considers him for a moment. She does not trust him, has never liked him, and there is a part of her that still feels like a child in his presence, small and afraid. But she is trapped in a deep hole and he is offering her a rope. There is nothing to lose by taking hold of it.

"Why?" she asks him.

Nigellus leans across the desk, resting on his elbows. "We have the same eyes, you know," he says. "I'm sure you heard the rumors in Bessemia, that you and your sisters were fathered by me."

If that was a rumor, it had never made it to Beatriz's ears. But he's right—his eyes are like hers, like Daphne's are, like Sophronia's were: a pure, distilled silver. Star-touched, the eyes of children whose parents wished for them using stardust or, in much rarer cases, when an empyrea wished on a star, causing it to fall from the sky. When Beatriz was sent to Cellaria, her mother gave her eye drops to hide the hue of her eyes, a hue that would mark her as a heretic in a country that viewed star magic as sacrilegious. When she was sent to the Sororia, she wasn't allowed to bring any possessions with her, including the eye drops, so her eyes have returned to their natural silver, but she supposes that after using a wish to break a man out of prison, star-touched eyes are the least of her problems.

As if reading her mind, Nigellus nods. "We have been touched by stars, you and I. Made, in part, by the stars. Your mother wished for you and your sisters, and I pulled down stars to make her wish come true. I assume my own mother used stardust to wish for me, though she died before I could ask her."

Your mother wished for you. It was a rumor Beatriz had heard, of course, but while wishing with stardust was relatively common, the wishes empyreas made on stars, bringing them down from the sky in the process, created strong enough magic to make miracles happen. Miracles like her mother becoming pregnant with triplets when her father had notoriously never before fathered a child, legitimate or not even with the assistance of copious amounts of stardust, in his eighty years. But even though an empyrea wishing on stars is rare, because stars themselves are a finite resource, Beatriz isn't surprised her mother crossed that line. If anything, it is one of the smallest trespasses she's made.

"And," Nigellus continues, watching her closely, "being star-touched sometimes comes with its own gift from the stars."

Beatriz forces her face to remain impassive, her thoughts sealed away. Twice now she has wished upon the stars and twice those wishes have come true, leaving stardust in their wake. One in ten thousand people can bring down the stars with magic—Beatriz never thought she'd be one of them, yet now she is sure of it. But they are in Cellaria, where sorcery is a crime punishable by execution, and Nigellus has already admitted that her mother wants her dead. She isn't about to hand him a dagger to turn on her.

"If every silver-eyed child were an empyrea, the world would be a mad place," she says after a moment.

"Not every silver-eyed child," he says, shaking his head. "Not every star-touched child—in most the talent lies dormant, like in your sisters, never woken. But it isn't dormant in you."

When Beatriz's expression doesn't change, his eyebrows lift. "You know," he says, leaning back in his chair and looking at her with appraising eyes. "How many times have you done it?"

"Twice," she admits. "Both times accidentally."

"That's how it is at first," he says. "The magic comes in fits, often brought on by extreme bouts of emotion."

Beatriz thinks of the first time she called on the stars, when she was so overcome with homesickness she thought it might break her. And the second time, when she wanted nothing more in the world than for Nicolo to kiss her. Painful as it is to admit now, in light of his betrayal, she knows she was quite overcome with emotion then, too. She was such a fool.

"It doesn't matter what talents I may or may not have," she says, pushing to her feet. "They suspect what I can do and so I'm kept in a windowless room all night. Unless you have a way of getting me out of this place—"

"I do," he interrupts, inclining his head toward her. "If you agree to my offer, you and I will walk out of here tomorrow night. You could be back in Bessemia in just a few days."

Beatriz tilts her head, eyeing him thoughtfully for a

moment as she weighs his offer. It isn't that it is a bad one, but she suspects she can push him further. "No."

Nigellus snorts. "You don't even know what I want," he says.

"It doesn't matter. I don't want you and me to walk out of here. If you're getting me out, you need to get Pasquale out as well."

Beatriz doesn't know if she's ever seen Nigellus surprised, but he's surprised now. "The Cellarian prince?" he asks, frowning.

"My husband," she says, because while the marriage has never been consummated—never will be consummated—they made vows to each other, both during and after their wedding. And they are vows Beatriz intends to keep. "He's being held by the Fraternia on the other side of the Azina River, just as I am here, on trumped-up charges of treason."

Nigellus gives her a knowing look. "From what I've heard, the charges had merit."

Beatriz clenches her jaw but doesn't deny it. They had plotted to overthrow Pasquale's mad father, that was true. Treason might even be considered a modest description—they'd also taken part in a jailbreak of another traitor, and Beatriz was guilty of violating Cellaria's religious laws by using magic. "All the same. If you can get both of us out, then maybe we can talk about your terms."

Nigellus pauses for a moment before nodding. "Very well. I will get you and your prince to safety, out of Cellaria."

She looks at Nigellus, trying to size him up, but it is impossible. There is no understanding Nigellus, and she would be a fool if she didn't expect that he is two steps ahead of her, playing a game she doesn't know the rules of. They are not on the same side in this, they do not have the same goals.

She should not trust him. But she doesn't have a choice.

"We have a deal."

Daphne

D aphne is getting married tomorrow and there are approximately a thousand things that need tending to. The wedding was already postponed to allow her to heal after she'd been shot in the woods outside the castle, but her wound is gone now—with a little help from the empyrea, Aurelia's, star magic—and everyone is anxious to see her and Bairre wed. No one more so, perhaps, than Daphne herself.

She wrote to her mother as soon as she'd returned to the castle, telling her about Bairre's and Aurelia's revelations, though she stopped short of recounting the moments she, Beatriz, and Sophronia had spent in one another's heads, or the nagging suspicion she has that she both heard and felt Sophronia die. She knows it's illogical, but as long as she doesn't put what she felt into words, it fails to be real.

Besides, there are seating charts to finalize and a gown that needs a final fitting and so many guests filling the castle from all over Friv who Daphne needs to socialize with. She has no time at all to think about her possibly dead sister.

Oh, Sophronia sneaks into her thoughts constantly—the florist suggests adding daisies to her bouquet, which were

Sophronia's favorite, a highland lord tells her a ghost story that would have terrified Sophronia, her maid picks out a dainty opal necklace for Daphne to wear that Sophronia bought her for their fifteenth birthday. At least a dozen times a day, Daphne finds herself mentally drafting a letter to her sister, only for the memory of their last conversation to stop her cold.

She doesn't *know* Sophronia is dead. That's what Bairre told her when the connection to her sisters snapped and she found herself back in Aurelia's cottage with Aurelia and Bairre. He tried so hard to reassure her and she pretended to let him, but when she met Aurelia's gaze, she knew the woman understood the truth of it just as well as she did.

The blood of stars and majesty spilled. Sophronia, with the blood of emperors and stars in her veins, was dead, just as the stars had foretold.

But Daphne cannot think about that now. Just as she cannot think about the fact that assassins have tried three times to kill her. Just as she cannot think about Bairre, with plenty of secrets of his own, who now knows a few of hers and still somehow wants her anyway. She cannot think about Beatriz, knee-deep in her own trouble in Cellaria. If she thinks about any of those things, she will fall apart, so instead she focuses on tomorrow, on finally accomplishing the one thing she was raised for and the one thing she can control—marrying the Crown Prince of Friv.

"I've never seen a bride looking so perturbed," Cliona says to her.

The other girl practically forced her into a walk in the snow-covered gardens of Eldevale Castle—Daphne would have preferred to stay inside, going over every detail of the planning for tomorrow and anxiously waiting for any word to arrive from Temarin, Cellaria, or Bessemia. It is a strange thing, to know her sister is dead but to be unable to mourn her yet.

"No?" Daphne asks, glancing at the other girl with raised eyebrows. "I don't think I've seen a bride looking anything but."

She can't help but glance back over her shoulder to where six guards now follow her every move. It was two the last time they walked in this garden, and before that there had been none at all, but with the wedding so close and someone so determined to kill Daphne, King Bartholomew has ordered her guard increased.

Daphne knows she should be grateful for it, but their constant presence chafes. Besides, Cliona has as good a reason to want her dead as anyone, and surely she could wedge a dagger between Daphne's ribs before any of the six guards could manage a step, if they even bothered, since Daphne would wager at least half are working for Cliona's father, Lord Panlington, the leader of the rebels.

The thought should alarm Daphne, but it doesn't. Enemies are everywhere, after all, and there is some comfort in knowing Cliona for what she is: the daughter of the head of the rebellion, every bit as deadly and manipulative as Daphne herself.

Maybe that's why Daphne likes her.

Besides, Daphne knows the rebels don't want her dead— not yet, at least. Not when they have Bairre himself on their side. Not when they think they have Daphne, too.

"Most brides are anxious, maybe," Cliona concedes. "But not ill—you're pale as a ghost."

"The Frivian weather is to blame for that," Daphne says, turning her gaze up to the gray sky. Now that winter has fully settled in, there isn't a hint of blue. "It's been so long since I've felt sunshine on my skin, I've forgotten what it feels like."

Cliona laughs, the sound light and breezy even as she drops her voice and gives Daphne's arm a squeeze. "Well, you'll be back in Bessemia soon enough, I'm sure."

Daphne cuts a sideways glance toward her—Cliona should know better than to speak like that in front of the guards. In fact, Cliona must know better. Which confirms her suspicion that at least most of the guards are on her side.

"I'm assuming, then," Daphne says, matching Cliona both in tone and volume, "that there isn't going to be a wedding tomorrow after all."

Cliona smiles. "Oh, the less you know about that the better, Princess," she says. "Do try to look a little more like the blushing bride you're meant to be, though, will you? It shouldn't be too difficult, given how cozy things have become between you and Bairre."

At that, Daphne does indeed feel a blush rise to her cheeks, but she tells herself it's only the bite of the Frivian winter wind. It has nothing at all to do with the memory of Bairre's lips brushing over hers or the way he said her name, full of reverence and the smallest hint of fear.

Over the last few days, there's been no time to talk about the kiss, or anything else, really. Her guards are usually present and it isn't a conversation either of them wants to have with an audience.

She's surprised that Cliona has managed to pick up on anything different between them, and she wonders with a blossoming horror if it's something she and Bairre have talked about. Bairre is working with the rebels, after all. He and Cliona have likely had a good many conversations about her. If she's lucky, that kiss is the worst of what they discussed.

"Oh, there's no need for that glower," Cliona says, rolling her eyes. "Just smile a little bit. I promise it won't kill you."

At that, Daphne lets her mouth twist into a sardonic smile. "A questionable choice of words, Cliona. All things considered."

Cliona shrugs. "Oh, after what I saw in the forest, I pity anyone who tries to kill you. It seems to be a dangerous pastime."

"I'm sorry, remind me which one of us slit a man's throat?" Daphne asks.

"I'm only saying I misjudged you, Daphne," Cliona says. "I didn't think you'd last a week in Friv, but here you are, doing quite well for yourself."

It's close to a compliment, and it makes Daphne uncomfortable. "Well, as you said, I'll be gone soon enough."

"Yes," Cliona agrees. "And I think I might just miss you."

The other girl says the words lightly, but a quick glance confirms she meant them. Something tightens in Daphne's chest and she realizes she'll miss Cliona as well. She's never really had a friend before, only sisters.

Before Daphne can respond, the head of her guard gives a shout and the rest of the men draw their weapons, their attention focused on a hooded figure approaching. Daphne can just barely make him out between the bodies of the guards that surround her, but she immediately knows who it is.

"It's only the prince," she says, just as Bairre pulls back his hood to reveal overgrown dark brown hair and his recognizable sharp features. The guards part and Bairre steps toward Daphne, his eyes on her even as he gives Cliona a quick nod.

"Daphne," he says, and something in his voice immediately sets her on edge. "There's a letter."

Her heart drops. "From Temarin?" she asks. "About Sophronia?"

She can't read it, she thinks. She can't read the words. Some part of her knows her sister is dead, but seeing it spelled out in an elegant hand with perfunctory sympathy? She cannot stomach it.

Bairre shakes his head, but the crease doesn't leave his brow. "From your mother," he says, and perhaps that should reassure her, but the way he says it, she knows he's already read it. And she knows it is far worse.

"Where is it?" she hears herself ask.

"In your bedroom," he tells her, glancing back at the guards. "I thought you'd want privacy."

My dearest Daphne,

It is with a heavy heart that I must tell you that our dear Sophronia was executed by rebels in Temarin. Fear not—this grave injustice has been repaid and I have already taken hold of the Temarinian throne and seen each person responsible for this heinous act put to death. I know this will bring you little consolation, but I am told her suffering was light and her death swift.

As a mother, there is no greater sadness than burying a child, though I know that what you are feeling now is certainly close. I know I will be relying on you and Beatriz all the more for comfort.

I am told that King Leopold managed to flee the palace before the rebels could execute him alongside Sophronia, though there has been no sign of him since. If word of him reaches you, please let me know, as I am sure he will be wanting his throne back.

Your devoted mama,
Empress Margaraux

Daphne reads the words three times, all the while aware of Bairre and Cliona watching her. The first time, she simply takes in the message—Sophronia dead, executed by rebels, Temarin under Bessemian rule, the rebels who killed her dead. The second time, she looks for a sign that it is coded, but finds none. On the third read-through, she focuses on what her mother says beneath the words themselves.

I have already taken hold of the Temarinian throne.

Well, that was always the plan, wasn't it? Admittedly, it was done quicker than Daphne thought possible, and Sophronia was meant to be there to welcome her mother's armies.

The thought sours Daphne's stomach, but she pushes it aside to focus on the letter.

I know I will be relying on you and Beatriz all the more for comfort.

That, Daphne is sure of, though she doubts comfort will play any part of it. No, without Sophronia, Daphne and Beatriz will have to work that much harder to aid the empress's plans. Daphne thinks of Beatriz—under house arrest at the Vallon palace, last she heard, in large part because she, like Sophronia, went against their mother's orders. If her mother didn't know of that when she penned this letter, she certainly does now, which means even more rests on Daphne's shoulders. She turns her attention to the part about King Leopold.

I am told that King Leopold managed to flee the palace before the rebels could execute him alongside Sophronia, though there has been no sign of him since.

So, Leopold escaped. Daphne hates him for that. How could he survive when her sister didn't? Sophronia did mention him the last time they spoke, saying that her friends were coming—Leopold and Violie. But surely they would go to Beatriz rather than her, given Leopold's family connections to the royal family there. Perhaps she should tell her mother that, but she doesn't know how she could without revealing all of Sophronia's final words, and the fact that she spoke them at all. The prospect of sharing those moments with anyone else makes Daphne feel ill.

One thing Daphne is sure of, though: her mother has no intention of giving Leopold his throne back, much as she might pretend otherwise. She also notices that there is no mention of Leopold's brothers, though Daphne knows he has two. If he is dead, the throne should by all rights pass to one of them, and Daphne knows her mother won't allow that to happen.

Daphne looks up from the letter, glancing between Bairre and Cliona.

"My sister is dead," she says.

It isn't the first time she's said those words out loud. She said them to Bairre and Aurelia as soon as she surfaced from her conversation with Sophronia and Beatriz, her voice then choked with tears. This time, she says the words calmly, though she still feels them threaten to strangle her.

Bairre isn't surprised, but Cliona is. Her brow furrows and she takes a step toward Daphne, like she might embrace her, stopping short when Daphne holds her hand up. Daphne doesn't want to be touched right now, doesn't want to be comforted. If anyone touches her, she will fall apart, and she cannot allow that. Instead, she draws herself up straight and crumples the letter in her hand.

"Executed by rebels," she adds. A touch of venom must leak in, because Cliona stumbles back a step.

It was a detail Daphne didn't know before, one that cuts all the deeper because here she is, conspiring with rebels herself. She knows it isn't logical, that Cliona and Bairre and the other Frivian rebels had nothing to do with Sophronia's death, but the spark of anger feels good. It is the only thing that does, so she clings to it.

"Temarinian rebels," Bairre points out, logical as always, but for once Daphne doesn't want logic.

"Sophronia was a gullible sort," she says, pushing her shoulders back. "She trusted those she shouldn't have."

She doesn't know how true that is, but as soon as she speaks the words aloud she believes them. It makes sense, it is a tangible thing she can latch onto, a place to lay blame. Sophronia trusted the wrong people. Those people are dead now. Her mother was right—the knowledge brings her little consolation, but consolation all the same.

"Daphne," Bairre says, his voice wary.

"I'm sorry about your loss," Cliona says. "But the Temarinian radicals were rash fools who had no plan beyond executing those they viewed as the elite. You know it isn't the same thing," she adds, tilting her head to one side. "Besides, it's a bit late to turn back now." The flash of tenderness is gone and Cliona is back to her usual sharp-edged self. Daphne is grateful for it.

"I think we're past that," Daphne says. "But still you should know that I am not my sister." Daphne can feel her hands start to shake, feel her throat begin to tighten. She is a mere breath from falling apart, and she refuses to do it with them here watching. The shame of that might just kill her.

Cliona watches her for a moment and gives a curt nod. "You'll want time to grieve," she says. "Bairre and I will pass the news along to the king and give your excuses for dinner."

Daphne nods, but she doesn't trust herself to speak. If she does, she isn't sure what will come out. Cliona slips out of the room, but Bairre lingers a moment longer, his eyes on Daphne.

"I'm fine," she bites out. "It isn't exactly a surprise, is it? I knew she . . . I knew she was gone."

Bairre shakes his head. "I knew Cillian was dying," he says, and Daphne remembers when they first met, mere days after he'd lost his own brother. "I knew it for a long time. But it didn't make it hurt any less when he was really, truly gone."

Daphne presses her lips together into a thin line. Part of her wants to close the distance between them and throw herself into his arms. If she did, he would hold her, comfort her. But to do so would show weakness, and Daphne cannot bear the thought of that.

"Thank you," she says instead. "I don't think your father will be keen to postpone the wedding again, what with all of the highlanders here already. Please assure him I will be well enough to go through with it tomorrow."

For a moment, Bairre looks like he wants to say something, but he thinks better of it. He gives another nod before slipping out of the same door Cliona passed through, closing it firmly behind him.

But even when he is gone and Daphne is well and truly alone, she can't cry. Instead, she lies in bed and stares at the ceiling and hears Sophronia's final words echo over and over in her mind.

I love you all the way to the stars.

Violie

I n her time working in the Temarinian palace, Violie grew used to a measure of comfort, even as a servant: her bed was always soft and large enough for her to sprawl out on with ease, her clothing was always freshly laundered, she bathed every other day. After five days in the Amivel Woods, she knows she will never take those little luxuries for granted ever again.

Still, she is at least managing better than King Leopold, who, Violie suspects, has never experienced a moment of even slight discomfort in his life.

Well, that isn't fair, she reasons with herself. She is sure he was uncomfortable enough when Ansel was holding him prisoner during the palace siege. When he first appeared out of thin air in the cave deep in the Amivel Woods where Violie and Sophronia had agreed to meet, his wrists were red and chafed raw from being bound for so long, and Violie used a strip of material from her dress and clean water from the nearby Merin River to tend to them while he told her what had happened.

Sophronia had lied to her—lied to both of them. She had never intended to save herself, only ever Leopold. Violie couldn't even bring herself to be truly angry about it—after all, she had lied to Sophronia more often than she'd spoken truth. Violie only wishes Sophronia had been selfish for once in her life, though that would be akin to wishing the stars didn't shine.

Violie watches Leopold now, as he sleeps on a bale of hay next to her in a small, empty barn beside a cottage that appeared abandoned—a farm, once, she supposes. There is no sign of life now—neither animal nor human.

But the barn remains, at least, and the few bales of hay left inside make a more comfortable bed than either of them has found over the last few days.

Sophronia was so enamored with Leopold, Violie thinks, watching his relaxed expression. His bronze hair tousled and dirtier than it's likely ever been, dark circles beneath his eyes, his mouth hanging open slightly. She was so in love with him that she gave her own life for his.

It isn't fair of Violie to resent him for that, but she does all the same. And now she is saddled with a useless king—a useless king with a bounty on his head, no less, and plenty of people who would rather kill him themselves than claim it.

Not for the first time, Violie considers leaving him behind. She could sneak away before he wakes up and he would never be able to find her, if he bothered looking at all. She would be free of him, free to return to her mother, free of any responsibility to anyone else.

Promise me that no matter what happens, you'll take care of Leopold.

Sophronia's voice comes back to her, extracting a promise

Violie never thought she'd have to keep, not like this. But she promised all the same.

Leopold's eyes flutter open slowly, a frown creasing his brow, just as it does every morning, as he takes in his strange surroundings. Then they find her and she watches again as the last six days filter back to him. She watches his eyes widen, his jaw tense, his heart break. Just as it does every morning when he remembers Sophronia is dead.

Violie doesn't have to remind herself. In her nightmares, she sees it happen again and again, watches as Sophronia, wan and unkempt from days as a prisoner, is led up the steps to the scaffold, watches as the executioner guides her head to the wooden block, wet with the blood of all those who came before her, watches as the silver blade of the guillotine falls, severing Sophronia's head from her body while the crowd around Violie and Leopold cheers.

Sophronia didn't even scream. She didn't cry or beg for her life. In that moment, she seemed to be miles away, and that, Violie tells herself, was the only small blessing the stars gave her.

No, Violie never forgets, not even when she sleeps.

"We'll reach the Alder Mountains today," she says, even though she's sure Leopold knows this. She needs to say something to fill the awkward silence that so often envelops them. They were strangers last week—Violie doesn't think he so much as glanced at her when she was Sophronia's lady's maid. Now, each of them is all the other has, the two of them bound together by Sophronia's final act.

Leopold nods but doesn't speak, so Violie feels compelled to continue, to fill the silence. "There's a popular trading route near the sea," she says. "We'll have better luck making our way through there than trying to scale the mountains themselves. We should take a look at the cottage before we leave, though. I don't think anyone has been here in a while, and perhaps there is some food or something we can sell—"

She breaks off at Leopold's horrified expression.

"You want me to steal from my own people?" he asks.

Violie grits her teeth. "They aren't your people, not right now, at least," she says. "And if you die in the Alder Mountains, you'll never rule Temarin again."

"I don't care, I can't just—"

"I promised Sophronia I would keep you safe," she says. "Are you going to let her sacrifice go to waste to honor principles that are, if you don't mind my saying it, entirely worthless at this point?"

It's a low blow, but it lands and Leopold's jaw clenches. Over the last few days, Violie has learned that the mention of Sophronia is a surefire way to silence him, though it's one that leaves her feeling a bit unmoored as well.

The urge to apologize rises up, but before she can, a sound outside the barn draws their attention—footsteps.

Violie hastens to grab the dagger she keeps in arm's reach always—this time it's embedded in the bale of hay just beside where she slept. On light feet, she tiptoes to the barn door and hears the low murmur of voices speaking . . . Cellarian?

Her mastery of the language isn't as strong as her knowledge of Bessemian or Temarinian, but she recognizes the sound of it.

She frowns, glancing at Leopold, who must hear it as well, because he looks equally perplexed. While they're close to the Alder Mountains, which serve as the southern border between Temarin and Cellaria, there isn't much travel back and forth between the countries apart from tradesmen, and they are far from any main roads tradesmen might take.

The footsteps and voices draw closer, and Violie presses herself to the wall beside the door, while Leopold crouches low behind a bale of hay, a large stick he's been using as a makeshift weapon in his hands.

The door creaks open and two men step inside, one who looks middle-aged and the other around Violie and Leopold's age. Both of them look the worse for wear, though Violie notes that their clothes are fine beneath the grime.

It doesn't matter who they are, Violie thinks. Everyone in Temarin is on the lookout for Leopold, the runaway king with a bounty on his head. If these people realize who he is, he and Violie will both be as good as dead. She tightens her grip on her dagger and prepares to pounce, but Leopold's voice stops her.

"Lord Savelle?" he asks, straightening.

The older man turns to Leopold, blinking rapidly as if expecting him to disappear before his eyes. "Your . . . Your Majesty?" he asks. "Surely that can't . . . King Leopold?" he asks, as if saying the name aloud will shatter the illusion.

Leopold drops the stick and shakes his head as if trying to clear it. "It's me," he says. "I thought you were in a Cellarian prison, or dead."

"And I thought you would be in your palace," Lord

Savelle says, looking Leopold over with a furrowed brow. "And much cleaner, too."

"Shortly after we received word of your imprisonment, there was a coup—we barely managed to escape the palace. We were on our way to Cellaria to seek refuge with my cousin."

The younger man shakes his head. "Pasquale and Beatriz were arrested for treason," he says. "We also just managed to escape."

"Stars above," Violie curses, looking toward Leopold, who clears his throat.

"Lord Savelle, this is—"

"No need for introductions, I detect that Bessemian accent," Lord Savelle says, offering Violie an attempt at a smile. "Queen Sophronia, I presume. Your sister saved my life at great cost to herself and I'm eternally grateful."

Violie's heart sinks. She knows she and Sophronia look alike, knows that this is at least part of the reason the empress recruited her, but now that knowledge turns her stomach.

"It seems that's something the girls in that family have in common," she says with a grimace. "I'm afraid Queen Sophronia did not escape the siege at the palace. I was her maid, Violie."

"Queen Sophronia is imprisoned too?" the younger man asks, the Temarinian words thick with a Cellarian accent. He's handsome, with the look of gentry—the sort of boy with soft edges and kindness that hasn't been filed away yet.

Violie and Leopold exchange a loaded look.

"No," Leopold manages after a moment. "No, she was executed."

It isn't something they've ever talked about, not since they rushed back into Kavelle after realizing Sophronia had lied to them about her plans.

Lord Savelle's and his companion's eyes widen. "Surely there must be a mistake," Lord Savelle says.

Violie swallows. Again, she sees the blade fall and Sophronia's blond head roll away from her body. There was so much blood.

"There isn't," she says before turning back to the boy. "Who are you?" she asks.

"Ambrose," he says. "I'm . . . I was . . . Pasquale and I are . . . friends," he manages.

"He helped me escape Cellaria," Lord Savelle explains. "Princess Beatriz used magic to get me out of prison and I met Ambrose and Prince Pasquale at the harbor. Our boat was nearly out of sight when we saw the guards come and arrest Prince Pasquale."

Violie glances at Leopold. "We'll need another plan, then," she says.

"And we will as well," Lord Savelle says. "We were on our way to you, though I suppose now you don't have armies about to invade Cellaria," he adds.

"He doesn't," Violie says. "But the Empress of Bessemia does."

Lord Savelle frowns, looking between Leopold and Violie. "What does Princess Beatriz's mother have to do with it?"

"It's quite a long story," Violie says. "And I certainly could do with a bit of food before telling it."

Ambrose holds up a knapsack. "We bought food with the last of our coin," he says. "You're welcome to it."

"Oh, we couldn't—" Leopold begins, but Violie is too hungry to be polite.

"Thank you," she says.

Over a breakfast of bread and cheese in the kitchen of the abandoned cottage, Violie tells them everything she dares— how the Princesses of Bessemia were trained as spies to further their mother's goal of conquering the continent, how Violie herself was recruited two years ago to spy on Sophronia, who the empress suspected was too weak to follow through, how Sophronia *did* go against her mother, and how the empress coordinated with Leopold's mother, Queen Eugenia, to overthrow Leopold and Sophronia and execute them both.

"I tried to help Sophronia escape, but she insisted she wouldn't leave without Leopold," Violie says as they eat the last of the bread and cheese. "The plan was for her to use a wish her mother had given her and her sisters to send both her and Leopold to meet me in a cave far from the palace—"

"But she knew all along that the wish would only be strong enough to save one of us," Leopold finishes, "and she used it on me before I could stop her."

"The wish . . . a diamond-like bracelet around her wrist?" Lord Savelle asks. Leopold and Violie nod. "Princess Beatriz used hers to save me."

"So we can't count on Cellaria for protection," Leopold says. "We can't stay in Temarin, and Bessemia can't be trusted. Perhaps Friv? Sophronia's sister there might offer help—Daphne."

Violie manages not to make a face, but everything she knows about Princess Daphne tells her that help against the empress would be unlikely. Leopold is right, though—unlikely is the best chance he has of finding protection. Violie, however, isn't interested in protection.

"You three should head to Friv," she tells them, pressing her finger to the wooden table to get every last crumb—who knows where her next meal will come from, after all. "I'll travel on to Cellaria to find Beatriz."

The three of them stare at her, shocked, but to Violie it is a perfect plan. By entrusting Leopold into Lord Savelle's care, she'll no longer have to nanny him, and half her debt to Sophronia will be cleared. If she could rescue Beatriz as well, Violie thinks, Sophronia would consider them even.

Lord Savelle is the first to break the silence, clearing his throat. "When we docked in Temarin, we heard a rumor among some sailors that Princess Beatriz and Prince Pasquale had been sent to a Sororia and a Fraternia in the Alder Mountains," he says. "We'd hoped to gain the support of Temarinian forces before seeking to free them. Trying to do so without an army is . . . well . . ."

"A death sentence," Leopold finishes. "The Alder Mountains alone claim a dozen lives a year, at least, and Cellarian Sororias and Fraternias are practically prisons. You can't simply walk in and out."

"I'll go with you," Ambrose says, taking Violie by surprise, though when she meets his steady gaze, she knows there will be no talking him out of it. She nods.

"No offense, Ambrose, but that isn't terribly reassuring," Leopold says.

Ambrose shrugs. "I'd have turned around and gone back for them as soon as we heard that rumor, but I needed to get Lord Savelle to safety, like I said I would. Violie is right—the two of you should continue on to Friv. We'll return to Cellaria."

"And do what?" Leopold asks.

Violie glances at Ambrose. "I don't know, but it's a few days' journey at least. Plenty of time to figure it out on the way."

Leopold stares at Violie, brow furrowed. After a moment, he gives a quick nod. "Fine, I'm going too."

Violie snorts. "You can't be serious," she says.

"I'm as serious as you are," he says. "You aren't the only one who owes a debt."

Deep down, Violie knows he's right, that she isn't the only one plagued by guilt and haunted by Sophronia's death. For all of Leopold's many faults, he loved her.

"You owe a lot of debts," she counters, pushing aside any sympathy she feels. "Don't you think they'd be better repaid in Friv?"

Leopold holds her gaze, but he doesn't fight back the way she expects. Instead, he sighs. "No," he says. "I don't. Sophronia wanted us to go to Cellaria, to find Beatriz and Pasquale. Their current peril wouldn't have changed her mind, and it doesn't change mine." He turns toward Lord Savelle, whose forehead is creased in thought. "Can you continue on to Friv on your own?"

"No one is looking for me. If I travel alone, I should avoid notice, but there is nothing for me in Friv. I have a distant cousin in the Silvan Isles—in Altia," Lord Savelle adds, naming one of the smaller islands. "I'll wait things out there, and if any of you have need of help or shelter, come find me."

"With what money?" Violie asks. "I thought you said you'd spent your last aster."

Lord Savelle offers her a half smile. "I'm not so old that I can't work for passage, my dear," he says. "I'll swab decks or clean fish if need be."

"Here," Leopold says, digging through his coat and producing a jeweled pin—the one he wore the night of the siege. It's one of the few things he still has, in addition to his signet ring, diamond cuff links, and his velvet cloak with the ruby buckle. While the items are worth enough to keep them fed for a year or more, selling them in Temarin is too risky. Lord Savelle is right, though—no one is looking for him, and after the journey he's had, no one will suspect he's part of the nobility. They'll assume he stole it, and likely praise him for it.

Lord Savelle takes the pin and pockets it. "And you three?" he asks.

"If you can work, so can we," Leopold says, shrugging.

"There was an inn we stopped at on our way here, at the edge of the mountains," Ambrose points out. "They let us wash dishes and muck stables in exchange for dinner and a bed."

"Sounds good to me," Leopold says, and Violie can't help but snort. She doubts Leopold even knows what mucking a stable means. He has no business making this trip. He'll only slow them down and likely complain all the while. She opens her mouth to protest again, but closes it just as quickly.

She promised Sophronia she would keep him safe. Keeping him longer in Temarin with Lord Savelle won't accomplish that, not when the entire country is looking for him. Cellaria is the safest way.

"We shouldn't dally, then," she says, pushing back from the table and standing up. "The cottage might be abandoned, but I don't want to risk crossing paths with anyone else— I doubt they'll be as friendly as you two turned out to be."

Beatriz

Back in her cell, Beatriz sits cross-legged on her cot, the skirt of her long gray dress spread around her and her eyes closed. There wasn't much time to go over everything she needed to know about this new power waking up within her, but Nigellus stressed the importance of concentration and patience—two things that have never been Beatriz's strong suits.

But at least if she sits completely still and keeps her eyes closed, she knows there is little chance she can miss Nigellus's signal. In one hand, she clutches the vial of stardust he passed to her before he left, the glass warm from her skin since she's barely set it down over the last day.

Any moment now, Nigellus will raise the signal. When he does, she has to be ready.

Any moment now.

Any moment.

She opens her eyes just enough to squint around the room. What if she missed it? Maybe it was too quiet to pierce the stone walls of her cell. Maybe—

Before she can finish the thought, a clap of thunder booms loud enough and close enough that the pitcher of water on her table rattles off the edge and shatters on the stone floor.

Beatriz leaps to her feet, unstoppering the vial of stardust and sprinkling it over her hand, remembering the wish Nigellus made her memorize, word for word so there would be no mistakes.

Wishes are tricky, he told her, as if she hadn't used stardust relatively often growing up. Beatriz knows that the key to a successful wish is specificity—magic is like water in a bucket: if any holes exist, magic will find its way through them.

"I wish lightning would strike my cell and make a hole the size of my fist," she says, the words coming out in a rush. As soon as they pass her lips, another clap of thunder sounds outside her cell and stone breaks off from her wall, falling to the ground in a cloud of dust.

Beatriz hurries toward it, her heart pounding in her chest. Already, she can hear the surprised shrieks of the Sisters, and it will only be a matter of time before someone comes to check on her. She peers through the hole in the wall, doing a quick inventory of the constellations she can see—the Lonely Heart, the Raven's Wing, and the False Moon. The Lonely Heart means sacrifice, the Raven's Wing means death—neither of those is a constellation she wishes to draw from tonight, or ever. The False Moon means duplicity—can that be twisted in a way to suit her purpose? She's sure the Sisters will consider her behavior duplicitous.

Before she can make that decision, though, another constellation edges into view from the north and Beatriz lets out a sigh of relief—the Queen's Chalice, which signals luck.

She can see the outline of a goblet, tilted just slightly, as if its contents are threatening to spill.

Well, she can certainly use all the luck she can get. She finds a star at the center of the constellation, the sort of small twinkle of light that fades if you try to look directly at it. The sort Nigellus assured her that few will notice missing, though because it's a smaller star, it will mean a weaker wish.

She was surprised Nigellus would allow her to pull a star from the sky intentionally—even outside Cellaria, that is a sacrilegious act, reserved for the direst of emergencies. But Nigellus pointed out that being locked away in a Sororia in Cellaria when her mother is determined to kill her qualifies as an emergency, and Beatriz wasn't about to disagree with him. There is a part of her, though, that suspects Nigellus could, perhaps, go about freeing her in a less sacrilegious way, with more stardust perhaps. There is a part of her that suspects this also serves as a test for her.

If that is the case, Beatriz can only hope she passes. The last few times she used star magic have been accidental, in moments of heightened emotion. In time, Nigellus assured her, she would be able to better control her power, but for now it will be simplest to replicate those prior incidents and channel her emotions. This time, homesickness and lust are far from her heart. This time, she reaches for anger.

It kindles within her in an instant, hot to the touch and easily stoked. She thinks of Sophronia, executed while she was hundreds of miles away and helpless; she thinks of Gisella and Nicolo, who she trusted only for them to betray her and Pasquale; she thinks of Daphne, who refused to help her or Sophronia and left them to fend for themselves. Anger comes easily, but it isn't enough. Beatriz can feel it, power just past her fingertips no matter how she tries to stretch.

Her heart pounds in her chest—there is no time for half measures, no time to hold back.

Beatriz keeps her gaze focused on the constellation and imagines what will happen when she sees her mother again. After two months in Cellaria, parts of Bessemia have already become a blur, but she sees her mother's face as clearly in her mind as if she is standing before her, perfectly coiffed and powdered, with that same smug smile she always wears.

Did she smile like that when she plotted to kill Sophronia? When she tried to do the same to Beatriz herself? Beatriz's hands clench at her sides as she imagines confronting her mother with that knowledge and laying all of those sins at her mother's feet. The empress won't care, of course, Beatriz knows that, but she will make her care. And then she will make her sorry.

Power wells up in her, filling her chest with heat in a way that feels vaguely familiar, though this is the first time she has recognized it for what it is. She takes a deep breath.

Clear your mind of everything but your wish, Nigellus told her, so Beatriz tries to do just that. She latches onto her wish, holds it tight, and forgets everything else.

I wish Nigellus, Pasquale, and I were far from here, together in the Alder Mountains.

She repeats the wish over and over in her mind, mutters it under her breath. She closes her eyes and sees the words on the backs of her eyelids. They burn themselves into her soul.

Frigid air blows over her skin and she opens her eyes once more, but she is no longer in her cell at the Sororia. Instead, she stands beneath an open, star-strewn sky, her bare feet buried in fresh snow and her wool dress blowing around her legs in the wind.

She is so cold, but she is free.

"Triz," a voice says behind her, and she whirls around, a laugh bubbling up in her throat before arms come around her, holding her tight—Pasquale's arms.

"Pas," she says, hugging him back. "It worked! It actually worked!"

"What—" Pas begins, but before he can say anything more, another voice interrupts.

"Yes, well done," Nigellus says, holding up two cloaks. "But it will have been a waste of a star if you freeze to death." He passes them each a heavy, fur-lined cloak before reaching into a satchel to pull out two pairs of boots that look to be roughly the right size. "Hurry up now, we've got quite a journey ahead of us, and I'll explain on the way, Prince Pasquale."

Pasquale shrugs on the cloak, but his eyes find Beatriz's, brow furrowed as it so often is. Beatriz realizes how much she missed him and his furrowed brow.

"Who . . . ?" Pasquale asks her.

"Nigellus," she tells him. "My mother's empyrea."

His eyes widen at that—not that Beatriz can blame him. Star magic is outlawed in Cellaria—he's likely never met an empyrea before. Well, apart from her, she supposes, though that label still doesn't feel like it fits her. She doubts it ever will.

"He helped us escape," she says.

"You trust him?" he asks, and Beatriz knows that Nigellus is only pretending not to hear.

"No," she says, quite clearly. "But we have little choice, do we?"

Daphne

Daphne has imagined her wedding often, for as long as she can remember. Her imaginings started off as skeletal daydreams, growing more solid once she attended a few weddings herself and taking on shading and color the more she learned about Friv and its customs. She imagined her wedding dress, how it changed with each season's trends. She imagined a ceremony under the stars, an audience of strangers, and a prince waiting for her at the end of a long aisle. The prince's face changed over the years too, an unrecognizable and unimportant blur that took on Prince Cillian's features once they began exchanging portraits.

As much as she thought about her wedding, though, she spent just as much time dwelling on all the things that would come after. Her mother's plans. Her orders. Her eventual return to Bessemia, triumphant and proven worthy of being the next Empress of Vesteria. Daphne ran over every facet of her future, not only the wedding, but as she stands here now, at the top of the aisle in the castle chapel with the stars shining down through the glass roof, she feels wholly unprepared.

Her gown is nothing like the frothy Bessemian gowns she ogled at the dressmakers' and in fashion plates—the spring-green velvet is unadorned and simple, except for a gray ermine trim at the hem and sleeves, and it hugs her figure without the usual layers of petticoats and cages. The audience is not made up of strangers, either, at least not entirely. She sees King Bartholomew and Cliona's father beside him. Cliona herself sits a row behind, Haimish beside her, though she is studiously ignoring him. There's Rufus, Bairre's friend, as well, seated with his five siblings. There are other courtiers too, ones she recognizes now. Ones she's even come to like.

And then there's Bairre, waiting for her at the end of the aisle, not a featureless face and certainly not Cillian. When his eyes find hers, he smiles slightly and she smiles back, clutching the bouquet of lilies and daisies she carries even tighter as she takes one step closer, then another.

She only glances away from Bairre for an instant, to look at Cliona again, but the other girl gives nothing away, which makes Daphne's stomach twist.

In all of her imaginings of this night, she always knew exactly what would happen. She would walk down the aisle. The empyrea would say a few words. She and her prince would exchange vows. And then it would be done.

But Daphne knows that Cliona and the rebels have something waiting. She knows she will not leave this chapel married. She only hopes she will leave it at all.

Oh, the less you know about that the better, Princess, Cliona said when Daphne asked about the rebels' plans for the wedding, and as annoying as it is to be kept ignorant, she knows Cliona is right. Daphne and Bairre have to be above suspicion, should anything happen.

And something will happen.

Won't it?

Daphne reaches Bairre and he takes her hand in his, but she barely feels it. Her mind is spinning and she's dimly aware of Fergal, the Frivian empyrea, beginning to talk about the stars and their blessings. Any minute now, something will happen. Rebels will charge into the chapel. Star-summoned lightning will strike. Someone will start a fire. Any minute now.

But as Fergal drones on, nothing happens, and some small corner of Daphne's heart stutters.

What if there is nothing? What if the rebels have changed their aims and no longer wish to prevent this wedding? What if they've realized that Daphne's letters about King Bartholomew and Empress Margaraux seeking to unite Friv and Bessemia through Daphne and Bairre were forgeries? What if—

Bairre yanks her toward him so hard that she feels like her arm leaves its socket and she crashes into him, toppling them both to the stone floor just as an explosion tears through the chapel, making her ears ring and raining down shrapnel over both of them. Something hard smacks the back of her head and pain erupts across her skull as her vision fractures.

"Daphne!" Bairre yells, and though she is sprawled over his chest, his mouth a breath from her ear, he still sounds miles away.

"I'm fine," she says, trying to shake off the pain in her head so that she can take an inventory of the rest of her body— her shoulder is bleeding and her ears are still ringing, but nothing feels broken, at least. She pushes up to look at his face. Some bit of shrapnel cut his temple, but apart from that he appears unharmed, though there could be all manner of injuries that can't be seen. "Are you?"

"Fine," he says, though he winces when he says it.

Daphne rolls off him, the pain in her head throbbing, but she forces herself to ignore it and instead take in the pandemonium of the chapel—guests huddled together, clothes bloody and torn, the ceiling above shattered, shards of glass and metal strewn over the ground. Her eyes find King Bartholomew first, but he is safe, crouched down beside Rufus and his siblings, checking on the children. Cliona and Haimish appear unharmed too, though Daphne must admit they are both doing a decent job of appearing startled. Cliona's father is as well, hurrying around the chapel to check on the injured.

Daphne lets out a breath. Everyone is safe, it was merely a stalling tactic . . .

Fergal's severed hand lies inches from her face, drenched in blood and identifiable by the empyrea ring he wears on his right thumb.

The ring he wore on his right thumb, Daphne corrects herself as she forces her gaze up. She sees a leg, then an ear, and then, finally, his head.

The last thing Daphne remembers is screaming.

Daphne comes to with weak predawn light filtering through her window and it takes her a moment to remember what happened—her would-be wedding day, Bairre pulling her out of the way an instant before the explosion, like he knew what would happen, the pain in her head, Fergal's body, blown to pieces.

She didn't know Fergal, really, she certainly won't mourn him, and yet . . .

Just last week, she, Bairre, and Cliona dispatched half a dozen would-be assassins and Daphne felt nothing.

But when she closes her eyes, she sees that bloodied hand right in front of her face. She sees Fergal's disembodied head with those lifeless silver eyes—star-touched, just like hers, just like Bairre's.

She shudders and forces herself to sit up, noticing as she does that the pain in her head is gone. All of her pain is gone. The glass ceiling shattered, pieces rained down, cutting her skin, but now there isn't even a scrape on her.

The room is empty and it takes only a second for her to realize why that unsettles her—the last two times she's woken up after grievous injuries, Bairre has been beside her.

Dread pools in the pit of her stomach as she reaches for the bellpull beside her bed, giving it a sharp tug. She hears the faint ring down the hall and forces herself to stay calm. Bairre was fine, he was conscious and talking. He had to be fine. He had to be—

The door to her room swings open and when Bairre steps in, Daphne feels herself sag with relief. An instant later, that relief is replaced with fury. When he closes the door behind them, ensuring they're alone, she reaches for one of the pillows piled around her and throws it at his head.

"You knew," she hisses, careful to keep her voice low.

Bairre catches the pillow with barely a flinch but doesn't deny it. "I couldn't tell you," he said. "It was for your own protection, the less you knew—"

"Yes, Cliona fed me that line as well," Daphne interrupts. "But we all know what the truth of it is—you don't trust me."

That, she expects him to deny, but he doesn't, and that hurts worse than Daphne expects it to. "You're keeping secrets too, Daphne," he points out, and much as she hates it, she can't deny he's right. "Are you going to pretend you trust me?"

Daphne grits her teeth. She told him pieces of her mother's plan, but there is plenty she's left out, too. Plenty that she can't tell him, that she won't because at the end of the day her loyalty isn't to him, it's to her mother and to Bessemia.

"I almost died," she says, fighting to hold on to her anger.

"You didn't," he said. "I made sure you didn't."

"Oh, am I supposed to thank you for that?" she snaps. "Fergal is dead. Any other casualties?"

"No," Bairre says, without so much as a flash of guilt. "We were careful about placing the bomb. There were a few injuries, but the new empyrea already healed them all, including yours."

"New empyrea? How did you find one so soon?" Daphne asks, struggling to process the information. "Wait, you wanted to kill Fergal. Why?" She doesn't know much about Fergal, but from all of her studies of Friv and her reading through intelligence provided by spies in the Frivian court, she was under the impression that Fergal was wholly uninteresting and uncontroversial. She isn't sure what anyone would have to gain by killing him.

Before Bairre can answer, the door opens again and Bairre's mother, Aurelia, sweeps into the room, Fergal's empyrea ring on her right thumb and a cheerful smile on her face.

"It's good to see you up, Princess. I must say, it feels like I am making a habit of healing you."

Daphne looks to Bairre again, and now she sees a hint of guilt in his gaze. Daphne realizes what, exactly, the rebels accomplished: not only the wedding postponed again but the royal empyrea killed and one of their own stepping into his place at the king's right hand. A king Aurelia already has quite a history with.

Beatriz

The Etheldaisy Inn is just barely on the Temarin side of the border, Nigellus explained, though if they crossed any kind of border, Beatriz didn't see it. Nigellus might have mentioned more but even though he talked for most of the hour's walk, Beatriz's teeth were chattering so loudly she barely heard him.

Pasquale has kept an arm around her shoulders, but by the time they finally reach the inn's great oak doors, Beatriz can barely feel her skin anymore. She's dimly aware of Nigellus ordering them rooms and hot baths, of Pasquale helping her upstairs, of a strange maid undressing her and helping her into water so blissfully hot that steam unfurls from its sudsy surface.

She must fall asleep at some point, because the next thing she knows she's burrowed under a mountain of blankets, in a bed much bigger than her cot in the Sororia but smaller than the bed she shared with Pasquale in the castle. *Pas.*

She sits up, blinking around the dark room, but she's alone. She wiggles her fingers and toes, relieved to find that her time trekking through the snow caused no harm, though a part of her wonders if Nigellus's magic helped with that, and if it's another debt she will owe him. It's a thought for another day.

She gets to her feet, determined to find Pasquale, since they couldn't speak more than a few words while they walked. She's sure they have much to discuss, but mostly she wants to assure herself that he's safe.

As if he's been summoned by her thoughts, the door opens and Pasquale steps inside, his eyes finding hers. He lets out a long breath.

"I thought I'd dreamt it all," he says, sagging against the doorframe. "I was in my cell at the Fraternia, picking maggots out of the gruel they'd given me, and then suddenly I was in the snow, with you."

He doesn't ask a question, but Beatriz knows he deserves an answer. After all the secrets they've shared, it should be easy, but Pasquale was born and raised in Cellaria, its customs are all he knows. He told her once that he didn't believe magic was sacrilegious, the way most Cellarians do, but it is one thing to say so in the abstract, quite another to be faced with it directly.

"Close the door," she tells him softly, sitting back down on her bed.

Pasquale does as she asks and comes toward her, his steps tentative.

"I'm not an idiot, Triz," he tells her before she can speak again. "I knew you were hiding something—and I assumed you'd used magic to help Lord Savelle escape."

"A wish," she tells him, shaking her head. "My mother had given it to me before I left, in case of an emergency. Magic, yes, but not mine. Not that time, at least."

He considers this. "The stardust on our windowsill?" he asks.

Beatriz remembers being dragged before King Cesare, accused of using magic. She denied it then, she even believed that denial, though now she knows better. She remembers the servant girl who was executed in her stead.

She nods. "That was the first time. I hadn't even meant to then. It took a while for me to realize I had. When I told you it wasn't me, I believed I was telling you the truth. But this time, I meant to."

She thinks about the star she wished on, the one she pulled down from the sky. There is one less star because of her. Several less, she supposes, if she considers the two she wished on by mistake.

"It was an emergency," she says, to him and to herself. "I had to do it."

She braces for judgment from Pasquale, but he only nods. "I'm glad you did, Triz," he says before glancing at the closed door behind him and then back at her. "And the empyrea? Nigellus? He can be trusted?"

"Stars no," Beatriz says with a scoff. "He's been my mother's lapdog since before I was born, and I certainly don't trust her." She relays the details of Sophronia's death and what Nigellus told her, that the empress had orchestrated it and had tried to have Beatriz killed as well.

"But why rescue you, then?" he asks. "If your mother wants you dead . . ." He trails off, brow furrowing. "Perhaps you were safer in the Sororia. It could be a trap."

"I thought about that," Beatriz says. "But Sophronia's

death was public, with an audience, and it gave my mother an opening to invade Temarin. Killing me in the Alder Mountains wouldn't serve that purpose. It could be their plan, but they won't enact it yet, and if they do, we'll be prepared." She pauses. "He wants to teach me how to control my power, and I need to learn. Empyreas aren't exactly commonplace."

He nods, but he still looks troubled. "I'm sorry about Sophronia," he says after a moment.

The words are kind, but Beatriz feels them like a knife between her ribs. She gives a curt nod. "She wasn't an idiot," she tells him. "My mother always said she was, but Sophronia was smart. It was the kindness. She was too kind, and it got her killed."

Pasquale must hear the warning in her voice—she hopes he does. She doesn't know what she will do if she loses him, too.

She clears her throat. "And then there's Nico and Gigi to worry about. I don't imagine they'll be thrilled to learn we've escaped."

Pasquale lets out something akin to a laugh. "I'd give just about anything to see their faces when they hear," he says.

Beatriz smiles too, but she still feels hollow. Not even the thought of Gisella's face, red with rage, or Nicolo's guilty eyes is enough to fill her with joy or anything close to it.

Pasquale's smile fades and he drops his gaze from hers. "You haven't asked me how the Fraternia was."

"Oh," Beatriz says, frowning. "I assumed it was like the Sororia, more or less. Lonely. Boring. Though I admit, bland as the food they served was, I never had maggots in mine."

"The maggots were the least of it," Pasquale says, shaking his head. He doesn't elaborate and Beatriz doesn't push him. When he speaks again, his voice is soft. "But in the hardest moments, I thought about what I would do when I got out. And the truth is, I didn't think about Nico and Gigi and revenge, I didn't think about Cellaria or being king. I just thought about Ambrose." He pauses. Considering his next words. "Let Nico be king—it isn't a duty I ever wanted."

"They betrayed us, Pas," Beatriz says, struggling to keep her voice level. "They banished us to the mountains to die— they'd have had us executed if they could have."

"I'm not sure about that," Pasquale says, his voice mild. "If I recall correctly, Nico tried to get you to marry him."

Heat rises to Beatriz's cheeks. She was such a fool over Nicolo, and both she and Pasquale have paid for it. "And I said no," she says.

Pasquale fixes her with a long look. "We never talked about it," he says. "About what, exactly, was between the two of you."

Beatriz doesn't want to answer that question. Whatever she thought was between her and Nicolo doesn't matter—it was never something with a future, even before he betrayed her. She knows Pasquale won't believe her if she claims she doesn't miss him, or even Gisella, so she cloaks her broken heart in thorns of anger.

"The only things between Nico and me were lies," she snaps.

"Triz, I have no interest in defending him, but the lies were yours as well," Pasquale points out.

Beatriz hates that he's right. "My lies never put him in danger," she replies.

"No," he agrees. "Only me."

She bites her lip. "What, then? You want to just . . . forgive him? Forgive both of them?"

Pasquale shrugs. "Not forgive, no. But I don't want to waste my life seeking vengeance against people who took something I didn't want. Honestly, Triz? If I never set foot in Cellaria again, I will die happy. I don't want to go back."

It's a radical statement, though not one that Beatriz is surprised to hear. Pasquale has never wanted to be king, and if she's honest, the role doesn't suit him. But if he walks away from Cellaria and the throne, he's also walking away from the only thing that truly binds them together.

"Where will you go, then?" she asks, trying to ignore the worry twisting in her gut. "I'm sure you'll want to find Ambrose."

He considers it. "If I knew where he was, I'd leave right this minute," he says. "But I don't, and I know myself well enough to know that I can't survive out there on my own." He hesitates. "Besides, Ambrose doesn't need me right now. You do."

Beatriz bristles at that—she doesn't need him, she doesn't need anybody. The very idea of it is mortifying.

"I'm the one who just saved you, in case you've forgotten," she tells him.

"I haven't forgotten," he says. "But we promised to look out for each other, didn't we? That goes both ways. If you're going to Bessemia, I'll be right there with you. Learn how to use your magic, figure out your mother's plans. And when the time comes to strike, I'll strike with you."

Beatriz's chest grows tight and all she can manage is a quick nod. "Then we'll strike together," she says.

Violie

It takes another day of travel for Violie, Leopold, and Ambrose to make it to the inn Ambrose mentioned, but in that time Violie learns more about their new companion than she could find out about Leopold in almost a week together. Though she would wager that Leopold would say the same thing about her—their days mostly passed in silence. Neither of them likes the other, and neither of them trusts the other, and so there has been little to discuss.

Ambrose, however, seems to like both of them right away, and he seems to trust them implicitly—a quirk Violie can't quite wrap her mind around. In just a day, Violie has learned about not just Ambrose's childhood in the Cellarian countryside but the names of his parents and their three dogs, and every detail of how he felt when his uncle named Ambrose his heir at the age of twelve and had him brought to court, where he met Prince Pasquale.

Though it's one detail Ambrose doesn't share, Violie suspects there is something other than friendship between the two—it's clear in the way Ambrose says his name, the slight color that touches his cheeks, the way he glances away. He isn't very good at keeping secrets, Violie realizes, and she finds that she envies him his lack of practice in that area.

Violie never had any choice but to be a good liar. She doubts she'd have survived this long otherwise.

When the chimney of the inn pokes out through the trees, Violie sags with relief. She doesn't care how many stables she needs to muck or dishes she has to clean—she'll happily cut off her own arm if it means she'll have a bed to sleep in tonight and a full belly.

"We should give you a name," Ambrose tells Leopold. "Technically, we're still in Temarin, after all. We have to make sure no one recognizes you."

Leopold frowns, considering it. "I could be Levi," he says. Violie winces and he gives her a sideways glance. "What's wrong with Levi? It's close enough that it should be easier for me to remember."

"Nothing's wrong with the name," she says. "But the second you open your mouth, they'll know you're nobleborn. Try not to say anything."

Leopold's jaw twitches and she knows if it were the week before, Leopold wouldn't let anyone speak to him that way, especially not a lowly servant girl. But after a brief hesitation, he nods.

"Fine," he says. "Though your Bessemian accent will raise eyebrows too."

Violie knows that's a fair point, even if she is good with accents. Tired as she is, she doesn't want to take that risk. "Fine," she echoes. "Then Ambrose will take the lead."

Ambrose looks uncomfortable with that idea, but nonetheless, he dips his head in assent.

The Etheldaisy Inn is small but well kept. As soon as Violie sets foot inside, a wave of heat hits her and she realizes just how cold she was, trekking through the snow all day. An assortment of mismatched rugs covers the floors, leading the way into a parlor whose walls are covered in cheery paintings of the snowcapped mountains outside. On a small table beside the door sits a clay vase filled with the inn's namesake flower—etheldaisies. Violie takes a step closer. She's never seen fresh etheldaisies before, only dried bunches merchants brought through the Bessemian markets, but she's always loved them. Delicate white flowers that appear fragile but can survive the fiercest of blizzards.

A woman bustles in from the hallway, brushing her hands off on a dusty apron, cheerful smile at the ready, though when her eyes fall on Ambrose, it slips away and she frowns.

"Didn't expect to see you back so soon," she says, her accent mostly Temarinian, but with a Cellarian lilt around the vowels. "Though I did warn you there was nothing good to be found in Temarin these days."

Ambrose glances at Leopold, then back at the woman. "Things have gotten worse, apparently. King Leopold's been overthrown and Bessemia's invaded."

The woman considers this. "Well, from the stories I've been hearing over the last year, that might just be an improvement over King Leopold."

This time, Violie glances at Leopold, but if the dig affects him, he doesn't show it. His expression remains placid.

"I see you traded your last friend for two new ones," the woman says, her gaze moving to Violie and Leopold.

"He and I parted ways when we heard the news," Ambrose says carefully. "But I met Violie and Levi and they're going the same way I am. It's safer to travel in groups, you know."

"It's safer not to travel at all, this time of year," the woman corrects, and the way she frowns, Violie suspects she's truly concerned about Ambrose's well-being.

Ambrose must see it too, because he smiles softly. "So you keep telling me, Mera," he says. "Is there any chance we can work off room and board for a night?"

The woman looks between the three of them. "I could use some help in the stables again," she admits. "I don't suppose any of you know how to bake? A girl staying here has a sweet tooth, and I'd like to keep her happy."

Violie blinks. She helped Sophronia with her baking a couple of times, enough that she learned some basics. "I can," she says, summoning her best Temarinian accent.

The woman's eyes fall on Violie and she nods. "Only one other group is staying here just now—a girl and a boy around your age and a man . . ." She glances back over her shoulder to ensure no one is listening before she drops her voice to a whisper. "He's the Bessemian empyrea, if you can believe it."

Violie's stomach plummets and before she can think twice, a name slips past her lips. "Nigellus?"

The woman's eyes narrow. "There isn't any other empyrea in Bessemia last I heard," she says.

Violie can feel Leopold's glare and Ambrose's worry, but

she forces herself to smile. "I've heard rumors, of course. I imagine everyone has. They say he has the ear of the empress herself," she says.

The woman keeps her eyes on Violie for a moment longer before giving a quick nod. "Steer clear of him—all of you. He isn't a friendly sort and I won't have you bothering him."

Violie nods quickly. The last thing she needs is to be seen by Nigellus—though they've only met once before, she doubts he's the sort to forget a face, and he'll surely have questions for her.

Then again, Violie has a few questions herself about what, exactly, the royal empyrea of Bessemia is doing so close to Cellaria, where a wrong look might lose him his head.

Mera shows the three of them to a small room with a small table holding a plain pitcher and a narrow cot set next to a washstand. Though the room is sparsely decorated, it's warm, and that's all Violie cares about at the moment.

"This is the best I can do," the woman says. "The empyrea and his companions are set up in my other three rooms—"

"It's perfect," Ambrose says. "Thank you, Mera. Let us know what needs to be done."

"Nothing tonight," she says. "You're of no use to me hungry and tired. We'll discuss it in the morning. Come down in an hour or so for dinner."

When she's gone and it's only the three of them, Violie lets out a long exhale. "Nigellus knows me," she says. "He can't see me."

Ambrose and Leopold exchange a look but nod. "I'm not certain he won't recognize me, too," Leopold admits. "He's seen portraits, I'm sure."

"If Mera requires any work that risks being seen, I'll do it," Ambrose says.

"I have to admit, though, I'm curious what he's doing here," Violie says. "He's loyal to the empress—I can't imagine what would bring him to Cellaria apart from Princess Beatriz."

Leopold takes in her words, his eyes widening. "If the empress was responsible for Sophronia's death—"

"He might be here to dispatch Beatriz as well," Violie finishes. "Mera mentioned companions, around our age. I know I wasn't the empress's only spy. Perhaps he has others with him."

Ambrose has turned pale. "The real question is, are they on their way to finish off Beatriz, or are they returning home having already done it?"

Daphne

Daphne spends the entire day after her would-be wedding in bed, resting, though she tells anyone who will listen that she's perfectly fine, every bump and bruise healed by Aurelia. No one listens, insisting that a little rest won't kill her. Daphne isn't so sure—the boredom alone makes death seem appealing, though she manages to write and code a letter to her mother, apprising her of the rebels' latest move and telling her everything she knows about Aurelia, Bairre's birth mother and an infamous empyrea in Friv who helped Bartholomew take the throne and end the clan wars. She considers telling her mother about Aurelia's talent for prophecies, including the one about Sophronia's death— the blood of stars and majesty spilled—but holds back. That information won't help the empress now, and Daphne doesn't want to write those words, to see them scrawled in ink.

The following morning, though, when Cliona asks Daphne if she'd like to join her for a shopping trip to Wallfrost Street, Daphne can't get out of bed fast enough. Their last trip to Wallfrost Street ended with a blade being held to Daphne's throat, but even that is preferable to another day in this stars-forsaken room.

And this time, Cliona tells her as they ride side by side through the thicket of woods that separates the castle from the surrounding city of Eldevale, they aren't merely going there in search of dresses and jewels.

"King Bartholomew wants to send a message that the attack at the wedding doesn't frighten him, or you by extension," Cliona says.

Daphne casts a glance at the ten guards who flank them—at enough of a distance to give her privacy, but close enough to send a message.

"The extra guards might undermine that message," she points out.

Cliona shrugs. "Well, he wants to appear bold, not idiotic," she says. "Someone did set off a bomb at your wedding, after all."

"*You* set off a bomb at my wedding," Daphne hisses.

"Don't be ridiculous, I don't know the first thing about explosives," Cliona says before pausing. "That was Haimish's job. And besides—you weren't the target. You were never in danger."

Daphne rolls her eyes. She believes Cliona means that, but it doesn't bring her much comfort.

"Bombs are unpredictable," she points out. "If Bairre hadn't pulled me away when he did—a second before the explosion, which I hope no one else noticed—I'm not sure we'd be having this conversation."

Cliona bristles. "No one noticed," she says. "The explosion served as enough of a distraction."

"It served as more than that," Daphne says. "You meant to kill Fergal."

She watches Cliona carefully, but no hint of guilt crosses her face. She shrugs again. "An unfortunate sacrifice," she says. "But we needed an opening."

The words turn Daphne's stomach, though she knows they shouldn't. The cool way Cliona is describing a murder she helped to arrange isn't so different from the way Daphne might. But when Daphne closes her eyes, she still sees Fergal's disembodied head. Was that necessary? she wonders. If she'd been in Cliona's position, would she have done the same?

Daphne knows the answer, and that unnerves her as much as anything else.

"Tell me," she says, pushing the thought from her mind. "How exactly did you convince King Bartholomew to name his former lover and Bairre's mother to the newly vacated empyrea post?"

"Necessity," Cliona says. "Empyreas are a rarity, and Bartholomew can't simply wait for another one to come along. Besides, Bairre's parentage is a rumor, and you're one of six people who know different."

Daphne does quick math—if she, Cliona, Bartholomew, Bairre, and Aurelia know the truth, that leaves one person remaining. Daphne is fairly certain it must be Cliona's father.

"Which begs the question: Why?" Daphne asks.

Cliona glances at her, the corner of her mouth kicking up in a smirk. "Last time we discussed it, Princess, you were saying you didn't trust me. So why, exactly, should I trust you?"

She digs her heels into her horse's sides and quickens his

pace, leaving Daphne to catch up. Daphne lets out a Bessemian curse beneath her breath and glowers at Cliona's back.

Daphne watches Cliona carefully after they dismount and turn their horses over to a stable hand before continuing down Wallfrost Street on foot, popping in and out of stores to browse, but even more so to be seen. Daphne is aware of the townspeople watching, peeking through windows and coming out to greet them on the street. A few are bold enough to call her name and wave. Daphne waves back, a smile pasted onto her face.

All the while, though, she keeps Cliona in her sights. The last time they came here, Cliona used the outing as an excuse to meet with Mrs. Nattermore, the dressmaker who also kept weapons and ammunition in her storeroom. But if Cliona has an ulterior motive for today's trip, Daphne can't find it. They make idle chat as they pass through stores—Daphne assuring anyone who asks that she and Bairre are perfectly fine, unfrightened, and looking forward to rescheduling the wedding as quickly as possible.

Cliona is free with her spending money, buying emerald earbobs, gray velvet boots, and an ermine cloak, but that in itself is unremarkable.

Eventually, they make their way back to the castle in time for dinner.

At the castle, dinner is a subdued affair—unsurprising, Daphne supposes, given the recent violence and the destruction of the castle chapel. The day before, she ate all of her meals in bed, so this is the first time she's seen the effect of the attack on the court and the handful of highland families who remain. The tone is a far cry from her betrothal ball, where the ale flowed freely and the guests were loud and rowdy. Instead, it is more reminiscent of a funeral. Conversations are relegated to mere murmurs and few people seem to be drinking.

Daphne herself is seated with Rufus Cadringal on her left and Aurelia on her right, with Bairre directly across from her, though he is deep in conversation with Cliona's father, Lord Panlington. Watching them, Daphne wonders what, exactly, they're discussing.

She glances at King Bartholomew, sitting on Aurelia's other side, at the head of the table. Does he feel a sword hanging over his head? she wonders. Does he know that the woman who pulled down a star to see him on the throne is the same one aiming to take it from him?

And Daphne still doesn't understand why Aurelia has aligned herself with the rebels at all. Aurelia told her it was because of prophecies told to her by the stars that spoke of a coming war, but she didn't tell Daphne exactly what they'd said apart from the blood of stars and majesty spilled, and that prophecy was fulfilled when Sophronia lost her head.

At the thought, Daphne's stomach lurches and she looks down at her half-empty plate.

"Are you all right?" Rufus Cadringal asks beside her. "You look a bit green . . ." He trails off. "You haven't been poisoned again, have you?"

Daphne forces herself to smile at Rufus, who looks genuinely alarmed. She can't blame him; he was there when she was poisoned before—his sister was the one to do it. "I'm fine," she assures him. She decides the truth is the safest course. "Just thinking about my sister Sophronia."

Rufus's eyes soften. "I haven't offered my condolences yet, but I'm very sorry for your loss," he says.

Daphne has heard similar sentiments—more over the last few days than she cares to count. Polite and perfunctory words to which she responds with a polite and perfunctory *Thank you.*

But there is nothing polite or perfunctory in Rufus's words. Daphne feels the weight of them, feels them burrow beneath her skin. She hates it.

"When I came here, I never planned on seeing either of my sisters again," she tells him, the truth as he understands it, though not the truth Daphne believed. "We went our separate ways, into separate lives. In a way, Sophronia died to me the second our carriages left the clearing in Bessemia."

"You wrote to each other, though," he says.

Daphne shrugs. "It isn't the same. I'd come to terms with the fact that I'd never see her smile again, never hear her laugh. I don't think . . ." She trails off. "It doesn't feel real yet. It doesn't feel permanent. Maybe it never will."

Daphne thinks of Beatriz and a thought suddenly occurs to her: Beatriz could die too. She could be dead already. Would Daphne even know if she was? What if she really, truly never sees her sisters again?

Suddenly, she remembers the night of their sixteenth birthday, when they'd escaped their party and hidden upstairs in their parlor, trading a bottle of champagne back and forth between them, arguing about which of them would be the first to execute their mother's plans and return home.

"To seventeen," Sophronia said, raising her glass of champagne.

Daphne remembers laughing. "Oh, Soph, are you sloshed already? We're sixteen."

But Sophronia only shrugged. "I know that," she said. "But sixteen is when we have to say goodbye. By seventeen, we'll be back here again. Together."

Daphne lifts her mug of ale to her lips to hide the expression she knows gives her away. It isn't that anyone would think it strange that she's upset, given everything that's happened the last few days, but Daphne feels like it would be a mark of weakness all the same, and she won't show off her vulnerabilities, not when she is surrounded by wolves.

She pushes all thoughts of Sophronia aside. Focus, she thinks before turning toward Aurelia, who has barely touched her food or ale. Instead, the older woman is looking around the table with her unwavering star-touched eyes. When her eyes meet Daphne's matching ones, a single thin eyebrow arches upward.

"An aster for your thoughts, Princess Daphne?" she says.

"I'm afraid my thoughts will cost you far more than that," Daphne replies, making Aurelia laugh.

"It's good to see that after so many mishaps, you're still as witty as ever," she says.

Daphne's smile is tight. "Tell me, how have you found court over the last couple of days?" she asks. "It doesn't seem like a place you would feel at home in, and I know you have gone to great lengths to avoid it."

Aurelia shrugs, taking a small sip of her ale. As she does so, Daphne's eyes are drawn to the royal empyrea ring she now wears on her thumb—the same ring Daphne saw on Fergal's severed hand.

"I think that you of all people would understand, Princess: we must go where we're directed," she says. "I'm sure if you'd had any say in things, you wouldn't have chosen to come here either."

Daphne can't argue that—she often envied her sisters their destinies. Cellaria with its lush weather and beaches and Temarin with its lavish metropolitan capital city seemed far preferable to dreary, desolate Friv.

"I did my duty," Daphne says, though the truth is she knows now that she might be the luckiest of her sisters. There may be people in Friv who want her dead, but they seem to be far less capable than those in the other countries.

"As did I," Aurelia replies evenly.

But my duty didn't involve killing anyone, Daphne thinks, though she isn't sure that's the truth. She killed several assassins in the woods, though that was in self-defense. Her mother prepared her to kill, though, and if she wrote to her tomorrow instructing her to kill, Daphne would do it.

Even if it were Bairre? a voice in her head asks. *Even if it were Cliona?* The voice sounds like Sophronia's.

Daphne doesn't want to answer those questions, so she shoves them to the back of her mind. It won't come to that, she tells herself.

Daphne glances around the table, but everyone is engrossed in their own conversations. Her eyes briefly catch Bairre's, but he glances away and goes back to speaking with Lord Panlington.

"Tell me," Daphne says, turning her gaze to Aurelia once more. "Have the stars been saying anything new to you?"

Daphne sees the way one corner of Aurelia's mouth pulls down, the way her eyes dart around, not searching for anything in particular.

"No," she says carefully. "Nothing new."

"You aren't a very good liar," Daphne tells her.

Aurelia's expression sharpens into a glare. "It isn't a lie. I've heard nothing new."

"But you've heard something," Daphne says.

"I've heard the same thing as ever, Princess," Aurelia says, holding Daphne's gaze. "The blood of stars and majesty spilled."

Daphne's stomach twists, and though she's eaten little tonight, she still feels like she might be ill. "That was Sophronia," she says. "That prophecy has already come to fruition."

"It seems the stars disagree," Aurelia says, but as casual as the words come out, Daphne sees the tension in her jaw. After all, Bairre himself has the blood of stars and majesty running through his veins. As does Daphne. As does Beatriz, and the last time Daphne spoke to her, she was under house arrest in Cellaria.

The blood of stars and majesty spilled.

As far as Daphne knows, the three of them are the only

people alive who are both royal and star-touched. Bairre, Beatriz, and Daphne. None of those are options Daphne will allow.

"The stars can disagree all they want," Daphne tells Aurelia. "But in this, they'll be wrong."

Aurelia considers Daphne for a long moment. "Well," she says finally, "there is a first time for everything, I suppose."

Beatriz

The public room of the inn, where meals are served, is deserted apart from Beatriz and Pasquale—a fact Beatriz is grateful for. She and Nigellus haven't spoken since arriving and she isn't sure who, exactly, she is meant to be here. An exiled princess? An empyrea in training? No one at all? But with only Pasquale, there is no need to pretend to be anyone other than herself.

"I'm almost looking forward to meeting your mother," Pasquale tells her, taking a bite of his buttered toast. She must give him a horrified look, because he snorts. He pauses while he chews, then swallows. "Don't misunderstand me— I'm terrified of the prospect, but after everything I've heard, it will be interesting to meet her in person."

Beatriz laughs before taking a long gulp of her coffee. "Interesting will be one word for it. She won't have you killed—she still needs you to take Cellaria—but I doubt you'll feel particularly welcome at the palace."

Pasquale shakes his head. "Right. Like I ever felt particularly welcome at the Cellarian palace. I only really had you and Ambrose and . . ." He trails off, and Beatriz knows he was about to say Nicolo and Gisella. His cousins were some of his only allies at court, until they turned on him.

"Well, you'll still have me," she says brightly, finishing her coffee. The innkeeper was frazzled this morning, tending to her myriad of duties, but she left a bell on the table in case Beatriz and Pasquale required anything. Beatriz reaches for it now, giving it a ring. She doesn't want to trouble the woman, but after her time in the Sororia, she feels like she could eat five whole breakfasts and not be sated.

"And you'll have me," Pasquale tells her with a lopsided smile. "But what, exactly, is the plan? It feels like walking into the lions' den."

"It is a bit," Beatriz admits with a sigh. "But I need to know exactly what she's planning, and even Nigellus doesn't seem to have those answers. It isn't only me in danger, but Daphne, too, and even if she doesn't believe . . ." Beatriz trails off. Pasquale's attention is suddenly focused over her shoulder, his eyes wide and his jaw slack. He looks like he's seeing a ghost.

Beatriz whirls around to see what he's looking at and feels the breath leave her body. There, standing in the doorway with a washrag in one hand and a pot of coffee in the other, is Ambrose—hair a little overgrown, face in need of a shave, but alive and whole and here.

Before Beatriz can make a move, Pasquale is out of his chair and he and Ambrose collide in the middle of the room. They only hold each other, but Beatriz feels like she's intruding on something private and she casts her gaze around the room until they break apart. Ambrose clears his throat, his cheeks flushing red.

"Princess Beatriz," he says, bowing low.

Beatriz's gaze returns to him and she smiles. "I've asked you to call me Triz, Ambrose," she chides, getting to her feet and giving him a hug of her own. "It's good to see you—but where is Lord Savelle?"

"On his way to the Silvan Isles," Ambrose explains. "Safe, last I saw him, and I have every reason to believe he'll stay that way. Temarin has fallen—"

"I know," Beatriz says, wincing at the thought of Sophronia.

"—But King Leopold is here too," Ambrose adds, lowering his voice though they're the only ones in the room. "We ran into each other on the way and—"

"Leopold?" Beatriz and Pasquale ask at the same time.

"Where?" Beatriz says.

"The stables," Ambrose says, frowning. "But—"

Beatriz doesn't give him a chance to finish before she hurries out the door and down the hall, not caring when she steps out of the inn and the cold air bites at her skin. King Leopold is here—he'll know exactly what happened to her sister. And if he's alive, then surely there's a chance that . . .

Beatriz's thoughts trail off as she approaches the stables. King Leopold is standing outside, leaning against the doorway with a rake in his hand. He looks so different from the last portrait she saw of him—older, yes, but rougher around the edges as well, in need of a bath and a haircut. But that isn't what stops Beatriz short.

He's deep in conversation with a girl whose back is to Beatriz, a girl with the same shade of blond hair as Sophronia. She's the same height, with the same curved figure. For the first time since she thought she felt her sister die, hope lights in Beatriz's heart.

"Sophie!" she shouts, quickening her pace to a run. Her sister is alive, and she's here, and Beatriz throws her arms open, ready to hold Sophronia tight and maybe never ever let go again and—

The girl turns toward her and Beatriz slams to a stop, her arms falling to her sides and her heart plummeting once more. She isn't Sophronia. There is a resemblance, but it isn't her. She swallows.

"I'm . . . I'm sorry," she manages. "I thought you were . . ."

She's dimly aware of Pasquale and Ambrose approaching behind her, of Leopold and the girl looking at her with a dawning understanding.

"Princess Beatriz," the girl says, her accent Bessemian. She looks every bit as surprised to see Beatriz as Beatriz was surprised to see her, before she realized her mistake.

"Who are you?" Beatriz asks her, injecting her voice with steel and drawing herself up another inch to hide the vulnerability she just showed.

"That's Violie," Ambrose says behind her. "And, well, I'm assuming you know Leopold, or of him at the very least."

Beatriz barely hears the words, barely feels Pasquale brush past her to greet his cousin with a hug and a handshake. Her eyes remain on Violie, who appears to grow more and more uncomfortable with each passing second.

"I've seen you before," Beatriz says. "You're from Bessemia?"

Violie looks more uncomfortable, but nods.

Fragments of memory slide into place—it isn't the first time Beatriz has thought this girl resembled Sophronia.

"You were at the brothel," she says, half to herself and half to the other girl. "Just outside the palace—the Scarlet Petal."

"The Crimson Petal," Violie corrects quietly. "Yes. My mother was . . . is . . . one of the courtesans employed there."

Beatriz visited a handful of brothels as part of her training, learning how to flirt and seduce, but even though she only went to the Crimson Petal once, the visit was notable because her mother accompanied her. She didn't supervise the lesson, and Beatriz never learned why she'd chosen to come along, or chosen that brothel in particular.

But it can't be a coincidence—not that visit then, or Violie's reappearance now. Not even the fact that Violie bears a striking resemblance to her sister.

"Your mother hired me," Violie blurts out before Beatriz can form the words herself. "I was placed in the Temarinian palace to spy on Sophronia."

Beatriz thinks of her sister's final letter to her, how Sophronia confessed that she'd gone against their mother, but their mother had been one step ahead of her, sending a declaration of war to Cellaria that had been forged. Someone in Temarin would have needed to forge that document and send it.

Beatriz takes one step closer to Violie, then another. Then she balls her hand into a fist and slams it as hard as she can into Violie's face.

Violie

Princess Beatriz knows how to throw a punch. Violie stumbles back a step, her vision fracturing into stars and pain exploding across her face. Leopold's arms come out to steady Violie, but she shrugs him off, her hand flying to her nose, and she winces as the pain sharpens at the slightest contact.

"I think you broke my nose," she says, dazed.

"And I think you killed my sister," Beatriz retorts. The other boy has his arms around her shoulders, and Violie suspects he's the only thing keeping Beatriz from hitting her again. Prince Pasquale, she assumes.

"She didn't," Leopold breaks in.

Violie spits on the dirt at her feet, noting it's more blood than saliva. The taste of copper fills her mouth. Finally, she drags her gaze back to Beatriz. "I didn't," she agrees. "But I am the reason she's dead."

Beatriz absorbs the words like Violie's dealt a physical blow, then begins to struggle against Prince Pasquale again.

"Would hitting me again make you feel better?" Violie asks her, taking a step closer, even as her body protests.

"Maybe not," Beatriz bites out. "But I'd like to find out for certain."

Beatriz manages to push Pasquale off her and lunges toward Violie again, but Violie holds her ground.

"Go on, then," Violie says, bracing herself. Maybe it will make Beatriz feel better—maybe it will make Violie feel better as well, maybe it will alleviate even a fraction of the guilt that has been threatening to drown her ever since the guillotine's blade fell on Sophronia's neck.

Violie closes her eyes and waits, but the blow never comes. Leopold throws himself between them, pushing Beatriz back gently but firmly.

"Stop it," he tells her. "If you're passing out justice, save some for me as well."

"Don't think I won't!" Beatriz snarls at him. "I'd heard you were an idiot and a coward, but how, exactly, are you standing here when she's . . ."

Beatriz trails off, her shaking hand lifting to her mouth as if she can keep the word sealed inside, as if not saying it will keep it from being true.

Dead.

"Because Sophronia wanted him to survive," Violie says quietly. "And she trusted me to ensure he did."

Beatriz swallows and Violie watches the fight leave her—almost. It lingers in her eyes as she looks between Violie and Leopold. Silver eyes, Violie notes, just like Sophronia's. Just like her own, now that the eye drops she was using in Temarin have faded completely. Leopold hasn't noticed the change, though he spends very little time looking at her.

"What exactly are you doing here?" Beatriz snaps.

Violie shrugs, struggling to ignore her nose—it is certainly broken. "Coming to rescue you, actually."

Beatriz snorts. "As you can see, you aren't needed."

Violie isn't entirely convinced of that. "You're traveling with Nigellus?" she asks.

Beatriz glances at Pasquale, a flash of uncertainty showing itself before she seals it away. "We are," she says, lifting her chin.

Violie could never see Empress Margaraux in Sophronia, no matter how she searched. She was the opposite of her mother in every way, for better or for worse. Beatriz isn't. The way she looks at Violie now makes her feel like she is back in the empress's presence, an inch tall. But Sophronia loved her sisters, and Violie can't let them meet the same fate she did.

"You shouldn't trust him," she tells her. "Or your mother."

At that, Beatriz laughs, but the sound is sharp enough to draw blood. "I can assure you, I have never in my life trusted my mother," she says. "And I have no intention of starting now." She looks at Violie a moment longer. "You know that she's responsible for Sophronia's death," she says.

Beside Violie, Leopold nods. "Sophronia knew it too," he says. "Before she . . . before we were separated, one of the rebels told her he'd been working with the empress, that it had all been orchestrated by her long before we married, including Sophronia's execution."

For an instant, Beatriz looks like she might be ill, but she manages to nod. "Nigellus told me the same, that if her plots in Cellaria had succeeded, I'd be dead as well by now."

"Nigellus told you that?" Violie asks, frowning. "Why would he do that? He's been plotting with her."

"With you, you mean," Beatriz corrects, though her voice is no longer laced with fury but with ice. Violie finds she misses the anger. "I haven't discovered the answer to that yet, but I will."

"But you can't trust him," Violie says.

Beatriz glances at Pasquale and the two of them share a silent conversation. They are close, that much is clear, but there is nothing romantic in the air between them, not like there was between Sophronia and Leopold. Unless Violie is mistaken—and she rarely is—Pasquale's heart belongs to Ambrose.

"At the moment, I have need of him," Beatriz says, and Violie can tell she chooses her words carefully. "But that is not the same thing as trust." She pauses. "As you can see, we are hardly in need of rescuing," she adds, glancing at Pasquale before turning back to Violie and Leopold. "So what will you do now?"

Violie shrugs, looking to Leopold, who appears just as uncertain.

"On to Friv," he says. "I'm not sure I'll find safety anywhere else."

"No, you won't," Beatriz agrees. "My mother wants you dead, and Nicolo's hold on the Cellarian throne is tenuous. If he can strengthen it by executing you, he won't hesitate. I'm not sure you'll find safety with Daphne, though. She is my mother's creature, through and through."

It's impossible to miss the bitterness in those words, but before Violie can ask what she means, Beatriz turns to her.

"And what will you do?" she asks. "Follow King Leopold to Friv?"

Violie smiles tightly. "It seems I have little choice," she says. "I made Sophie a promise and I intend to see it through." She hesitates, a question rising to her lips that she knows she has no right to ask. "I'm sure I'm low on the list of people you would do a favor for," she says carefully.

Beatriz raises her eyebrows. "Bold to assume you're on the list at all," she says coolly.

Violie ignores the insult. "I started working for your mother because she promised she would heal mine. She has Vexis. Nigellus used star magic to cure it, but your mother made it clear that if I went against her . . ." She trails off, but Beatriz understands her meaning well enough. "Her name is Avalise Blanchette. She's still at the Crimson Petal last I heard."

"If I know my mother, I'll be watched," Beatriz says, and despite everything, she does sound sorry. "She can't know our paths have crossed."

"I won't be," Ambrose points out, nodding at Violie. "I'll seek her out as soon as I'm able. Is there anything you'd like me to tell her?"

Assuming she's still alive, Violie thinks before she can stop herself. Her stomach twists as she thinks of the woman who raised her, who braided her hair each night, who taught her how to sing and dance and lie. She cannot think about living in a world without her mother, of letting her die alone. She'll go mad if she does. She clears her throat. "Just . . . that I love her. And I'll see her again soon."

Beatriz

L ater that night, over dinner, Nigellus is not quite pleased when Beatriz tells him Ambrose will be joining them on their journey in the morning, though he isn't exactly upset either. He seems to absorb the story of Ambrose's fortuitous appearance at the inn, though Beatriz isn't sure if he truly believes it or not. His eyes move from Beatriz, to Pasquale, to Ambrose, before darting back to Beatriz.

"I don't suppose you can be talked out of it?" he asks mildly.

"No," Beatriz replies. "I'll also need another vial of stardust and fifty asters."

That causes a frown to tug at Nigellus's mouth.

"Why?" he asks.

Beatriz only smiles. "Debts Ambrose owes, isn't that right?" she asks, glancing at him.

For an instant, Ambrose looks confused, but then he nods. "Yes, that's right. I owe Mera . . . er . . . the innkeeper."

"Fifty asters is a lot of money," Nigellus points out, his voice so flat that Beatriz isn't sure what, exactly, he's thinking. "To say nothing of the stardust—how long exactly have you been at this inn, Ambrose?"

"He gambles," Pasquale blurts out. "Compulsive gambler. I've tried to get him to stop, but since we parted ways, he's apparently gotten into trouble again." He affects a heavy sigh, and while he isn't a great liar, Beatriz has to admit he isn't a bad one. Certainly not as bad as he used to be. The thought is a relief, but it also leaves her feeling sad.

"It shouldn't be much trouble," Beatriz says to Nigellus with a smile. "I'm sure you have that and plenty more, even if my mother isn't funding this particular trip."

Nigellus narrows his eyes at her slightly before shaking his head. "Very well, I will settle your debts with the innkeeper before we depart tomorrow."

"No need for that," Beatriz cuts in before lowering her voice even though they are the only ones in the public room. "Apparently the innkeeper isn't supposed to be gambling. She's terribly embarrassed by the habit. She asked that I bring her the payment in private, tonight, when her husband and children won't be about."

Nigellus looks at her for a long moment and now she has no doubt that he sees through her lie—it isn't a very good lie, after all, but under the circumstances it is the best she can do. In the end, though, it doesn't matter if he believes her lie, so long as he gives her the money and the stardust, and she knows that for the moment, at least, he's highly motivated to keep her on his side.

After what feels like an age, he reaches into the inner

pocket of his cloak, withdrawing a velvet drawstring bag. Beatriz watches as he counts out five ten-aster silver pieces.

"And the stardust?" she asks. "You have more, don't you?"

In truth, it isn't strictly necessary, but she feels slightly guilty about Violie's broken nose.

Nigellus lets out a belabored sigh before reaching into another pocket and pulling out a small glass vial of shimmering silver dust. He slides the coins and the vial over to Beatriz, but when she reaches for them, he lays his other hand on top of hers, trapping her.

"Consider it a loan, Princess," he says.

Beatriz doesn't flinch. "All of this is a loan, Nigellus," she tells him. "You saving me, saving Pasquale, our passage back to Bessemia, you training me. It's all a loan. We both know that. Add it to my debt."

Nigellus doesn't respond, but he releases her hands and lets her gather the coins and the stardust, tucking them into the pocket of her own dress before she pushes back from the table.

"Now, if you'll all excuse me, I'm not feeling well and I'd like to get a good night's sleep before we resume our journey north."

Before she leaves the table, she glances at Ambrose and Pasquale, both of whom give her an almost imperceptible nod—they know their duty: to keep Nigellus at the table by whatever means necessary for the next twenty minutes.

Violie answers the door after Beatriz's knock, and a quick glance around the small room behind her confirms that she's alone.

"Where's Leopold?" Beatriz asks, brushing past Violie into the room without waiting to be invited.

"Helping with dishes," Violie says, closing the door and sealing them in an uncomfortable silence. Her nose is a mottled black-and-blue mess, but if she's in pain, she hides it well. Beatriz gets the feeling it isn't the worst thing the other girl has endured. "It's still a risk," she continues. "But Nigellus has met me in person, and Leopold he only knows through illustrations and paintings. We thought it best I stay hidden."

"I'm sure your nose would raise a few questions as well," Beatriz points out mildly.

Violie's eyes narrow. "Come to revel in it?" she asks, touching her nose gingerly and flinching. "It was a good punch, I'll admit that."

"It was well deserved," Beatriz volleys back before reaching into her dress's pocket and withdrawing the vial of stardust and coins. "For your journey north," she says, pressing the coins into Violie's hand. "You can book passage to Friv in the Avelene Harbor."

Beatriz suspects that if she tried to give the money to Leopold, his pride would force him to refuse it, but Violie takes the coins easily enough. "Thank you," she says, before her eyes dart to the vial of stardust, though she makes no move to take it.

"As I said, your nose will raise questions and draw attention," Beatriz says. "Have you used stardust before?"

When Violie shakes her head, Beatriz sighs. "It's important to phrase it right or it won't work. I'll help you."

Violie stares at Beatriz a second longer, a frown creasing her brow. "Why?" she asks.

It isn't a question Beatriz wants to answer. "You tried to save her," she says after a moment. It isn't a question, but Violie answers regardless.

"Yes," she says, her voice hoarse. "She didn't want to be saved, not if it meant Leopold died."

Beatriz chews so hard on her bottom lip she worries she'll draw blood. "She was a fool for him before they even met, you know," she says before laughing. "I'm sure you did, actually. That's part of why my mother sent you."

Violie doesn't deny it.

"I heard he was an idiot," Beatriz continues. "He ran Temarin into the ground."

"He did," Violie agrees tentatively. "But it was a bit more complicated than that. His mother was—"

"Yes, I know," Beatriz interrupts. "Sophie told me all about how Eugenia was using Leopold's throne to ruin the country. Sophie thought she was working with King Cesare, but she was working with Pas's cousins instead. Still, Leopold isn't blameless, is he?"

Violie considers the question for a moment. "No," she says. "But for whatever it's worth, I believe he loved Sophie as much as she loved him." She pauses. "When he arrived in the cave we were supposed to meet in, alone, he was screaming her name. Despite the danger of it, he insisted we return to Kavelle, determined to save her. We arrived just in time to watch the blade fall."

Beatriz closes her eyes tight, breathing suddenly an effort. "You saw it, then," she says quietly.

"Yes," Violie says.

Beatriz forces her eyes open and looks at the other girl. She doesn't want to ask the next question, but she needs to hear the answer. "I still can't believe she's truly dead. I keep thinking that maybe it's a trick, that she escaped, that they executed the wrong girl, thinking it was Sophie. It's not logical, I suppose, but I didn't *see* it, so I can't help but think maybe . . ." She pauses. "You saw it, though. She really is dead? There is no miracle waiting to be revealed?"

"No," Violie says quietly, a shudder wracking her. "No, she's . . . I saw her die. There is no mistaking that."

Beatriz nods, pressing her lips together tightly. She won't cry, not here in front of this stranger who is, by her own admission, partially responsible for Sophronia's death.

After a moment, Beatriz speaks. "My mother always said Sophie was the weakest of us, but she was the best," she says, her voice coming out quiet. "And I won't stop until my mother pays for what she did."

Violie nods slowly. "I'm with you," she says. "Leopold will be too. And when we get to Friv and speak to Daphne—"

Beatriz interrupts her with a laugh, cold and hard-edged. "I asked Daphne for help already," she tells her. "So did Sophie. But Daphne's a ruthless bitch and her loyalty is to our mother. Seek shelter from her, she's the only hope you have now, but for the sake of the stars, don't trust her." She pauses, turning the vial of stardust over in her hands and weighing her next words carefully. "My mother recruited you for a reason," she says. "Clearly you were good at going unnoticed, at gathering information. You know how to code?"

Violie nods. "I had the same lessons you did, albeit truncated versions," she says.

"Good," Beatriz says, pursing her lips as she uncorks the vial of stardust. Without warning, she smears the black dust over the back of her hand. "I wish Violie's nose were no longer broken. Try not to scream."

"Wha—" Violie begins before breaking off with a sharp gasp, her hands flying to her nose once more as she lets out a string of curses in both Bessemian and Temarinian. Beatriz says nothing, waiting for the other girl to get ahold of herself. After a moment, Violie goes quiet and her hands drop away from her face, revealing a nose that, while still mottled purple, is straight once more.

"By tomorrow, it should be back to normal," Beatriz says. "And you work for me now. I want you to keep an eye on my sister. I want to know everything she's doing. If you can intercept letters between her and my mother, all the better." Beatriz swallows, thinking of the Daphne she's known her entire life, the one who drove her mad but who she loved anyway. The one she always believed, deep down, would be on her side to the end. The one who did nothing and let Sophronia die.

"But when the time comes, if she proves to be a threat, you will stop her. By whatever means necessary," she finishes, the words coming out cold.

Violie's eyes widen ever so slightly. "You want me to kill her?" she asks. "She's your sister."

"She is," Beatriz tells her. "And I love her, but I don't trust her and I won't make the mistake of underestimating her." It isn't only Beatriz's life at stake now, it's Pasquale's and Leopold's as well, it's Ambrose's and Violie's by extension, and so many others. "My mother sharpened us into weapons, you understand that better than most. I won't let her wield Daphne to hurt anyone else I care about."

Daphne

Daphne lets loose another arrow, watching with mounting frustration as it lands on the rim of the target. A very unprincesslike curse rises to her lips, though she manages to tamp it down. After all, she has an audience. She glances behind her where six guards wait, three observing her, three standing with their backs to her, monitoring the surrounding woods for any sign of a threat.

She understands why they're there—part of her is even grateful for their presence, after the last few attempts on her life—but she knows their watching eyes are a large part of the reason she's shooting so poorly today. Unlike Beatriz, Daphne doesn't flourish with an audience.

Lifting the bow again, Daphne forces herself to take a deep, steadying breath and tries to ignore the guards entirely. They aren't there. It's only her, the bow in her hand, and the target before her. Nothing else exists. Nothing—

Just as she releases the arrow, one of the guards gives a shout and her shot goes wide.

"Stars above," she snaps, whirling toward the guard, though her annoyance dies as soon as she sees a figure riding toward them. Bairre, appearing unsettled.

For a moment, Daphne thinks he might be coming to join her. It's been weeks since they practiced together, but she finds she misses his company. Him watching never affected her aim. But when he pulls his horse to a stop beside her and her guards, he doesn't dismount.

"My father is requesting your presence," he tells her, an unreadable look in his eyes that makes Daphne's heart clench.

"Is everything all right?" she asks him, her mind already whirling through the myriad of things that could have gone wrong since she left the castle just an hour ago.

"Fine," he assures her quickly. "Everything's fine. But there's a visitor."

"A visitor?" Daphne asks, even more perplexed. Many of the highland clans left after the failed wedding, and she can't imagine they'd have returned so soon. And as for visitors from the south . . . well . . . no one visits Friv.

"From Temarin," he tells her.

The air leaves Daphne's lungs. Sophronia. It isn't. It can't be. Sophronia is dead. But for the barest sliver of an instant, Daphne's heart lifts in hope. Bairre must see it, because his expression softens.

"No," he says, shaking his head. "No, not . . . it's someone else."

Embarrassment claws at Daphne's skin. Of course it isn't Sophronia. She was a fool to hope that it might be, even more foolish to let anyone see her hope. She seals her disappointment away behind a cool mask and lifts her chin. "Who, then?" she asks.

Bairre clears his throat, glancing at the guards around them, who are only pretending not to listen.

"Queen Eugenia and her two sons," he tells her, lowering his voice to a murmur. "They've come seeking political asylum."

Daphne clutches the bow tighter in her hand.

"Her sons," she echoes. "Does that include King Leopold?" The Dowager Queen of Temarin has three sons, Daphne knows, and if King Leopold were among them, surely Bairre would have mentioned him first, but she has to ask. She has to be sure.

"No," Bairre says. "The younger two—children, who look like they've seen the stars go dark."

Seen the stars go dark is a Frivian expression, and one Daphne doesn't fully understand the origin of, but she gets the meaning all the same. It seems apt now, describing children who lived through a coup.

How did they survive the coup? Daphne wonders. And why are they here, of all places? Friv has never been known to be kind to outsiders. Surely Eugenia would have better luck in her homeland of Cellaria.

Well, there is only one way to find out what she's doing here. Daphne slides her bow back into its place in her quiver and steps toward Bairre, holding her hand out. He grabs hold of her palm with one hand, elbow with the other, and hoists her up to sit in front of him. The saddle isn't made to ride sidesaddle, but with Bairre's arm secure around her waist, it'll do for the short ride back to the castle.

Upon Daphne and Bairre's arrival back at the castle, he leads her through the labyrinth of halls that she is finally beginning to know her way around. When he makes a left instead of the right Daphne knows will take them to the throne room, her steps falter. Bairre notices, but he gives her arm a gentle tug, urging her to follow him.

"It's a private audience," Daphne says, noting that he's leading her toward the royal family's wing. "Your father doesn't want the court to know of their arrival. Not yet, at any rate."

Bairre doesn't answer, but Daphne knows she's right. It makes sense. Friv prides itself on its independence from the rest of the continent, and King Bartholomew is aware that many of his people already think he's relying too much on other countries—Bessemia, in particular, given Daphne's betrothal to Bairre. So of course he doesn't want it known that the Dowager Queen of Temarin is seeking asylum with him.

Daphne files that information away, wondering if she can use it.

Bairre leads her to the library, pushing the door open and ushering her inside.

The library is Daphne's favorite room in the castle—a cozy space with floor-to-ceiling windows and overstuffed sofas clustered around the largest of three fireplaces. It is King Bartholomew's favorite place in the castle too, and she often comes across him there early in the mornings or in the evenings, reading a volume of poetry or a novel—books Daphne's mother would have said were far too impractical to bother with.

Now Bartholomew is standing by the bay window, the thick velvet curtains drawn, casting the room into darkness only alleviated by the three burning fireplaces. The room is warm enough, but a woman sits on the overstuffed sofa, fur blankets piled on her lap and a boy on either side of her. Queen Eugenia and her younger sons, Daphne notes.

She searches her memory for everything she knows about the woman. Eugenia was born a Cellarian princess, the younger sister of King Cesare, and married off to King Carlisle of Temarin at the age of fourteen—a union that ended the Celestian War between the two countries and ensured a tentative peace. By all accounts, the marriage hadn't been consummated until she was sixteen and King Carlisle was eighteen, and even after that, she and the king had never been more than passingly polite. Passingly polite, however, was far kinder than the rest of the Temarin court had been to her.

But Eugenia had survived it, and when King Carlisle died, leaving behind a fifteen-year-old Prince Leopold to succeed him, Eugenia had ruled in her son's stead. Daphne remembered the empress referring to Eugenia as the most powerful person in Temarin.

Sophronia was supposed to supplant her, to exert her own influence over Leopold however necessary.

So why, Daphne wonders, her eyes raking over Queen Eugenia, is Sophronia dead and Eugenia here, looking no worse for wear? Well, that's not entirely true, she notes, her eyes finding a large bruise on the woman's left temple.

Another thing Daphne can't ask about, not yet. Instead, she pastes a smile over her face and crosses toward Queen Eugenia, holding out her hands to grasp the older woman's and giving them a squeeze.

"Your Majesty," Daphne says, dipping into a curtsy. "It is such a relief to see you made it out of Temarin safely. Word of the uprising has reached Friv and we have all been terribly worried."

"Princess Daphne," Queen Eugenia says, her eyes scanning Daphne's face. "You are the very image of your dear sister, stars bless her soul."

It's a lie—the only notable similarity between Daphne and Sophronia is their silver eyes. Daphne's hair is black where Sophronia's was blond, her features are sharp where Sophronia's were soft, her figure stick-straight where Sophronia was plump and curvy. Anyone who didn't know them would think they were strangers.

"Thank you," Daphne says, casting her eyes down as she makes a show of swallowing back tears. "And these must be my young brothers-in-law," she says, looking to the two boys flanking the queen, one around fourteen, the other twelve or so. Gideon and Reid. Both of them look at her with wide eyes, though they don't speak. Daphne makes a mental note to seek them out later, alone—children, she knows, are prime sources of information, often without the slightest idea of what they're meant to keep secret.

Behind her, King Bartholomew clears his throat. "Queen Eugenia is seeking asylum here in Friv," he says. "She believes if she returns to Temarin, she will be executed as well."

As well as Sophronia, Daphne thinks, though she appreciates that King Bartholomew doesn't say so out loud.

"Oh," Daphne says, furrowing her brow and glancing at Bartholomew. "I was under the impression that my mother had taken control of Temarin, no? She wrote to me that she would turn its rule over to Leopold once he was located—do you know where he is?"

There it is—a slight narrowing of the nostrils that tells Daphne that Eugenia is hiding something.

"Dead, I fear," Eugenia says, clutching her younger sons closer to her in a way that strikes Daphne as more performance than anything. "And I have written to your mother as well—while her troops have quelled the worst of the rebels, it is her belief that it is not yet safe for us to return. She suggested we come to Friv until it is."

"Did she?" Daphne asks, struggling to hide her confusion—surely her mother would have mentioned that to her?

"I have a letter from her, in fact," Queen Eugenia says, reaching into a pocket of her dress and withdrawing a rolled bit of parchment, then passing it to Daphne, who unrolls it and scans the words. It is a few short lines, written in her mother's hand—she'd recognize the writing anywhere—but the letter raises more questions than it answers.

Dear Eugenia,

We must proceed with caution—seek out my dove Daphne in Friv. I trust that she will give you shelter for as long as you need it. Let me know if you hear word from King Leopold—I shall keep his throne warm until I hear from him.

Your friend,
Empress Margaraux

Even if Daphne didn't recognize her mother's handwriting or the echo of her mother's letter to her, Daphne would know the letter is genuine. Her mother only called Daphne, Beatriz, and Sophronia her doves in private. But the letter doesn't tell her what, exactly, she is meant to do with Eugenia. She considers this as she passes the letter back to Eugenia.

"Daphne," King Bartholomew says behind her, his voice low and level. "A word, if you please."

Daphne nods and turns away from Queen Eugenia, following King Bartholomew to a quiet corner of the library, out of earshot of the queen and princes. Bairre follows them, the furrow in his brow deeper than usual.

"Daphne," King Bartholomew says again. "Friv has a long tradition of abstaining from the conflicts of the rest of the continent, and for good reason."

"Yes, of course," Daphne says quickly, the wheels of her mind turning. She might not know what to do with Eugenia, but it's clear her mother wishes her to stay here. Which means she needs to convince King Bartholomew to allow it.

Quickly, she runs through her tactics and how likely they are to work—there is little strategic reason for Bartholomew to help Eugenia. It won't benefit Friv or him and, in fact, many people at court would resent him for it, and Bartholomew can't afford to lose any more allies to the rebellion. Eugenia has little to offer and nothing that would counterbalance that. But King Bartholomew is a good man, and that is a weakness she has exploited before, with success.

So Daphne bites her bottom lip, casting a glance over her shoulder at Queen Eugenia and her sons.

"I'm sorry, Your Majesty, I know it's a lot to ask but I . . . I can't help but think that my sister is watching me from the stars, that she would want me to help keep Eugenia from meeting the same fate as she did and . . .” She trails off, swallowing and turning her gaze back to King Bartholomew, who appears unsettled. “And you heard her—her own son is likely dead. I understand it isn’t an ideal situation, but I can’t bear the thought of throwing a grieving mother to the wolves when we could offer her and the children she has left some measure of protection.”

It is cruel, using King Bartholomew’s own recently dead son as leverage, but it is a cruelty that works. Daphne sees the flicker of horror in his eyes, the way he glances at Queen Eugenia with pity and understanding.

“Of course, I wouldn’t dream of that,” he says quickly.

Bairre is staring at Daphne like he doesn’t know her, but he manages to tear his gaze from her and look at his father. “I’m not sure it’s the best idea—the last thing Friv needs is to insert itself into a war it has no stake in,” he says.

King Bartholomew shakes his head. “It is less than ideal, certainly,” he says with a sigh. “But I cannot see another option here. We will keep their presence quiet. No one need know who they are. We can make up a story, tell people that she is the Temarinian widow of some highland lord.”

“No one will believe that,” Bairre says. “They’ll figure out the truth soon enough.”

“By which time we will hopefully have a better idea of what to do,” King Bartholomew says. “But they’ll be staying and that’s final, Bairre.”

Without giving Bairre a chance to respond, King Bartholomew makes his way back to Queen Eugenia, offering her a smile and Friv’s protection.

Daphne slips out of the library and into the hall, Bairre at her heels. He reaches for her hand, but she pulls it from his grip and keeps walking, her eyes darting to the guards waiting to escort her back to her room safely.

"Daphne," Bairre says, his eyes glancing between the guards as well. Is he sizing them up? she wonders. Noting which of them is on the rebellion's side—his side?

"Not now," she snaps, and he falls silent. When they reach her room, Daphne isn't surprised that he follows her in, closing the door behind him and blocking them from the guards' prying eyes and ears.

"You shouldn't do that," she tells him with a heavy sigh as she removes her cloak and drapes it over the back of the armchair near the fire. "The last thing we need is gossip about us being alone together."

"I don't care about gossip," he says, and Daphne snorts out a laugh.

"Of course you don't," she says. "The gossip would affect me far more than it would you."

He doesn't answer right away, but Daphne sees the muscle in his jaw jump and she knows he understands what she means. "Should I go, then?" he asks.

"The damage is done, you might as well join me for tea," she says, sitting down at the small wooden table where a servant has laid out afternoon tea and pastries for her. She gestures for Bairre to sit. "Of course, if the wedding hadn't been interrupted, we'd be able to be alone whenever we pleased."

Even to her own ears, Daphne's words sound waspish

and curt, not the way she imagines Beatriz might say them, looking up at Bairre through lowered eyelashes with a coquettish smile, her voice a purr. But as unseductive as the words might be, Bairre's face still flushes red as he takes the chair across from her.

"What exactly are you playing at, Daphne?" he asks, pouring tea for her, then himself. "Everyone in the castle will know who Eugenia is by supper, and my father—"

"Will find himself even less popular than he is now," Daphne says, taking a sip of her tea. "Was I mistaken in believing that would suit the rebellion's aims quite well?"

He shakes his head. "That isn't . . . there's a reason we don't get involved in the squabbles of other countries," he says. "I'm not inclined to hurt Friv to prove its leadership is faulty."

It is not lost on Daphne that that is exactly what her mother is doing, but then, her mother has no loyalty to Friv and neither does she. Daphne won't forget that—she can't.

"What would you have done, then?" she asks. "Cast that woman and her sons out in the cold, sent them back to Temarin, where they would be killed as soon as they stepped over the border, like my sister was?"

Bairre shakes his head. "There are other places—she has family in Cellaria, and your mother offered her your hospitality, but what of her own?"

Both are good suggestions, and both make far more sense than Friv, and yet Eugenia is here, at her mother's urging. The empress isn't a fool, she would have thought of all options, weighed them carefully. There is a reason Eugenia is in Friv.

"I don't know," she admits. "But I'm sure my mother

wouldn't have sent her to me if she thought there was a better option."

Bairre looks at her for a long moment. "You aren't telling me the truth," he says finally.

Daphne holds his gaze. "No more than you are me," she replies, her voice coming out softer than she intends it to.

A long moment stretches out between them in silence as they sip their tea. Daphne opens her mouth several times to say something, but the words never come. She feels the secrets lying between them, creating a chasm that grows wider with each breath they take.

Let it, a voice whispers in her mind that sounds like her mother's. *Keep your distance. Use his affection if you can, use him, but don't let him use you.*

Bairre's hand reaches across the table to take Daphne's, and this time she doesn't pull away. Instead she laces her fingers with his and pretends that simple touch is enough to bridge the space between them, to cross the mountain of secrets and lies they've erected.

Daphne is not Sophronia, she knows there is no happy ending where she and Bairre will sit side by side on thrones and rule together—not least of all because Bairre himself doesn't want that future. She knows there is no place for him at all in the future she and her mother want to build, and that means there is no place for her feelings, either. She knows that eventually—soon, even—he won't look at her like he is now, with tenderness and adoration, if a little frustration, too. Soon, when he realizes what she and her mother are really working toward, he won't look at her with anything less than hate.

Daphne knows this, but right now he is looking at her like he would set the stars on fire if she asked it of him, like he will do anything for her except tell her the truth, and suddenly the truth doesn't matter as much as it should, not for either of them. Soon it will matter, but soon is not now.

Now she sets aside her tea but keeps ahold of his hand as she gets to her feet and walks toward him. Without saying a word, he pushes his chair back and gives her hand a soft tug and she lets herself be pulled down to sit on his lap, her arms going around his neck and his anchoring her around the waist, holding her tight against him.

She isn't sure which of them initiates the kiss, but it doesn't matter, not really. He kisses her and she kisses him and when his tongue traces the line of her lips, she opens to him, deepening the kiss. Still, it doesn't feel like enough. Even when her hands tangle in his dark overgrown hair, even when he lets out a low groan that Daphne feels echo in her own throat, it isn't enough.

Daphne presses herself closer to him and feels his hands bunch in the skirt of her dress.

A knock at the door cuts through the fog of her mind and Daphne forces herself to pull away. She feels like she's been on an hour-long horseback ride, and Bairre appears similarly out of breath, his eyes a darker shade of silver than usual and locked on hers.

Without a word, she reaches up to smooth his hair, mussed from where she ran her fingers through it, and he leans into her touch.

The knock sounds again and Daphne drops her hand,

forcing herself to stand up from his lap and return to her seat, Bairre reluctantly releasing her as she goes.

"Come in," Daphne calls out, equal parts surprised and relieved when her voice comes out steady.

The door opens and a guard pokes his head in, eyes darting around the room before landing on Daphne and Bairre. "Apologies for interrupting, Your Highnesses, but Lord Panlington sent a messenger looking for Prince Bairre."

Bairre lets out a low curse, getting to his feet. "I was supposed to meet him for a ride into town," he says. "I'm sorry, Daphne, but I have to go."

Lord Panlington is Cliona's father and the head of the Frivian rebellion—King Bartholomew's closest friend and greatest enemy. The sound of his name brings reality crashing down on Daphne—a reminder of who, exactly, Bairre's loyalties are to. He chose Lord Panlington and the rebellion over his own father, after all; she knows better than to think he will ever choose her. Which is just as well, she reminds herself.

"It's all right," Daphne says, forcing herself to smile. "I owe my mother a letter anyway."

She watches a curtain fall behind his eyes, feels the chasm open up between them once more, as wide as ever.

"I'll leave you to it, then," he says, giving her a stiff bow before exiting without another word, closing the door firmly behind him.

Violie

iolie and Leopold leave the Etheldaisy Inn as the first hints of the sun's rays are cresting over the mountaintops, and they don't make it to noon before Violie is missing Ambrose's presence, if only because he had a way of filling the heavy silences that always stretch between Violie and Leopold when they're alone.

At first, she suspected it had something to do with the fact that she was a servant and he was a deposed king who in all likelihood had little experience talking to servants more than strictly necessary. But he's acted as a servant himself now, back at the inn, and though the innkeeper was beneath him in status, he had no issue conversing with her.

Which means the issue is with Violie, and it likely goes much deeper than the difference in their classes.

"Has it been long since you've seen your cousin?" she asks him when the sun is high overhead and the silence becomes unbearable. They should reach the harbor by dusk if they take minimal breaks to rest.

For a long moment, Leopold stays silent and she thinks he'll actually ignore her, but eventually he sighs. "About a decade," he says.

"A long time," Violie says, casting a sidelong glance, but his expression gives nothing away.

"Yes," he says, and silence envelops them once more. Violie has just about given up altogether when he speaks again. "What happened to your nose?"

Violie's hand flies up to touch the appendage in question. It's still tender, but it doesn't hurt as much as it did yesterday, or even this morning. Leopold didn't mention it when they woke up and she assumed that in typical male fashion he hadn't even noticed something was different, just as he didn't notice when her eyes went from blue to star-touched silver the day after he arrived in the cave.

"Princess Beatriz healed it with stardust," she says. "When she gave me the asters." The asters, at least, he knows about, though not because he asked. Violie explained the plan to buy passage on a boat bound for Friv before they left the inn.

"Kind of her, considering she's the one who did it," he says, and Violie thinks she hears a hint of amusement color his voice.

"I don't hold that against her," Violie says with a shrug, and though it's the truth, it doesn't mean she wouldn't have ducked if she'd known Beatriz's aim, or how hard the princess could hit. "Don't tell me you didn't think of doing the same thing when I told you the truth about my employment with the empress."

At that, Leopold looks at her with wide eyes. "I would never hit a lady," he says, horrified.

"Lucky for you, I'm not one," she points out. "But the fact of the matter is, I'm responsible for Sophronia's death. I know that, you know that, and now Princess Beatriz knows that. I'm sure Princess Daphne will deal me a blow of her own when we meet."

Leopold goes quiet again and Violie thinks that will be the end of that. She focuses on the path ahead. If she squints into the distance, she can just make out the Iliven River on the horizon, a ribbon of blue cutting against the gray mountains.

"I don't know that," Leopold says, so quietly she almost doesn't hear him. Puzzled, she glances sideways at him. He clears his throat. "I don't know that it is your fault. No more than it's mine, at least. If I hadn't been such a terrible king, the rebellion never would have flourished like it did; if I hadn't trusted my mother, she wouldn't have been able to betray Sophie and me so devastatingly; if I'd somehow stopped Sophie before she . . ." He trails off, shaking his head. "The lion's share of the blame is mine, Violie."

Violie doesn't speak for a moment, but when she does, her voice is soft.

"You couldn't have stopped her, Leopold," she says, realizing belatedly that it's the first time she's called him that. "Sophie knew when we hatched our plan that she was going to sacrifice herself to save you. It wasn't a spur-of-the-moment choice, and if there is one thing I've learned about Sophie and her sisters it's this: when they hatch a plan, the stars themselves aren't enough to stand in their way."

Leopold considers this for a moment. "If you had refused to assist the empress, at the beginning or when she ordered you to forge the declaration of war, do you imagine she would have simply given up?"

It's a question Violie has never considered before. She opens her mouth, then closes it again. She doesn't have an answer, she realizes, though Leopold doesn't seem to expect one.

"If you were her secret weapon, I'd wager she had more. We know she had my mother on her side. How many others do you think there were?"

Again, Violie doesn't answer, though the question raises the hairs on the back of her neck. Leopold continues.

"From what Sophie told me before she . . . well, before, the empress has been planning her attacks since before they were even conceived. That's seventeen years. Seventeen years of looking at things from every angle, of plotting and arranging pieces on a chessboard. Do you think she would leave anything to chance? Even you?"

Violie swallows. "I hadn't thought about it that way," she says.

"You said it yourself—if Sophie and her sisters hatch a plan, the stars themselves can't stand in their way. Where, exactly, do you think they learned that from?" he asks.

That, at least, is a question Violie knows the answer to, though she suspects it's a rhetorical one. She would be lying if she said Leopold's words didn't ease her guilt, if only a fraction, but they unsettle her even more. She never expected that going against the empress would be an easy task, but as they make their way closer and closer to the harbor, closer and closer to Princess Daphne and Friv, Violie suspects it just might be an impossible one.

Violie and Leopold make good time to the harbor, in large part thanks to a farmer they meet on the road who offers them a ride along with the bushels of wheat he's bringing to sell to a merchant ship. Violie is ready to give the man payment, but when he doesn't ask for any, she holds her tongue. The journey to Friv won't be easy, and they will need every last aster Beatriz gave them.

Leopold lets Violie take charge of finding them passage to Friv, which Violie is grateful for. She doubts Leopold knows the first thing about bargaining, or even what an aster is worth, and she doesn't need his high-born accent to complicate matters.

After they ask around for a Frivian ship, the name everyone gives her is Captain Lehigh of the *Astral,* a cargo ship that ferries various goods among Cellaria, Temarin, Bessemia, and Friv. She and Leopold find Captain Lehigh at one of the pubs near the harbor, already several pints of ale deep. He's in his fifties, with a round, ruddy face and a full red beard. When Violie asks him about passage, he narrows his eyes, his gaze darting between her and Leopold.

"And what business do you have traveling to Friv?" he asks, his accent Frivian, but worn down by his travels.

Violie shrugs. "Family," she says, which she supposes is close enough to the truth. It simply isn't her family. It is technically Leopold's, she supposes, if only through marriage.

"You don't sound Frivian to me," Captain Lehigh points out.

"I'm Bessemian," she admits. "My husband is Temarinian," she adds, nodding toward Leopold. "But neither of us is keen on risking our necks or livelihood staying in a country in such tumult. My sister married a Frivian farmer, near the Ester River," she adds, remembering the maps she was forced to study. "It seems as good a place to start over as any."

Captain Lehigh considers her for a long moment, his eyes a little too glassy from the ale to be called shrewd. "Fifteen asters," he tells her. "Each."

Beatriz gave her fifty asters, which means they'd have twenty asters to get them from the Frivian harbor to the castle. Doable, maybe, but Violie isn't keen on risking it. She decides to bluff.

She shakes her head. "Never mind," she tells him, pushing back from the table. "Another ship offered to take us for fifteen total. Not as nice a ship as I've heard the *Astral* is, but—"

Captain Lehigh grabs her wrist and Violie freezes. Next to her, Leopold stiffens. "Twenty total," he says. "That's my final offer."

Violie wrenches her arm out of Captain Lehigh's grip—an easier feat than she'd expected. He releases her readily enough. She pretends to consider it for a moment before she nods. "Deal," she says.

"I'll take the payment now," he says, holding his hand out, palm up. He has a tattoo of an anchor on the side of his thumb, a tradition Violie has heard of for captains who believe it keeps their ships from sinking.

Violie reaches into the pocket of her dress, pulling out a single ten-aster coin and dropping it into his hand. "Ten now, the other ten when we reach Friv safely."

Captain Lehigh looks ready to argue, but seems to think better of it. "We leave at dawn—if you aren't on the boat by then, we leave without you." He doesn't wait for Violie to reply, instead waving over the barmaid and ordering another drink, effectively dismissing them.

Beatriz

Beatriz, Pasquale, Ambrose, and Nigellus depart the Etheldaisy Inn in far more comfort than they arrived, bundled into Nigellus's private carriage with several fur blankets between them and hot bricks at their feet to stave off the cold. The carriage, its driver, and its two white horses left Nigellus at the Sororia in the mountains and took the long and winding roads in order to make it to the inn safely just hours after Violie and Leopold departed. The driver suggested they all stay another night to let the horses rest.

When the sun creeps over the mountains the next morning, though, they depart. While the first few hours of the journey pass with some polite conversation—comments about the blistering cold weather, compliments for the basket of breakfast the innkeeper packed them—Beatriz notes with relief that Pasquale and Ambrose are appropriately wary of saying too much in front of Nigellus.

Nigellus, for his part, doesn't pay any of them much mind, either keeping his silver gaze out the window as they make their way down the winding road or thumbing through a well-worn copy of last year's *Astral Almanac*.

When they stop for a late lunch at another inn, Nigellus leads them into the public room, nodding toward the innkeeper who approaches them, this one a middle-aged man, bald, but with an impressive mustache.

"The gentlemen will dine here, but I'll need a private room for the girl and me—just for an hour," he says smoothly.

Beatriz stiffens, her gaze darting to Nigellus. He's shown no interest in bedding her, but surely he must know how that sounds and what the innkeeper will think. Sure enough, the innkeeper looks uneasily between the two of them.

"And is that what the lady wishes?" he asks carefully.

Nigellus frowns and opens his mouth, but Beatriz gets there first, offering the innkeeper a bright smile.

"Oh yes," she assures him, looping her arm through Nigellus's "I've a fear of crowds, you see, and my dear uncle indulges me."

The innkeeper is visibly relieved and nods. "I'll see if we have a spare room for you, then," he says before hurrying down the hall. As soon as he's out of earshot, Pasquale turns to Beatriz and Nigellus.

"Where Beatriz goes, I go," he tells Nigellus, his voice coming out stronger than Beatriz expected it would. Though she's touched by his standing up for her, she isn't afraid of Nigellus. Whether that makes her brave or foolish, she isn't sure. She releases her hold on Nigellus's arm and reaches out to touch Pasquale's.

"It's fine," she assures him with a smile. "Nigellus and I have things to discuss."

Pasquale doesn't look terribly reassured, his brow still

creased in a frown, though he nods once, looking back at Nigellus. "If you lay a hand on her—"

"I can assure you, I've no interest in children," Nigellus replies, his voice colder than the weather outside.

"I'll be back in an hour," she says when Pasquale's frown deepens. "Go, enjoy a good lunch with Ambrose."

The innkeeper leads Beatriz and Nigellus to a small room, sparsely decorated, with a narrow bed and a round table set with two chairs. He promises to bring them drinks and lunch as quickly as possible, then departs, leaving Beatriz and Nigellus alone.

"This is to be my first lesson, I take it?" Beatriz asks, circling the room as if inspecting it, though there is little to inspect. Moving calms her, though, just as it always has.

"Yes," Nigellus says, watching her with weary eyes. "*You* didn't think I was planning to seduce you, I hope."

Beatriz laughs. "No," she assures him. "You're familiar with the training I had in Bessemia—I know when I'm wanted like that. But I'm glad the innkeeper ensured I wasn't in danger, and Pasquale . . ." She trails off, thinking about Pasquale's father, King Cesare, who made no secret of his attempts to bed her. The thought of his hands on her makes her shudder. The man is dead now and Beatriz hasn't mourned him for a moment. The world is better off rid of him.

She doesn't say any of that aloud, but Nigellus's eyes trace over her expression.

"It shouldn't surprise you that your mother has spies

in the Cellarian court," he says after a moment. "From what they had to say, Prince Pasquale was not nearly so . . . protective then."

Beatriz grits her teeth, the insult to Pasquale digging beneath her own skin. "I didn't need him to be," she says. "It was only what I'd been raised for, after all." She tells herself it's the truth, but talking about it needles at her. "I didn't realize you were so terribly interested in my personal trials and tribulations," she says, forcing her voice to stay light and unbothered. "Would you like to dissect my diary, or can we get to the lessons?"

Nigellus stares at her with uncomfortable intensity for a moment before one corner of his mouth lifts ever so slightly. "Come now, Beatriz—we both know your mother taught you never to commit your thoughts to paper where anyone can read them."

He reaches into the pocket of his cloak and pulls out the *Astral Almanac* he was studying in the carriage. He holds it up so she can see the cover—cornflower-blue leather, embossed with gold script. "You're familiar with these?" he asks.

Beatriz shrugs. "Passingly," she admits. "Daphne and Sophie have always been more interested in horoscopes than I am and I never saw the point in looking at horoscopes past."

"Ah," Nigellus says, sitting down at the table and gesturing for her to sit across from him, which she does. "But that is how we find the patterns. And once you understand the patterns of the past, you can spot them in the future. Of course, this would be a more instructive lesson if we had the night sky to study, but that will have to be saved for another time. For now . . ." He thumbs through the pages, landing on one in particular and passing the book to her. "What do you notice here?"

Beatriz takes the book and examines it—not only the page, but the book itself. It's well-worn, though only a year old. The page he's opened to is a midsummer night, with a list of the constellations that appeared, their proximity to one another, and interpretations of what it could mean. Beatriz squints.

"The Thorned Rose is one of my birth constellations," she tells him, noting its presence on the list. She and her sisters were born beneath the Thorned Rose, the Hungry Hawk, the Lonely Heart, the Crown of Flames, and the Sisters Three. "It symbolizes beauty, and this says it appeared beside an upside-down Queen's Chalice, which would signal misfortune. Their close proximity would indicate that these things are linked, no?" she asks, glancing up at Nigellus, who is watching her intently. "What happened on this date?"

Nigellus's eyebrows rise. "You don't recall?" he asks her.

Beatriz searches her memory. Midsummer, last year. She was still in Bessemia, still spent each and every day in the company of her sisters, still had never seen more of the world than palaces and the gleaming cities around them. The days all blended together in her mind.

"You broke your nose," Nigellus tells her.

Beatriz blinks. She *did* break her nose last summer, during hand-to-hand combat practice with Daphne. It wasn't the first time such practice had led to injury, and Nigellus himself healed it so quickly with a pinch of stardust that it didn't leave much of an impression on her.

"A misfortune that affected my beauty, however briefly," Beatriz says wryly, passing the book back to him. "I'll admit, I feel quite flattered that the stars saw fit to mark the occasion."

If Nigellus understands her humor, it has no effect on him. "I'm sure others were affected as well, in different ways. And as you said, it is one of your birth constellations, so you would be more affected by its presence in the sky."

"And my sisters', though I don't recall them suffering similar incidents," she says before pausing. "That isn't true. Daphne woke up with a pimple the size of the moon on her chin. And Sophie . . ."

"That would have been the day the newest portrait of King Leopold arrived. Your sister was quite taken with it, if you remember."

Beatriz did. All day, Sophronia talked of little else. By the time the sun set, Beatriz thought if she heard another word about his handsome face and kind eyes, she'd take a dagger to the canvas herself.

"And her infatuation turned out to be an unlucky thing indeed," Beatriz finishes, though as she speaks, she remembers Violie's words. *For whatever it's worth, I believe he loved Sophie as much as she loved him.* It was difficult to imagine her sister falling in love with the hapless king—infatuation, certainly. Beatriz herself wasn't blind, and even covered in more than a week of grime, she could acknowledge that Leopold was handsome. But love was something else, wasn't it?

Though she doesn't mean to, she thinks about Nicolo. That wasn't love. She didn't make Sophronia's mistake there, though she can't help but think that was more due to Nicolo's betrayal than any restraint on her part. A few more weeks and perhaps she'd have thought herself in love with him, too.

"So all of us were affected in different ways," Beatriz says, pushing Nicolo from her thoughts and focusing on Nigellus. "Though no offense to Daphne's unfortunate pimple, but is that really comparable to a broken nose? And I hardly think we can blame the appearance of a couple of constellations for Sophronia's death—that was my mother's doing."

"Everything ties together, Beatriz. Especially where the stars are concerned," Nigellus says mildly. "But you aren't wrong. You were the most affected that day, and by other appearances of the Thorned Rose, and there is a reason for that. It took nearly two hours from when you took your first breath to when Sophronia took hers. You're triplets, your births stretched on some time, so I marked each constellation that appeared overhead during the labor. The Thorned Rose reached its peak as you drew your first breath. It was still in the sky when your sisters came along, but it is strongest in you."

It might be new information to Beatriz, but it doesn't surprise her. She's always been told that her beauty is her greatest asset—by her mother most of all. She's well acquainted with the rose and its thorns.

"And my sisters?" she asks. "What signs would you

say belonged most to them?" She almost regrets asking the question as soon as it leaves her lips, but she suspects the answer.

"I'd like to hear your guesses," Nigellus says, leaning back.

Beatriz grits her teeth. "I'm sure I don't know," she says, but it's a lie, and he seems to know it.

"Your mother never saw fit to give you the lessons your sisters had in star reading," he tells her. "She thought the more you knew of it, the more likely it would be that you would say the wrong thing in Cellaria and get yourself killed."

"Isn't that what she wants, though?" Beatriz asks, another wry comment that Nigellus doesn't acknowledge.

"For the right ends, not for a slip of blasphemy on your first day in the palace," he replies. "But my point is that you have no formal education in star reading, so I'm curious what your instinct tells you."

Beatriz rolls her eyes. "The Hungry Hawk seems very like Daphne," she says. "To take it literally, I suppose, there's something a bit hawkish about her. And she is more ambitious than Sophie and I."

Nigellus doesn't agree with her, but he doesn't correct her, either. "And Sophronia?"

Beatriz swallows. "She was born beneath the Lonely Heart, wasn't she?" she asks. "It symbolizes sacrifice."

Now Nigellus nods. "The other two constellations, the Crown of Flames and the Sisters Three, were never directly overhead, yet present nonetheless," he says. "But yes, you have the right of it."

Beatriz laughs. "There are plenty of ugly children born

beneath the Thorned Rose," she tells him. "Everyone knows birth constellations are to be taken with a grain of salt."

"Under normal circumstances, yes," Nigellus tells her. "But we've already established that the circumstances of your birth were anything but normal."

"Because my mother wished for us?" Beatriz asks.

"Because it wasn't only one wish," Nigellus says. "There was the original wish for her to fall pregnant with triplets— that I made on the Mother's Arms." The Mother's Arms is a constellation that resembles a pair of arms holding a swaddled infant. "But the larger wishes had to be made when each of you took your first breaths, to tie your fates to the fates of the countries you would one day call home."

Beatriz blinks. "If an empyrea could so easily conquer countries, how has no one else done it before?" she asks.

Nigellus shakes his head. "It *is* far too big an undertaking, even when wishing on stars," he says. "But your mother didn't rely on the stars alone to make her wishes come true. She planned carefully for seventeen years and made sure every piece was in place for her plots. The wishes we made on the day you and your sisters were born aren't responsible for those plans, they were simply meant to ensure a greater chance of those plans' success."

Beatriz processes this, not speaking for a moment. "It didn't work, though. Not for me. Or Daphne, apparently."

"Because wishes require sacrifice, and her sacrifice of you and Daphne is as yet incomplete," Nigellus says. "But as I was saying, your mother wished on a separate star upon each of your births. I had to pull a star from each of those constellations in order to make her wish come true. There is a piece of the Hungry Hawk inside Daphne, just as there was a piece of the Lonely Heart inside Sophronia. Small stars, the kind I told you to look for because few would notice them missing, and those who did knew better than to ask questions."

"So the constellation you took my star from was what?" she asks. "The Thorned Rose?"

It's a disappointing revelation. Though Beatriz's beauty is the first thing anyone remarks upon when meeting her, she believes it is quite possibly her least interesting trait.

Nigellus leans back in his chair, folding his hands on his lap and surveying her. "No," he says after a moment. "From another constellation that edged its way into the sky when you were born, ever so slightly. Not present enough to be worth mentioning in your zodiac, especially when it was gone before your sisters followed you."

Beatriz's chest tightens. "And what constellation was that?" she asks.

Nigellus smiles. "The Empyrea's Staff."

The Empyrea's Staff, for magic.

Beatriz's mouth suddenly feels dry. "You planned this, then," she says slowly. "You planned me."

"Yes," he says simply.

"Why?" Beatriz asks.

For a moment he doesn't respond. "The stars don't only give blessings and twist fate, Beatriz," he says finally. "They demand balance. As an empyrea, you will come to understand that, to hear that demand as clearly as you hear my voice now. And you will come to know how to answer it. When the stars sent the Empyrea's Staff overhead during your birth, I understood it for the demand it was."

Goose bumps rise on Beatriz's skin. She wants to laugh at how melodramatic he sounds, at the very idea of the stars demanding anything with regard to her, but her mouth is still dry. It takes a moment for her to speak and when she does, she manages only one word. "Why?"

"Because the stars require a balanced world. It's why wishes come with sacrifices, why you feel terrible after pulling stars down. There's an ages-old prophecy, from some empyrea whose name has long been lost. To unbalance the world is to darken the stars."

Beatriz repeats the words under her breath, frowning. "That doesn't sound like a prophecy," she says.

"Given how many times the words have been translated from one language to another and back, that isn't surprising. But the meaning remains. The stars are good to us, but they require balance. Creating you and your sisters threw the stars off-balance—I should have known then that your mother was asking too much, but I was young and foolish and too curious for my own good. But when the stars made their demand, I knew we'd gone too far. Your mother was creating weapons to use against the world, and so the stars demanded a weapon of their own."

"And that weapon is supposed to be me?" Beatriz asks, not bothering to mask the skepticism in her voice. Nigellus's eyes narrow.

"These lessons will go much faster if you don't fight everything I tell you," he says.

Beatriz wants to argue that point, but she realizes that would be proving his point. "Fine," she says. "I am a weapon, created by the stars. To do what, destroy my mother? Certainly if the stars truly wished to stop her, there would have been easier ways of doing it seventeen years ago."

"Ah, but you aren't listening, Princess," he says, shaking his head. "The stars aren't on your side, or hers, or mine for that matter. The stars aren't soldiers in anyone's war—they are the battleground, and they prefer to keep it as even as possible."

Daphne

I t isn't that Daphne wanted to poison Queen Eugenia, but she was left with little choice. Over the course of the tea Daphne had arranged for them to enjoy together two days after Eugenia's arrival, the dowager queen hid far more than she revealed about her ordeal in Temarin, and what little she did reveal struck Daphne as lies.

Most notably, Daphne knows for a fact that Sophronia was executed nine days ago, and yet Queen Eugenia claims she's spent the last week making her way from Kavelle to Friv.

The journey would take four days by carriage, but as Eugenia's pace may have been hindered by the fact that they had to avoid notice for much of their trip, a week is plausible.

But that doesn't account for the two missing days.

And then there is Eugenia's wound. She tries to hide it with cosmetics and the swoop of her dark brown hair, but in the bright afternoon light coming through the windows, Daphne can just make out the angry bruise on Eugenia's left temple. Judging by the size and shape of the wound, Daphne would guess it was caused by the butt of a pistol.

Given the lengths to which Eugenia has gone to hide the injury, Daphne would wager she won't give an honest answer about how she sustained it. Posing the question also certainly won't endear her to the dowager queen, and Daphne needs to ensure that the woman is on her side, at least for now.

So when Queen Eugenia turns to ask a servant for more tea cakes, Daphne reaches across the small table, dropping a sprinkle of powder from her hollow ring into Eugenia's tea just before she takes the cream and pours a splash into her own cup.

It isn't enough to cause her any harm, or even raise her suspicions. As small a dose as Daphne gave her, it should simply leave her exhausted, something she will likely attribute to a lingering exhaustion from her trying journey north.

Daphne returns to the dowager queen and her sons' temporary chambers an hour after their tea ends, under the pretense of bringing a book of Frivian history she made a passing mention of over tea for just this reason. When a maid tells her that Eugenia is napping, Daphne feigns surprise and disappointment.

"Well, I can leave it here with you for when she wakes," Daphne says before making a show of peering around the maid to the sitting room, where Prince Reid and Prince Gideon are playing with wooden swords. The maid has already moved the furniture aside to make room for them. "Would the princes be happier playing outside?" Daphne asks, loud enough to get their attention.

"Can we?" the elder, Gideon, asks. He is fourteen and gangly, with blond hair and freckles on his nose and cheeks. Reid, two years younger, stands beside him, his hair a bit darker, his skin a shade paler. Both of them look like their brother, King Leopold, or at least the paintings and illustrations Sophronia received of her betrothed.

"Your mother said you should stay indoors," the maid says, shaking her head before turning back to Daphne. "I'm sorry, Your Highness, but they aren't accustomed to the weather here yet. It wouldn't do for them to fall ill."

"Oh, of course not," Daphne says, widening her eyes. "It was quite a shock to me as well when I arrived here, but it isn't so bad if you're properly dressed for it. I'm certain we can dig up some of Prince Bairre's old clothes and get them properly attired."

"I'm not sure . . . ," the maid says, frowning.

"Please, it won't be any trouble. I was going to go for a walk myself and I'm sure you have plenty of unpacking to do." She glances past the maid to Gideon and Reid. "Have you ever seen snow? Quite a bit fell last night, enough for a snowball fight."

Reid's eyes grow wide as asters. "Please, please, please, Genevieve," he begs the maid. "We'll be good, won't we, Gideon?"

"So good," Gideon promises, before looking back at Daphne. "Can Bairre come too?"

Daphne winces internally, though she isn't entirely surprised. Of course a boy Gideon's age would look up to Bairre. It might even be helpful to have him around, to put the boys at ease so that they feel comfortable sharing information, but she hasn't seen him since their tea two days before, and she is dreading seeing him again.

"We can ask him," Daphne says before looking back at the maid, Genevieve. "They've had a difficult few days, haven't they? Fleeing their home, losing their brother. They need a bit of fun, don't you think?"

The maid hesitates, glancing over her shoulder at the closed door that must lead to the queen's bedchamber. "All right," she says, turning back around. "But you both must do whatever Princess Daphne says, and be back before supper."

Daphne gives the maid her sweetest smile. "I'm sure they'll be on their very best behavior."

Bairre agrees to help her show the young princes around the grounds and finds some heavy coats and boots for them, hidden away in the back of his wardrobe. They're still a bit big on the boys, but at least they'll be warm.

"I promised them a snowball fight," Daphne says as the four of them make their way outside. The snow stopped early in the morning, but Daphne awoke to a thick blanket of fresh snow outside her window. As they walk up the hill on the edge of the forest, trailed by six guards who keep at a distance, Gideon and Reid are in awe of the footprints they leave behind, Reid taking particular joy in stomping each step.

"Have you never seen snow before?" Bairre asks them, and they both shake their heads.

"It doesn't snow in Temarin," Gideon says.

"Oh, you're in for a treat," Daphne tells them. "It snowed very rarely in Bessemia, but every time it did my sisters and I had such fun throwing snowballs at one another. I was always the best, of course."

"Of course," Bairre echoes, shooting her a lopsided smile.

"You and Sophie had snowball fights?" Reid asks, wrinkling his nose. "I can't imagine that."

"Oh yes," Daphne says, smiling at the memory of a young Sophronia, face red and nose runny from the cold, holding a snowball in mittened hands, her gaze fixed on Daphne. "I'm sure you think Sophie was too kind to throw snowballs at me, but she was quite vicious when she wanted to be."

Gideon looks skeptical about that, but Reid gives a loud sigh. "I miss her," he admits.

Daphne bites her bottom lip. "I do too," she says, aware of Bairre watching her. She won't fall apart in front of him again, she's done so too many times already. She focuses on the task at hand. "You must miss your brother as well," she says, glancing back at the guards. They're far enough away not to hear, and most of their attention is focused away from Daphne, Bairre, and the princes, scanning for threats.

Reid nods. "Mama says he's dead," he says.

"He's not," Gideon tells him, his voice sharp.

"No?" Daphne asks, glancing at the elder prince. "Have you had word of him, then?"

"No," Gideon says, frowning. "I just know, is all. Did you know Sophie was dead? Did you feel it?"

Daphne frowns, opening her mouth and closing it again as she struggles to find the words. Bairre beats her to it.

"I felt it when my brother died," he says. "Cillian was ill for a long time, but it never felt real. Until it did."

Daphne glances at him, the desire to reach out and take his hand catching her by surprise. Instead, she clenches her hand into a fist at her side.

"See?" Gideon says, triumphant. "I would know if Leopold were dead. He isn't."

Daphne isn't sure how much faith to put in feelings, but she's fairly sure that if Leopold is alive, his mother and brothers don't know about it.

"It must have been very frightening," she says after a moment. "Fleeing the palace in the middle of a siege. I know I would have been terrified. You're very brave."

Gideon and Reid exchange a look so brief Daphne almost misses it.

"Yes," Gideon says, lifting his chin. "It was terrifying."

He doesn't elaborate. It could be because the events of the night left them traumatized, too shaken up to speak of it, or . . .

She stops in front of Reid, bending slightly to straighten the collar of his coat. She meets his gaze and gives him a warm smile.

"Unless you weren't at the palace at all that night," she says lightly. "Perhaps you were already far away from the danger by then. Somewhere else."

Reid frowns. "I—"

"No, we were at the palace," Gideon interrupts. "It was terrifying, just like I said. Are we going to have a snowball fight or not?"

Daphne's eyes search Reid's face a second longer before she

reaches down to the snow beneath her feet, balls up a handful, and throws it square at Gideon's shoulder with a grin.

"Got you!" she says, but Gideon and Reid are already laughing, reaching down to make their own snowballs.

After half an hour of lobbing snowballs back and forth, Daphne and Bairre surrender and the brothers turn on each other, running deeper into the woods, their laughter echoing. Five of the six guards stay with Daphne and Bairre while one follows the boys.

"Stay close!" Daphne calls after them. When she turns back to Bairre, she finds him watching her.

"You think they're lying?" he asks her. "About the siege?"

"I know they are," Daphne says, leaning back against the trunk of a great oak tree. "They aren't very good liars. Reid would have broken if I'd had him alone, but Gideon seemed . . . afraid."

"But why lie?" Bairre asks. "Are they trying to protect Leopold, wherever he is?"

Daphne shakes her head. "No, I believed them when they said they hadn't had word of him. They're lying because their mother told them to. I haven't the slightest idea why. And before you ask, yes, that's the stars' honest truth."

Daphne isn't sure he believes her, but after a second, he gives a quick and decisive nod.

"If she's a friend of your mother's, can't you ask her?" he says, and though his voice is mild enough on the surface, it is not an idle question.

"I'm not sure they are friends, but they did become family

when Sophie married Leopold," Daphne says, and that at least is the truth. "And the letter she arrived with was in my mother's hand, and in hindsight, I suppose they have a bit in common, both tasked with running countries that were hostile toward them."

"Your mother's hold on Bessemia is strong, though," he points out.

Daphne nods. "In my memory, it always has been, but when I was a baby, just after my father died, there were many who refused to bow to a woman who'd been born a tailor's daughter, many who thought they themselves would be better suited to the throne."

"But your mother triumphed," he points out. "She didn't end up fleeing to a foreign land with you and your sisters in tow."

Daphne has never thought about that path, what might at one point have seemed a likely one. How different her life might have looked, if that had happened. It might not have been a very long life at all. In the distance, she hears Gideon and Reid laughing as they play.

She pushes the thought aside. "My mother always triumphs," she tells Bairre with a smile. "She made the right allies, and she had her empyrea, Nigellus, on her side. Now every person who tried to overthrow her is dead, or imprisoned, or has made appropriate amends, and the last sixteen years of my mother's reign have seen Bessemia flourish."

"Perhaps more tailors' daughters should find themselves crowned," Bairre says before glancing sideways at her. "You miss her," he says. "Of course you do, that isn't surprising, but when you talk about her, you light up."

Daphne nods. She always knew she would leave Bessemia, leave her sisters and her mother, too. The empress certainly never minced words about that. She raised them to leave her. But especially with Sophronia's death still an open wound, Daphne doesn't think there is anything in this world she wouldn't give to find herself in her mother's arms once more.

"She's a remarkable woman," she tells Bairre. "I've always wanted to be just like her."

Bairre's hand finds hers, entwining their fingers together. He opens his mouth to speak, but before he can form words, a scream pierces the air, followed by another.

Ice floods Daphne's veins as she drops Bairre's hand. "The princes," she says, already starting after them.

Bairre falls into step beside her, as do the guards, as they begin to run. Daphne's eyes search the woods around them, but there is no sign of either boy apart from footsteps in the freshly fallen snow.

"They can't have gone far," Bairre says, though he sounds like he's convincing himself more than her. "These woods have been patrolled ever since . . ."

Ever since we were set upon by assassins here, Daphne thinks. The thought isn't terribly reassuring.

"Gideon!" she calls out. "Reid!"

But only silence meets her cry. She and Bairre continue to shout the princes' names as they follow the footprints, but there is no response. The prints weave through the trees, circling and crisscrossing in a maze before ending in the middle of a small clearing, where the body of the guard who accompanied them lies, blood staining the snow beneath him red.

Two more guards run to him, but Daphne knows by the look of him that he's dead.

"Horses," Bairre says, pointing out hoofprints in the snow. "At least five of them."

Daphne lets out a curse under her breath, her heart thudding in her chest. The princes have been kidnapped.

Violie

After just a day on board the *Astral*, Violie can't remember what not being ill feels like. Her stomach is constantly rioting, and despite the chill in the air, her skin is cloaked in a thick layer of sweat. Getting out of the narrow bed in the small cabin she and Leopold share is an effort that seems to require the favor of the stars, but staying in bed is pure misery. Every fiber of her being is exhausted, but no matter how she tries, she can't manage more than an hour of sleep at a time. A bucket has taken up residence beside the cot, which she empties her stomach into often, though she can't bring herself to eat more than a nibble or two of stale bread.

Violie isn't aware of much outside of her own misery, but she knows that someone dabs her face with a cool, wet rag from time to time. Someone forces her to take sips of water from a glass and small bites of bread. Someone empties the bucket of her vomit.

Someone, she supposes, must be Leopold, but even when her thoughts fray at the edges, she has a difficult time imagining the King of Temarin acting as her nursemaid.

Violie wakes at dawn, if the faint light streaming through the single porthole in the cabin is anything to go by. Two days. She's been on this boat for two days and it feels like an eternity. It takes her a moment to recognize the scent hanging heavy in the air.

"Ginger," she mumbles, rolling over on her side.

Leopold is sitting on the wooden floor beside the cot, a mug of steaming tea in his hands.

"Among other things," he says, looking at the mug. "The cook brewed it for you—she said it is a foolproof cure for seasickness. Can you sit up?"

It's a struggle, but Violie manages to pull herself up, leaning against the understuffed pillow. Leopold passes her the mug of tea, but her arms feel so weak she can barely hold it. He helps her bring it to her lips and though it's hot, she manages three small sips.

Violie gives a sputtering cough as she lowers the mug and winces.

"The cook said it isn't the best-tasting thing, but it does its duty."

"The cure might just be worse than the sickness," Violie says, but she manages to lift the mug on her own and force down another sip. "Thank you."

Leopold nods. "The ship is making good time," he tells her. "Captain Lehigh says the stars and weather are on our side. We should reach Glenacre port by sundown tomorrow."

"I think my stomach can survive that, if only barely," she says. She means the words as a joke, but Leopold frowns.

"Is there anything you need? Do you want to try some more bread?"

The thought of food makes Violie want to vomit, but she merely shakes her head. "I'm fine. Well, I'm surviving, at any rate."

"The cook also said fresh air would help," Leopold says. "When you finish the tea, I could help you up to the main deck."

Violie shakes her head. "I'm sure the crew will be busy up there."

Leopold laughs. "Trust me, after the festivities last night, I think most of them will be sleeping for another hour at least."

"Festivities?" Violie asks, taking another sip.

"Captain Lehigh's birthday," he explains. "You won't be the most miserable person on this boat today by a nautical mile."

Violie manages a smile and takes another sip of tea, then another. It is helping, she realizes. She still doesn't feel like herself, but her stomach has calmed down significantly. She sits up a little straighter and manages to drain the cup in a few more sips.

"Fresh air sounds perfect," she tells Leopold.

The deck of the ship is largely deserted, though Violie notices a scattered handful of crew members about, doing their various duties to ensure that the *Astral* keeps sailing while everyone else sleeps. The clear sky overhead is just beginning to lighten, though the stars are still visible, strewn over the pinkening sky like the diamonds Violie used to polish for Sophronia. She knows, vaguely, what clusters of the stars represent, but she's never completely sure which constellation is which.

"That's the Tumbling Water," Leopold says when Violie asks him if he knows, pointing to a cluster of stars to the east. "It's supposed to look like a waterfall."

Violie squints, but she doesn't quite see it. She takes his word for it, though. Growing up a prince, he had access to the best teachers for that sort of thing.

"Tumbling Water for . . . inevitability?" Violie asks, frowning.

"Sort of. I always heard it as fate," Leopold says, shrugging. "The water can't help but go where it's meant to."

They stop at the ship's railing and Violie leans her entire body against it. She's only been on her feet for a moment, but she feels like she's been running for miles.

"Is it helping?" he asks. "The fresh air."

"With the nausea, yes," she admits. "Thank you. For the tea and . . . well . . . taking care of me like you have been."

"I don't think I've done a good job of it," he admits, leaning against the railing beside her. "I've never been around ill people, really."

"Not surprising for a king, or crown prince for that matter," she points out. "What would Temarin have done if you'd gotten ill and died?"

He gives her a sidelong look. "Been just fine, I'd imagine," he says.

Violie isn't sure what to say to that. She knows she should tell him it isn't true, but she doesn't have the energy to reassure him just now. Before she can say anything at all, a new voice breaks the silence.

"Hey, Leopold!"

Hairs rise on the back of Violie's neck—not because she recognizes the voice but because she doesn't. Because Leopold has never known what it is to fear the sound of his own name, so of course he turns toward it without a bit of hesitation.

A man stands just a few feet from them, dressed like a member of the crew in rough-spun trousers and a tunic that is more oil stains than clean linen. His face is ruddy and covered in stubble and his eyes are dark and beady, locked on Leopold. In his right hand, he holds a pistol, aimed right at them.

"I thought I recognized you," the man says, coming a step closer. "I'm sure you don't remember me, though."

"I think you have me confused with someone else, sir," Leopold says, moving to place himself between the gun and Violie, a gesture Violie appreciates—not because she needs his protection but because it allows her cover to reach beneath her skirt to where a small knife is strapped to her thigh. She moves slowly to avoid notice, hoping Leopold can at least keep the man talking for another moment.

The man laughs. "Do you really think I would forget the face of the boy who forced my family from their home? I assure you, *Your Majesty*, I know exactly who you are."

Violie moves quicker, her fingers fumbling with the strap. Suddenly, the man shooting Leopold seems far more likely. His desire for personal vengeance might just outweigh the bounty on Leopold's head. She glances around the deck, but there is no one else nearby. The night crew must have retired while she and Leopold were talking, and the day crew hasn't yet come on deck.

"I never forced . . . ," Leopold begins before trailing off. "You lived in that village. Hebblesley."

"*Hevelsley*," Violie hisses. *Hevelsley* was the name of the village Leopold had seen demolished so that he could build a new hunting lodge. Violie remembers because it was right after she arrived at the castle, and the details of that disaster made up her first coded letter to Empress Margaraux.

"Hevelsley," Leopold amends. "I'm sorry, truly I am. There is no justification for it. I was told few people lived there and that everyone who did had agreed to move and been compensated for the inconvenience, but that was a lie, wasn't it?" he asks.

Violie is surprised at how level his voice is, even with a gun aimed at him. She didn't think the pampered king had it in him. Her fingers close around the knife and she straightens. She has one throw—one chance to hit a man pointing a gun at them. They're poor odds, poorer still given how ill she feels. The knife feels impossibly heavy in her hand, the strength it takes to lift it almost unfathomable.

"A lie," the man says with a snort. His hand is shaking, but Violie doesn't find that fact comforting. He's leading with emotion and it makes him erratic. It makes his behavior unpredictable, and there is nothing comforting about that. "We were given no money. My family and all of our neighbors were forced onto the streets, carted into Kavelle and left to fend for ourselves. I took this stars-forsaken job because it was the only one I could get, but I doubt my children will survive long enough to see me return."

Violie tightens her grip on the knife and steels herself. She sees the throw she needs to make, notes the best place to strike.

"I'm sorry," Leopold says again, and Violie knows he means it. She knows that if it were up to him, he might just let the man shoot him. But Violie made Sophronia a promise to protect Leopold, and she intends to keep her word. Even if she has to protect him from himself.

She throws the knife with all the strength she can muster and she and Leopold both watch as the blade embeds itself in the man's throat. He slumps to the deck, the gun falling with a clatter that echoes in the silence, though mercifully it doesn't go off. The man dies, quickly and quietly, just as Violie intended.

Leopold drops down beside him, a scream lodging in his throat as he pulls the knife from the man's neck and uses his hands to try to quell the blood.

"He was going to kill you, Leopold," Violie says, her voice level.

"So you killed him instead?" Leopold asks, looking at her over his shoulder with horror in his eyes. Violie tries not to let that look bother her. It's better, she tells herself, that he understands who she is and what she is capable of.

"If I'd hit him in the arm and made him drop the gun, what would have happened?" she asks Leopold, struggling to keep her voice calm. Any moment now, the crew will finish their breakfast and come up to the deck.

When Leopold speaks, his voice is hoarse. "He would have told the captain and anyone who would listen who I am."

"They would have fallen all over themselves to take you back to Temarin to collect the bounty on you," Violie says, nodding. "I couldn't allow them to do that. There was only one true option and I took it."

"You killed him," Leopold says again, turning back to the man. "He was right to be angry with me. He was right to want revenge. You should have . . ." He trails off.

"I should have what?" Violie asks, because she needs him to realize that there is no right answer, no good answer. They left the possibility of right and good behind when they watched Sophronia's execution. "If you want to be a martyr, you're welcome to try, Leopold. But your fate is tied to mine. If you're caught, I'll be executed right beside you. I'm not willing to make myself a martyr to ease your guilt."

He doesn't answer, but the deck is so silent that she hears him swallow. Finally, he pushes himself to his feet and lifts the man's body into his arms. With a blank expression, he carries the body to the railing and tosses it overboard. They both listen as the body hits the water with a splash barely audible over the sound of waves crashing against the ship's hull.

Violie turns to the deck, where the man left a trail of blood. She crouches down to retrieve her knife.

"We'll need a bucket of water, quickly," she tells Leopold. "Hungover or not, the sailors will be coming up soon."

Leopold nods, his face still ashen but some of the shock leaving him. "And when they notice a crew member missing?" he asks.

Violie shakes her head. "The most plausible explanation will be that he had too much ale and fell overboard," she says. "Let's not give them any reason to look for a less plausible explanation."

He nods, the movement jerky. "I saw a bucket and mop down by the galley," he tells her, moving to walk away.

"Leopold," she says, her voice soft. He hears her, though, and turns back, only for Violie to realize she doesn't know what to say. She opens her mouth, then closes it, before trying again.

"It wasn't . . . ," she starts, but she can't tell him it wasn't his fault. He wasn't blameless; he made choices that ruined the man's life, knowingly or not. But Violie made the choice that ended it. "It was necessary," she says, and that, at least, is the truth.

Beatriz

Beatriz doesn't recognize the moment the carriage passes into Bessemia until Nigellus tells her as much. There are no signs to mark the border, no physical change in the terrain, no shift in the air to welcome her home. Home. She didn't expect to return to this place for months yet, and she always imagined the journey would be filled with triumph and excitement, that she would be reunited with her sisters.

But no sisters are waiting for her in Bessemia now, and there is no triumph in her wake. The only thing she has to look forward to is a reunion with a mother who wishes her dead and more training with an empyrea she doesn't trust. And a comfortable bed, she supposes. That, at least, holds some appeal.

"It isn't safe for Pasquale and Ambrose to arrive with us," Beatriz says when they enter the Nemaria Woods—the same place where she last saw Sophronia and Daphne. She remembers Sophronia as she last saw her, dressed in that frilly yellow Temarinian gown and piled into that open-topped carriage, surrounded by strangers and looking terrified. Beatriz closes the curtain to block out the window beside her and turns toward Nigellus. "I'm sure you can arrange secure lodgings for them." It isn't a question.

"It isn't safe for you, either," Pasquale points out. "Your mother does want you dead."

"On Cellarian soil, by Cellarian hands," Nigellus says. When Beatriz, Pasquale, and Ambrose turn to look at him, he frowns. "Did I leave that part of the magic out?"

"You did, yes," Beatriz says. The revelation makes her feel somewhat better, though it certainly doesn't mean her mother can't hurt her. Or put her in chains to deliver her right back to Nicolo, who would have no choice but to kill her now.

"It won't serve her to have Prince Pasquale killed in Bessemia, either," Nigellus continues, so unbothered by his omission that Beatriz genuinely believes he simply forgot to mention it. "He's a bargaining chip with Cellaria's king, and she'll use him as one."

Cellaria's king. Beatriz still can't hear those words without thinking of King Cesare rather than Nicolo. She tries to picture the boy she kissed wearing that heavy crown and fails. She hopes it crushes him beneath its weight.

"I'm not keen on that, either," she says.

"Well, I'm not keen on any of this," Pasquale points out with more force than Beatriz expected. "But since you're insisting on this stars-forsaken plan, I'm not letting you go about it alone." His gaze slides to Ambrose, whose brow is furrowed.

"Both of you are too important to kill," Ambrose points out. "I'm not."

Beatriz knows he's right, just as surely as she knows how difficult it will be for Pasquale to choose her over him. She suspects he would, though—after all, Pasquale made her a promise.

"Then you'll be too insignificant to notice," she says, looking at Nigellus. "He can be a servant—your servant. A footman, perhaps, or a valet."

Nigellus says nothing for a moment, his eyes resting on Beatriz's with uncomfortable intensity. Finally, he gives a nod and Beatriz imagines he is mentally adding another debt to the ledger before him.

Hapantoile looks the same as Beatriz remembers, as does the palace at the center of the city—the same gleaming white stone walls, the same golden gates inlaid with an array of jewels, the same sky-blue flags waving from the turrets. It should be comforting to see that the place where she was raised hasn't changed in her absence, but instead Beatriz finds herself disconcerted. After all, she is not the same person she was when she left this place.

The gates open and the carriage continues inside, and only then does Beatriz suck in a breath. Not at the marble steps that lead up to the main palace doors, not at the crowd of familiar noblemen and noblewomen gathered to greet her, but at the lone figure standing on the top step, hands clasped before her and dressed head to toe—comically, to Beatriz—in black.

Empress Margaraux. Her face is veiled, but Beatriz would know her anywhere. She knows that beneath the black lace, her mother's eyes are the same deceptively warm shade of amber, that her mouth has been painted her signature red and is pursed, as it always is when she looks at Beatriz, like she is a problem that can't be solved.

A footman opens the carriage door and Nigellus steps down, followed by Pasquale, who holds out a hand to her. Beatriz spares one last glance at Ambrose, who will remain in the carriage and out of sight until it returns to Nigellus's private residence. She doesn't know Ambrose terribly well, but he offers her a small, reassuring smile and Beatriz is grateful for it.

She takes Pasquale's hand and lets him help her from the carriage, her heeled slippers touching down on the pavement the only sound audible. She lifts her gaze to her mother, standing a dozen steps above her, and drops into a deep curtsy. Beside her, Pasquale and Nigellus both bow.

"Oh, my child," her mother says, her voice loud enough for everyone gathered to hear as she lifts her gown to descend the steps. "Oh, I'm so glad you are safe."

Beatriz has barely risen from the curtsy when the empress folds her into a hug, holding her tight. The sobs are a bit much, Beatriz thinks, but she is careful to hold her mother just as close, to let fake tears well up in her eyes as she buries her face in her mother's shoulder. This is a performance, after all, and if there is one thing Beatriz knows how to do it is put on a show.

"Mama," she says, pitching her voice just as loud as the empress's and adding an edge of hysteria. "Oh, I was so frightened, so terribly frightened."

"There, there, my dear, you are home and safe with me," her mother says, brushing a rebellious strand of auburn hair away from Beatriz's face. She keeps hold of Beatriz's arm and turns back to the courtiers, watching and whispering. "After the tragic loss of my darling Sophronia, I'm grateful that Nigellus could bring Princess Beatriz and her husband, Prince Pasquale, back safely." She takes Nigellus's hand in hers and lifts it up, cueing applause from the crowd, though it is halfhearted at best. Still, Beatriz must admit, it's the warmest greeting she's ever seen for Nigellus, and he seems perturbed by it.

"Come, my dove," the empress says, leading Beatriz up the stairs and giving Pasquale and Nigellus no choice but to follow. "I'm sure you've had a trying journey, but there is much to discuss."

In a matter of moments, the empress has stripped away Beatriz's only defense, having a servant show Pasquale to his chambers so he can rest. She sends Nigellus away too, though Beatriz isn't sure whether she should be grateful for that or not—he certainly didn't count as a defense, but he was, if nothing else, a buffer.

Now, when the empress leads Beatriz into the throne room and closes the door behind her, Beatriz finds herself completely alone with the woman who killed her sister—the woman who would have killed Beatriz, if her plans hadn't been ruined by a couple of scheming twins with an eye on the throne.

"So, you've failed," the empress says now, pushing the veil back from her face. Every trace of the grieving mother has disappeared, the performance over. The empress steps onto the dais and sinks onto her throne, crossing her ankles.

Beatriz half expected her mother to take her somewhere else—a parlor, perhaps, somewhere cozier. But then, her mother intends to lecture her, and there is no place better to do that than from her throne.

"We were outmaneuvered," Beatriz says, lifting her chin.

"By a boy and girl of such little importance, I still can't bring myself to recall their names," her mother says, each word frozen in ice.

"Gisella and Nicolo," Beatriz supplies, though she knows her mother didn't ask. "*King* Nicolo now, I suppose," she adds.

"You're slouching, Beatriz," her mother replies, but Beatriz makes no move to straighten up. Her mother rolls her eyes. "How, exactly, did that happen?"

Because I trusted them when I shouldn't have. Because Sophronia asked for my help and I gave it to her. Because I sabotaged the plans you spent seventeen years making.

But Beatriz can't say any of that—her mother doesn't know the truth of what went wrong in Cellaria, how Beatriz sought out Gisella and Nicolo's help in getting Lord Savelle out of prison to prevent war from breaking out between Temarin and Cellaria. If she did, Beatriz is sure they'd be having a very different conversation, if it were a conversation at all. Beatriz thinks quickly, spinning a lie as close to the truth as she dares.

"King Cesare was mad," she says with a sigh. "I found out afterward that Nicolo and Gisella had been poisoning him with small, regular doses of cyanide from ground apple seeds. It's what eventually killed him." That much is true, but from here, Beatriz deviates. "Mad as he was, though, he had decided not to execute Lord Savelle—a decision he'd entrusted only to Pasquale and me, as far as I know. I'd tried to convince him otherwise, but reasoning with a madman was enough to drive me mad myself. So I thought to visit Lord Savelle in the dungeon, to use the wish you'd given me to further incriminate him," she says, lifting her bare wrist to indicate the place where her bracelet once hung. In truth, she used the wish to help Lord Savelle escape, transporting him to the docks where he met Ambrose at his uncle's boat.

She isn't sure whether her mother believes her; her expression remains infuriatingly impassive. But Beatriz has no choice but to continue weaving her tale.

"I couldn't get to the dungeon myself, so I solicited help—my fatal error, I'm afraid. Like you, I'd thought Gisella harmless and I told her I wanted a moment to speak to my . . . lover." It's a struggle not to choke on the word *lover,* but that was what her mother had sent her to become to Lord Savelle, and for all the empress knows, she succeeded. "She said she would help me, but instead she brought the guards in to arrest me for treason. I tried to use the wish to save myself, but Lord Savelle knew what it was somehow and took it from me, using it to escape."

The empress leans back in her chair, surveying Beatriz with cold eyes.

"That's interesting, Beatriz," she says. "From what I'd heard, Nicolo himself was your lover."

Beatriz tries to hide her surprise—she and Nicolo weren't lovers. They only kissed twice, and both times Beatriz was sure no one had seen, so how did that information reach her mother's ears? She forces herself to smile brightly.

"Well, Mother, you didn't say I could only have the one, did you?"

The empress looks at Beatriz like she sees straight past that smile. "I didn't think I raised a fool, Beatriz, and I refuse to believe I raised two."

The allusion to Sophronia causes Beatriz to ball her hands into fists, though luckily, her full skirt hides them.

"Sophronia wasn't a fool," she says, careful to keep her voice light, not to let venom leak in. She can't show her hand too early, certainly not within moments of being in her mother's presence. She can't blame her mother for Sophronia's death, not yet. She recalibrates. "Nigellus said you'd laid claim to Temarin with no issues. I trust those responsible for Sophie's murder have been killed?"

Her mother schools her expression into one of grief so flawlessly that Beatriz herself would be fooled if she didn't know better. "All except one," she says, a frown creasing her unnaturally smooth forehead—the product of copious amounts of stardust. "King Leopold managed to escape somehow."

Beatriz frowns like this is news to her, like she didn't see King Leopold with her own eyes, hollowed out by grief as he was. "What did Leopold have to do with Sophie's death?" she asks, assuming even as she asks the question that her mother's answer will be a lie.

Her mother winces, like the thought physically pains her. "I have it on good authority that the boy sacrificed Sophronia to save his own skin. Of course, if she'd listened to me in the first place, he would have been in no position to do so, but your sister always had a weakness where he was concerned. I did everything in my power to prevent it, but . . ." She trails off with a mournful sigh.

It takes all of Beatriz's self-control not to launch herself across the room and wrap her hands around her mother's neck.

"The point remains, though," her mother says, straightening up, "that King Leopold is still at large, though my people have picked up several promising leads. I have that well in hand. What I *don't* have is Cellaria."

Beatriz shrugs, clasping her hands in front of her and trying to appear unbothered—the insolent, rebellious princess her mother believes her to be. "I doubt Nicolo's reign will be a long one—the court isn't with him, not really, and once you have Friv under your control, you should have no trouble using your combined militia to take it quite easily. It simply requires patience."

Her mother snorts. "Patience is rich advice coming from you, Beatriz," she says, shaking her head. "No, I don't have any plans to wait. It doesn't matter what a mad king proclaimed on his deathbed—Pasquale is his heir and the rightful King of Cellaria. The two of you will simply have to return to Cellaria to claim the throne. Have the usurper and his sister executed, along with anyone who tries to support him."

Beatriz stares at her mother, unblinking, for a long moment. "That," she says slowly, "would be suicide."

The empress rolls her eyes. "Always so dramatic, Beatriz. I didn't raise you to fail."

She raised you to die, Nigellus's voice echoes in her mind. If Beatriz had any doubt that he was telling the truth, it evaporates now.

"You can't be serious," she says. "Power doesn't come from technicalities; you know that better than anyone."

Her mother ignores her. "I will, of course, be sending some of my troops with you to support your claim," she adds as an afterthought. "Though I can't very well pull them all out of Temarin at the moment, nor leave Bessemia defenseless, so it will be a small army, but I trust your ability to manage the situation."

So, this is her mother's plan for her, then, Beatriz thinks. Sending her back into the lions' den and slaughtering the lions in her name when she's immediately devoured. If her mother has set her mind to it, there is no use arguing, though every star in the sky will fall before Beatriz sets foot in Cellaria again.

She lets out a long exhale as if she's considering her mother's words. "We'll need time to regroup," she says finally.

"Two weeks," her mother replies. "Now, if you don't mind, I have dinner with the Frivian ambassador to prepare for. You can find your way back to your rooms, I'm sure."

And just like that, she's dismissed. Beatriz is nearly to the door before her mother's words hit her and she stops.

"I'm a married woman," Beatriz points out. "Surely I should be housed in quarters with my husband."

The empress looks up at her with a wry smile and Beatriz realizes that a handful of kisses with Nicolo are the least of what her mother knows. "Please, Beatriz, don't insult me. If you insist on acting like a child, you can sleep in your childhood rooms."

Daphne

The castle has spent the last day in chaos, the woods around it and the bordering town of Eldevale searched for any sign of the lost princes—not that most people in the castle know Reid and Gideon are princes, which makes their disappearance all the stranger. What would be the motive for kidnapping the sons of a dead Frivian nobleman and his foreign wife?

Queen Eugenia, for her part, is distraught. Or, at least, Daphne is told she's distraught, since she hasn't left her room and her maid claimed she needed to be sedated with a tincture of eddleberries and ground vestalroot.

After a night and day of searching, there is still no indication of who took the princes or why. The hoofprints Daphne and Bairre noticed appeared to lead in circles before disappearing altogether, and after another heavy snowfall, even those are gone, leaving no trace of the princes at all.

Daphne didn't need to ask Bairre if he knew anything about it—she knows him well enough by now to know that he would never put children in danger and that his shock and horror following their kidnapping was genuine. That doesn't mean, however, that the rebellion isn't involved.

Bairre must have told someone the princes' true identity, and they wouldn't have taken kindly to Friv involving itself in the matters of a foreign country.

She doesn't have a chance to ask him if he knows anything more before he leaves with a group of scouts to search the surrounding villages for any information that might reveal the boys' whereabouts.

So, asking after Cliona, Daphne is directed to the stables, where she finds the other girl brushing out her mare, a tall creature, every inch of her black apart from a white mark on her forehead that reminds Daphne of a crown. Cliona doesn't seem surprised when Daphne appears, barely interrupting her brushing to give a nod of acknowledgment.

Daphne sees no point in wasting time with small talk—the stables are otherwise empty of humans, she ensured it herself.

"Did your people kidnap the princes?" she asks.

Cliona's expression doesn't change. "Princes?" she repeats, her voice ringing a little too innocent to be believable, at least to Daphne. So Bairre did tell her the princes' true identities, or someone did.

"You really are a terrible liar," Daphne says, stepping farther into the stable and reaching up to scratch behind the mare's ear. The horse leans into Daphne's touch and lets out a low whinny. It isn't quite true—Cliona is a perfectly fine liar, Daphne is simply better at reading people.

Still, the insult digs beneath Cliona's skin and her lips purse. "Fine, then let me say this perfectly clearly," she says, looking up and meeting Daphne's silver eyes with her brown ones. "Neither I nor any rebels had anything to do with the kidnapping of those boys."

Daphne's eyes search hers for a moment, but she's telling the truth—at least she believes she is. Cliona claims she knows every move the rebels make, every plot they have brewing, but Daphne knows that Cliona's father is the head of the rebels, and there are some things he might not wish to burden his daughter's conscience with.

"But you did know who they were," Daphne says, knowing better than to pull that particular thread with Cliona.

Cliona snorts. "Of course," she says. "I know the king underestimates his people, but I'd have thought you knew better by now."

"Then you must have had a plan to get rid of them and their mother," Daphne says. "What was it?"

Cliona rolls her eyes. "Nothing so dastardly as you're imagining, I'm sure," she says. "We were simply going to leak the information about their true identities and let the people of Friv put pressure on the king to send them back to Temarin."

"And, of course, if he still refused, it would only incite more opposition to his rule," Daphne adds.

Cliona shrugs. "Either way, it was a win for us," she says. "We had no reason to extract those boys from the castle." She pauses, eyes settling on Daphne. "Just as we had no reason to want you dead, Princess," she adds.

"So you say, after threatening to kill me," Daphne reminds her, but the point remains. Cliona and the rebels weren't responsible for the attempts on her life, and Daphne never found out who, exactly, was. It stands to reason that if there is another element at play here, it might be responsible for both the attempts on her life and the boys' kidnapping.

"Your assassins lured us to the very woods where the princes were kidnapped," Cliona says, as if reading Daphne's mind.

"There have been no further attempts on my life," Daphne says, shaking her head. "We killed every assassin there—what makes you think there are more?"

"Because I've learned a little something about underground movements over the last few years. There are always more people involved than you think, and more often than not, they're right under your nose."

It isn't reassuring, but Cliona's words rarely are.

"Speaking of which," Cliona continues, "I didn't ask where you learned to fight. I've never met a princess who could wield a knife like you do."

"Apart from me, you've never met a princess at all," Daphne points out. "Besides, I assumed you and Bairre didn't ask questions because you didn't want me to ask questions of my own," she adds, turning back to the door and walking away. She nearly makes it before Cliona speaks again.

"Sooner or later, Daphne, you're going to have to trust someone," she says.

Daphne's steps falter for just an instant and she's tempted to respond. She trusts her mother, and that's all she has ever needed or will ever need. She will not make her sisters' mistakes. But the words die on her tongue and she walks away, leaving them unspoken.

Bairre and his scouting party return that evening, and when Daphne goes to her room after dinner, Bairre is waiting for her, sitting in the green velvet armchair that Daphne has come to think of as his on account of the nights he's spent there while she's been ill or injured. Those nights have added up to too many, she thinks.

He took a bath after arriving and his chestnut hair is still wet, the smell of his soap—something with bergamot, she thinks—thick in the air.

"Any sign of them?" she asks, closing the door behind her. She's sure if he'd found the princes, word would have spread through the castle in the time it took him to bathe, but she has to ask anyway. When he shakes his head, her heart still sinks.

"My mother said she would listen to the stars again tonight, but they haven't spoken to her about the princes yet," he says.

"We were meant to be watching them," Daphne says, shaking her head and leaning back against the closed door. "I just never thought—"

"No one could have," he says, getting to his feet and coming toward her but stopping short a few steps away, as if he's afraid to get too close.

He should be, Daphne thinks, even as she wishes he would close the distance between them and take her in his arms.

"Cillian and I played in those woods all the time when we were younger and we were never in danger, and all of Friv *knew* we were princes. Those woods should be safe," he says.

"But it isn't the first time they haven't been," she points out, her conversation with Cliona coming back to her. "I can't help but think the two events are related. Cliona swears the rebels had no part in it—"

"Of course they didn't," Bairre says, shaking his head. "I would never let them hurt children."

That steals Daphne's words—not because his heroism is touching, but because he's naïve enough to believe he would have a say in the rebellion's plots. Bairre might be the reluctant Crown Prince of Friv, but he isn't in charge of the rebels. Not even close.

"But murdering an empyrea is all right?" Daphne asks. "Tell me, what was Fergal's crime? It must have been something truly heinous for him to die so horribly."

That makes Bairre frown. He opens his mouth to speak but thinks better of it.

"You might be one of them, Bairre, but you don't make their rules," she says softly before pausing and letting him absorb her words. "But in this, I think you're right: they had nothing to do with kidnapping the princes. There was a time I thought the rebels were the ones responsible for trying to kill me."

Daphne expects him to balk at that notion again, but he doesn't. At least he isn't completely oblivious to the lengths the rebellion will go to in order to succeed. "They weren't, obviously," she says. "So, we have to assume there is a third faction working within Friv to hurt us—though I'm not sure who us is. Me, certainly. And I don't think it's a coincidence that both the fight with the assassins and the princes' kidnapping happened in the woods."

"You were poisoned in the woods as well," Bairre points out.

Daphne frowns. That had to have been a coincidence, didn't it? After all, Zenia had been given the poison to use against her long before she'd set foot in the woods. The location she'd chosen to use it had to have been a happenstance. Except . . .

"When my saddle girth broke, I was in the woods as well," she says. "I was supposed to be riding alone. The assassin who cut the girth didn't know I was meeting Cliona."

"The same assassin we followed, who said you were supposed to follow him alone instead of with Cliona and me?" he asks.

Daphne nods, feeling ill. That assassin is dead now, she saw him die, saw his body lifeless and cold. But someone else is still out there, she knows this as surely as she knows her own name, and that someone has Gideon and Reid.

"The pattern breaks with Zenia," she says. "Zenia poisoned me with six other people around."

"Zenia was following orders," Bairre points out. "She's ten—it's possible she misunderstood what she was supposed to do."

Daphne considers this. "That or she simply didn't care," she says. "Is she still in the castle?"

Bairre nods. "Rufus and the rest of his family are supposed to leave tomorrow afternoon," he says. "Zenia's still skittish. She feels guilty for the part she played—I'm not sure how open she'll be to talking about it more."

"She'll talk to me," Daphne says. Her mother always told her she could talk a snake into eating its own tail. Bairre doesn't seem surprised by her confidence.

"You're good at getting information from people," he tells her, his voice lowering.

Daphne looks at him for a long moment. First Cliona

pushing her about her fighting skills, now this. She would suspect it was a coordinated attack, but she knows Bairre well enough to know he wouldn't do that. He's too blunt; scheming and manipulating aren't his style. But she thinks of their conversation before, about the secrets between them. Perhaps this one, she can let him have just a sliver of.

"My mother thought it was an important talent for my sisters and me to cultivate, especially since she was sending us to countries that might just be hostile toward us. She'd faced hostility early on in her own reign—she always said she survived mainly on the secrets she'd wormed out of her enemies, or those close to them. She thought we should be able to defend ourselves as well, for similar reasons. I'm hardly the first royal bride with a target on her back."

Bairre takes this in, though she can't tell if he believes her or not. He doesn't look at her, but suddenly she's desperate for him to. She wants him to look at her the way he did in his mother's cottage—like lightning, she remembers, or even like he did over tea, just before he kissed her. She can feel the space between them yawning open again, filling up with secrets both of them are keeping. It's good distance, necessary distance, she tells herself. Sophronia cared too much about Leopold and that made her foolish. It got her killed. Daphne won't make the same mistake, but suddenly she understands why Sophronia did. Suddenly, Sophronia seems a little less foolish.

"It'll be best if I talk to Zenia alone," she says, pushing the thought away. "I'm sure Rufus won't be keen on letting her out of his sight, though."

"I'll distract him," Bairre says before pausing. "Daphne . . . ," he starts, trailing off. She hears an ocean of words in that silence. A thousand questions she can't answer. A thousand statements she doesn't want to hear, even though she also does, so desperately she can't think straight.

And that's exactly the problem with Bairre—where he's concerned, she can never think straight.

"You shouldn't be here," she tells him, injecting her voice with false brightness. "Thanks to your rebel friends, we aren't married yet, and if you're caught here—"

"They'll what? Force me to marry you?" Bairre asks, taking a step closer to her, pausing, then taking another until they are toe to toe and the scent of bergamot soap and Bairre threatens to overwhelm her. He's so close that if she just tilts her head up an inch her lips will meet his. "I think that ship's sailed," he says, the words ghosting over her cheek before he brushes his lips over hers.

It's a gentle kiss—barely enough to be properly called a kiss at all—but it steals Daphne's breath all the same. She brings a hand up to Bairre's chest, torn between pushing him away and pulling him closer. Her good sense wins out, this time at least, and she pushes him back a step, grappling for a reason to keep him at arm's length.

"It hasn't, though," she tells him. "Sailed, that is. You've no intention of marrying me. You've made that perfectly clear, Bairre."

Bairre falters for a moment. "That doesn't mean I don't—"

"Don't what?" she asks. He's been knocked off-balance,

but now she needs to finish it. "Don't want to kiss me? Bed me?"

He stumbles back another step. "Daphne, I . . . ," he says, but if he has more words to offer her, they die on his tongue.

"You don't want a throne, Bairre. But I do. Friv might be a dead end in that regard, but that doesn't mean I'm going to waste time with a bastard rebel masquerading as a prince."

For just one breath, Daphne wants to take the words back, but she can't. She watches them land like punches, watches Bairre's expression turn to shock, then fury. Watches him barrel past her to the door without sparing her a second look.

And then he's gone and the words Daphne spoke echo in her mind. They were true, all of them, but that doesn't mean they didn't feel like razor blades in her throat.

Violie

Violie and Leopold avoid leaving their cabin as much as possible for the next day and a half, Leopold sneaking down to the galley only twice for their food rations. The second time, he tells Violie he overheard the cook warning a deckhand not to drink too heavily before his shift, lest he go overboard like Aylan.

While it's a relief that the man's death is assumed to be an accident, Violie wishes Leopold hadn't heard the man's name. His voice cracks when he says it and she knows those two syllables will haunt his sleep.

Violie never knew the name of the first person she killed; she'd barely even seen his face. She'd been walking home from her lessons at the palace in Bessemia one night, a few months after the empress had recruited her, and a man had leapt from the shadows and attacked her. She'd stabbed him with the penknife she kept in her boot, reaching around to embed the blade in the back of his neck, severing his spinal cord and reducing him to a motionless heap at her feet in a matter of seconds. Her hand had shaken the entire time, but she'd succeeded in killing him. She remembers the man's dead eyes and the blood that pooled beneath his fallen body.

She suspected then that the empress had arranged it, a way to test Violie's skills as well as her stomach for violence. Now she is sure of it.

When the ship docks in Glenacre port, on Friv's southeastern shore, Leopold and Violie disembark, paying the captain the rest of what they owe him. Violie manages small talk, spinning her story about the fictional sister she's staying with and promising to try the raspberry jam tarts from a bakery in town the captain recommends. Leopold, however, hangs back silent, though Violie supposes that's for the best, given his accent.

They find an inn to stay the night in, on the outskirts of Glenacre, though they only book a single room in an effort to save money. At dinner, they go over their plans for the next day.

"I found a mail cart leaving for Eldevale at dawn. The driver said he wasn't supposed to accept passengers but would make an exception if we could pay fifteen asters each. I tried bargaining, but he wouldn't go lower."

Violie's stomach sinks. After the inn in Temarin, passage on the ship, and their room and dinner at the inn tonight, they only have twenty asters left. It's also a full day's journey from Glenacre to Eldevale in a carriage, and Violie assumes food isn't provided by the mail cart.

"Is there another way to get there?" she asks.

Leopold shakes his head. "A private carriage will cost more. There's a passenger carriage that would be eight asters a person, but it doesn't leave for another five days."

"During which time, we would run through all of our asters on room and board anyway," Violie says with a sigh.

Leopold nods. "We're out of Temarin now," he says. "I can sell my ring or my cloak."

"Your ring is still too recognizable," she says. "Especially in a port town where Temarin's news reaches more easily. I'm not sure you'll find any interest in your cloak here, either."

"Why not?" Leopold asks, frowning. "It's a perfectly good cloak."

"*Too* good a cloak," she says. "An impractical cloak. There isn't much heft to it, and the ruby buckle adds nothing in the way of warmth. Frivians are practical sorts. You're better off keeping it for now."

She doesn't add that flimsy as the cloak may be, he'll certainly be grateful for the warmth once they're tucked away in the mail cart.

"What, then?" Leopold asks as Violie scans the inn's public room, darting over a group of sailors drinking, a young man and woman sitting close together and speaking softly, a group of four playing dice. "You can try to bargain with the driver, but he seemed stubborn—"

"No need for that," Violie says, her gaze lingering on the group playing dice. They were there when she and Leopold sat down, and if the collection of empty ale glasses and the red tinge to their cheeks are anything to go by, they've been there for quite a while now. One of the men is a sailor, judging by his suntanned skin and weather-beaten face. The other man is older, with gray hair and a long beard. The two women are courtesans—Violie has no tangible way of knowing this, but she spent enough time around courtesans growing up to recognize that they're at work.

"How are you at dice?" she asks, not taking her eyes from

the table. One of the women leans close to the older man, whispering something in his ear that must distract him thoroughly, since he fails to notice the other woman swapping a die for an identical one from her pocket.

"Good," Leopold says, following her gaze. "I win all the time."

Violie resists the urge to laugh at the confidence in his voice. If there's one thing she knows about dice, it's that there is no being good at them, and if Leopold did, indeed, win all the time, it had more to do with not wanting to best a spoiled king than any talent on his part.

"Let's put those skills to work, then," she says, passing him the bag of asters.

Leopold falters. "But if I lose . . . ," he starts.

"You won't," she says with a smile, starting over toward the table and letting Leopold follow in her wake. "Any chance my husband can join your game?" she asks, and though she directs the question at the men, her eyes linger on the women, who exchange a wary look. "We'll even buy a round of drinks," she adds. "Will one of you help me carry them?"

The men agree easily enough, welcoming Leopold to the table with boisterous shouts and slurred words. The younger woman follows Violie toward the bar, her forehead creased in a frown. She introduces herself as Ephelia.

"We want no trouble," Violie tells her as they wait at the bar for six pints of ale. "You have a good game going. How many weighted dice do you have?"

The woman glares at her. "Four," she admits.

"Of course," Violie says with a smile. "You have to switch

them out to avoid suspicion. Even drunks have a stroke of sense from time to time."

"What do you want, if not trouble?" Ephelia asks.

"I want in," Violie says with a shrug. "Not for much, fifteen asters—let's make it twenty, since I'm buying this round of drinks."

"I don't suppose we have much of a choice," Ephelia says. "If I say no, you'll give us up, I assume."

Part of Violie wants to deny it, but she can't. She leans her hip against the bar and fixes the woman with a long look. "Yes," she tells her. "But I can offer a little extra, too, for the trouble. A ruby, this big." She holds her hand up to demonstrate. She's not sure why she does it—blackmail is more than enough to get her the asters she needs—but the idea of taking coins from women who need them, women like her mother, leaves her feeling ill. Leopold's conscience might be rubbing off on her, she thinks, which is unfortunate, since a conscience is something neither of them can afford any longer.

"And I'm supposed to take your word for it? For all I know it's nothing but paste, if it exists at all," Ephelia says.

"Might be," Violie says with a shrug. "But it's plenty more than you'll have if I walk over to that table and tell those men you've been fleecing them."

"Fine," the woman bites out.

The barkeep sets a tray laden with six flagons of ale in front of them and Violie passes him an aster and moves to pick up the tray.

"Wait," the woman says, reaching into a pouch strung

around her waist and withdrawing a small vial of pale green powder. It would take a more thorough inspection for Violie to know for certain what it contains, but she has a hunch.

"Adettel root powder?" she asks. While adettel leaves are edible and commonly used across the continent in soups and stews, the roots of the plant can be toxic if ingested in large quantities. A small pinch of powder, though, is enough to render a person ill for the next few hours. Though Violie learned most of what she knows of poisons from the empress's lessons, adettel root powder was her mother's preferred method for dealing with troublesome customers without losing any pay.

Ephelia shrugs, holding Violie's gaze and daring her to say something about it. Violie holds her tongue, though, and watches as Ephelia pours the powder into two of the flagons.

"Be sure you and your husband don't drink from those," Ephelia tells him. "Or you'll be in for a rough evening. It'll take hold in half an hour—hopefully that's enough time to win you your asters."

Not keen to take any chances, Violie picks up two of the untainted flagons and makes her way back to Leopold, passing one to him.

He glances up at her, cheeks red. "I might not be as good at dice as I thought," he whispers. "I never lost before, but—"

"They let you win before," she whispers back. "How much did you lose?"

"Five asters," he tells her.

Violie nods, taking a sip of the ale and nearly retching. It's warm and bitter. "Don't worry, your luck is about to change."

By the time the first man makes a mad dash out the door for the outhouse, Leopold has managed to win twenty-three asters. He manages an extra two before the other man makes his escape too.

"You'd best leave now," Ephelia tells them, her and her companion—Gertel, Violie has learned—counting their own coin. "If they suspect they've been had, they'll likely blame two foreigners before a pair of strumpets."

Violie suspects she's right, but she hesitates a moment. "Will you be all right?" she asks. Again, she's unsure why she does. The woman seems surprised as well, exchanging a look with her friend.

"Mind your business," Gertel says, her voice hard-edged. "Let us mind ours."

Violie opens her mouth to protest but quickly closes it again, considering her words. "Frivian girls are a rarity in Bessemian brothels," she says after a moment. "If you can make your way there, you might find yourselves with more customers to choose from. The Crimson Petal offers security and the madam is a good woman who takes care of her girls. Tell her Violie referred you."

"Mind your business," Gertel says again, her voice sharpening, but Ephelia meets Violie's gaze, curious. Violie isn't sure that curiosity will be enough to convince the woman to leave her home, but it's out of Violie's hands now.

"Give me the cloak," she says to Leopold, who's been watching the exchange with a furrowed brow. She wonders how much of it, exactly, has pierced the bubble of ignorance he's been enclosed in since birth. He hands the cloak over without a word and Violie uses her dagger to cut off the ruby buckle, passing it to Ephelia. "It is real," she tells the girl. "But wait as long as possible before trying to sell it."

The woman has no reason to trust her, just as Violie has no reason to trust that Ephelia won't try to sell the jewel within the hour—though it is late enough that Violie suspects most shops are closed—but when Ephelia nods, Violie decides she does trust her, just this much at least.

She and Leopold make their way upstairs to their room—a small space set up with a narrow cot, a washbasin, and a threadbare rug. Leopold has already said he would sleep on the floor, and Violie knows there is nothing to be gained by arguing with his chivalry.

"They poisoned them," he says slowly.

Violie nods, sitting down on the bed to remove her shoes. "Just a little," she says. "They'll be fine in a few hours' time."

"Why?" he asks.

Violie considers how best to explain it. "There were courtesans aplenty in the Temarinian court," she says. "Did you ever . . ."

"No!" he says, face flushing red. "No, I'd never."

"There's no shame in it," she says, shrugging. "My mother is one, you know. Most of the men are decent sorts, she's even liked a few of them. But some . . . well, addettel root powder helps. Take payment for the night, serve a nightcap, add a little powder to the man's cup . . . next thing you know, he's too sick to continue, but he can't very well request a refund."

Leopold stares at her like she's just begun spouting

nonsense and he can't wrap his brain around it. She knows he doesn't understand—how can he, given the life he's led?—but she doesn't like the idea of him casting judgment on Ephelia and Gertel, on her mother, on her, in some respect.

"It's survival," she tells him, her voice low. "It isn't pretty or moral or just. Sometimes, all you can do is get through in one piece, however you can."

The sun is barely cresting over the horizon when Violie and Leopold leave the inn the next morning, Leopold leading the way through Glenacre's twisting, narrow streets to where the mail cart is parked beside a small white building with a wooden sign hanging on its front that reads GENERAL POST OFFICE. A tall wooden box with a slot for letters to be dropped into stands beside the door.

Leopold pays the driver thirty asters and he and Violie climb into the carriage, stacks of letters and boxes all around them so that there is barely any room to move. Violie sets a basket between them, full of stale bread and dried meats and a hunk of cheese she used the last of their money to buy from the inn's cook.

The driver warns that he'll be making few stops on the way to Eldevale, but neither Violie nor Leopold complains. By this evening, Violie will be face to face with Princess Daphne.

Beatriz

Beatriz doesn't doubt that her mother intended that banishing her to her childhood rooms would serve as a punishment. It is that, though not, perhaps, in the way the empress intended. In some ways, Beatriz prefers the comfort and familiarity of the cream walls and pink accents and dainty furnishings—especially compared to the inns she's stayed at during the journey or her cell at the Sororia. She might even prefer it to her rooms at the Cellarian palace, which never truly felt like home.

It's Sophronia's presence, and her absence, that threaten to drive Beatriz mad. It started with the stain on the carpet in the sitting room—barely noticeable, unless you know to look for it. And Beatriz knows. She remembers Daphne opening a bottle of champagne, the night of their sixteenth birthday, spilling it on the rug, and how Sophronia hastened to clean it up.

If she closes her eyes, she almost feels like she's back there, on that night. She can smell Daphne's freesia perfume. She can hear Sophronia's soft voice—*Sixteen is when we have to say goodbye. By seventeen, we'll be back here again. Together.* Whenever she sits down on the sofa, she can feel her sisters on either side of her, as if they could press close enough together to prevent their ever being separated.

But they are separated, and if Beatriz sees seventeen at all, it won't be with Sophronia. She has a difficult time imagining she'll see it with Daphne, either, and the thought of that sends another pang through her heart.

She hasn't spoken to Daphne since they felt Sophronia die. Beatriz doesn't even know what she could possibly have to say to Daphne. Anytime she tries to imagine it, her words come out full of anger and spite and blame. If Daphne had helped them, if she'd grown a backbone and stood against their mother for once in her life . . .

Deep down, though, Beatriz knows that even if Daphne had done those things, Sophronia still wouldn't be here.

When she wakes up in her childhood bedroom her second day in Bessemia, she knows what needs to be done—what Sophronia would tell her to do, if she were here. She puts it off for as long as she can, eating breakfast in her room before meeting up with Pasquale to show him around the palace. It's only after lunch that she returns to her haunted chambers.

She crosses the room to the desk that now seems too small and writes a letter to the only sister she has left.

Daphne—

I'm safe—or as safe as I can be—in Bessemia, at the palace. I know we don't see eye to eye on many things, and you may not believe me, but you need to be careful. You'll likely say I'm being dramatic, but I've every reason to believe Sophie's death was orchestrated by an outside force, and the person *responsible will come for us next. Contrary to what you like to think, you aren't invulnerable, and our opponent isn't to be underestimated.*

Sophie told us she had friends coming to find us. They found me, but I can't keep them safe so I am sending them on to you. Please protect them—if not for me, then for Sophie.

Being back in this palace, in our old rooms, I miss you and Sophie so much it makes my heart ache. It still seems impossible to believe that I'll never see her face again. I'll never forgive you if you meet the same fate.

—Beatriz

It's a sentimental letter—Daphne will surely roll her eyes at that—but Beatriz doesn't change it. Let Daphne mock her for it if she wants to. There are many things Beatriz wishes she could say to Sophronia that she'll never be able to, and that isn't a mistake she'll make twice.

Perhaps, though, she should be more explicit about the threat Daphne faces. She considers naming the empress as the person responsible for Sophronia's death, but she stops herself short. Daphne won't believe her, not without proof, and maybe even then she wouldn't be able to see the truth. No, if Beatriz points the finger at their mother, Daphne will disregard the letter entirely. Better to keep her on guard against an unknown threat, if nothing else.

She folds the letter into an envelope and seals it with wax, letting it harden before she slips the envelope into her pocket. Her mother will never let the letter out of the palace if she reads it, and there isn't a code she could put it into that her mother would be unable to break, but she can give it to Pasquale to pass on to Ambrose, who will be able to post it in the city with fewer eyes watching.

She walks into the sitting room and her eyes fall on the mantel with its gilt-inlay constellations. The Thorned Rose, the Hungry Hawk, the Lonely Heart, the Crown of Flames, and, finally, the Sisters Three. Crossing toward it, she lifts her hand to brush the tips of her fingers over the Sisters Three, the stars arranged to form the figures of three dancing ladies. While Beatriz has always seen the constellations as far more abstract than their names imply, the Sisters Three is one she's always seen clearly. She's always seen herself there, with Daphne and Sophronia.

She shakes her head and drops her hand, looking toward the clock hanging on the wall above the mantel.

Nearly sundown, now. In a few hours it will be time for another lesson with Nigellus.

The sun has just left the sky when Beatriz steps into Nigellus's laboratory in the palace's highest tower. She pushes the hood of the cloak she borrowed from Pasquale back from her face and looks around the room—one of the few places in the palace that she's never set foot in. There's a telescope beside the largest window, and the ceiling is made of glass to allow a full view of the stars. The table that dominates the room is laden with equipment. Some, like microscopes and scales, Beatriz recognizes, but there are other things she cannot fathom the purpose of: shining silver disks of various sizes, stacked on top of one another, rings of gold and bronze that interlink, dozens of beakers and vials containing an opalescent liquid she's never seen before.

"Princess Beatriz," a voice behind her says, and Beatriz whirls to find Nigellus standing in the doorway she just stepped through, watching her. "You're late."

"Only by a few minutes," she says, shrugging. "My mother is having me watched, unsurprisingly, and it took longer than expected to get past her spies unnoticed."

"I take it that's the reason you're dressed that way?" he says.

Beatriz glances down at the cloak, breeches, and shirt she borrowed from Pasquale in order to better avoid notice. "It seemed prudent," she says.

While her rooms have been outfitted with a full wardrobe, a well-stocked jewelry box, and every luxury Beatriz could want, one thing is conspicuously missing—a vanity case. There hasn't been much need for cosmetics, since Beatriz has mostly kept to her room and there are no balls or other social events on her schedule, but she is sure the omission is intentional on her mother's part. Beatriz has always excelled at the art of disguise, after all, and the empress wouldn't want to risk that talent being wielded against her.

It's a compliment, in a way, to know her mother fears her enough to try to hobble her, but it's annoying all the same.

"What is all this?" she asks Nigellus, nodding toward the table of gadgets and equipment. When she imagined Nigellus's laboratory before, she imagined a simpler place where he could commune with the stars, pull them down if absolutely necessary, and perhaps make a few of the wish items he is known for—like the bracelets the empress gave Beatriz and her sisters when they left Bessemia.

Beatriz's bracelet is gone now, its wish used to help Lord Savelle escape Cellaria. Sophronia used hers, too, before she was killed. Daphne likely still has hers, Beatriz thinks. She's always been the most prudent of the three of them—she'll probably save it until she is, quite literally, at death's door. Maybe not even then, if she's feeling particularly stubborn.

Nigellus glances at the table Beatriz gestures to and his brow furrows. "My practices might differ from other empyreas, but I believe the key to harmony with the stars is understanding them," he says.

"That hardly seems controversial," Beatriz comments.

"It depends on the methods, I suppose," he says, brushing past her to cross to the table and pick up one of the beakers of opalescent liquid. "Study of the stars is often seen as a spiritual endeavor."

"Isn't it that?" Beatriz frowns.

Nigellus shrugs. "I believe so, yes, but I also believe it is a science." He glances at her. "Science, I'm sure, wasn't one of the things you studied under your mother's tutelage."

Beatriz bristles. "As a matter of fact, we studied chemistry."

"Only as far as the mechanics of various poisons, though," he says, and Beatriz can't deny that, even if she detests admitting to a weakness.

"Not much point in providing a more thorough education to a sacrificial lamb, I suppose," she says instead, keeping her voice light. It's nothing to joke about, but doing so makes her feel better for a moment.

Nigellus doesn't so much as smile, though. Instead, he holds the beaker out to her, and she takes it.

"What is it?" she asks him, examining the liquid inside as it sloshes around.

"To explain that, I need to go back a few steps," he says. "You know what stardust is, of course."

"Fallen stars," she echoes automatically.

"Yes," Nigellus says before pausing. "And no. At least not in the way we think of stars. These fall from the sky, it's true, but there are never fewer stars in the sky after a star shower, not the way there are when an empyrea pulls a star down. But having examined stardust and a piece of a star I pulled down myself, I've confirmed they are made up of the same matter, more or less."

"I'm assuming there is significantly less, considering how much more powerful magic is that comes from a star that's been pulled down."

Nigellus inclines his head in agreement, turning to make his way toward the telescope by the window. Unsure of what else to do, Beatriz follows.

"I've spent the last decade and a half trying to bridge that gap," he says. "I believe it's imperative that we find a way to harness the raw magic of the stars in a renewable way. I've made strides, like with your wish bracelet, but even that was weaker than a star itself."

"You never said what stardust is," Beatriz reminds him. Nigellus doesn't seem accustomed to talking with other people, constantly dropping the thread of conversation and getting lost in his own mind.

Nigellus blinks and turns to look at her, as if he'd forgotten she was there. "We lose hair," he says.

Beatriz frowns. If she could have placed a bet on what he would have said next, she wouldn't have guessed that in a million years. "We do?" she asks.

"A few strands a day, surely you've noticed that. When you brush your hair, if nothing else. We shed skin cells as well. Nail clippings, eyelashes, tears, spit—"

"And?" Beatriz interrupts, sure he could go on for days if she let him.

"And," he says, looking mildly annoyed at her interruption, "all of those things contain part of us, no? I have a theory that stardust is to stars what shed hair and skin cells and whatnot are to us."

Beatriz considers this for a moment. "So, stardust," she says slowly, "is actually star spit?"

"In a manner of speaking. It explains why it's so much weaker, even though it contains the same properties."

It does explain that, but even though Nigellus's explanation makes sense, something about it underwhelms Beatriz. The world seems a little less magical all of a sudden.

"I'm sure I don't have to tell you to keep my theories to yourself," he says, and though his voice is conversational, it takes on a hard edge. "Your mother knows about them, but there are plenty of others who would see me burned alive for even saying these things."

"I spent two months in Cellaria with silver eyes and unpredictable magic," she points out. "I know how to be discreet."

Nigellus merely raises an eyebrow. "You were arrested

for treason—and accused of witchcraft even before that, I believe."

Beatriz rolls her eyes. "Lessons were learned both times," she says tightly. This time, for instance, she knows better than to trust a handsome face and charming words.

"Let's hope so," Nigellus says. "We'll start with stargazing tonight. Tell me what you see in the telescope."

Beatriz crosses toward the telescope, trying to squash her annoyance at the thought of Nicolo's betrayal, and the embarrassment that followed. Next time they cross paths, she'll make him pay for that.

She bends to press her eye to the telescope, blinking as the stars come into focus. It takes her a moment to adjust the dials on the side in order to see a full constellation.

"The Glittering Diamond," she tells Nigellus. "The signal of strength and prosperity—I'm sure my mother will be pleased to hear of its presence."

"As will the rest of Bessemia," Nigellus points out. "What else is near it?"

"The Slithering Snake," she tells him, moving the telescope. "Hardly surprising, given my mother's and my being under the same roof. Either of us could be considered a snake to the other, and the betrayal it promises seems imminent in one way or another."

"Not everything is about you, Princess," Nigellus says. "Betrayal seems to be in the air for everyone. Look closer, near the snake's tongue. Do you notice anything amiss?"

Beatriz frowns, spinning the dials to get a closer look, but all she sees are stars in the rough shape of a snake's forked tongue.

"I don't think I'm familiar enough to notice a change in the constellation," she admits. "I've never paid much attention to it before."

Nigellus picks up a book from the shelf and flips through it, bringing it toward Beatriz. "Here, this is what the Slithering Snake usually looks like."

Beatriz pulls back from the telescope to look at the illustration. She frowns, then looks through the telescope again.

"There are extra stars around the tongue," she says. "Three. Where did they come from?"

"The more accurate question is *Who do they belong to?*" Nigellus replies.

Beatriz's frown deepens and she fiddles with the dials again. "It's a branch of the Twisted Trees," she says. The Twisted Trees are a constellation of two trees with their branches entwined together—a sign of friendship. "So, the two are connected? Friendship and betrayal?" Despite herself, she thinks of Pasquale and Ambrose, the only friends she has left in the world. If they betray her, she isn't sure how she'll stomach it.

"That is what the stars say," he says. "I'll make a note of it. Keep on looking."

Beatriz bends her head to the telescope once again and searches for more constellations as they slowly arc across the sky. Her heart seizes in her chest when she catches sight of the Lonely Heart—Sophronia's sign, Nigellus told her. The one he pulled a star down from to create her. It's the shape of a romantic heart rather than an anatomical one, a shape so simple Beatriz can make it out with no difficulty.

But.

She frowns, looking closer. It isn't right. The Slithering Snake she never paid much mind to, but the Lonely Heart has been emblazoned on the mantel of her fireplace throughout her childhood. She knows the stars that form it as surely as she knows the lines of her hand. One is there that shouldn't be. She fiddles with the dials again, trying to see what other constellation is linked with it, but none come close.

"There's an extra star in the Lonely Heart," she says, straightening.

"What other constellation is nearby?" Nigellus asks, not looking up from where he's scribbling in his notebook.

"None," Beatriz says. "It's just one star, where the heart dips. Look."

Nigellus furrows his brow, but he motions for Beatriz to step aside so he can peer through the telescope himself.

Beatriz watches as his spine goes rigid. When he steps back from the telescope, his face is pale.

"That isn't possible," he says. For the first time in her life, he sounds unnerved.

"What isn't?" she asks, feeling unsettled herself. Nigellus looks at her and hesitates. "Oh, just tell me," she says. "I'm already keeping plenty of your secrets."

Nevertheless, Nigellus is quiet. He glances up at the sky, where the Lonely Heart can still be seen. Without the telescope, though, the extra star is hardly visible at all.

"I told you I pulled a star from the Lonely Heart to create Sophronia," he says, his voice hoarse. "That is the star I chose. It fell from the sky more than sixteen years ago, I held its dying embers in my hands."

Beatriz feels her own skin go cold, and she looks back

up at the sky, at Sophronia's constellation. Stars cannot re-appear in the sky—everyone knows that. Once they are pulled down, they are gone forever. It is why empyreas are only supposed to do so in grave emergencies. What does it mean that one has suddenly reappeared? And *that* star, too?

The question is on Beatriz's lips, but looking at Nigellus, she knows he can't give her an answer. Nigellus, who seems to know everything about the stars, is, for the first time in Beatriz's life, at a loss, and that is a terrifying realization.

Daphne

Daphne can't help but feel a bit of trepidation as she walks with Zenia through the Trevail Forest the following day. She is careful to keep a close eye on the girl, and she isn't even annoyed at the six guards who surround them at a respectful distance. After two children were taken under her watch it feels like tempting the stars to bring a third here, but Daphne needs answers, and she suspects Zenia has them.

Zenia, for her part, is wary. As they wind their way through the forest, she keeps casting Daphne sidelong glances. With her blond hair in braids on either side of her round, freckled face, she looks even younger than her ten years.

Daphne clears her throat. "I know you and your family are going back north today, Zenia, but I do hope we can part as friends," she says, offering the girl a smile. "I want you to know that I don't blame you for the poison."

"You don't?" Zenia asks, her wariness shifting into confusion. "But I tried to kill you!"

"Yes, and I'd rather you didn't try to do that again, but I don't think you will. Because you never wanted to kill me in the first place, did you?" Daphne asks.

She already knows that Zenia was pushed to poison her, and that she did so because her nanny told her to, promising to use star magic to bring back the dead.

"I thought I had to," Zenia says quietly.

"Perhaps," Daphne says, casting a quick glance at the guards who surround them, all far enough away to allow them a private conversation. Still, Daphne pitches her voice lower. "But I think you knew it wasn't right, even then, and that's why you didn't follow all of the instructions your nanny gave you."

Zenia swallows. "I already told my brother everything about that day," she says.

Daphne knows she's hiding something, but getting her to give it up won't be easy. If she didn't tell her own brother, Daphne can't imagine she would tell her.

"It was an overwhelming day for both of us," Daphne says. "I wouldn't be surprised if you forgot something."

"I didn't," Zenia says.

"Might I tell you what I think, to see if it refreshes your memory?" Daphne asks.

Zenia shoots her a skeptical look but doesn't protest.

"I think your nanny told you to get me alone before you gave me the poisoned water. Though with Bairre and all your siblings about, that would have been all but impossible. I understand why you didn't wait."

For a long moment, Zenia says nothing.

"Zenia," Daphne prompts, reaching out to touch the girl's arm. "You know that two boys were taken from these woods, don't you?"

Zenia glances around before giving a quick nod.

"I believe that whoever is responsible for that might also be the people who passed on those instructions to your nanny. I'd like to find the boys before they're hurt, but it would help if I knew exactly what you were meant to do."

Zenia looks at her for another few breaths. "It won't help," she says.

"It might," Daphne replies.

Zenia bites her bottom lip. "I don't want to get in any more trouble," she says quietly.

"It will be your secret and mine," Daphne promises, though she doesn't for one second believe it is a promise she will keep. Zenia still looks unsure. "What if I tell you a secret in return?" Daphne asks. "That way, we're even and neither of us can tell."

After a moment of consideration, Zenia nods. "You first," she says.

Daphne has no intention of revealing a real secret to a child she barely knows, but she doesn't think Zenia is a fool, so she needs to make sure her secret is believable. She decides to share one that just might benefit her if Zenia decides to tell it.

"The boys who were kidnapped?" she says. "They are the Princes of Temarin."

Zenia rolls her eyes. "They are not," she says.

"I swear in the name of the stars they are."

Zenia's eyes grow large as saucers. She hesitates a few seconds more before speaking. "I was meant to befriend you, then say I was tired and ask you to sit with me while the others hunted," she tells Daphne, her voice dropping to barely louder than a whisper. "But I was supposed to do it at a certain place, where the stream meets the star stones."

"The star stones?" Daphne asks, frowning. "Did you know what that meant?"

Zenia shakes her head. "But Nanny showed me a map and made me memorize it," she says. "I could see it in my mind, just as it was on paper, but once we were in the woods, it was so much more confusing."

"I'm sure," Daphne says, her mind awhirl. "Can you still see the map in your mind?" she asks.

Zenia hesitates before nodding.

Daphne pauses in the middle of a small clearing where the ground is largely dirt. "Why don't we draw a picture?" she asks, loudly enough that the guards hear her. She finds a fallen stick at the base of an oak tree, and another a few feet away. She hands one to Zenia, who eyes her uncertainly but presses the sharper end of the stick into the dirt.

"This is where we entered from the castle," she tells Daphne, making an *x*. She draws a squiggling line above it, cutting from the bottom left to the upper right. "That's the Stillwell Stream."

Daphne nods, having come across the stream before, on previous trips into the woods. While it runs for miles, it's a narrow thing, easy enough to jump over in places.

"And here," Zenia says, drawing another *x* near the upper right corner, over the stream, "are the star stones."

Daphne examines the map. "And what are star stones?" she asks.

Zenia shrugs. "Never seen them myself," she says. "But

that's what Nanny called them. She said they'd be sharp so I should be mindful not to hurt myself."

Such care the nanny showed to a girl she tried to set up for a murder, Daphne thinks. Though the woman is dead now. Daphne isn't sure Zenia knows that, but she has no intention of telling her.

Daphne eyes the map Zenia drew, committing it to her own memory. She won't bring Zenia there now, not when she doesn't know what she'll find. And at any rate, the girl is supposed to be leaving for home soon with her siblings.

She brushes the toe of her boot over the dirt, erasing Zenia's map.

After returning Zenia to her brother's care, Daphne claims to have a headache and goes to her room, leaving the guards on the other side of her door. Rather than lying down to rest, though, she changes into a pair of men's riding breeches and a tunic hidden away in the back of her wardrobe for an opportunity such as this. She takes her daggers as well, strapping one around her calf, the other on her left arm. Once she's dressed, she crosses to the window on the far side of her room, where Cliona once left her a letter. She suspects the rebels have used the window when they've snuck into her room on other occasions as well, and with good reason—the large oak tree growing alongside the palace provides both leverage and coverage. Both of which Daphne now has need of herself.

She has plenty of experience scaling walls—she and her sisters did it often enough in Bessemia, and their rooms there were on a much higher floor. In just a few short minutes, Daphne's feet hit solid ground almost silently. She pauses. It's barely noon, and the chances of there being courtiers or guards milling about the castle grounds is high, but after a moment of listening, Daphne hears nothing, and she takes off toward the edge of the woods on quick feet.

Zenia's map indicated the star stones would be found to the northeast, and she continues on foot for nearly an hour before she hears the sound of the stream. She follows that east for a while longer, her eyes scanning the stream ahead for anything that might be described as star stones. When she sees them, she stops short.

A pile of rocks sit over the stream, looking at first glance like any other rocks Daphne has seen. But as she approaches and the sunlight filters through the canopy of leaves above, the rocks begin to sparkle and shine—like stardust, she realizes. And, as Zenia said, their edges are sharp enough to draw blood. These must be the star stones, but after she's examined them for a moment, dread pools in the pit of Daphne's stomach.

She looks around the woods, suddenly sure she's been here before, though she can't quite recall. She remembers being carried through here, hearing the sound of the stream, feeling Bairre's arms around her, his heart pounding as he ran. When she looks north, she spots the chimney poking out from the top of the canopy.

Aurelia's cottage, she realizes. The star stones are mere yards away from Aurelia's front door.

Beatriz

When the empress sends a messenger to inform Beatriz that she and Pasquale are required in the throne room immediately, Beatriz's first instinct is to take her time. Pasquale, however, hurries her along, all but dragging her down the hall as they follow the messenger. She supposes he's used to catering to his own father's whims—at any moment, Cesare could have been in the right mood to have them executed for the fun of it. Beatriz knows her mother well enough to know just how far she can push her before she snaps, and dawdling has only ever been enough to annoy her.

"It's smart to stay on her good side," Pasquale says with an apologetic smile when she tries to tell him as much.

Beatriz knows he's right, but she can't help but want to needle her mother every chance she gets. Every time she manages to make the empress's mask fall, even for an instant, Beatriz takes it as a personal victory. But she knows, logically, that in doing so she isn't doing herself or Daphne any favors.

The messenger ushers them through the doors of the throne room, but that is as far as they can go. The throne room is so packed with courtiers that Beatriz can barely make out the top of her mother's head where she sits on her throne, a silver-and-pearl crown resting atop her jet-black hair. The empress's eyes find Beatriz for just an instant before cutting away and focusing again on whoever stands before her.

Beatriz frowns—why would her mother summon her and Pasquale here, only to ignore them? She opens her mouth to speak, but the empress gets there first.

"Let me see if I understand this, Lady Gisella," her mother says, her voice booming, loud enough to be heard throughout the throne room. Beatriz gasps at the name, and beside her, Pasquale goes stiff, his neck craning to get a better look. Beatriz envies him his height—from her vantage point, she can see nothing.

"You're telling me," the empress continues, "that my daughter, Princess Beatriz, and her husband, Prince Pasquale, were . . . overcome with a sudden bout of piety and elected to forgo their claim to King Cesare's throne in order to voluntarily commit themselves to a Sororia and Fraternia in the Alder Mountains. I must confess, I have difficulty believing it."

"I don't blame you, Your Majesty," Gisella's voice replies, the sound of it enough to make Beatriz's hands ball into fists at her sides. Even here, lying to the Empress of Bessemia, Gisella's voice is smooth and melodic. Beatriz is sure she's smiling as she does it. "But Cellaria had quite an effect on the princess. She became an entirely different person in the few weeks she was there—and if you'll forgive me for saying so, she took Lord Savelle's imprisonment very hard. She wasn't the same afterward. My brother—the king—and I didn't wish to see her and Pasquale leave court, but try as we might, we couldn't change their minds. I'm sure you know how stubborn the princess can be when she's made her mind up."

A murmur goes through the crowd, though a few of the courtiers standing close to Beatriz and Pasquale have taken notice of them now, appearing as confused as Beatriz feels. So this is the story Gisella and Nico are spinning in an attempt to avoid Bessemia's wrath. She finds she's a bit disappointed— even if Beatriz hadn't beaten Gisella here, she doubts anyone would have believed her story. The idea of Beatriz choosing to live in a Sororia is laughable.

Rather than confronting Gisella about the lie, though, her mother purses her lips, as if she's considering her words. "Beatriz, in a Sororia," she says. A few titters erupt from the crowd. "You're right, of course, that she's stubborn, and if this is the course she and the prince have chosen we surely must accept it. What path forward did your brother have in mind with this . . . new development?"

When Gisella speaks again, Beatriz can hear the smugness leaking into her voice. It's almost comical, how unaware she is of the trap she has wandered into. If she were anyone else, Beatriz might even pity her for it. "King Nicolo would be honored if the treaty between our countries would hold. He's aware that you've taken control of Temarin and would offer you his support there— Unlike King Cesare, he has no interest in expanding his own reach."

"Yes, I'd imagine a young upstart boy barely out of the schoolroom would have enough difficulty running one country, never mind two," the empress says, earning more laughter from the courtiers, and Beatriz thinks she would give just about anything to see Gisella's face. "Nevertheless, that is generous of him. Perhaps I ought to consider it." She pauses and her eyes find Beatriz's in the crowd once more. At a gesture of her hand, the crowd in front of Beatriz parts and she gets her first glimpse of Gisella, standing before her mother dressed in a striking gown of red-and-gold brocade, her white-blond hair styled into an elaborate plait that drapes over her shoulder.

"What do you think, dearest?" the empress asks Beatriz, and even though she doesn't trust her mother, she knows she's being given a gift, and one she isn't about to waste. She steps through the crowd, the heels of her satin slippers clicking against the stone floor as she walks toward Gisella, Pasquale at her back.

"I think," Beatriz says, enjoying how Gisella's shoulders stiffen at the sound of her voice, even before she turns to look at Beatriz, dark brown eyes wide and mouth twisting, "that Lady Gisella is very lucky that our palace dungeon is more comfortable than a Cellarian Sororia."

Even though Gisella looks like she's smelled rotting meat, she drops into a curtsy, her eyes never leaving Beatriz's.

"Your Highness," she says before her gaze darts to Pasquale. "Your Highness," she repeats to him, staying in her low curtsy. "I see there's been a . . . miscommunication."

"Oh?" the empress says, a single eyebrow arching up. "Then by all means, Lady Gisella, please explain why you believe my daughter and her husband went voluntarily into a Sororia and Fraternia, when they claim you and your brother sent them there by force in order to steal a throne that is rightfully theirs?"

Gisella's eyes dart between Beatriz, Pasquale, and the

empress. She opens her mouth, then closes it again, but no words come out.

"I thought as much," the empress says, gesturing again. Guards approach Gisella, who allows them to bind her hands behind her back with a set of gold manacles.

Beatriz savors the sight of them leading her away, and a quick glance at Pasquale confirms that he's enjoying it too. They'll take their joy where they can find it, Beatriz thinks before turning back to her mother.

"It was very kind of her to fall into our laps," Beatriz says. "She'll make an excellent hostage—she and Nicolo are very close. I'm sure he would do just about anything to get his sister back."

The empress waves a hand and the courtiers file out of the throne room. When only she, Beatriz, and Pasquale remain, she stands up from her throne and steps down from the dais onto the stone floor.

"It's a boon we won't waste," the empress says. "I'll write to this imposter king to let him know."

"Oh, allow me to," Beatriz says, unable to hide a grin. Her mother narrows her eyes. "Please," Beatriz adds, and she can't remember the last time she begged her mother for anything. For this, though, she'll beg.

"It isn't a love letter, Beatriz," the empress says.

Beatriz glances at Pasquale, realizing that if her mother is mentioning that in front of him, she has a clearer understanding of their marriage than Beatriz thought.

"You once told me how important it is to know an enemy's weaknesses," she tells her mother instead. "I know

Nicolo's weaknesses." *I am one of them,* she adds mentally, thinking about how he stood outside her bedroom window after being named king, begging her to be his queen.

She won't tell her mother that, though. It would mean opening up a path toward her victory that doesn't require keeping Pasquale alive, and Beatriz won't risk that.

"Very well," the empress says. "Visit our new prisoner as well, would you? See if you can't extract a few secrets out of her."

Dear Nicolo,

I'm sure that by now you've received word of Pasquale and me escaping the Alder Mountains. It is a shame that news did not reach your sister before she sought an audience with my mother. Don't worry—I'll extend the same courtesy to her that you extended to us: imprisonment, but not death.

I told you once that I'd carry the memory of you as I last saw you, drunk, desperate, and disappointed, into my darkest hours, and rest assured that it's brought me great joy. But I believe the sight of Gisella being dragged away by palace guards just may have supplanted it.

Enjoy your throne, while you still hold it.

Yours,
Beatriz

After sending the letter to her mother for approval, Beatriz takes Pasquale down to the dungeon to visit Gisella, even arranging to have tea brought for them to enjoy. Much as she might like to deprive Gisella of all human comfort, the way she was at the Sororia, she knows that the show of kindness will knock Gisella off-balance far more than cruelty, and Beatriz will need every advantage she can take.

And sure enough, Gisella isn't quite able to hide her bewilderment as servants file into her cell, bringing a table, chairs, a silk tablecloth, and a painted porcelain tea set. As they set up, Beatriz glances around the space—bigger than her room in the Sororia, but similarly devoid of windows. There is a narrow bed in one corner with a thin quilt draped over the foot, as well as a washbasin and a desk with a spindly wooden chair. Sparse, Beatriz thinks, but nothing for Gisella to complain about, all things considered.

"I suppose you're here to drag information from me," Gisella says when the servants file back out. Beatriz and Pasquale take their seats at the table, and after a moment of hesitation, Gisella does the same.

"It seems there's much to catch up on," Beatriz says, reaching across the table to pour tea into the three cups. "I've written to Nicolo to apprise him of your . . . situation."

"Am I being held for ransom?" Gisella asks.

"Not quite," Pasquale says. "Much as Nicolo might love you, we all know he wouldn't surrender the Cellarian throne to get you back safely. And I'm afraid Beatriz's mother will settle for nothing less."

"Execution, then?" Gisella asks, and despite the breeziness she tries to inject into her voice, Beatriz hears a real thread of fear beneath the surface.

"It hasn't been ruled out," she lies, simply to keep Gisella on her toes. Beatriz takes a sip of her tea and sets it down on the saucer. "The tea is quite good," she says.

Gisella frowns at the cup in front of her. "Poisoned, I expect?" she asks.

Beatriz laughs as if the idea is ridiculous. "I drank it myself, didn't I?"

"My cup could have been poisoned," Gisella points out. "Paint the bottom with a thin layer of poison paste, let it dry. When the hot tea is poured in, the poison dissolves."

"My, that sounds like the voice of experience," Beatriz says with a grin before looking to Pasquale. "Perhaps we should be taking notes."

Pasquale smiles back before reaching across the table to take Gisella's cup. He looks at Beatriz for just a second, giving her the opportunity to stop him, before he takes a sip of Gisella's tea.

"You see?" he says, handing it back to her.

Pasquale's blind trust in Beatriz takes her by surprise for an instant before she realizes she trusts him just as much. A frightening thought.

Gisella glances between the two of them, her brow still furrowed in uncertainty.

"Oh, go on, Gigi—you must be parched from your journey here, and we've already established that we don't want you dead."

"Yet," Gisella adds, but she lifts the cup to her lips and takes a long sip.

Beatriz can see her tasting the tea, searching for anything that might be poison. When she finds none, she takes a longer sip.

"How long did you stay in Cellaria after we were sent away before coming to see my mother?" Beatriz asks.

"Oh, are we getting right into the interrogation?" Gisella says, taking another sip. "I left a week after you did. There was some debate about sending a letter, but we thought sending me to personally appeal to the empress would be a show of trust and good faith."

"That was a misfire," Pasquale murmurs, earning a smirk from Beatriz and a glower from Gisella.

"And in that week," Beatriz continues, "how was Nicolo's court receiving him as king? I can't imagine he didn't ruffle a few feathers."

Gisella's jaw tightens, but she holds Beatriz's gaze. "Oh, he's very well liked," she says before breaking off to cough. When she's done, she continues. "He's spent years making friends, and, of course, my father has spent decades doing it. Cellaria is happy to have Nico as a king."

She coughs again, and Beatriz schools her expression into one of concern. "Oh, it sounds like you're getting sick, Gigi—luckily you'll have plenty of time to rest and recover, I suppose."

Gisella glares at her and takes another sip of tea.

"I have a question," Pasquale says, surprising Beatriz. His eyes are on his cousin, not hostile, the way Beatriz suspects she looks, though not with the open expression he used to look at Gisella, either. "When did you decide to turn on us?"

Gisella blinks, the question taking her by surprise. Beatriz finds herself curious about the answer too—not that it changes anything, she reminds herself. But still. She is curious.

"You served me an opportunity on a silver platter," Gisella says. "I won't apologize for taking it."

Beatriz frowns. "You're saying that you had no plans to betray us until we told you about our plan to break Lord Savelle out of prison?" she asks.

"It was a foolish plan," Gisella says. "We would have been fools not to take advantage of that."

"But you and Nicolo started poisoning King Cesare long before then," Pasquale says.

"Well, yes," Gisella says with a shrug. "You can't pretend to mourn him—I know you better than that."

"Then your plan doesn't make sense," Beatriz says. "You were planning to kill the king and conspire with Queen Eugenia . . . for what?"

"Oh, you puzzled that part out, did you?" Gisella asks, sounding unbothered. "We didn't particularly care what the endgame was there—if Pasquale ended up on the throne, our status as his favorite cousins meant that we rose with him. If Eugenia succeeded in her plot to drive Temarin and Cellaria to war and managed to take the throne here, surely she'd reward us for our help."

"You were playing both sides, then," Pasquale comments. "How noble."

"We were surviving," Gisella corrects, her voice coming out sharp. "Beatriz, you barely spent two months in the Cellarian court and even you know that is no easy feat. Yes, we poisoned a cruel king. Yes, we stepped on your necks to rise a little higher, become a little safer, a little more untouchable. You aren't really mad at me for that, you know."

"I beg to differ," Beatriz snaps, but Gisella ignores her.

"You're mad at yourself for letting me—for letting Nico."

Beatriz doesn't respond to that, in large part because she suspects Gisella is right. She finishes her tea and pushes back from the table, Pasquale a beat behind her. "Don't forget my advice, Gisella," she says with a saccharine smile. "I told you that you climbed so high the fall would kill you—I suggest that now is the time to brace yourself for impact."

After leaving Gisella's cell, Beatriz and Pasquale return to Beatriz's room, careful not to speak again until they are safely behind closed doors.

"Was the tea poisoned?" Pasquale asks, looking at Beatriz with a dose of fear that makes her uncomfortable.

"Only with a truth serum," she says, shaking her head.

He frowns. "I thought as much, but she did lie . . . didn't she?"

Beatriz gives a snort and shakes her head. "Oh, several times," she says. "But try to tell a lie right now."

Pasquale looks uneasy. He opens his mouth to speak and coughs. When it passes, he continues. "I trust Gisella."

Beatriz grins. "There, did you catch it?"

"The cough," Pasquale says. His eyebrows arch up. "The cough precedes the lie. No wonder she kept doing it."

"Precisely. If I'd given her a truth serum that prevented her from lying, she would have known. This way, she'll never have a clue. It's more subtle—we don't know what the truth is, but we know what she's lying about."

"The court is turning against Nicolo," Pasquale says. "That's certainly interesting."

Beatriz nods. "Though not necessarily surprising," she adds. "The Cellarian court is temperamental at best, and Nicolo inheriting the throne would have ruffled plenty of feathers. I expect there are a few families planning a coup."

"Your mother will be happy to hear that," Pasquale says, grimacing.

"I'm sure she would, but she won't hear it from us," Beatriz says. "I'm not keen on giving her any more information that will encourage her to send us back to Cellaria at her earliest convenience. There's more I need to learn from Nigellus, and if she tries to make a move against Daphne—"

"I understand," Pasquale says. "But can you keep the truth from her?"

Beatriz frowns. Maybe a few weeks ago, she would have said yes, but now she knows better than to underestimate her mother. And she understands what, exactly, is at stake if she fails. "I'll have to," she says, shaking her head. "There's no other choice."

Daphne

D aphne returns to the palace an hour before supper, re-entering her room the same way she left it—through the window. From there, she hurries to change into her dress, shoving her men's clothes back into her wardrobe, all while mulling over her suspicions.

If Zenia was meant to bring Daphne nearly to Aurelia's door before poisoning her, that asks more questions than it answers, but at the same time, Daphne wouldn't be surprised if Aurelia was the reason behind the assassination attempts. She said herself that she'd foreseen the death of someone with the blood of stars and majesty and feared it would be Bairre. Daphne can almost believe that Aurelia might have tried to have her killed as a way of keeping that prophecy from touching her son.

But what does that have to do with the princes? Aurelia said she was still hearing the same prophecy, but that had nothing to do with Gideon and Reid—they might have the blood of kings in their veins, but they aren't star-touched.

Perhaps the two things are unrelated, she tells herself. Perhaps Zenia bringing Daphne to that place would have been a coincidence as well. But to Daphne's mind, even one coincidence is too many.

There is someone in Daphne's bedchamber when she comes back from supper, she is sure of it. The window is open even though it's snowing again, and both she and her maids have been keeping it closed. Then there is the indent in the plush rug that stretches just below the window, as if someone crouching on the window's ledge had jumped down.

Maybe the assassins aren't bound to the woods after all. Maybe they're getting bolder. Or lazier. Or perhaps just more desperate.

Tempted as she is to step back into the hall and shout for help, Daphne isn't sure she can trust the guards stationed throughout the royal wing. And besides, if the assassin is working for the same people who took the princes, she has a few questions she'd like to ask, and that's best done without interference.

She pauses in the doorway, reaching down to adjust her boot and sliding her dagger from its hiding place before straightening up and closing the door behind her. She waits to see if the assassin will take the opportunity to attack, but they don't. She scans the room, looking for potential hiding places—a person could fit beneath the bed, but the position would render them more vulnerable than she is, making it a doubtful choice. The wind blows through the curtains, showing that there is no one hiding behind them. Which leaves her wardrobe—the only place a fully grown adult could hide.

She tiptoes toward the wardrobe, quiet as a cat, dagger poised and ready to strike. Her heart hammers in her ears, drowning out all thoughts but that of the danger before her. There can be no hesitation: she will strike or be struck, and she's spent too many days close to death since she arrived in this stars-forsaken country.

In a quick, fluid movement, she throws open the door of the wardrobe and plunges the dagger inside, letting out a cry of rage as she does. She stabs again and again, only on the fourth try realizing she is maiming nothing but the gowns hanging there. Several now have holes—something Mrs. Nattermore is bound to be annoyed about.

Daphne spins back to the room, sagging against the wardrobe and struggling to catch her breath. The hand holding the dagger falls to her side while her free hand goes to her heart, as if she can calm its rapid beat.

No one is there. She's seeing ghosts, she thinks, shaking her head. She pushes away from the wardrobe and crosses toward the window, closing it with a slam.

It's only then that she feels the cold press of metal against her throat.

"Drop the dagger, Princess," a voice says—a female voice, a Bessemian voice. Daphne is so startled by that last detail that she does as she's told and lets the dagger fall to the floor.

"I mean you no harm, but I needed to speak with you alone," the voice says. "I'm going to drop my dagger, but the instant you reach for yours, I'll bring it back. All right?"

Daphne nods, though already her mind is spinning. As soon as that dagger is away from her throat, she'll lunge for her knife. As soon as she has her knife—

"Your sister sent me," the assassin says as she lowers her blade, and Daphne's plan falls away with it. She whirls to face the assassin and finds herself looking at a girl around her own age, and for the slightest instant, she's reminded of Sophronia. They have the same blond hair, the same stature, but she isn't Sophronia.

"Which one?" Daphne bites out, keeping a close eye on where her knife fell. She doesn't trust the girl, but it's clear she isn't an assassin—if she were, Daphne would be bleeding out right now.

"Sophronia first," the girl says, holding Daphne's gaze. Her eyes are like Sophronia's, too, like Daphne's as well—star-touched silver. "Then Beatriz more recently."

"You're lying," Daphne says.

The girl seems to expect this reaction. She shrugs. "Beatriz is left handed I know because she punched me, though she was kind enough to get stardust to heal me afterward. She also called you a ruthless bitch."

That was certainly Beatriz, Daphne thinks. "And Sophronia?"

The girl hesitates, her eyes darting away. It's the perfect moment to dive for her dagger, but Daphne doesn't move. She waits, eyes on the girl.

"Sophronia liked to sneak into the Temarinian kitchens to bake when she couldn't sleep," the girl says after a moment. "I believe she had the same habit in Bessemia."

Daphne feels like a sail when the wind stops blowing. How many times did she find Sophronia in the kitchens, apron tied around her nightgown, with flour dusting her skin and hair and a beaming smile as she pulled a tray from the oven? "Who are you?" she asks, struggling to keep her wits about her.

"My name is Violie. Your mother sent me to accompany Sophronia in Temarin." The girl pauses. "And spy on her."

Violie. Daphne knows that name—Sophronia said it just before she died. She'd told Daphne and Beatriz that friends were coming to find her—Leopold and Violie. Leopold, Daphne knew, but Violie she didn't. But even if Sophronia considered this girl a friend, Daphne knows her sister was far too trusting.

"My mother wouldn't—" Daphne begins before stopping herself. Her mother would send someone to spy on Sophronia. It would have been the prudent thing to do. "And Beatriz?" Daphne asks. "You said she hit you?"

The girl—Violie—reaches up to touch her nose, though as far as Daphne can see there's nothing wrong with it. Her eyes dart away and Daphne knows before she speaks that she won't be telling the entire truth.

"It was deserved," she says carefully. "We came across her fleeing Cellaria with Prince Pasquale. It's my understanding she'd been sent to a Sororia there by a new king who had usurped the prince's place in the line of succession."

Daphne frowns. "Is that even possible?" she asks.

"Anything is possible for a mad king, which I understand King Cesare was," she says. "They were on their way to Bessemia, but she told us to come to you."

"Us?" Daphne asks. "Who is us?"

Violie hesitates, twirling her dagger in her hand—a nervous tic, Daphne thinks. "King Leopold," she says finally.

Daphne laughs—she can't help it. There is nothing funny

about the situation, but the fact that King Leopold, the most wanted man in the continent, has just fallen into her lap is truly laughable. "Where is he?" she asks, already mentally drafting the letter she'll write her mother. The empress will be so pleased, so proud of Daphne for securing Temarin for her.

"I don't believe Sophronia would want me to tell you," Violie says.

Daphne feels like she's been kicked in the stomach. "What?" she asks, shaking her head. "You came here for my help, didn't you? Allow me to help—"

"By doing what?" Violie asks. "Writing to your mother? You do that and his days are numbered. Sophronia gave her life to keep him alive, and I intend to honor that sacrifice."

Daphne is careful not to let Violie know just how close she came to guessing her thoughts. "I loved my sister, but she was a sentimental fool sometimes," she says, keeping her voice level. "From my understanding, Leopold was an awful king. My mother believes she can rule Temarin better—"

"She believes she can rule all of Vesteria better," Violie interrupts.

Panicked, Daphne casts her eyes around the room, reassuring herself that they're alone, before hushing Violie. "I don't know what you think you know—"

"I know what your mother told me," Violie says, interrupting again. "In her own words, when she sent me to spy on Sophronia."

Daphne grits her teeth. "Fine," she snaps. "But the point stands—Leopold had no business being king. My mother wishes to ensure her rule in Temarin, yes, but if he simply renounces his claim—"

Violie interrupts her once more, but this time with a laugh, harsh and mirthless. "Please tell me you don't genuinely believe that," she says.

Daphne crooks a bitter smile. "I see Beatriz got to you with her conspiracy theories—she's always been dramatic."

"Beatriz didn't need to get to me," Violie says. "Sophronia already had. She'd have told you as much herself, but your mother had her killed."

The words are a bucket of ice water dumped over Daphne's head, but she holds fast to her composure. "A Temarinian mob killed Sophie," she says through gritted teeth.

Violie searches Daphne's face for a moment, lips pursed. Finally, she nods. "All right, then," she says, picking up Daphne's dagger and backing toward the window. "Beatriz was right—there's nothing more we need to discuss."

"I beg to differ," Daphne says, following her to the window and shouldering in front of her, blocking her escape route. Violie might have both daggers, but Daphne is certain now that the girl won't hurt her. "Where's King Leopold?"

"Safe," Violie says, trying to push past Daphne, but Daphne holds firm.

"If you truly have him—which I'm beginning to doubt—I'm sure his mother would like to know that he's well, at least," Daphne says. She doesn't expect the sentimentality to affect Violie—she doesn't strike Daphne as that sort—but she's unprepared for the shock and fury that ripple over Violie's face.

"Eugenia is here?" she asks, her voice low.

"Arrived a few days ago with Leopold's brothers. They were . . . taken," Daphne admits. Violie's eyes sharpen and Daphne wishes she'd held back that particular detail. "She's lost two sons, would you keep her from him, too?"

Violie laughs again. "And here I was led to believe you were clever," she says. "Did you fall for her mourning mother act? She forgot to mention the fact that she worked with the mob and your mother to execute Sophie and Leopold. She won't be relieved to know he survived, she'll be disappointed."

"You're lying," Daphne says, though some part of her knows that this, at least, is true. She knew there was something not right about Eugenia, and this bit of information fits into the gaps Eugenia left in her story. But how can she believe that without believing her mother had a hand in it as well?

"Am I?" Violie asks. "The next time you see Eugenia, mention my name and see her reaction."

Daphne opens her mouth to speak, but before she can, Violie reaches out and grabs her wrist and she feels a sharp jab. Looking down, Daphne sees that Violie is wearing her ring—the one that keeps a dose of sleeping poison.

"How dare . . . ," she begins, but before she can finish the thought, the world goes black.

Violie

After climbing back down the castle wall, Violie makes her way into the woods that surround the castle, twisting the poison ring she stole from Princess Daphne's jewelry box as she goes. She's grateful she took the opportunity to rifle through the box while she waited for Daphne to return from dinner—even more grateful that she chose to hide on top of the wardrobe rather than inside it, as she'd initially chosen to do. If she had, she'd be cut to ribbons right now.

Princess Beatriz was right, Daphne can't be trusted, and what's worse, Queen Eugenia is currently in residence at the castle. In Violie's wildest imaginings, she wouldn't have expected that. She'd assumed Eugenia would have fled south to Cellaria, where she was born and raised and likely has allies.

But apparently, she has made an ally of Daphne—a discouraging thought.

There was that flicker of doubt, though, when Violie told Daphne that her mother was responsible for killing Sophronia. Daphne didn't believe her, of course, but there was a part of her that didn't think the idea was ludicrous. It's a start.

But it was also plain that Daphne wouldn't hesitate to turn Leopold over to her mother at the first available opportunity. Violie is determined that she won't get that opportunity, not until Violie is sure she can be trusted.

It takes some time to retrace her path through the woods—careful to use a fallen tree branch to obscure the prints she leaves in the snow—but she finally comes across the cave she and Leopold picked out when the mail cart dropped them off in Eldevale a few hours ago. She hoped it would be a stopping point before they settled in the castle, but those plans have changed.

Leopold appears in the dark mouth of the cave, eyes questioning, though he must see something in her expression, because his shoulders slump.

"Beatriz was right about her sister?" he asks, leading her farther into the cave, out of sight of anyone who might wander by.

"Worse than that," Violie tells him, shaking her head. "Your mother is staying in the palace, a refugee guest of King Bartholomew."

Leopold stops short, whirling to face her. Violie can't see his face, but she can feel the spark of fury, burning so hot it radiates from him like heat from a fire.

"My mother?" he asks, the two words spoken dangerously low.

"That's what Daphne said, yes. She thought it would tempt you to come to the castle, to reunite with her."

"It tempts me to go to the castle, if only to get my hands around her throat," he growls. "Were my brothers with her?"

Violie swallows. "They arrived with the queen, but . . ."

She trails off. She knows telling him will break his heart, and he's faced more than his share of heartbreak lately. She realizes she doesn't want to hurt him any more, a disconcerting thought. She pushes past it. "They were kidnapped a few days ago."

"Kidnapped," he echoes.

Violie nods before realizing he can't see her in the dark. "Yes. Apparently your mother is distraught."

"I'd wager my mother had something to do with it," Leopold replies. "She already tried to kill me, clearly she has no reservations about filicide."

"It's possible," Violie agrees, though privately she suspects the kidnapping has Empress Margaraux's fingerprints all over it. Leopold doesn't need reason just now, though, he needs anger, so she lets him have it.

"We can't stay here tonight," she tells him. "I've heard enough stories about the size of Frivian bears to haunt my nightmares, and I have a feeling Daphne will search the woods first when she wakes up."

"Wakes up?" Leopold asks.

Violie holds up her hand with the ring on it. "I stole it from her jewelry case, along with a bag of asters. Sophronia had one like it—it contains a sleeping draught and a needle to inject a person. She'll sleep until morning."

She half expects Leopold to wring his hands over the fact that Violie used poison, but she supposes he must be getting used to the way she handles things, because he doesn't even blink.

"Where will we go?" he asks instead.

"We'll have a better chance of avoiding notice in town,"

she tells him. "There will be a lot of people around, hopefully two travelers with strange accents won't stand out too much. And I stole enough asters to get us a room at an inn for a few nights, at least."

"And then?" Leopold asks.

Violie bites her lip. "I don't know," she admits. "But I told Beatriz I would spy on Daphne for her, and I'll need to be in the castle to do that."

Violie and Leopold make their way to the Wallfrost Inn on the outskirts of Eldevale. All the while, Violie's mind is awhirl, thinking up a plan. After she uses the asters she stole from Daphne to secure a room, they sit down for dinner in the public room.

"You speak Frivian well," she tells him. "But your accent is atrocious."

Leopold looks vaguely affronted. "I'll have you know my Frivian tutor said I was the best pupil he'd ever taught," he said.

Violie snorts. "Yes, well, you were going to be his king. I'm sure he hoped to flatter you."

Leopold frowns, though he doesn't look surprised at the idea. She supposes it's a reality he's had to face often since they fled Temarin—Leopold is woefully underprepared for this life that he was never supposed to live.

"I suppose you can do better?" he challenges.

Violie smirks and waves the barmaid over, ordering another round of the hot cider she and Leopold have been enjoying—with a healthy dose of cinnamon, it feels like drinking liquid fire, and after spending the evening out in the snow, that prospect is appealing. The barmaid smiles and she and Violie make brief conversation about the snow before she leaves to fetch the ciders.

Leopold looks at her like he's never seen her before. "How did you do that? You sounded like a local."

Violie shrugs. "I told you my mother was a courtesan," she says. "Many of her colleagues grew up in other countries. I used to enjoy mimicking the way they spoke." She pauses for a moment. "I used to think it would be a helpful skill to have as an actress."

"You wanted to act?" Leopold asks, eyebrows rising.

Violie shrugs. That version of her feels like a complete stranger now. "I was a child—my acting phase fit in somewhere after being a princess and before being a dancer. But spying utilizes many of the same talents as acting, accents among them."

"You have a plan, don't you?" he asks, looking at her over the rim of his mug. "That's why you want me to pass as Frivian."

"Well, if nothing else, it will help us fit in here. Friv is a reclusive country, they don't trust outsiders. And if Princess Daphne sends anyone looking for a Temarinian, you'll be easy to find."

Leopold nods, his brows drawn close together. "Right," he says. "Can you help teach me?"

The barmaid returns, passing them their fresh mugs of cider.

"Anything else?" she asks them.

Violie considers her plan for a second—impulsive it may

be, mad it certainly is, but it's a plan nonetheless. "Would you happen to know somewhere we can buy stardust?"

The barmaid raises her eyebrows. "My brother's friend's sister has a shop. It's closed now, but I can have a vial brought up to your room tonight."

Violie rustles through her bag of asters and withdraws ten, passing them to the barmaid. "I trust that will suffice?"

The barmaid counts the coins and nods. "I'll have it for you in a few hours," she says before heading back behind the bar.

"Stardust?" Leopold asks. "You must know that whatever she's going to get at this hour for ten asters will hardly be strong."

Violie shrugs. "It doesn't need to be strong," she says. "It just needs to change the color of your hair."

"My hair?" he asks, alarmed, running a hand through it.

"When she wakes up in the morning, Daphne will have everyone looking for a boy matching your description. We need to ensure *you* don't match it, especially if we're going to get jobs in the castle."

Leopold raises an eyebrow. "Isn't that a bit like walking into the lions' den dressed in slabs of meat?"

"Daphne and your mother are the only people who will recognize us—and even Daphne might not know you in person, especially with different hair, though I'm not keen to test that theory. If we can find work somewhere like the kitchens, I should be able to learn enough about what Daphne's doing to keep Beatriz apprised while still avoiding notice."

Leopold appears to consider it for a moment, staring

into the mug of cider he holds, a plume of steam rising from the top. "It still seems risky," he says.

Violie snorts and takes another gulp of her cider. "At this point, Leopold, even breathing is risky."

That night, Violie and Leopold sit cross-legged on the narrow twin bed that takes up most of their room at the inn. Leopold has already set up a makeshift bed on the small patch of floor next to it, but they've been sitting together while they practice his accent.

His problem, Violie realizes, is that he keeps the edges of his words hard, the way Temarinians do, but Frivians have a tendency to let their words crash into one another. It is a difficult habit to erase, but by the time the barmaid arrives at their door near midnight with the promised vial of stardust, his accent is almost passable.

"You shouldn't speak unless necessary," she tells him when the barmaid is gone, closing the door and crossing back to the bed with the stardust in hand.

"I could simply not speak at all," he offers, but Violie shakes her head.

"The last thing we want is for there to be anything notable about either of us. It was one of the first things I learned working for the empress—how to be invisible. And no one is more invisible than a servant."

Leopold snorts. "That's not true. I paid attention to the servants."

Violie laughs. "Please—when you arrived in that cave and found me there, you didn't even recognize me."

"Well, you were Sophie's maid. It wasn't as if we crossed paths often."

Violie stares at him. "Leopold, we were in the same room almost daily, usually multiple times. You spoke to me often enough, though never by name."

"I did not," he says, frowning. "I'm sure I would have remembered."

"But you didn't," she tells him. "Because no one notices the servants."

Leopold's frown deepens and she senses he wants to argue with her more, but she isn't terribly concerned with soothing his guilt at the moment.

"It's a good thing they don't," she says. "That's what we're counting on."

Leopold looks like he wants to argue the point further, but after a second, he nods.

Violie holds up the vial of stardust. "Now, let's take care of your hair."

Daphne

Daphne wakes up just as dawn light is streaming through her still-open window, making her head throb. It takes her a moment to remember why that is— a lingering headache is an aftereffect of the knockout poison in her ring. The ring that was stolen by the Bessemian girl who claimed to know her sisters. Violie.

The next time you see Eugenia, mention my name and see her reaction.

Daphne sits up in bed, leaning back against the pile of plush pillows and realizing that she's still dressed in the gown she wore to dinner last night. Violie tucked the covers up to her chin so that when her maid came to help her undress, she'd appear to have done it herself and fallen asleep early. A thorough plan, given that Violie would have largely been acting on instinct. She couldn't have expected to find the poison ring in Daphne's jewelry case.

Which begs the question how she knew the ring contained poison. It was designed to look like any piece of jewelry, though Daphne knows Sophronia and Beatriz had the same rings. She doesn't believe much of what Violie told her, but she was at least telling the truth about knowing her sisters—Sophronia's love of baking isn't widely known, and Violie's description of Beatriz referring to Daphne as a ruthless bitch had to have come from the source. Besides, Beatriz does have a mean left hook—one Daphne has been the target of several times herself.

But the rest? That the empress was responsible for Sophronia's death? That was a lie. The real question is whether it's a lie Violie herself believes, or whether she has some ulterior motive for trying to turn Daphne against her mother.

And then there is the matter of Eugenia—who Daphne doesn't trust but who is, at the moment, a grieving mother. That situation requires a delicate hand if she's going to get any worthwhile answers.

Ignoring her throbbing head, Daphne climbs out of bed and strips off her rumpled gown, leaving it in a pile half under the bed where her maid might believe she missed it last night in the dark. She rings the bell beside her bed, and when her maid appears a moment later to help her ready herself for the day, she instructs her to send an invitation to Eugenia for tea.

"It's my understanding that Lady Eunice has declined all social invitations since the disappearance of her sons," the maid says, using the false name King Bartholomew gave Eugenia to keep his court from knowing he's harboring a Temarinian dowager queen.

"Of course," Daphne says, all wide eyes and sympathy. "But I confess I'm worried for her well-being. If Lady Eunice wishes to refuse me, I must insist she does so face to face."

Tea is set up on the winter terrace, which is enclosed by glass walls and a glass roof that allow visitors to view the falling snow without enduring the cold. Three braziers are set up around the small table at the center to keep the space warm and comfortable, though Daphne knows as soon as she sets foot on the terrace that Eugenia will still find it too cold.

Daphne's surprised to realize that she no longer does— a thought that disconcerts her. She doesn't want to acclimate to Frivian temperatures.

She has barely sat down at the table when Eugenia bursts through the door, and when her eyes fall on Daphne, there's a flash of fury before she manages to cover it with a congenial mask.

"Your Highness," Eugenia says, ducking into a brief curtsy before sitting across from Daphne, who motions for the servants to bring out the tea and cakes.

"I'm so glad you could join me," Daphne tells her, her own smile affixed to her face.

"I don't believe I had much of a choice," Eugenia says, barely masking the bitterness in the words. "I won't be staying long—I can't abide company these days, I'm sure you can understand that."

"Of course," Daphne says smoothly. "Why, when I received news of Sophronia's death, I could barely stand to leave my room."

"You understand, then," Eugenia says, appearing to relax.

"Well," Daphne says, still smiling, "my sister was slaughtered. As far as anyone knows, all three of your sons are still breathing. Unless you have reason to believe different?"

Eugenia must hear the test in her words, because she falters for just an instant before collecting herself.

"You're young," she says. "I envy you your hope. If the villains who kidnapped Reid and Gideon intended to keep them alive, they would have tried to extract a ransom by now, and Leopold could not possibly have survived the brutal siege."

He did, though. That's another thing Violie said that Daphne is sure is the truth. She considered sending scouts into Eldevale to search for him, but many of those scouts would doubtlessly be loyal to the rebels, and she doesn't trust their motives. She'll write to her mother this afternoon, though, to let her know that Leopold is nearby.

She thinks about Violie's directive to mention her name to Eugenia and presses on with the line she spent the morning crafting.

"Tell me, I've been wondering about another person in the Temarinian palace—a friend my sister mentioned in her letters," she says.

Eugenia frowns in confusion. "You'll pardon me for saying so, Your Highness, but Sophronia had no friends. It wasn't her fault, Sophronia was a dear girl, but Temarin has always been hostile toward foreign queens who lord it over them, and Sophronia had let her power as queen go to her head."

That doesn't sound like Sophronia at all, but Daphne bites her tongue and focuses on her task. She can't let Eugenia distract her.

"It was a Bessemian girl, actually," she says. "A maid, I believe. Her name was Violie."

Daphne studies Eugenia's response closely—the flare of her nostrils, the sudden stiffness in her posture. She knows the name, and hearing it makes her uncomfortable.

"I do remember Sophronia being fond of her maid," she says carefully. "Though if you're asking what happened to her after the siege, I confess I haven't a clue. I always suspected, though . . . no, I shouldn't say."

"Say," Daphne encourages, her voice coming out sharper than she intends.

Eugenia makes a show of hesitating, but Daphne understands that a show is exactly what it is.

"I always suspected," Eugenia goes on, lowering her voice, "that she was working with the mob who besieged the capital. There was a rumor that she was . . . romantically involved with the young man leading them—Ansel, I believe his name was. I must confess that I've heard other rumors from some very reliable sources that she was the very person who captured Sophronia as she was fleeing the castle."

Eugenia leaves moments later, not even finishing her tea or pastry, but before Daphne can do the same, Bairre steps onto the terrace, raking a hand through his hair and glancing around, his eyes lighting on her. From the look of his wind-mussed hair and dirty riding clothes, he's come straight from one of the search parties that have been sent out looking for the princes.

"Any sign of them?" Daphne asks, getting to her feet, but Bairre shakes his head and she sinks back into the chair with a sigh.

Bairre fills the chair Eugenia just vacated, but Daphne wishes he wouldn't. She knows what he's going to ask her.

"Did you learn anything from Zenia yesterday?"

In all of the chaos with Violie, Daphne hasn't quite forgotten her conversation with Zenia, but she's no closer to knowing what to do with the information.

"We were right," she tells him hesitantly. "There was more to Zenia's instructions that she didn't share originally."

"What was it?" Bairre asks, leaning forward across the table.

"She was supposed to get me alone before giving me the poison, and she was supposed to take me somewhere. Her nanny had drawn it for her on a map. I went there myself yesterday to see if I might learn something."

"Clearly, you learned nothing if you traveled into those woods alone," Bairre says, but Daphne ignores him.

She bites her lip. "The place she was supposed to take me was just beside your mother's cottage," she tells him.

Bairre goes still, his forehead creasing. "The woods are vast," he says, shaking his head.

"They are," Daphne agrees. "But that's where Zenia's nanny told her to take me before giving me the poison."

"Zenia got the location wrong," Bairre says, shaking his head. "Or you did."

"Does that make more sense to you?" Daphne asks him. "That I misread the map Zenia made, and in the forest you yourself just described as vast, I somehow ended up at your mother's cottage? What would the chances of that be?"

"It's more likely than the alternative," Bairre snaps. "Are you forgetting that my mother saved your life?"

"Of course not," Daphne says, keeping her voice level. "But I do wonder if she would have done so had you not been there, asking it of her."

Bairre doesn't speak, his jaw tense. Daphne forces herself to continue.

"She knew that a person both royal and star-touched would die. Perhaps she wanted to ensure it wouldn't be you," she says, as gently as she can.

"She wouldn't—" Bairre starts, but he breaks off with a scowl. Daphne realizes that he knows she would. Maybe two weeks ago he wouldn't have believed it, but his mother and the rebels had Fergal killed. Why wouldn't she want Daphne killed too, if she thought it would protect Bairre? "She wouldn't hurt those boys," he says instead. "Do you still think the assassination attempts and the kidnappings are related?"

"I'm not sure they aren't," Daphne says carefully. "But there are too many pieces missing from this puzzle."

Bairre drops his head into his hands, rubbing his temples. "We're still searching for them. There were whispers of two boys that matched their description near Lake Olveen."

"Lake Olveen?" Daphne asks, alarmed. "That's all the way to the east."

"A doable journey, if only just," Bairre agrees. "The real question is why send them to Lake Olveen. There's nothing out there."

It's a fair question, but not one she can answer.

Violie

It's easier than Violie expected to secure employment at the castle. She and Leopold arrive at the castle kitchen the next morning and recite an elaborate tale they concocted of their travel from a small village in the Crisk Mountains, a remote enough area that it is unlikely anyone will be able to contradict their story. Violie has even forged reference letters from a made-up inn, recommending her for employment in the kitchens and Leopold for work in the stables—two places where they would best be able to avoid notice from Princess Daphne and Queen Eugenia.

It's Violie's understanding that Princess Daphne did frequent the stables in Bessemia, enjoying at least one daily ride, but the royal stables in Friv are large enough that Leopold should go undetected. And if they did happen to cross paths, Daphne only knows Leopold from an outdated painting, and with his hair darkened to nearly black, it's not likely that she would look at him long enough to recognize him.

As it turns out, though, all of Violie's plans aren't necessary. No sooner do Violie and Leopold show up at the servants' entrance to the kitchen than the head cook—a woman in her sixties with frizzy gray hair and dark brown eyes heavy with exhaustion—offers them employment with her, Violie as a kitchen helper and Leopold assisting in transporting supplies from town to the kitchens.

"I'm sure a strapping lad like you would be welcome in the stables as well," she tells Leopold. "But I'm quite desperate after that disaster of a wedding, and if you work for me, you and your wife can lodge together and work similar shifts."

Which is how Violie and Leopold find themselves in the kitchen at dusk after their first day of work, exhausted but too smart to complain about the labor or ask exactly what the disaster of a wedding the cook mentioned was. Leopold goes back and forth from the cart outside to the pantry, carrying large bags of grains, flour, and produce, and rolling barrels of ale. Violie keeps an eye on the great pot of stew the cook has set about making, stirring it and adding spices. She thought it sounded like an easy enough task, but after an hour her arms are aching. Not nearly as much, though, as Leopold's must be, she thinks.

Leopold is just bringing in two large milk pails when the cook drops the rolling pin she has been using to roll out short crust pastry.

"Oh, Your Highness!" she calls out, and Leopold and Violie both freeze. For a moment, Violie fears she's addressing Leopold; then her mind turns to two other people who might be addressed by that title, both of whom Violie and Leopold need to avoid. But when Violie glances behind her, she lets out a sigh of relief: the cook is addressing a young man around her own age with dark brown hair and a moody expression.

Violie assumes he must be Prince Bairre—King Bartholomew's bastard son and the accidental heir to Friv's throne. And Princess Daphne's betrothed.

"I've told you not to call me that, Nellie," he says to the cook, though his voice is soft and his smile kind. "You've known me since before I could walk."

"True as that might be, you are a prince now. What can I do for you, Your Highness?" the cook replies.

Prince Bairre rolls his eyes, but again the gesture is more affectionate than anything. "Have you seen . . ." He trails off, glancing at Violie and Leopold, who pretend to be focused solely on their tasks. "Have you seen Aurelia?"

Aurelia is the new empyrea, Violie has surmised from other kitchen chatter she's overheard today. She thought the Frivian empyrea was called Fergal, but the change seems to be a recent one.

"Can't say I have, today," the cook says. "Though a friend of mine in the stables said she left for the highlands yesterday—said she felt a starshower coming."

Prince Bairre lets out a huff of a sigh before shaking his head. "Just as well—I'm heading in that direction myself in the morning."

"Not another scouting party?" the cook asks. "You'll forgive me for saying so, but there's been no sign of those boys, Prince Bairre. I'm not sure another scouting party will suddenly change that."

Violie stiffens and glances at Leopold. Though his back is to her, she can see the sudden tension in his shoulders, the way he is hanging on every word even as he pretends not to pay attention.

"There have been some sightings of two boys matching their description near Lake Olveen," Bairre says.

The cook doesn't reply, though Violie is sure she's thinking the same thing Violie has thought since hearing of the princes' disappearance—if they haven't been discovered by now and no ransom note has been sent, it's likely they're dead. The sightings very well may be no more than rumors, but if the princes did make it to Lake Olveen, it raises even more questions. There is nothing that far east but the Whistall Sea.

"It isn't your fault, Prince Bairre," the cook says instead, her voice softening. "The attack seems to have been planned—they would have been taken no matter who was watching them."

"They should have had more guards," Bairre replies, his voice turning gruff.

"For two little highland lairds?" the cook asks, her eyes cutting to Violie and Leopold and narrowing. Bairre catches her warning and nods quickly.

"Of course, that would have been deemed unnecessary," he says briskly. "But as it happens, I'm going to Lake Olveen on an unrelated matter. My father can't leave Eldevale at the moment, but someone needs to take Cillian's ashes east."

Violie frowns. Cillian, she knows, is the Frivian prince who died, Bairre's brother, though that was months ago now. Admittedly, she doesn't know anything about Frivian death traditions, but it seems like a long time to let pass before scattering ashes.

"We'll need provisions, if you can spare them," Bairre continues.

"Of course I can spare them," the cook says, her voice softening. "Now out with you, we have a dinner to serve."

Bairre gives the cook a small smile and offers his thanks before ducking out. Leopold only hesitates a second before following him, and Violie knows deep in her bones that he is going to do something reckless. She moves to follow him, but the cook steps in her way.

"You aren't due another break until after dinner," she says, her voice full of steel.

Violie thinks quickly, putting her hand to her mouth and feigning illness. "Please, I'm going to . . ." She fakes a gag and the cook is too quick to jump out of her way, letting Violie run past her and after Leopold.

By the time she reaches the hallway, though, it's too late. Leopold and Prince Bairre are already deep in discussion.

"I grew up north of Lake Olveen," Leopold is telling Prince Bairre, still clinging to the accent they worked so hard on. It isn't perfect, but close enough that Bairre might just attribute the flaws to regional differences. "It would be an honor to accompany you on Prince Cillian's starjourn."

The word *starjourn* is distantly familiar to Violie, and while she's sure it has something to do with Prince Cillian's ashes, she doesn't know more than that, though Leopold seems to.

"I appreciate the offer, but we're traveling light. We don't require any more servants."

As Bairre begins to walk away, Leopold speaks again. "What about trackers?" he asks. Bairre pauses, looking back over his shoulder with a furrowed brow. "You said you were still looking for those boys—I've been hunting my whole life, I'm good at tracking."

"Game," Prince Bairre is saying. "Not people."

"Similar idea, though, isn't it? Looking for tracks, listening, et cetera," Leopold says. "If there's a sign of them near Lake Olveen, I'll find it."

Violie wants to shake him. She knows that Leopold wants to find his brothers, she understands that, but she can't let him risk his own safety. Though as soon as she thinks it, she realizes that sending Leopold out of the castle might be a sensible choice—it means there is less likelihood of him crossing paths with his mother or Princess Daphne, and gives Violie a chance to keep an eye on both of them without worrying over him. If she could find some proof of Eugenia's part in Sophronia's death, she might just earn Daphne's trust by the time Leopold returns.

"As I said, we leave first thing in the morning from the stables," Bairre says, extending a hand, which Leopold takes in a firm shake.

The cook is understandably frustrated that Leopold is leaving so soon, but she is more exhausted than angry.

"I won't tell you your job won't be here when you return—I doubt I'll fill it before then," she says with a sigh.

When they're back in the servants' room they're sharing that night, Violie turns to face Leopold, watching as he bundles up his single change of clothes.

"This is a risk," she tells him. "You know this is a risk."

Leopold doesn't answer for a moment, continuing to pack. Finally, he sighs. "They're my brothers—the only family I have left. If there's been a sign of them—"

"Your mother's alive. She's here," Violie points out, even as she knows that isn't a winning argument. She hesitates a second longer. "Leopold, do you really think it's possible that she's responsible for their disappearance?"

Leopold, to his credit, doesn't dismiss the idea as quickly as he would have once, but after a moment, he shakes his head. "I don't see why she would have done such a thing," he says. "If she wanted them dead, she would have left them in the palace with me during the siege. She went to great trouble to get them out beforehand. Why do all that, then cart them all the way to Friv, to have them"—he hesitates—"to have them kidnapped?"

Violie considers it. "She's in league with Margaraux," she reminds him. "The kidnapping of two Temarinian princes, the last remaining heirs to the throne, as far as most know, might be enough of an excuse for Bessemia to declare war."

"For foreign princes?" Leopold asks, doubtful.

"Not foreign anymore, though. Not really. Margaraux 'saved' Temarin from the rebels there, and she's claiming to have every intention of turning the throne over to you if you're found, or presumably Gideon. As of now, though, Temarin and Bessemia are under her rule. She could position an attack on your brothers as an attack on Bessemia, should she be inclined to. If they're heading as far east as Lake Olveen, she could be trying to get them on a ship heading somewhere far away, though I admit that seems a bit merciful for her."

Leopold considers that, his face going a shade paler. He does realize, Violie thinks, that his brothers are likely dead. He might not be ready to face that fact, but he does know, deep down, that the chances of finding them alive are slim.

Violie has to stop herself from reaching out to touch his shoulder. Instead, she balls her hand into a fist at her side.

"What is a starjourn?" she asks him.

He clears his throat. "Seems strange, that there's something I know that you don't," he comments. "I feel like you're constantly teaching me things."

"I never learned much about Friv," Violie says with a shrug. "I don't think Margaraux could have anticipated I would find my way here."

"A starjourn is part of the funereal process, though it has to be done during the aurora borealis," Leopold explains.

That Violie has heard of, though she's never been able to picture it, and any paintings or illustrations she's seen have always seemed fake, in some way. Something so beautiful couldn't possibly exist in nature.

"They only happen in late fall into winter, though there's never a guarantee of exactly when," Leopold continues. "But it's customary in Friv to bring ashes of lost loved ones to scatter in a body of water under an aurora borealis, as a way of sending a lost soul back to the stars they came from. I've heard that the ceremonies are beautiful, though obviously, I've never been to one myself."

"Why Lake Olveen?" Violie asks. "There are bodies of water aplenty nearer to the castle."

Leopold shrugs. "The aurora borealis is best seen farther north, from what I've heard, and it might be that there's a personal significance in the lake," he says before pausing. "I exchanged a few letters with Cillian growing up, before he . . ." He pauses again. "I didn't know him well, I wouldn't pretend to. The letters my parents forced me to write to him and Pasquale and even Sophie, at first, seemed like a chore. I'm sure they felt the same. But he seemed kind, and clever." He shrugs.

Violie isn't sure what to say—she didn't know Cillian at all, whether he was kind or clever doesn't matter to her.

"While you're gone, I'll work on Daphne," she says after a moment. "I'm not sure all the proof in the world will convince her of her mother's involvement in Sophie's death, but maybe I can prove Eugenia's involvement at least." When Leopold doesn't respond, Violie presses on. "She's your mother—you know her better than anyone, I expect—" She breaks off when Leopold gives a snort.

"I don't think I know her at all, all things considered," he says, shrugging. "If I did, Sophie would still be alive and we wouldn't be freezing to death in Friv."

Violie bites her lip. "But she is your mother—is there a weakness to exploit? A secret I should know? Anything that might come in handy?"

For a moment, Leopold says nothing, cinching the tie that holds his knapsack together. "She's superstitious. It was a point of contention between her and my father—she believes in ghosts and hauntings and curses and he mocked her for it." He pauses. "And despite everything else, I believe she does love me and my brothers. Perhaps she views me as a lost cause now, but I believe she would go to great lengths to protect them."

Violie nods, turning this over in her mind. It's a cruel card to play and part of her is surprised that Leopold suggested it, but she supposes even his moral compass goes wonky where his mother is concerned.

"You should get close to Prince Bairre, if you can," she tells him. "I don't know much about him, but since Daphne has proven difficult, we might have better luck appealing to him. At the very least, he might provide some insight into her."

"I'll try," Leopold says. "But I'm not good at this, not like you are. Manipulating and lying and using people."

Violie isn't sure what to say to that, not sure if he intended the words as a compliment or an insult. "You haven't had to be," she says after a moment. "But you know what's at stake now. Not only your life but mine as well, and your brothers', not to mention all of Temarin. I don't believe you'll fail easily with that weight on your shoulders."

Leopold swallows, but after a few seconds, he nods. "You should be careful here as well," he says. "Underestimating my mother would be a mistake."

Violie thinks about Sophronia, who made that mistake. "Underestimating me is a mistake too," she tells Leopold. "And it's one I hope your mother makes."

Daphne

aphne reads Beatriz's letter, rolling her eyes when she realizes that once again, her sister didn't bother coding it as she should have. Unlike the last one, this one isn't even written with any kind of hidden meaning. Though Daphne reasons that if she's sending it from Bessemia, there's no reason to expect someone would read it there. The Frivians very well may have, though as far as she can tell they didn't—something that doesn't surprise Daphne. Security in Friv has always been a bit lax, as far as she's seen.

It's kind of Beatriz to worry about her safety, she supposes, but after three assassination attempts and a bombing, the warning is a bit late.

I've every reason to believe Sophie's death was orchestrated by an outside force makes Daphne hesitate. Sophronia's death was orchestrated by the mob who executed her, which is enough of an outside force for Daphne, but Violie's claim echoes in her mind—that the empress caused Sophronia's death. Surely that can't be what Beatriz means—even by her standards it's ridiculous.

But the letter does mention Violie, though not by name. *Sophie told us she had friends coming to find us. They found me, but I can't keep them safe so I am sending them on to you.* That can only be Violie and Leopold. *Please protect them—if not for me, then for Sophie.*

Daphne's stomach twists into knots at that and she thinks of the letter she already sent to her mother, telling her that she believed Leopold was in Friv. It was the right thing to do, she tells herself, but she suspects Beatriz might have a point. Sophronia wouldn't have wanted her to.

Sophronia is dead, she reminds herself. She trusted the wrong people—and it's quite possible Violie and Leopold were among them. Daphne isn't about to make the same mistakes.

Still, she rereads the last paragraph until her eyes blur.

Being back in this palace, in our old rooms, I miss you and Sophie so much it makes my heart ache. It still seems impossible to believe that I'll never see her face again. I'll never forgive you if you meet the same fate.

Daphne crumples the letter in her fist, blinking away her gathering tears. She throws the page into the dying fire and watches as it blackens and curls, her sister's words turning into nothing but ash and smoke, though the echo of them lives on in her mind.

It's only then that her eyes catch on another letter sitting on her desk, this one unmarked, though Daphne knows who it's from even before she breaks the plain seal and pulls the single page from the envelope.

My dove,

I do hope you're staying warm in Friv this time of year. Should you find yourself catching a chill,

I've heard the waters of Lake Olveen can be quite restorative. Write back soon, your poor mother worries over you so. You have always been my stone in the storm.

The letter bears her mother's signature, but Daphne knows there is more to it. Lake Olveen, she thinks as she crosses the room to her jewelry box, rifling around for a yellow sapphire pendant the size of an overripe strawberry—far too big for Daphne's taste in jewelry, though it wasn't designed to be worn.

Returning to her desk, she smooths the letter flat and brings the taper closer. She bends over the desk so her face is mere inches from the letter and lifts the yellow sapphire to her right eye, closing the left.

More faint words come into focus through the yellow tint of the stone, also written in her mother's hand. As Daphne reads them, her stomach twists like a fish on a hook before finally sinking.

I've received word that the kidnappers who have captured the princes of Temarin intend to flee Vesteria on a ship from Tack Harbor but, due to the weather, no ships are leaving for another week. They should be hiding somewhere near Lake Olveen until then.

Temarin's rebels are beginning to rear their heads again, and I fear that some of the same villains who executed our dear Sophronia are still at large, intending to find and use the princes as weapons

against us in order to reclaim Temarin for their own.
The only way to protect yourself, Beatriz, and me is
for the princes to disappear altogether.

You must find them first and leave nothing to
chance. Do it as you see fit, but Sfelldraught would
be the most merciful, should you be so inclined.

Daphne reads the message three times, sure she has misunderstood before finally convincing herself that she hasn't, that her mother is truly giving her instructions to kill Gideon and Reid.

Sfelldraught would be the most merciful. If she had any doubt about what her mother intended, it disappears now. Sfelldraught is one of the more merciful poisons Daphne learned about in her lessons, and one of the easiest to administer. Just a few drops mixed into water—scentless, tasteless, quick. It isn't easy to acquire, but Daphne knows there is a vial of it in the false bottom of her jewelry case—enough, certainly, to kill two boys with.

She doesn't doubt her mother's intelligence about the boys being near Lake Olveen. She wouldn't have sent word to Daphne unless she was absolutely certain. And Daphne has enough confidence in herself to know that she will be able to find them there with relative ease.

No, the finding and the poisoning will be easy enough to accomplish, all things considered, but still the idea weighs down on Daphne's shoulders until she feels she might collapse.

Kill Gideon and Reid.

She tries to imagine it, the boys she met only briefly, dead. Dead by her own hand.

Daphne was raised for this, she reminds herself. And it will hardly be the first time she's killed, but this will be different.

The only way to protect yourself, Beatriz, and me is for the princes to disappear altogether.

Those words send a shudder down Daphne's spine. Her mother has never been prone to dramatics. If she is saying that, it's the truth. Daphne has already lost one sister—could she stand to lose anyone else? Is there anything she wouldn't do to prevent that?

The question leaves Daphne feeling nauseated. She moves to throw the letter into the fire, just as she did with Beatriz's, but pauses, hand stretched out toward the low flames, letter dangling between her fingers.

It doesn't feel real to her, that this is what her mother has instructed her to do. If she burns the letter, it will be easy to convince herself that she never received it, that her mother never asked her to kill two innocent boys. She needs to remember just how real it is.

Rather than burning the letter, Daphne folds it into as small a square as possible. She goes back to her desk and finds her sealing wax, heating it over a candle before letting a drop spill onto the folded letter. Before it dries, she opens one of the small drawers on the right side of the desk and presses the letter to the top of the drawer, holding it there until the wax dries and the letter sticks, hidden from sight.

Daphne tries not to think about her mother's letter over dinner in the banquet hall, instead focusing on keeping a close watch on Eugenia, though she pretends not to. She notices, though, how several widower lords pay Eugenia special attention, offering to refill her ale and fretting about her each time she shivers.

It isn't surprising, Daphne supposes. Eugenia is quite pretty, and she's sure the Frivians find her blend of Cellarian and Temarinian accents charming. The surprising thing is how shocked by it all Eugenia is. Each time a man pays her a compliment, Eugenia looks like she expects him to douse her with ice water at any moment.

Daphne filters through the information she learned about Eugenia in Bessemia. She wasn't privy to the same intelligence Sophronia was given, since surely her mother didn't foresee their paths ever crossing, but she remembers the basics, if only because her mother would often use Eugenia's story as a warning to Daphne and her sisters.

Eugenia had been in the Temarinian court since she was only fourteen, though her marriage to King Carlisle wasn't consummated until she was sixteen, but she'd never fully assimilated to life there, in large part because the courtiers refused to let her. They still saw Cellaria—and by extension Eugenia—as the enemy. The more Daphne thinks about that, the more sense it makes. Daphne is quite sure that even after King Carlisle died, no man dared flirt with the widow he left behind.

Daphne doesn't pity Eugenia, not for that at least, but it does add another layer of understanding for the woman.

It doesn't, however, give her any clearer idea of whether or not she should trust her. In all likelihood she should. Her mother's letter recommended her, and Eugenia didn't break into her bedchamber, threaten her life, and then knock her unconscious with Daphne's own poison ring. Eugenia said Violie was the one responsible for Sophronia's death, and Daphne has no reason not to believe her.

And yet. There is something not right, some piece of the puzzle Daphne is missing, compounded by her mother's letter and instructions to kill Eugenia's younger sons. And on top of that, Beatriz's letter implied that she should trust Violie, and protect her. Daphne doesn't know what to make of it all.

"Did you hear a single word I said?" Bairre asks from beside her.

Daphne blinks, realizing he's talking to her, has been talking to her for quite some time, apparently. She offers him a guilty smile.

"I'm sorry. My mind is elsewhere tonight, I'm afraid," she says.

"Seems to be a habit," he mutters, but before Daphne can respond, he speaks again. "I was telling you that I'm leaving tomorrow morning for Cillian's starjourn."

"Oh?" Daphne asks, focusing more on what Bairre is saying. She learned about the starjourn during her studies of Friv—a mourning ritual where the ashes of the dead are scattered beneath the northern lights. Frivian folklore says the northern lights are the dead, reaching down from the stars. There are stories of the dead's making contact, but those stories were listed right along with tales of fairies and talking animals, so Daphne doesn't give them much credence. Still, she can appreciate the tradition, and the northern lights are said to be an indescribable spectacle—one she is curious to see for herself.

"My father can't go," he says. "There's too much to do here. But I need to."

"Is it northern lights season already?" Daphne asks, blinking. As soon as she says it, though, she realizes it is. She's been in Friv for more than two months now and winter has arrived in full force.

"I should have gone earlier, but with the wedding, it wasn't feasible. Though, doing it now, I can be back before we try again."

The way he says it, he doesn't even bother making it sound real. He knows there will never be a wedding, and Daphne still hasn't figured out how to force one.

"Where will you go?" she asks, wondering if his absence will be a boon to her or a curse.

"Lake Olveen," Bairre says, and Daphne nearly drops her glass in surprise.

"Lake Olveen?" she echoes, struggling not to laugh. What are the chances of that? "Is it necessary to travel so far?"

"Cillian and I spent many summers at the palace there. He loved it, so it seems an appropriate resting place," he says, shrugging before taking another sip of his ale. "And," he adds, lowering his voice, "it will serve a double purpose—I told you there were rumors of the princes being seen near Lake Olveen, and they've only gotten louder."

Daphne hides her expression by taking another sip of her drink.

He misreads her silence as skepticism. "They can't simply have disappeared into thin air."

Daphne isn't so sure about that. There are many ways to dispose of bodies, after all, and more than a few that leave nothing behind but dust, ash, or animal excrement. Yet if her mother and Bairre have received word that the princes are near Lake Olveen, that word must be solid.

"Were you planning on inviting me to come along?" she asks, keeping her voice neutral.

Bairre frowns, glancing sideways at her. "You would hate it," he says, shaking his head. "You're constantly shivering here—Lake Olveen is far colder this time of year. And besides, Cillian—"

"Was my betrothed," she interrupts. "Did it not occur to you that I would like to say a proper goodbye myself?"

"It didn't," Bairre says, and the words irk Daphne, though she has to admit that had her mother not instructed her to go to Lake Olveen, there wouldn't have been enough stardust in the world to convince her to do so.

"Well, I would," she tells him.

Bairre still shakes his head. "The aurora borealis is unpredictable," he says before pausing. "There's no telling how long we'll be gone—a day, a week, a month."

"Goodness," Daphne says, forcing a flirtatious smile that even Beatriz would commend. "You're telling me that we might be together, away from the prying eyes at court, in an empty castle for a whole month."

Bairre's cheeks flush, but he looks away from her and clears his throat. "Not alone," he says. "A small party is coming along with me. Rufus, Cliona, Haimish—people who knew Cillian well."

That isn't all those people have in common. Daphne assumes Cliona has at least tried to turn Rufus to the rebellion by now, and she knows Cliona can be quite persuasive. She wonders if they're going to Lake Olveen for more than the starjourn—and for more than the princes.

She turns to look at Bairre fully. "I'd like to go," she tells him.

Bairre's gaze searches her face. "Why?" he asks, sounding truly perplexed.

Daphne forces a nonchalant shrug, trying not to think about her mother's letter, about Gideon and Reid and what she is meant to do. "When else am I going to see the aurora borealis?" she asks him.

Bairre lets out a belabored exhale, shaking his head. "Then you'd best go pack," he tells her. "We're leaving at first light and I won't make an exception to my plans by waiting for you."

Beatriz

B eatriz remembers the first time she and her sisters were allowed to enter their mother's study. They were fourteen at the time and until then, the room had been strictly off-limits to them and, it seemed, everyone else in the castle, apart from Nigellus. Beatriz had hatched a plot to sneak in once, a few years before, but in the end even she hadn't dared to try.

As it was, when they'd finally been invited into that room, it had been something of a letdown. There were no state secrets spelled out on the walls, no treasure trove of crown jewels on display, no secret garden of rare orchids— nothing they'd spent years theorizing about. It was, actually, fairly plain, without the ornate décor that could be found in every other room of the palace. The desk at the center was plain oak, the bookshelves stocked with practical historical texts, the only ornament on the walls a single map of Vesteria, bordered by an assortment of constellations.

Now, standing in her mother's office two years older, without her sisters at her side, Beatriz struggles to keep her eyes on her mother rather than let them drift to the map behind her. It isn't only the additions to the map that distract her—how Temarin is now shaded the same blue as Bessemia, the silver pin stuck in Friv's capital of Eldevale, which she imagines must represent Daphne the same way the gold pin stuck here in Hapantoile represents Beatriz herself. It isn't that she's wondering what color pin Sophronia was and what, exactly, her mother did with it. At least, those aren't the only things about the map distracting her. She also keeps stealing glances at the constellations surrounding Vesteria.

Someone else might say they were coincidental, a choice of the mapmaker, but Beatriz knows nothing her mother does is coincidental.

"Beatriz, I assume you know I didn't bring you here to stare at a map you surely have memorized," Empress Margaraux says, and Beatriz forces her gaze back to where she sits behind her great oak desk.

"I assume you brought me here to find out what I learned from poisoning Gisella yesterday," she replies, injecting her voice with enough flipness to make her mother's eyes narrow. It's a small shift in her expression, but Beatriz feels like she's scored a point.

Her mother leans back in her chair, surveying Beatriz. "The coughing truth serum was a clever touch," she says.

Beatriz shrugs. "Gisella is no stranger to poisons, she would have detected anything more straightforward, perhaps even trained herself to lie through it, just as Daphne, Sophronia, and I did."

"The real question is how effective it was, considering it narrowed the scope of truth in her answers," her mother says.

"It was effective enough," Beatriz says, bristling. In the last day, she's weighed just how much she should tell her mother—things the empress is bound to find out herself, from her spies in Cellaria, but not so much that her mother might believe that marrying Beatriz to Nicolo is the best path toward her end goal. No matter what else happens, Beatriz will keep Pasquale safe, from her mother and from anyone else who means him harm. "Nicolo isn't well liked at court. His ascension was sudden. Admittedly, the court wasn't terribly fond of Pasquale, either, but he was King Cesare's only living legitimate child, so they tolerated him. But I'd imagine many feel that if the throne was contested and open to claims, they themselves might be better suited than Nicolo and Pasquale both."

"Hmm," her mother says, watching Beatriz in silence just long enough that she begins to feel herself sweat. Did she say too much? Not enough? Just when Beatriz is about to speak again, the empress continues. "My spies in Cellaria say the same, though that isn't all they say about young King Nicolo."

The way the empress says it, Beatriz knows she is laying a trap, hoping to see Beatriz show weakness, or any sign that she cares for Nicolo more than she should. Luckily, it's a trap she can avoid easily. She simply looks at her mother and waits for her to elaborate, using the woman's own trick against her—silence.

"They say," the empress says after a moment, drawing the words out, "that he is pining." When Beatriz still doesn't react, she continues. "Many say he pines for you."

Once, when Beatriz and her sisters were young, they snuck away from their lessons to climb up to the castle roof, taking turns walking along the edge, balancing carefully. All it would have taken was one misstep—or even a strong breeze—and they would have fallen to their deaths. They didn't, which in hindsight strikes Beatriz as nothing short of a miracle, but here and now she feels the way she did then, standing at a great height, balancing for her very life.

She forces a laugh, something she learned from courtesans—how to convincingly laugh at jokes that aren't at all funny. "I suspect it's less about pining and more about guilt."

"Oh?" the empress asks, raising a single eyebrow.

Beatriz sighs, biting her lip. "I'll confess, Mother, you were right before: we did have a . . . flirtation that crossed the line. From what I'd heard, extramarital affairs were quite common in Cellaria and I didn't think much of it, but Nicolo was absolutely mad with guilt over it. He and Pasquale were close, as I'm sure you know."

"Hmm," the empress says, and Beatriz isn't sure whether that hmm indicates interest or disbelief. "Curious, though, that he would be so guilt-ridden over a few kisses with his cousin's wife but not over stealing his throne?"

Beatriz shrugs. "If you're hoping I can explain the way the male mind works, Mama, I fear you'll be disappointed," she says. "Though it is my understanding that Gisella was the power behind the coup, Nicolo hardly more than a puppet for her to control."

"If that is true," the empress says, "it will be fascinating to see how the puppet behaves with his strings severed. And speaking of which, I read the letter you wrote, alerting King Nicolo to Lady Gisella's situation. I assume it will irk him?"

Beatriz smiles. "I believe so, yes," she says.

"Well, it matters little," her mother says, shrugging. "You'll be leaving for Cellaria soon, just as we discussed."

Beatriz stiffens. "You can't still mean to send Pasquale and me back to Cellaria—not now. Wouldn't it be more prudent to see how he responds to our having Gisella? That gives us leverage."

"I never thought to hear you advocating for being prudent, Beatriz," her mother replies dryly.

Beatriz clenches her jaw to keep from saying something she will regret. She takes a deep breath and steadies herself. "Sending Pasquale and me back into Cellaria without the entirety of Bessemia's army behind us is a death sentence," she says.

She knows that's the point, knows her death at Cellaria's hands is exactly what her mother needs to take the country for her own, but still she needs to say it. She needs to see her mother's reaction. But, of course, her mother gives no reaction at all.

"Only if you fail," she says instead, her voice cold. "Do you intend to fail, Beatriz?"

"Of course not, but—"

"Then don't," she says, as if it's that easy.

Beatriz opens her mouth to argue, more out of habit than an expectation that she'll change her mother's mind, but before she can, there's a knock at the door.

"Come in, Nigellus," her mother says without asking who it is. But then, who else would dare enter her mother's study?

The door opens and Nigellus sweeps in, looking perplexed. When he sees Beatriz, he stops short.

"It's fine," Empress Margaraux says, waving a hand.

"Beatriz and I are done here. Keep an eye on that husband of yours, my dove. He might be more tenderhearted toward his cousin than you are."

Beatriz decides not to respond to that, in large part because she isn't certain her mother is wrong about Pasquale. She turns toward the door and passes Nigellus, who gives her a brief nod, as friendly as he usually is, Beatriz supposes. They haven't spoken since he discovered that the star he took down from Sophronia's constellation—the Lonely Heart—had reappeared. She's supposed to meet him in his observatory for another lesson tonight and she is both looking forward to it and dreading it.

Beatriz just makes it to the door when her mother speaks again. "Oh, Beatriz, I almost forgot. There was a letter from Daphne."

Beatriz turns back toward her mother, who is holding out a folded piece of cream parchment. "Daphne wrote me?" she asks, eyeing the letter.

"Oh. No, actually," her mother says, frowning. "The letter was written to me, but I thought you might be interested in its contents all the same."

Beatriz masks her disappointment and crosses back to her mother's desk, taking hold of the letter, though her mother doesn't release it.

"I must say, it's a relief to have one daughter, at least, who isn't a disappointment."

The empress finally releases the letter and it takes all of Beatriz's self-control not to crumple it in her hand.

A dozen bitter words rise to Beatriz's lips and she knows she's going to say something she'll regret—knows too, somewhere deep down, that her mother wants her to speak in anger now, to show all of her cards. She opens her mouth, but before she can speak, Nigellus clears his throat.

"I beg your pardon, Your Majesty, but it is imperative we speak at once. I bring word from your friend in the north."

Empress Margaraux's eyes cut away from Daphne and land on Nigellus. "Go," she says, and though she doesn't look in her direction, Beatriz knows the words are meant for her. She hurries from the room before she can lose more than her temper, though two questions nag at her—who is her mother's friend in the north, and why did Beatriz get the feeling Nigellus had just saved her from herself?

Beatriz waits until she reaches her room before she sits down at her desk and smooths out the letter from Daphne. Though she feels a touch of guilt, reading words that weren't meant for her, she reasons that her mother did give her the letter, though Beatriz knows she had her own motivations for doing so. Still, seeing Daphne's elegant and neat handwriting digs beneath her skin.

The letter, written in a hidden ink that only shows when the correct solution is applied to the paper, has already been revealed.

Dear Mama,

Queen Eugenia has arrived with a letter that I believe is from you, though if it is a forgery, please tell me so. Shortly after she arrived with her two younger sons, the boys were kidnapped, though Prince Bairre and King Bartholomew are doing everything they can to locate them. I will let you know if they succeed.

As to King Leopold, I've heard some whispers that have yet to prove true, though I will keep you apprised of that situation as it unfolds as well. I believe he is in Friv, though I'm sure you know how rumors of his whereabouts have spread over these last weeks. I know how important it is that he is found as soon as possible and don't want to distract you with false leads.

Your dutiful daughter,
Daphne

When Beatriz finishes the letter, she wishes she could reach through the paper and give her sister a shake. Though Daphne doesn't say as much, Beatriz would bet her favorite pair of shoes that the whispers of Leopold's whereabouts she mentioned came from Violie—at least Beatriz is relieved that Violie was smart enough to withhold Leopold himself, especially with Queen Eugenia loose in the castle.

And the young princes have been kidnapped—something Beatriz is sure her mother is at least partly responsible for. *Your friend in the north,* Nigellus said, and now Beatriz has several suspicions about who that might be—either Queen Eugenia, or whoever is responsible for kidnapping her sons.

Another thought occurs to her—what if her mother's friend in the north is Violie? It's possible—Violie worked for her mother before, she admitted as much, and after falling for Nicolo's and Gisella's lies, Beatriz doesn't have the same confidence in her ability to read others that she used to. But as she follows that line of thought, she realizes that if Violie were working for her mother, she would have simply delivered Leopold to her rather than traveling first to Cellaria and then to Friv.

No, the most likely candidate for her mother's friend in the north is Eugenia.

Beatriz arrives at Nigellus's laboratory just shy of midnight, dressed once again in Pasquale's clothes, with the hood of his cloak drawn up over her head to hide her red hair. When she opens the door and slips inside, Nigellus doesn't look up from his workbench, a vial of stardust in one hand and a beaker full of some gray liquid in the other. Beatriz closes the door behind her firmly, but still Nigellus doesn't glance up, instead studying the gray liquid closely, turning the beaker this way and that.

"Who is my mother's friend in the north?" she asks him.

At that, Nigellus spares her a glance, though he doesn't answer, instead setting both the stardust vial and the mysterious beaker down. "You're early," he points out. "I didn't think such an occurrence was possible."

Beatriz ignores him. "My mother's friend, in the north," she presses. "Who is it?"

He shrugs. "Your mother has many friends, some of whom reside north of here," he says. "But you aren't here to discuss your mother, you're here for lessons."

Beatriz clenches her jaw. "Very well," she says. "Then I

have another question: Why is Sophie's star back in the sky? You said yourself it was impossible."

"Surely many things seem impossible until they've been done," Nigellus says with a shrug. "As to the why of it, I don't know enough to speculate, but I will find out."

"I'm starting to believe you don't know much of anything, Nigellus," she says, more to rib him than because it's the truth. As is often the case with Nigellus, though, he shows no reaction to the barb.

"You came here for a lesson, Beatriz, not an interrogation," he says mildly. "Come, sit," he adds, gesturing to the chair on the other side of his worktable, which Beatriz begrudgingly takes. He moves away, turning his back to her as he searches the bookshelf against the wall, trailing his fingers over several spines before taking down a tall, slim volume. "You know why empyreas don't use their magic to bring stars down, except in the direst of emergencies," he says.

"Because stars are finite," she answers automatically. "They are a resource to be preserved. Though in Cellaria, of course, it is because it is viewed as blasphemous. The stars are gods, and taking one from the sky is an act of deicide."

"Do you view the stars as gods?" he asks, his tone shifting from lecturing to merely curious.

Beatriz blinks, considering it. The stars control the way the world turns, she believes this, but does that make them gods? Does it make them sentient?

"I haven't spent much time thinking about the stars at all," she admits. "Apart from what they say in horoscopes, I suppose, or when it comes to wishing on stardust."

"Which is to say that you don't think about the stars unless it is in how they can serve you," he infers, and though the words raise Beatriz's hackles, there is no judgment in his tone. When she doesn't respond, he continues. "There are different schools of thought in regard to what, exactly, the stars are, and those who believe pulling stars down is sacrilegious aren't only in Cellaria. Many empyreas vow to never intentionally do so."

"You did," Beatriz points out. "Not just with my sisters and me, but during the drought a few years ago."

He nods, once. "It was a decision I weighed carefully, one many people disagreed with, many empyreas disagreed with. The royal empyreas in Friv and Temarin both refused to do it, though I suspect they were grateful that I did. They reaped the benefits, but the blood was only on my hands."

"Is it a decision you regret?" Beatriz asks.

Nigellus shrugs. "I don't know if the stars are sentient or not," he says. "I don't know if they are gods or souls or anything else people believe. I do know that every day the drought continued, people died. People I *knew* were sentient, people I *knew* had souls. So no, I don't regret the decision."

Beatriz agrees with Nigellus, though she won't give him the satisfaction of saying as much. "What's in the book?" she asks, nodding toward the volume he is still carrying.

Instead of answering, he opens it, finding the page he's searching for and laying it out on the table between them. Beatriz looks down, though it takes her a moment to make sense of what she's looking at—a star map, but with more stars than she's ever seen. Almost more stars than sky are depicted.

"The first recorded star map," Nigellus says. "The date

of origin is unclear, but it's believed to date back a thousand years or more."

Beatriz frowns and looks at the map again. She spies some familiar constellations—the Clouded Sun, the Hero's Heart, the Broken Harp—but they are almost lost among a sea of stars she has never seen before.

"There are so many," she says, her voice coming out mostly breath.

"There were," Nigellus corrects. "Not only stars are gone but entire constellations. There are some references in ancient texts about constellations that no longer exist—the Bones of the Dead, for instance," he says, drawing his finger to connect six stars in the upper corner of the page. "You'll note that it's much smaller than the Hero's Heart," he continues, pointing at that constellation, which contains at least two dozen more stars, a few that Beatriz knows aren't in the Hero's Heart she's seen in the sky itself.

Beatriz studies the map in silence for a moment, struggling to reconcile the image before her with the sky she's seen her entire life. She knew, logically, the cost of bringing a star down from the sky, but it never seemed a truly dire cost—what did it matter, after all, if the sky was missing a handful of stars, when there were so many? But looking at the map of what the sky once was frightens her now. Suddenly, it seems all too easy to imagine a world where there are no stars left in the sky at all. What will the world become then?

"You understand," Nigellus says softly, withdrawing his hand from the book. "There is a cost to magic, and we aren't the only ones who pay it."

Beatriz nods but can't bring herself to speak. She clears her throat, tearing her eyes away from the star map to meet Nigellus's gaze. "What of the stars I took? By accident in Cellaria, and then . . . on purpose. To escape the Sororia?"

For a moment, Nigellus doesn't respond, and for the first time in her life, she notes a touch of emotion in his eyes. Pity. She wishes he would go back to the cold, vacant expression he usually wears. He turns to the bookshelf and brings forth another book—another star map, she realizes, when he opens the book to a page and lays it out atop the other book.

"Here," he says, pointing at a star in the Queen's Chalice, the star Beatriz remembers selecting for her wish in the Sororia. At the time, she thought it a small thing, dimly lit and lost among a constellation full of others. Now, though, the sight of it twists her stomach. That star had been there since the dawn of time and now, because of the trouble Beatriz got herself into, it isn't.

Nigellus opens to another page featuring the Wanderer's Wheel—to one star in particular on the wheel's axle. Beatriz didn't focus on a particular star then, the first time she used her magic, but she thought she noticed one missing the next day. There it is, confirmed now, another star Beatriz took. Killed, even. It doesn't matter that it was by accident, she still did it.

Nigellus flips to another page, and Beatriz finds that she's holding her breath. She doesn't recall what stars were out when she wished that Nicolo would kiss her, what constellation she used. This, if anything, is worse than the others because though she did wish by accident, it was such a frivolous wish, one that didn't save her life, only broke her heart. *I wish you would kiss me.*

Beatriz looks at the constellation depicted and can't help but let out a small, sharp laugh. The Stinging Bee—which signals either surprise, pain, or both. In regard to Nicolo it was certainly both.

"Which star?" she asks, surprised that her voice comes out even.

Nigellus points to the star at the end of the bee's stinger. She blinks.

"That isn't a small star," she says. "How did no one notice it missing?"

Nigellus shrugs. "Plenty of people did, I expect," he says. "Most likely wrote it off for what it was—a new empyrea learning her power. You aren't the first and you won't be the last."

Perhaps it should make Beatriz feel better, but it doesn't.

"Come back in two days and we'll resume your studies," Nigellus says, closing the book.

"Come back?" Beatriz asks, blinking. "I only just arrived."

"In the state your mind is in, you're useless to me," he says before hesitating. "I don't know any young empyrea who isn't shaken after comparing star maps."

Beatriz shakes her head. "I knew the cost of pulling a star from the sky," she says. "I just didn't realize how many had already been lost."

"And how few, by comparison, remain," Nigellus adds.

"But what am I supposed to do for two days?" she asks. "Every passing hour brings us closer to my mother attempting to ship me back to Cellaria, to whatever scheme she has planned for Daphne in Friv. I'm not content to sit idle and wallow in my feelings about dead stars."

For a moment, Nigellus says nothing, his unsettling silver eyes resting on her. "I'm sure you'll find something to keep you occupied. Between your mother, your husband, and Lady Gisella, I don't doubt your hands will be quite full indeed."

Beatriz opens her mouth to argue but quickly closes it again. He's right, but that's exactly the problem. She doesn't *want* to think about her mother's plots or how Pasquale is relying on her or that needle of sympathy she feels for Gisella, or Daphne's silence. For all of the stars' complexities, Beatriz understands where she stands with them more than anyone else.

"What of my debt?" she asks instead.

"Your debt?" he asks, frowning.

"You rescued me from the Sororia and brought me here," she reminds him. "And then you paid, er . . . Ambrose's gambling debts. I was under the impression those weren't gifts given from your magnanimous heart."

Nigellus hesitates, seemingly speechless for a moment. "I rescued you because it was clear the stars had plans for you, and in making you an empyrea you became my responsibility," he says, his voice full of censure. "And officially, I brought you here because I convinced your mother that your dying as a disgraced princess rather than a throned queen of Cellaria didn't suit her needs."

"But once you helped me escape the Sororia, I could have gone to Friv," Beatriz points out, mostly to be contrary, but Nigellus laughs.

"Oh? And you think you would be safer under your sister's roof than your mother's?"

Beatriz doesn't respond, but her silence is all the answer Nigellus needs.

"Come back in two days, Princess," he says, turning away from her and returning to his work.

And just like that, Beatriz is dismissed.

Daphne

Daphne felt half asleep when their party of seven left the castle, the sun just barely risen. Now, she guesses it is close to noon and they are on horseback deep in the Trevail Forest. The forest takes up a large swath of central and eastern Friv, bleeding into the Garine Forest toward the west, though Daphne isn't quite sure where the line between them lies. It stretches all the way to Lake Olveen near the eastern coast.

If her mother's intelligence is correct, that eastern coast is where the kidnappers are taking Gideon and Reid, in order to get them on a ship out of Friv. Wherever Bairre has gotten his information, he doesn't seem to know that part yet, but Daphne knows Bairre well enough by now to know that he'll figure it out sooner rather than later. Her mother made it plain that Daphne needs to get to them first.

Her stomach lurches at the thought, but she shoves it down, focusing on Bairre. On his horse ahead of her, Bairre is deep in conversation with Haimish and a boy Daphne doesn't recognize, though he looks close to Bairre in age, with hair as black as her own and what looks to be a permanent furrow between his brows. There is something familiar in his face, but try as she might, she hasn't been able to place him. She knows she couldn't have met him before, though—his accent is notably from the highlands, and she's certain he wasn't one of the highland guests at her failed wedding. But he seems to be a servant and it's entirely possible she's merely seen him around the castle and not heard him speak.

She shifts her gaze to Bairre, and as if feeling her eyes on him, he turns to look over his shoulder and gives her a small smile that she tries to return, even as the thought of what her mother has tasked her with continues to weigh her down.

He'll never forgive you for it, a voice that sounds like Sophronia's whispers in her mind. Daphne tries to dismiss it—after all, there are plenty of other things Bairre won't forgive Daphne for when he discovers them—but it isn't so easy. Daphne isn't quite sure she'll be able to forgive herself for murdering two innocent boys.

"I'm surprised you wanted to come along," Cliona says beside her, jerking Daphne out of her thoughts. She turns to look at the other girl, riding her jet-black mare. Cliona doesn't bother trying to mask her suspicion, and Daphne can't quite blame her for that—in fact, if Cliona did believe Daphne truly wanted to make this trek in the freezing cold of winter, Daphne would be terribly disappointed in her.

"I might say the same," Daphne says, deciding that the best way to throw off suspicion is through deflection, "given how you plotted against Cillian and his family. Did your father put you up to it?"

"No, actually," Cliona says, turning her gaze back ahead of them. "But contrary to whatever you may think of me and my aims, I did care for Cillian. We were friends. I'd known him for as long as I could remember."

Daphne glances at her sideways, unsure if Cliona is in earnest or if this is some new manipulation. If it's the latter, Daphne isn't sure what is to be gained by showing vulnerability. Cliona certainly can't expect that it will cause Daphne to lower her guard or underestimate her. But if she is earnestly expressing regard for the dead prince, that's even more bewildering, though Cliona herself has pointed out that they are friends, or at least something resembling friends.

Before the wedding, Daphne almost agreed, despite the fact that she'd never had a real friend before, but now it seems laughable. If Cliona knew what Daphne's mother had tasked her to do, even she would turn on her.

"You have some way of honoring that friendship," Daphne says.

"My work with the rebellion was never about him personally," Cliona says, shrugging. "I like to think he would have understood it, supported it even in time—Bairre thinks he would have."

Daphne's eyes drift back to Bairre, who is now focused on the boy she doesn't know, nodding along to something he's saying.

"Who is that?" Daphne asks, nodding toward him.

"I believe his name is Levi," Cliona says, following her gaze. "A servant in the castle kitchens, though not one I've seen before."

There's a thread of suspicion there that Daphne picks up on.

"Is that unusual?" she asks. She hardly knew all of the servants at the Bessemian palace, and while the castle in Friv is smaller, with a smaller staff, knowing everyone on sight would be quite a feat.

"Perhaps, or perhaps not," Cliona says. "There was quite a bit of turnover after the wedding."

"The bomb, you mean," Daphne corrects. "I can see how many people would find the castle an unsafe place to seek employment after that."

Something that might be akin to guilt passes over Cliona's face, but it's gone before Daphne can say for sure. Daphne doesn't want Cliona's guilt, though. If anything, she'd prefer a reminder that the two of them are cut from the same swath of stars—ruthless and cold, doing what their parents decide is best without question. Certainly without guilt. Cliona can't falter in that now, and neither can Daphne.

"Why is he coming along?" Daphne asks to change the subject. They brought a handful of guards with them— primarily for her benefit, she would guess—but no other servants. Not even her lady's maid, to her disappointment.

Cliona shrugs. "That was Bairre's decision, though Levi claims to be from near Lake Olveen," she says, something in her voice setting Daphne on edge.

"Claims?" she asks. "You don't believe him?"

Cliona watches Levi a moment longer, a frown tugging at her mouth. "I'm not an expert on every Frivian accent—

I doubt anyone out there is—but I can't say I've ever heard that one before."

Daphne follows Cliona's gaze to Levi and frowns. "Who do you suppose he really is, then?" she asks.

"I don't know," Cliona admits, seeming to hate saying those words aloud. "But I can assure you, I'll find out. Will you help me?"

Daphne glances at her, surprised. In this, though, they are on the same side, she supposes. "What did you have in mind?" she asks.

The starjourn party has stopped for the night at an inn about a mile south of the Notch River, nestled in a clearing in the forest. A limited number of rooms is available, so Daphne and Cliona share one, while Bairre, Haimish, and the six other men traveling with them split two more rooms between them. After changing out of their riding clothes and taking turns bathing in a copper tub behind a trifold screen, Daphne and Cliona make their way down to the public room, where the rest of their party is already seated around a large table laden with mugs of ale and bowls of stew.

Daphne has eaten so much stew since coming to Friv that she believed herself sick of it, but after a day of riding, the smell of spiced beef makes her mouth water as soon as she joins the table, sitting between Bairre and Cliona, directly across from the unfamiliar servant boy—Levi, Cliona called him.

As Bairre passes her a bowl of stew and a mug of ale, Daphne notices that Levi is watching her—not staring outright, but his eyes keep darting over her, sometimes accompanied by a small frown. Perhaps it is only because she is a princess, and Bessemian, and he quite likely has never met a person who is either of those things before, let alone both.

"At the pace we're traveling, we should make it to Lake Olveen by tomorrow night," Bairre is saying to the table, dunking a piece of bread into his stew. "The summer castle isn't officially open this time of year, but my father sent a letter ahead of us, so they'll be readying a wing of it for our stay."

Daphne recalls the map that hung in their mother's office, how Friv's summer castle sat on the eastern edge of Lake Olveen. It had been her hope that her time in Friv would be short enough that she'd never see it in person. She is, however, looking forward to seeing the northern lights. She finds herself thinking that she'll tell her sisters about them one day, before she catches herself and remembers Sophronia. It is still such an easy thing to forget, still impossible to wrap her mind around. She pushes Sophronia to the back of her mind once more and hopes that this time, she stays there. It is difficult enough to think about what she is meant to do in Lake Olveen—the last thing she needs is the ghost of Sophronia here to judge her for it.

And Sophronia would judge her for it, she knows. Beatriz would too. But that is why their mother relies most on Daphne, why she chose her to be her heir. Daphne can't let her down and put them all in danger.

As the conversation at the table breaks off into different groups, Daphne turns to Levi, eyeing the mug of ale in his hand—his first of the evening, she would reckon, though if Cliona's plan is going to work, it won't be his last.

"I don't think we've met," she says, offering him her most charming smile. "Lady Cliona says you work in the kitchens?"

"Aye," he says, his eyes darting around the table as if he is looking for rescue, which strikes her as odd, though again she attributes it to his being unused to royalty. He seemed to have an easy enough time speaking with Bairre, but then, Bairre still balks anytime someone treats him like a prince rather than a bastard.

"I can't imagine what could have brought you on this somber journey," Daphne comments, never losing her smile, though Levi seems utterly uncharmed, even wary of her. Nevertheless, she presses on. "Did you know Prince Cillian?"

Bairre must sense Levi's discomfort, because he turns away from his conversation with Haimish and toward them. "He's from near Lake Olveen," Bairre explains. "He's familiar with the area, and he offered to join us."

"Oh," Daphne says, glancing between them with raised eyebrows before her gaze settles on Levi. "Will you be wanting to visit your family, then? Is their town on the way?"

"Afraid not," Levi says. "They have a farm to the west of the lake."

"Well, perhaps we can pass by on our return," Daphne says, looking to Bairre. "It wouldn't take much longer."

Bairre stares at her like he's never seen her before in his life, though after a moment, he shakes his head. "It will depend on the timing of the northern lights. They may show up tomorrow night, or not for another month, but if it tends to the latter we'll be in a hurry to return to Eldevale."

"Well, we'll keep our fingers crossed, then," Daphne

says, turning back to Levi. "Do you have any siblings there, or is it only your parents?"

Levi appears a little flustered by the question, but after a second he gathers his wits. "I have a sister," he says, and now his eyes don't dart away. He holds Daphne's gaze. "Her name is Sophie."

Daphne feels like the air has been knocked from her lungs—it isn't an uncommon name, not the shortened version, though she would imagine it's short for Sophia rather than Sophronia. Still, it takes her a moment to find her voice again.

"Oh," she says, dimly aware of Bairre reaching out to touch her arm. "Older, or younger?"

"Younger," he says without missing a beat.

"How old?"

"Fifteen." His answers are coming quicker now, without much thought to them, which is exactly what Daphne wants. She pushes aside her discomfort over the name of his sister and continues.

"And how long has it been since you were home?" she asks.

"Six months," he answers. "My wife is from farther north, near the Tack Mountains, but the cold isn't good for her lungs and we decided to travel to find work in Eldevale, where the weather is more agreeable."

Daphne can't imagine Eldevale weather being called agreeable, but she supposes anything is warmer than the Tack Mountains.

"And your wife didn't wish to join?" Daphne asks.

"Not in this weather, no," he says. "She's just getting settled in her job at the castle so we decided it was best she remain there."

"And have you worked in kitchens before?"

"No, actually," he says. "I was hoping for a job in the stables, but the cook required more assistance after what happened at the wedding." He pauses, frowning. "I actually don't know what happened at the wedding, since I arrived afterward and no one really said. They only talked around it."

Daphne's smile tightens. "A bomb went off," she tells him. "Planted by Frivian rebels. The royal empyrea, Fergal, was killed in the explosion."

He nods, considering this. She watches his expression closely, wondering if, perhaps, he is working for the rebels after all, or at least sympathetic to them. Cliona claims to know everyone loyal to her father, though unless the rebellion is even smaller than Daphne believes, Cliona must be exaggerating. But instead of discomfort or sympathy, a flare of anger brightens Levi's blue eyes before he smothers it.

"I'm sorry to hear that," he says after a second, taking another drink of his ale. "But I'm glad no one else was harmed."

Daphne glances at Cliona next to her, where she is pretending not to eavesdrop on their conversation. For just an instant, Cliona meets her gaze.

"I am as well," Daphne says.

"Especially after what happened in Kavelle," Levi adds.

Daphne sits up a little straighter, struggling to hide her frown, though she can see the confusion on Cliona's face as well. Most people in Friv, regardless of status or education, care little about what happens outside its borders, and they speak of it less—yet for a farm boy from northern Friv not only to know about the rebellion in Temarin but also to know the name of its capital city? It stretches the limits of Daphne's imagination.

There is no doubt left in her mind—Levi is not who he says he is.

Daphne leaves dinner halfway through to allow Cliona time to perform her own interrogation of Levi. By the time Cliona makes it back to the room they're sharing, it's past midnight. At her entrance, Daphne stops her pacing and looks up.

"Well?" she asks her.

Cliona sits down at the edge of the large bed, removing her shoes and stockings. "Someone trained him with a false history," she says. "But after a few drinks, he did forget the details. He said his sister was thirteen, that his wife was from the Crisk Mountains, not the Tack Mountains, and he was very emphatic that we not go out of our way to travel by his farm so that he could visit his family."

"And there was his knowledge of Temarin," Daphne adds. "How many farm boys do you think know the capital of Temarin?"

"I would wager most nobles don't," Cliona says, shaking her head. "He isn't a rebel spy—even if he was and I somehow didn't know him—"

"His distaste for the rebellion was genuine," Daphne finishes.

Cliona nods, her brow furrowed. "We should tell Bairre," she says. "It isn't safe to keep traveling with someone whose motivations we don't know. You said yourself that whoever wanted you dead might still be out there."

Daphne suspects she has a point—if he was sent to kill her, that might explain his discomfort around her—but still she shakes her head. "It's better to keep him close so that we can keep an eye on him. If Bairre knows, he'll dismiss him. He's less of a risk if we understand exactly where he is."

Cliona chews her lip, considering this, but after a second she nods. "There was something else he mentioned to you that I thought peculiar," she says carefully.

Daphne frowns, searching through her memory of the conversation for anything suspicious, but nothing noteworthy comes up.

"He said his sister's name was Sophie," Cliona says. "Isn't that the nickname you used for your own sister?"

"A coincidence, I'm sure, but there are plenty of Sophies in the world," Daphne says.

"Perhaps," Cliona allows. "But not in Friv. It isn't a name I've heard of anyone here having, because . . . well . . . what does it sound like in Frivian? So-fee?"

Daphne has to think about it, though as soon as the answer hits her, her cheeks warm. It sounds like the Frivian word for a male appendage.

"Exactly," Cliona says, reading her expression. "It's difficult to imagine someone choosing to call their daughter that."

"Then why . . ." Daphne trails off, a theory slamming into her that would explain everything—including why he would insist on coming on this journey. It would be a foolish decision, but from what she's heard, King Leopold is a fool several times over.

"You know who he is?" Cliona asks, her voice sharpening.

Daphne thinks quickly, because if she is correct, the last thing she wants is for Cliona to know the truth. She decides to hew as closely as possible to the truth in her lies. "Bairre mentioned that there were rumors of the princes being seen near Lake Olveen," she says. "Perhaps Levi isn't Frivian at all but Temarinian—sent by Queen Eugenia to search for her sons."

Cliona frowns. "It doesn't make sense, though. Why not simply send him to Lake Olveen on his own? Why put up the farce?"

"Because she must suspect we had something to do with their disappearance," Daphne says. "Bairre and I were the last people to see them, after all."

Cliona shakes her head. "It doesn't make sense," she says.

"She's a grieving mother," Daphne says, shrugging. "I don't expect her actions to make sense. But it does answer every question, doesn't it? Even his distaste for the rebellion—he's just lived through a rebellion of his own in Temarin."

"Once again, they are not the same," Cliona replies.

Daphne rolls her eyes. "Assuming I'm right, he doesn't mean us harm," she says.

"Assuming you're right," Cliona echoes, doubt lacing each syllable.

Let Cliona doubt her, Daphne thinks. She needs to see Levi again to be sure, but it explains why he looked so familiar to her. And if she is right, she needs to tread carefully—if he suspects she knows his true identity, he'll run, and Daphne doesn't expect he'll fall into her lap a second time.

Daphne mentally drafts a letter to her mother as she tries to fall asleep that night, imagining how proud she'll be when she learns that Daphne has solved her most pressing issue. But as she does, she realizes she knows exactly what her mother will tell her to do to keep Leopold from undermining their plans.

Her mission for this trip has gone from killing two Temarinian royals to killing three.

Violie

By the evening after Leopold leaves with Bairre, Violie has overheard two other servants gossiping about how Princess Daphne decided to join Prince Bairre on Prince Cillian's starjourn. To hear them discuss it, one might believe the choice is romantic, though whether that's in regard to Daphne and Bairre, or Daphne and Cillian, Violie isn't sure. In truth, she doesn't suspect Empress Margaraux left much room in Daphne's heart for romance.

Part of her is tempted to leave the castle immediately after hearing the news, stealing a horse from the royal stables and riding as fast as she can until she overtakes the starjourn party . . . but then what? Haul Leopold away from Daphne? She doubts he would go with her willingly, and in doing so she would only risk raising Daphne's suspicions about his true identity.

No, all she can do is write to Beatriz to inform her of everything that's happened since she arrived in Friv, wish on all the stars she can see that Leopold avoids Daphne's detection, and focus on Queen Eugenia—or Lady Eunice, as she's known in Friv.

It only takes a day and a few conversations with her fellow servants for Violie to learn Eugenia's schedule—she stays in her room mostly, leaving only for a morning and evening turn about the gardens, each of which lasts only ten minutes before she grows too cold and returns indoors. She receives no visitors and plays the part of a bereaved mother.

The rest of the servants don't seem to think much of her, apart from passing pity. They certainly don't appear to know who she is, even though it seemed as though the castle cook did when she was talking to Bairre. It strikes Violie as curious, though she doesn't have enough information yet to begin assembling that puzzle.

There is, however, one way to gather more information, though she will only have ten minutes to do so.

The maids mentioned that Eugenia's morning walk takes place shortly after the sun rises, and since in the evenings Violie is too much needed in the kitchens to slip away unnoticed, she forces herself out of bed before dawn and slips through the castle hallways, passing bleary-eyed servants who spare her no more than a glance.

This was why the empress hired her in the first place—Violie is very good at going unnoticed, even among those whose job it is to go unnoticed.

She finds the hallway that leads to Eugenia's quarters and hides nearby, drawing a dustcloth from her apron pocket and pretending to polish the picture frames that line the hallway. It's a risk, to be so close to where she knows Eugenia will walk when she leaves for the garden, but she will be able to keep her back toward her, and Violie knows that Eugenia has never once paid attention to a servant.

Sure enough, as Violie watches the sun rise through the large window beside the picture frame she polishes, the sound of a door opening echoes down the hall, followed by a familiar voice that makes Violie's grip on her dustrag tighten in anger.

"I would like my breakfast waiting for me when I return, Genevieve," Queen Eugenia says.

"Of course, Your—my lady," another voice says, this one familiar as well, though less so. The door closes and footsteps start down the hall toward Violie.

Though she was careful to choose a place where she would go unseen, Violie's heartbeat still picks up as the dowager queen's footsteps draw closer and closer. She ducks her head, careful to keep her face hidden as she continues polishing the picture frame, though at this point it might just be the best-polished frame in the entire castle.

Queen Eugenia walks directly behind Violie—a mere two feet away—and it would be so easy for Violie to whirl around, to snatch the dagger she keeps in her boot, to stab it through Eugenia's heart and finish what Sophronia started on the Temarin palace's terrace.

That wouldn't solve anything, a voice in Violie's mind cautions, and she isn't sure if the voice belongs to Sophronia or Empress Margaraux.

Violie manages to keep from turning toward Queen Eugenia as she strides past her, not giving her a first glance, let alone a second. When she rounds a corner and disappears from sight, Violie exhales, tucking her dustrag into her apron and starting down the hall in the opposite direction, toward Eugenia's rooms.

At the door, she pauses and knocks. When the door opens, she finds herself face to face with Eugenia's maid, Genevieve, a middle-aged woman with a severe expression and her dark brown hair swept back in a tight chignon. While they crossed paths once or twice back in Temarin, it was always with a crowd of others and they were never properly introduced. Sure enough, there is no spark of recognition in Genevieve's eyes when they sweep over Violie.

"May I help you?" she asks, her words Frivian, but heavily accented.

"I work in the kitchen," Violie says, maintaining her Frivian accent and affecting a polite smile. "The cook sent me to inform you that she ran out of eggs—would porridge suffice for Lady Eunice's breakfast?"

"It would not!" Genevieve exclaims, her eyes going wide and her mouth twisting into a grimace. "My lady detests porridge. In the three decades I've been her maid, she has only ever eaten eggs for breakfast."

Violie, who remembers Eugenia's strict dietary preferences and the chaos the Temarinian kitchens were often thrown into to cater to them, bites her lip. "I'm sorry, but there is nothing I can do. If you would like to speak to the cook—"

"Oh, I most certainly would," Genevieve says.

"Do you know the way?" Violie asks, tilting her head. "There are others I must inform about our egg shortage."

Genevieve waves a dismissive hand at her before stalking down the hall toward the kitchen and leaving Violie alone in front of Eugenia's door. After a quick glance to be sure that the hallway is truly deserted, she slips inside, closing the door behind her.

Violie has seen enough of the Frivian castle to know that the chambers King Bartholomew set Eugenia up in are quite generous, though the size and splendor of them pales in comparison to what the dowager queen was used to in Temarin. The sitting room is a small space furnished with a two-seated velvet sofa set near the fireplace, a round table just big enough for four, and a wooden desk set beside a window that overlooks the gardens below. Two doors lead off from the sitting room, and Violie would guess that one goes to Eugenia's bedchamber and one to the princes'.

Looking around, she is sure she can give the place a thorough search before Eugenia or Genevieve returns.

She begins with the desk, though she is fairly sure that it is too obvious a place to keep anything important. Sure enough, she finds drafted letters to a few Temarinian nobles who must have been away from the capital when the siege occurred, assuring them that Eugenia has everything in hand and asking for their continued loyalty to the crown. There is a letter to King Nicolo of Cellaria that piques Violie's interest, though it is only a few lines long and innocuous, congratulating him on his ascension to the throne. She does a cursory search for some sort of code but finds nothing suspicious.

Careful to leave everything as she found it, Violie closes the desk drawer and moves on to the sofa, feeling beneath the cushions for anything out of place, but her fingers find nothing but dust and a few errant crumbs. She looks underneath the sofa as well before moving to the bookshelves along the wall.

Amid rows of books on Frivian history, her eyes snag on

a navy-blue leather spine, emblazoned with gold lettering that reads *Anatomy of Livestock*. Normally, such a book wouldn't give Violie pause, but the words are in Temarinian, not Frivian. She pulls the book from the shelf, but as she begins to open it, she hears voices outside the rooms.

"I told them you required eggs for breakfast," Genevieve's voice says, and Violie freezes, panic seizing her. "And I was assured it would not be an issue."

"Very good," Eugenia's voice replies. "My walk chilled me to the bone—see to it my tea is as close to boiling as possible."

"Of course, my lady."

The doorknob to the sitting room begins to turn, and Violie has no choice but to dash into the princes' room, closing the door behind her as quietly as possible. Her heart beating loudly in her chest, she scarcely dares to breathe as Eugenia's footsteps sound against the sitting room floor. Looking down, Violie realizes she is still clutching the Temarinian book in her hands. She can only hope Eugenia won't note its absence until she has managed to escape.

Violie hears the sound of a chair scraping against the stone floor, and she imagines that Eugenia is settling in at the dining table. Violie tucks the book into the pocket of her apron, casting a glance around the dark room, lit only by a small window between two narrow beds. The sun has barely risen, dousing the room in a dim and ghostly light. Her first thought is to climb out the window—they are only on the second floor, and Violie can see a shadowy outline of a tree just outside. But she doesn't think she can open the window without drawing Eugenia's attention.

There is no help for it—she will have to wait here until Eugenia leaves. She knows Eugenia takes a second walk in the evening, but Violie guesses she will retire to her bedchamber at some point, allowing Violie to slip out unnoticed.

She gingerly lowers herself to one of the narrow beds and withdraws the book from her pocket. She opens the book to the first page and grins, a bolt of triumph rushing through her. The book is hollow, and here, within the cutaway hiding place, are folded letters bearing the seal of Empress Margaraux.

As soon as she lifts the first letter out of the hollow, though, her triumph evaporates. Two-thirds of the letter breaks away into dust as soon as she touches it, leaving behind a small square of solid parchment, with just a few words scrawled in Margaraux's familiar handwriting.

... Daphne will always ...
... for your sake and the ...
... hope next time you ...

It amounts to nothing. Violie reaches for the next letter, knowing already what will happen when she does. She lifts it as carefully as she can, pinching the corner gingerly between her fingers as she lifts it, but it still crumbles into dust on her lap, so fine that it almost disappears entirely. This time, only one word survives.

Leopold.

She doesn't bother with the third letter, instead placing the book back in her pocket. Perhaps, once she is back in her room with more time and proper tools, she can manage to preserve more than a word or two, but she doubts it. The empress wrote the letters on verbank sheets—like paper in every way that counts, but over time the material dries out and becomes brittle, breaking apart. It's the same method the empress used for sending Violie messages, as if Violie would ever have dared to save the empress's letters anyway. Not when her mother's life was at risk.

It does tell Violie one thing useful, though—Eugenia attempted to keep the letters, meaning she doesn't trust the empress. As always, though, the empress is two steps ahead. Eugenia might not understand that yet, but she will.

As soon as Eugenia turns in for a nap around noon, sending Genevieve to bring a basket of laundry out, Violie hurries out of the dowager queen's chambers and back down to the kitchen, where Nellie is equal parts exasperated and glad to see her.

"There you are, Vera," she snaps. "I've been looking for you all day!"

"Apologies," Violie says, ducking her head and trying to appear chastened. "I got lost in the east wing."

She isn't sure if Nellie believes her. "Lady Eunice's maid is being a right pain," she says, lowering her voice. "She stormed in here all aflutter this morning, ranting about our being out of eggs. I told her we had plenty, but she was awfully snippy about her mistress's preferences. I'm not keen on saying a thing about a grieving mother, mind you, but . . ." Nellie trails off, shaking her head.

Violie takes the opening she's given. "I've heard it said that Lady Eunice adores cakes," she says. "Perhaps that would cheer her up?"

Nellie laughs. "We're busy enough without adding another cake to our list," she says.

"But if I wanted to make one," Violie presses, "after my other work is done. Could I?"

Nellie frowns, giving her a once-over with narrow eyes. "I don't see why not."

Violie smiles, already beginning to plan what she's going to bake up for Eugenia—and the note from a ghost that will accompany it.

Beatriz

The day after her lesson with Nigellus, Beatriz can't stop thinking about the stark difference between the ancient star map and the current one. Yes, stars are only killed by inexperienced or desperate empyreas, but she's been both three times already, and there are roughly a dozen other empyreas in the world at any given time. How long will it be before the stars disappear entirely?

"Triz," Pasquale says, drawing her out of her thoughts as they step into the bright and cheerfully decorated teahouse. The two of them are meeting Ambrose here, just off Pellamy Street—Hapantoile's busiest shopping area. After spending the morning dragging Pasquale from shop to shop, she feels fairly confident they've slipped whatever spies her mother sent to follow them. The guards, who Beatriz is sure will report to her mother as well, have been instructed to wait outside the front door, which means they won't notice Ambrose, who should be here when they arrive.

Sure enough, Beatriz sees him in the otherwise empty back room, at a table in the corner, pouring from a pot of tea into a porcelain cup. The table beside him is empty, so

Beatriz and Pasquale slide in to sit there. Beatriz offers Ambrose a polite if distant smile, as if they are strangers.

When a woman bustles over, Beatriz orders a pot of cinnamon black tea. Beatriz and Pasquale watch the woman walk away, and when they are alone, the three turn toward one another.

"I'm glad you two are safe," Ambrose says, just as Pasquale asks how he is and Beatriz asks if he was followed.

After they get the pleasantries out of the way, Ambrose glances around the room uncomfortably. "I went to visit Violie's mother yesterday, as I told her I would," he says.

The way his voice drops tells Beatriz it isn't good news, and while her feelings about Violie are still mixed at best, she feels her chest tighten.

"Dead?" she asks.

"Nearly," Ambrose says. "She won't last the week."

Violie won't be able to see her again, then. Even if Beatriz could get word to her today, she wouldn't arrive in time to say goodbye.

"Nigellus was supposed to cure her," Pasquale says.

"You're assuming my mother isn't cruel or petty enough to retract her gift when Violie retracted her loyalty," Beatriz says. "If she kept her word in the first place—why should she, when Violie would have had no way of knowing the truth until it was too late?"

Ambrose stares at her for a moment, brow furrowed. "Surely she wouldn't," he says.

Beatriz isn't sure whether to envy or pity him. Even after spending years in the Cellarian court, Ambrose has lived a soft life, with kind parents and books about heroes triumphing over villains. He can't fathom someone like her mother existing in reality, let alone without a hero to check her.

"She would," Beatriz says. "Oh, and Gisella is in Bessemia."

That causes Ambrose's eyes to widen and he glances at Pasquale, who nods. "Making herself at home in the dungeon, luckily, where she can't do any harm."

Beatriz snorts. "I think you may be underestimating your cousin," she says. "Though my mother is planning on shipping us back to Cellaria with a paltry army at our backs, so I doubt she'll have a chance to cause too much trouble before then."

Pasquale stares at her, agog. "You didn't tell me that!" he says.

Beatriz shrugs, though a touch of guilt niggles at her. It wasn't that she intentionally kept the information from him, but between dodging her mother's barbs, Nigellus's late-night lessons, and worrying about Daphne, she simply forgot.

"It isn't as if we're actually going to return to Cellaria," she says before pausing. "We'll go to Friv instead." When Ambrose and Pasquale exchange a look Beatriz can't read, she lets out a heavy sigh. "Unless either of you has a better idea?"

"Is it an idea?" Pasquale asks. "Or is it simply the only possibility left?"

Beatriz opens her mouth and closes it again. "It's both," she manages. "I need to speak with Daphne myself . . ." She trails off. Even as she says the words, she doesn't believe them. She could go before Daphne with proof of their mother's misdeeds, proof that she was behind Sophronia's death, and Daphne would still take their mother's side.

"If I were your mother," Ambrose says after a second, "wouldn't I know that you had no intention of returning to Cellaria?"

Beatriz frowns. She wants to say no, but the more she thinks about it, the more she wonders if he's right. Her mother insisted that Beatriz go to Cellaria, against all reason. And Beatriz has never been one to do as she's told, her mother knows that better than anyone. Could this threat to send her back to Cellaria be an altogether different trap? And if so, where is her mother trying to lure her? Friv, or somewhere else?

"Something my mother and Gisella have in common is that it is all too easy to underestimate them," Beatriz says after a moment. "I'll see if I can find more information on what her true plans are."

"Any word from Violie yet?" Pasquale asks, looking to Ambrose. Violie sending letters to the palace would be too risky, so she's been directed to send them to Nigellus's address instead, where Ambrose has been staying.

"Not yet," Ambrose says.

"Daphne sent my mother a letter after their encounter—at least I'm almost positive it was about Violie and Leopold. There should be one from her soon. Send a note as soon as there is," Beatriz says.

Ambrose nods. The server appears in the doorway with a tray holding a teapot and two cups, as well as a small plate of biscuits. Immediately, Ambrose turns back to the book open on his table and Beatriz and Pasquale pretend to be deep in conversation about the shopping Beatriz did earlier in the day.

When the server leaves again, Beatriz pours both Pasquale and herself a cup of tea, idly dunking a biscuit into her cup before taking a bite. The biscuit is perfect—buttery and just sweet enough, it melts in her mouth. She finds herself thinking that she'll have to bring Sophronia here, before she remembers and sets the biscuit down.

"My mother has layers of plots," she says after a moment. "It feels impossible to understand what she's going to do next, how she will react to moves we haven't yet made."

"It's chess, with a grand master," Ambrose says.

"Chess with five grand masters, conspiring together," Beatriz corrects before pausing. A solution appears, one she's shocked she never thought of before. She blinks, casting a glance around the room to be sure they're completely alone.

"What if . . ." She trails off, unable to believe she's about to speak these words. She lowers her voice to a whisper. "What if we . . . what if *I* killed her?"

Silence follows her words, and for a moment, Beatriz worries she's horrified them, that for all of her mother's evil acts, Pasquale and Ambrose will see killing her as somehow more immoral. She isn't sure it isn't. What sort of person discusses the murder of their mother in a teahouse? But then she thinks of Sophronia, of Violie's mother, of the countless others her mother has hurt to hold on to her power. She thinks of the threat she poses to Pasquale, to Ambrose, to Daphne—to Beatriz herself.

She isn't naïve enough to believe that killing her mother

will solve all of her problems, but she isn't sure she can solve any others while her mother continues to draw breath.

"Could . . . could you?" Ambrose asks. "I mean, it's difficult to imagine that others haven't tried."

They have. Beatriz remembers three separate attempts in her childhood—poison that left her mother violently ill for a week, a trespasser discovered in the royal wing of the palace with a dagger on his person, a bullet shattering the window of their carriage as they returned from the summer castle. She remembers too what followed each attempt, her mother taking her and her sisters to witness the assassins' executions. Those were Beatriz's first experiences with death.

She wonders now if that was another lesson from her mother, a warning of what would come if any of them found themselves considering what Beatriz is considering now. She knows, beyond a shadow of a doubt, that if she fails, her mother will show her no mercy. Her life will be forfeit. But then, her life is forfeit anyway, isn't it? In many ways, assassinating her mother is her best chance at surviving her.

"They failed because they didn't know her, not like I do," Beatriz says, shaking her head. "There will only be one chance at it, though. I need to make sure I do it right." Already, she is thinking of how she might do it, but her mother is always one step ahead of her, and Beatriz doesn't trust her own instincts.

She lets out a low curse under her breath.

"What is it?" Pasquale asks, frowning.

"I just realized the one person I know who has experience killing a monarch," she says, watching as understanding dawns on his and Ambrose's faces. "And I'm not keen on asking for her help."

That evening, Beatriz pretends to be too tired to attend dinner with the rest of the Bessemian court, while Pasquale attends just long enough to make an appearance at the first course before leaving early under the guise of checking on her. She meets him in the hall outside her rooms, dressed again in his spare set of clothes and a long black cloak, the hood drawn up to cover her hair and face.

"Why do you look better in my clothes than I do?" Pasquale mutters.

Beatriz manages a brief smile, though her mind is too distracted to put much meaning behind it. "Let me do the talking with Gigi," she tells him. "Cornered beasts are always the most dangerous, and she's not to be trifled with." Beatriz knows that she fell for Gisella's tricks as hard as he did, and though Pasquale must know that too, he doesn't say it aloud. For that, Beatriz is grateful.

It's still a sore spot. The fact that Gisella and Nicolo were able to fool her so thoroughly, that her gullibility very nearly cost her her life, floods her with a deep embarrassment. She knows she is better than that, and there is a part of her that is itching for a chance to prove it.

Beatriz knows all of the hidden tunnels the servants use to get around the palace quickly and quietly and knows too that the majority of those servants will be tending to the dinner in the banquet hall or cleaning bedchambers while their employers are dining, so she leads Pasquale down the narrow, dimly lit halls, winding down staircase after staircase until they find themselves in the dungeon. Gisella is being kept well away from where the common folk are, her cell twice as large as any other.

Gisella has made herself at home in her cell, lounging on her narrow bed with a bóok in hand and a stack of others on the small table beside her. Beside the books, a candle burns, casting enough light to read by.

Gisella doesn't look up when Beatriz and Pasquale approach, instead turning her page and continuing to read. Still, Beatriz knows that Gisella is aware of their presence and that even this is a battle. So she waits, even when Pasquale begins fidgeting.

After a long moment, Gisella's eyes dart up and she affects shock, setting her book aside but not standing or even straightening up from her slouch.

"Well, isn't this a surprise," she drawls. "Come with more of that truth serum? My throat was sore for hours after all that coughing."

Beatriz shrugs. "If you didn't lie as often as you drew breath, that wouldn't have been such an issue," she replies.

Gisella laughs. "You can hardly judge me when you aren't exactly a beacon of honesty, Triz," she points out. "You've lied to me as much as I've lied to you—I've just done it better."

Beatriz opens her mouth to retort but quickly snaps it shut again. She isn't sure Gisella is wrong about that.

"And me?" Pasquale asks, his voice so soft that Beatriz nearly doesn't hear it. Gisella does, though, and her spine stiffens.

"I did what was necessary," Gisella says, and if Beatriz didn't know better, she'd think there was a trace of guilt in

Gisella's voice. "And that includes the lies I told. But whether you believe me or not, I am sorry that you had to fall so that Nico and I could rise."

"Not exactly an apology, is it?" Beatriz asks. "All three of us know you'd do it all again if you had to."

"Would you rather I say I was sorry for all of it?" Gisella asks, raising a single eyebrow. "Would you rather I tell you how I would never in my life betray you again, how guilt over it keeps me awake at night? How I regret it all? It would be another lie."

Beatriz clenches her jaw to keep from saying something she would surely regret. "When did you decide to poison King Cesare?" she asks instead.

Gisella blinks, looking for the first time truly surprised. "More than a year ago now, I suppose."

"After he had Lord Savelle's daughter killed for using star magic?" Beatriz asks. Between Lord Savelle and Pasquale, Beatriz had an understanding of what had happened that night—King Cesare had accosted Fidelia, just as he had so many other women and girls before, and though they were in a crowded banquet hall, though she struggled against him, no one had helped her. So Fidelia had caught sight of a star flickering through an open window and, in a fit of desperation, uttered six words: *I wish you'd let me go.* Innocuous enough, if Fidelia hadn't been, like Beatriz herself, a fledgling empyrea with no control over her gift. Lightning had struck through the window, creating such a distraction that King Cesare had been forced to release her. But having heard what she'd said and seen the effects, he'd had her executed for using magic.

"That," Gisella says with a shrug, "was a drop in the bucket. I'm sure Pasquale can tell you better than I can."

For a moment, Pasquale says nothing, but then he clears his throat. "I don't mourn my father, and I won't pretend he was a good man or a good king," he says, his voice coming out even. "Was it your decision, or Nicolo's?"

That earns a snort from Gisella. "Mine, of course," she says. "Nicolo was content to bide his time, earn the king's favor. He would have been happy with a seat on his council and never reached for more. The poison was my idea, though my brother was the one who began corresponding with Queen Eugenia, first as Cesare, then revealing himself."

"And the wine was the perfect vessel for the poison, as Cesare always had a glass in his hand," Beatriz says. "But why the small dose? You could have killed him right away."

"It was tempting," Gisella admits. "But for one thing, it would have raised suspicions, and as cupbearer Nicolo would have borne the brunt of them. For another, it wouldn't have accomplished enough—Nicolo needed to rise higher before Cesare was removed, and a mad king is as malleable as he is dangerous."

"If you'd waited for me to become king, I'd have raised Nicolo's position. There was no one at court, apart from Ambrose, that I trusted more," Pasquale says, and Beatriz is surprised to note how angry he sounds—not quite yelling, but closer than she's ever heard him.

"That's just it," Gisella says, her gaze snapping to meet his. "How long do you think you'd have held the throne? Days? Weeks? Perhaps you'd have managed longer, after Beatriz arrived, I'll admit that much. But when you did eventually fall, we would have fallen with you. You would have made an awful king, Pas. And you would have hated every moment of it. So yes, we made other plans, with the poison and with Eugenia."

Pasquale doesn't reply, and Beatriz is beginning to wish Gisella would go back to lying. She steps forward, drawing Gisella's attention back to her.

"Would I be wrong to assume you'd like to get out of this cell?" she asks.

Gisella shrugs, affecting disinterest, but Beatriz catches the flash of yearning in her eyes. "I'm sure I will be soon enough, once Nicolo bargains for my release."

"From what you said—or rather, didn't say—I wouldn't think he had much power left to bargain with," Beatriz muses, and Gisella's silence tells her that she's struck the truth of it. "Nicolo will be too busy saving his own skin to spare you a second thought." This, Beatriz doesn't truly believe—Gisella and Nicolo are loyal to each other over everyone—but she sees the words find their mark in Gisella's insecurities.

"I told you this would happen, didn't I?" Beatriz continues when Gisella remains silent. "You've climbed far, but you have all the further to fall because of it, and countless people who will be only too glad to push you off the edge."

"Including you?" Gisella retorts.

"Oh, especially me," Beatriz says before pausing. "But not today."

Gisella's jaw tightens. "Why exactly are you here?" she asks.

Beatriz and Pasquale exchange a look.

"Did you mix the poison for King Cesare yourself?" Beatriz asks rather than answering.

"I did," Gisella says, her voice wary.

"It was clever," Beatriz admits. "Using ground apple seeds. Even if someone were looking for poison, they very well might overlook that altogether."

"You didn't," Gisella points out.

"My sister didn't," Beatriz corrects. Daphne was always better at poisons than Beatriz, though she knows she can't ask her sister for help with this one. "If I were to ask you for another poison, one that would kill quicker but be just as undetectable, what would you suggest using?"

Gisella's eyebrows lift a fraction of an inch, though the rest of her expression remains placid. "And who would the target be?" she asks.

"Not you," Beatriz replies. "Which is all you need to know."

Gisella's mouth purses. "I'd need to know some things about the target in order to recommend a suitable poison—age, weight, any health conditions they might have."

Beatriz doesn't know the exact answer to the first two queries, but she hazards a couple of guesses. "Healthy, rarely ill."

"If they drink often, the apple seed mixture I used with Cesare would work—you might need to up the dose to kill them quicker, though that would increase the likelihood of detection—"

"And it still wouldn't be quick enough. It would need to work in less than a week," Beatriz interrupts.

Gisella stares at her. "You're asking the impossible," she says.

Beatriz holds her gaze without blinking. "Then I suppose you'll die in this cell," she says.

Gisella's chin lifts. "And if I tell someone about this conversation?" she asks.

"Then you'll die here all the faster," Beatriz replies. "I might not have your talent for poisons, but I have my own two hands and quite a few daggers."

Gisella tries to mask her fear, but Beatriz sees it flicker in her eyes. Good, she thinks.

"I'll be back soon, should an epiphany strike," Beatriz says before she and Pasquale leave Gisella alone once more.

Daphne

The morning after Daphne and Cliona discuss Levi's identity, Daphne watches him closely as they ride east, trying to recall the details of the portraits of King Leopold she's seen. She never studied his picture as closely as she studied Cillian's—there was no point since, in all likelihood, they would never cross paths. Leopold would be Sophronia's enigma to unravel; Daphne had her hands full enough already. But she remembers he was handsome, with strong features and a toothy smile, reminding her more of a puppy than the prince he was at the time. She remembers that she never understood why Sophronia was such a fool for him, blushing as she read his letters dozens of times apiece, sometimes until the paper broke apart in her hands.

Eyeing Levi as he rides ahead of her, deep in conversation with Bairre and Cliona, Daphne searches for similarities between the boy in the portraits and the one before her. His hair is different—longer and darker—but that isn't the main difference. It takes her a moment to realize what exactly the difference is: that puppy-like quality is gone. In every portrait she's seen, Leopold has seemed cheerful, even when he's been attempting a serious pose. His eyes have always sparked, even when his mouth has been unsmiling.

Now, though, that spark isn't there. He's closer to a thundercloud than a puppy, quicker to glower than grin.

But it *is* him. The more Daphne watches him, the surer she is of this. Not necessarily because of any similarity to the portraits she's seen, but because there is something unmistakably royal about his bearing and the way he speaks, even with that atrocious accent. Lost royalty isn't exactly in short supply at the moment, but only one matches Levi's description, hair color aside.

It isn't even a good alias, she thinks, as they continue east. Levi instead of Leopold. But by the same token, someone unaccustomed to assuming a fake identity would have an easier time responding to a name vaguely like their own. That must have been the servant girl's idea—Violie, Daphne remembers with a dose of distaste.

When the sun is directly overhead, their group stops to eat a packed lunch and let the horses graze and drink from a nearby stream. Daphne approaches Levi where he stands beside his horse, rummaging through his saddlebag. She feels almost like a lioness on the hunt. It isn't an unfair comparison, she realizes, the thought souring in her stomach. If he is Leopold, that does make him her prey, along with his brothers.

She needs to be careful, and she needs to be smart. If he knows she even suspects his true identity, he'll run and then there will truly be no finding him. She can't imagine the mortification of having to tell her mother that Leopold slipped through her fingers for a second time.

But her mother's orders aside, Daphne desperately wants

answers, and Leopold is the only one who can give them. Namely, she needs to know why he is standing here before her when Sophronia is dead. Even thinking that floods her veins with fury. She doesn't know all of the details of what occurred in Temarin, but she knows that the mob there was caused by Leopold himself—a foolish king who ran his country into the ground.

Sophronia didn't cause that, she even sought to help right it, against their mother's wishes. She'd always been ruled by her emotions, but that was a step too far even for Sophronia. Daphne knows that Leopold was responsible for that, too, for turning her sister against her family and the purpose they had been born for. The fury in her quadruples.

Patience, her mother's voice whispers through her mind.

Leopold must feel her eyes on him, because he turns toward her. "Can I help you with something, Princess?" he asks, bowing his head.

Daphne shakes herself, forcing a pleasant smile that doesn't feel like it reaches her eyes.

"Yes, actually. I caught sight of some apple trees just back there," she says, gesturing to the way they came. "But I'm afraid I can't reach the apples. Might you be willing to help?"

He glances over her shoulder, where she knows Bairre is standing with Haimish and Cliona. He must be wondering why she's asking him—a fair question, she supposes, but not one she has an answer to. "I thought the horses might enjoy a snack, but if you're too busy I can ask someone else."

She gets a few steps away before he speaks. "No, I can

help," he says, still looking perplexed, but he falls into step beside her as they walk toward the apple trees. She needs to earn his trust, she thinks, though it occurs to her that for the first time she's at a loss as to how to charm someone. All she really knows about him is that he seemed to truly care for her sister, but that doesn't do her any good. Daphne is as different from Sophronia as two people can be.

The questions she wants to ask rise to her lips, but she forces them down. There will be time for those later. "I have a sister named Sophie as well, you know," she says instead. "Well, Sophronia, but those of us who loved her called her Sophie—Sophronia was awfully stuffy for a girl who spent her free time baking cakes in the kitchens."

She watches his face carefully and is rewarded with a nearly imperceptible flinch. For whatever it's worth—and to Daphne it is worth very little—Leopold did love her sister. Perhaps the route to charming him lies there, showing him how much she, too, loved Sophronia. Which means the role she needs to play is frightfully simple. She needs to be the grieving sister, something she hasn't let herself be since learning of Sophronia's death.

"She died," she tells him, the words sticking in her throat as if they don't wish to be spoken, don't wish to be true. "Just over two weeks ago now."

She feels him glance sideways at her, though she keeps her gaze straight ahead, on the horizon. Bairre and Cliona both gave her condolences, and she knows that Bairre empathizes with her more than most people could, as someone who recently lost a sibling himself, but she realizes that talking to

Leopold about Sophronia is different because to him, Sophronia isn't a stranger. Daphne lets out a heavy breath.

"I still can't quite believe she's gone," she tells him. "That I'll never hear her laugh again. She had a wonderful laugh, you know. Our mother hated it—she said Sophronia laughed too loudly, that she sounded more like a pig rolling in mud than a princess."

It's only when Daphne says the words that she realizes she'd forgotten about that, forgotten how Sophronia's face would fall every time their mother made that remark, how she tried so hard to soften her laugh, even if, to Daphne's secret relief, she never quite managed to do so.

For a moment, Leopold doesn't say anything. "That's cruel," he says finally.

Daphne blinks. "I suppose it was," she says, shaking her head. "They never quite got along."

Her mother was cruel to Sophronia. That isn't new information to Daphne—she recognized the cruelty even while they were living through it. Daphne and Beatriz were on the receiving end of that cruelty as well, it was simply how their mother was, but Sophronia got the worst of it. More than that, she felt the cruelty more harshly than Daphne and Beatriz did.

Daphne told herself it was because Sophronia was weaker than they were, that she hadn't yet developed as thick a skin. She told herself that in some way, Sophronia deserved the cruelty, that if she'd worked harder, done as she was told without question—if she could just be stronger—their mother wouldn't be so cruel to her.

Now, thinking about that causes the seeds of guilt in her to sprout. She remembers the last letter Sophronia sent her:

I need your help, Daph. You must have seen how wrong she is now, how wrong we are to do her bidding.

Again, Daphne thinks of the difficult task her mother has set before her, the lives she's demanded Daphne take, including that of the boy standing beside her. Surely, Sophronia would feel that this is wrong as well, but their mother said it was the only way to guarantee their safety. Could something be both wrong and necessary?

"Our mother is a difficult person," she says, pushing that train of thought to the back of her mind, and her guilt with it. "But only a difficult—and yes, sometimes cruel—person can hold a throne the way she has for nearly two decades. Sophie understood that."

"I'm sure she did," he says softly. "But it couldn't have been easy, growing up with a mother like that. For any of you."

Daphne stiffens. What did Sophronia tell him? Or was it that servant girl, Violie? "My mother raised her daughters to be as strong as she is," she says coolly. "I'm grateful for that every day."

"Of course," he says, a bit too quickly. Daphne wishes he'd push back just a bit more, let the mask he's wearing slip, but it isn't time for that yet. He is playing his role, and she needs to remember to play hers.

"There," she says, stopping in front of a tree and pointing up to the apples that hang from its branches. "If you can gather a dozen, I'm sure the horses would be grateful."

"Of course, Your Highness," Leopold says with a bow of his head.

"There's no need to torment him," Bairre says to her when they are riding again—the last leg of their journey before they reach the summer castle at the southern edge of Lake Olveen tonight.

"Torment who?" she asks, though she has an idea of who he's talking about. She wouldn't say she's tormented Leopold, but she's certainly spoken to him more than Haimish, Rufus, or the two guards today.

"Levi isn't here to fetch apples for you," he says.

Daphne laughs. "The apples were for the horses," she says. "And besides, that is precisely what he is here for, considering he is a servant. He's here as part of his job, which encompasses fetching things, including but not limited to apples."

Bairre frowns and doesn't reply. Glancing sideways at him, Daphne smothers a sigh. Despite growing up so close to the throne, Bairre is still so idealistic. Or perhaps it's his history with the rebels that did it. As soon as she thinks it, though, she knows it has nothing to do with them. After all, Cliona is as ingratiated with the rebels as a person can be, and she has no hesitation about employing or utilizing servants.

"Still," Bairre says after a moment, "you're paying an awful lot of attention to a servant."

Daphne flashes him a smile. "Jealous?" she asks.

She thinks his cheeks flush, but it might just be the winter chill in the air.

"Suspicious," he says after a moment, and Daphne's stomach sinks.

"What is there to be suspicious of?" she asks, hiding her worry with a laugh. "He's a servant from the highlands.

Unless you think he's actually working for my mother?" She laughs louder as if it's a ridiculous thought, which it is, if not for the reasons Bairre might think. "Or is he one of the assassins who tried to kill me, but I've managed to convert to my side?"

It's another ridiculous idea, but Bairre doesn't smile. "I don't know, Daphne," he says with a sigh. "But you said yourself you were keeping secrets—"

"No more than you are," she retorts, annoyance sparking in her. Bairre isn't the naïve boy she once believed him to be, and she won't be made to feel like the only dishonest one of them. "Unless you're ready to tell me the truth about what the rebels are planning, you have no room to speak on what secrets I choose to keep to myself."

"That isn't fair—"

"I beg to differ," she interrupts. She realizes their voices have risen only when the others riding ahead turn to look at them. Daphne forces a smile and waves. "Just a lovers' spat," she calls out.

"Ugh, is there another term you can use?" Cliona yells back, wrinkling her nose. "I hate the word *lover.*"

From where he's riding beside her, Haimish leans over to say something to her, quiet enough that only she hears it. In response, she shoves him so hard that he nearly falls out of his saddle, though both of them are laughing.

Watching them makes Daphne's heart clench. She and Bairre have never been destined for that sort of romance, the kind made up of jokes and teasing and easy lightness. But Cliona and Haimish are both entrenched in the rebellion, both fighting on the same side, with their interests wholly aligned. There is a future for them that they are steadily moving toward, with the possibility of forever on the horizon.

That isn't the case for Daphne and Bairre. Maybe before, when Daphne didn't know who Bairre really was or that he was working for the rebellion, she thought there might be a future there. When he was just a hapless reluctant prince who had no desire to rule and no interest in politics. Then, Daphne thought perhaps that when her mother conquered Vesteria, Bairre could be convinced to fade into the background and stay with her as consort once she succeeded her mother as empress.

It was, she realizes now, a foolish hope. Looking at him, she can't imagine a world where he would stay with her after he realized the extent of her betrayal. And if she's honest with herself, she can't imagine a world where her mother would let him.

The thought sours in her stomach. Her mother won't kill him, she tells herself. But he would be banished to some other land, never allowed to return to Vesteria. He would be dead to her, just as she surely would be to him.

That's what she's told herself her whole life, at least. But that was before her mother gave her orders to kill Leopold and his brothers. Bairre might not be important enough to have killed, his claim to the throne far more tenuous, but Daphne knows that killing him would certainly be cleaner, and her mother has always preferred to be tidy in her plots.

The thought haunts her as they continue to ride in silence. She imagines what her future looks like now: her returning to Bessemia triumphant, having delivered Friv to her mother; her reuniting with Beatriz, their differences forgotten; her mother telling her how proud she is of her, Daphne one day ruling all of Vesteria. Before, the thought of the future would have buoyed her, filled her with giddiness and a sense of purpose. Now, though, it leaves her hollow.

There is no longer a Sophronia in that future. There is no Bairre, no Cliona, and it seems more and more likely there will be no Beatriz, either.

The future Daphne has always been heading toward since she took her first steps now strikes her as incredibly lonely.

The summer castle isn't nearly as grand as the name led Daphne to expect, though her standards for grandeur have plummeted since she arrived in Friv. It is, she concedes, a very grand manor, stretching up three floors, but referring to it as a castle is quite a stretch. She guesses it would fit inside the Bessemian palace at least ten times over.

Bairre mentioned that it had only just been opened up by the small staff of servants there, the bed linens changed, the candles lit, the rooms aired out, but as a maid gives Daphne a tour of the west wing, where her bedroom is, she is struck by how stale the air feels. She supposes it went unused this past summer, with Prince Cillian so ill, so it has been quite some time since anyone walked these halls.

The room the maid leaves Daphne to is at first chilly, but with the fire roaring in the hearth, it grows tolerably warm, and after a day spent riding, she can't bring herself to complain. The large four-poster bed at the center of the room is piled high with silver furs.

"I'll arrange for a bath to be drawn for you, Your

Highness," the maid says, bobbing what Daphne thinks must be her twentieth curtsy in the last half hour. "Is there anything else you need?"

"Yes," Daphne says, turning back toward her. "Parchment and pen. When does the mail go out? I'll need a letter sent to Bessemia at the earliest opportunity."

She's tarried too long already, her mother will need to know about Leopold.

The maid's eyes go wide and she stutters. "Oh, um . . . w-well, Your Highness, in the winter, it is difficult for the mail cart to get through the snow. We have riders for local mail, of course, but I don't think anyone will be able to get a letter to Bessemia for weeks—not until the frost melts."

Daphne stares at the girl for a long moment, feeling her temper flare. "Weeks," she echoes.

"Unfortunately, yes," the maid says. "You see, we don't have much cause to send mail to Bessemia. I fear you'll be better off waiting to send the letter until you return to Eldevale."

Daphne closes her eyes and grits her teeth. "Fine," she says on an exhale. "Fine, a bath will do. Thank you."

The maid scurries out of the room, closing the door behind her, and Daphne sinks down onto the bed. Annoyed as she is that she won't be able to tell her mother she knows exactly where Leopold is, there is a part of her, deep down, that is relieved as well.

Violie

Violie doesn't have Sophronia's skill or practice in baking, but she manages a perfectly respectable imitation of the cake she and Sophronia made back in Temarin, which Sophronia then served to Eugenia: a light and fluffy cinnamon-spiced cake. In Temarin, Sophronia had studded it with fresh blueberries, but those aren't available in Friv this time of year so Violie substitutes a cup of red currants.

It's the early hours of the morning when the cake is baked and cooled and Violie finds a piece of parchment and a quill among Nellie's kitchen supplies, for when she makes shopping lists for the errand boys. Violie memorized Sophronia's handwriting long before she'd ever met the girl face to face, though she never had cause to use it, and as soon as she sets the quill's nib to the parchment, it comes flowing out.

Dear Genia,

I'd ask if you missed me but I know the answer to that. I suspect there are two people you do miss quite terribly right about now and I will

give them your regards. Perhaps if you
properly atone for your misdeeds against
me, you will see them again. Rest assured
that in the meantime, they will be quite safe
with me.

∫

Violie reads the words twice through, a crease in her brow. The content of the letter doesn't sound like Sophronia at all— Violie can't imagine her threatening anyone, let alone children, but that is the Sophronia that Violie knew. Eugenia, on the other hand, saw Sophronia as a threat virtually since the first time they met. To her, Sophronia is the villain.

Ignoring the content of the message, Violie can hear the message read in Sophronia's voice. She isn't sure whether or not the other girl would approve of Violie's using her memory in this way, but the more Violie thinks about it the more she believes Sophronia *would* approve of this charade. It might be a morally gray area, but by the standard of things Violie has done even in the last week it is surely on the lighter end of the spectrum.

Violie manages to sneak into Eugenia's rooms again, this time an hour before dawn, when the castle is fast asleep. She picks the lock to enter the sitting room and tiptoes in on light feet, leaving the cake and the note on the dining table before hurrying toward the door again. She has her hand on the doorknob when a voice cuts through the silence.

"Genevieve?" Eugenia calls out. "Ring for my coffee, would you?"

Panic seizes Violie, but she forces herself to stay calm.

"Yes, ma'am," she replies, in her best imitation of Genevieve's stuffy Temarinian accent.

She slips out the door and closes it firmly behind her.

It isn't twenty minutes later that Genevieve storms into the kitchen, eyes wide. Violie is quick to busy herself with stirring the vat of porridge that will be served for breakfast, though her heart is beating rapidly. In truth, she's surprised and impressed that Eugenia sent Genevieve to investigate the kitchens after finding the cake, though she shouldn't be. Still, her timing is unfortunate—just two minutes later and Nellie would be doing her daily check of the pantry's stock and Violie would have been alone to assure Genevieve that no, no one in the kitchen made a cake last night at all, and how odd it was that one appeared in Lady Eunice's room, but did she know that the castle was haunted?

Instead, it is Nellie who goes to speak with Genevieve in hushed tones, and Violie braces herself for an accusation, which will surely lead to her being discovered. Perhaps if she makes a run for it now, she can reach the forest before . . .

The door closes behind Genevieve as she leaves the kitchen, and silence stretches between Violie and Nellie for a long moment before the woman crosses the kitchen to stand beside Violie.

"I don't know what game you're playing, but I'd advise you to play it more carefully, and preferably outside my kitchen," she says softly.

Violie's heart slows, if only slightly. "You didn't tell her it was me?" she asks.

Nellie pauses. "I told you I was desperate for workers after the disaster of a wedding," she says. "I'm not about to toss the only one I've found to the wolves so quickly. You aren't Frivian, are you?"

"What makes you say that?" Violie counters.

"You know Queen Eugenia for who she is, and I'd wager she would know you as well. You're Temarinian?"

Violie hesitates, trying to decide whether to embrace the half-truth or confess the whole truth.

"I worked in the Temarinian palace," she manages after a moment. "The queen hurt a friend of mine, so I decided to give the notorious Frivian ghosts a hand in haunting her for it."

Nellie pauses again and Violie wonders if she hears the gaps in her story, the things Violie doesn't say, or if she just senses it's the truth and accepts it at that.

"You know she's a dowager queen, not a dowager lady," Violie says, hoping to deflect before Nellie can question her further.

"I know enough," Nellie says. "For what it's worth, she was apparently quite distressed upon seeing the cake and a note left with it."

"Good," Violie says.

Nellie looks at her for a long moment and Violie gets the feeling that Nellie is very good at reading most people, but Violie isn't most people and she knows it. She meets Nellie's gaze with a carefully erected edifice of blankness. Nellie's lips purse.

"Only a fool believes they're the smartest person in the

room," she says. "And you would be a fool to bring that trouble into my kitchens again. Understood?"

Violie can only nod, managing to suppress her eye roll until Nellie turns her back.

When Violie's shift in the kitchen is over, she doesn't follow the other servants back to their quarters. Instead, she hangs back from the crowd, pretending to adjust the laces on her boots before slipping down another hallway and up the stairs, grabbing a pile of folded white bedsheets from the laundry room and meandering through the narrow, dimly lit halls. She makes her way to the royal wing. The guards standing at the entrance stop her, but when she tells them she's been sent to refresh the linens in Princess Daphne's room, they exchange a look.

"Don't you people ever speak to one another?" one guard asks with a scoff. "Someone did that this morning."

"Someone *attempted* that this morning," Violie corrects with a charming laugh. "The silly thing accidentally replaced the dirty linens with *other* dirty linens. I've been sent to correct the error."

The guards exchange another look before one of them nods. "Be quick about it, then," he says, stepping aside so Violie can pass.

She makes her way to Daphne's chambers and steps inside, bumping the door closed with her hip before setting the pile of linens on top of the small sofa by the dead fireplace. The evening light coming through the window is barely enough to see by, but Violie can make do. She quickly gets to work searching the room for anything that Beatriz might find interesting.

Violie knows that Daphne will have burned any letters the empress sent her, but she sifts through the ashes in the fireplace anyway, looking for any scrap that might have survived the flames. There is nothing but ash. She combs through the sitting room and bedroom, searching all of the places the empress instructed her to hide things—beneath the mattress and the slats of the bed, between loose bricks in the fireplace, under the plush rugs. She also searches the places the empress told Violie that Sophronia was likely to hide things, like the false bottoms of her jewelry and cosmetic cases, in the linings of the gowns and coats hanging in her wardrobe, in the hollow heels of her shoes.

But Violie finds little that will interest Beatriz—little that interests her, either. She does find a vial of stardust in the lining of Daphne's winter cloak that she pockets, but other than that there is nothing.

Violie has all but given up when she decides to give Daphne's desk another look, rifling through the drawers. When she closes the one on the right side, she hears a strange, soft sound. Frowning, she opens the drawer again, and again she hears the sound. One of the quills, she realizes, is catching against something at the top of the drawer—paper, by the sound of it.

Heart leaping into her throat, Violie reaches into the drawer and feels around. Her fingers glance over a folded-up piece of paper attached to the roof of the drawer, and a zing of triumph bolts through her as she pulls it out and unfolds it.

She can barely read in the low light, so she crosses to the window, letting the glow from the stars illuminate the page.

The letter is in the empress's handwriting, but the excitement over that discovery dulls as soon as Violie reads the words.

"Stars above," she mutters under her breath before shoving the letter into her pocket and hurrying out, her mind so scattered that she barely remembers to take the pile of linens with her.

She needs to catch up with Leopold and Daphne. Now.

Beatriz

Beatriz makes her way down the palace hallway, two guards following her every step. One guard has been constant, following her, more or less, since she arrived back home—ostensibly for her own protection, though Beatriz is sure that isn't their only assignment from her mother. The other post has been rotating among three other guards so far. While none of them have been particularly chatty, she's managed to extract some information from the head guard over the last few days.

Well, she knows his name is Alban, at any rate, and judging by how utterly impossible to charm he's been, she would guess that his loyalty to her mother is absolute. Which is a shame, because he's young and handsome and she would have had a good deal of fun trying to lure him to her side if she thought there was a chance he could be swayed.

She is on her way back from tea with a distant cousin on her father's side—more out of boredom than anything else, as the woman prattled on about her gardening for more than an hour—and as she walks down the crowded hallway, a servant bumps into her, catching her arm to steady her.

"Apologies, Your Highness," a voice says—a familiar

voice, speaking in Bessemian but with a noticeable Cellarian accent. A piece of paper is pressed into her palm and she just catches sight of Ambrose's face before he disappears again into the crowd.

"Are you all right, Princess Beatriz?" Alban asks.

"Fine," she says, subtly tucking the paper into her pocket. She told Ambrose to let her know as soon as Violie's letter arrived, and she would bet several bottles of stardust that's exactly what he's just given her. "I'm perfectly fine," she adds.

She has to remind herself not to hurry, which would surely raise questions, but as soon as she is back in her room alone, she takes the letter from her pocket and opens it, her suspicions confirmed when she notes the unfamiliar hand-writing in an all-too-familiar code.

She takes the letter to her desk and sits down, reaching for the quill in the inkstand and getting to work decoding. In the end, the letter reads:

Dear B,

You were right—D was less than welcoming upon our arrival, but I've managed to secure a position working at the castle. L did as well, just before he volunteered to accompany D, Prince Bairre, and some Frivian nobles on a trip to Lake Olveen. I tried to stop him, but couldn't. He is in disguise, but I worry your sister will see through that quickly enough.

While I have no other news to report about D, Queen Eugenia is here in Friv, though I don't know why. I would wager it has something to do with your mother. I will keep as close an eye on her as I can, though I must be careful as she will surely recognize me.

> *More soon,*
> *V*

Beatriz immediately rises from her desk and crosses to the fireplace, tossing the letter in. As she watches the flames swallow Violie's words, she turns them over in her mind.

She doesn't like the idea of Leopold being so close to Daphne and knows that if her sister hasn't uncovered his identity yet, she will soon, though there is nothing she can do about that short of trying to intercept any letters Daphne tries to send their mother. But that is a risk she can't take, not when getting caught would put her and Pasquale at risk. No, Leopold made his choice and he will have to see it through.

Then there is the matter of Eugenia and her presence in Friv, something Daphne mentioned as well, confirming that it was, in fact, the empress's plan.

Beatriz returns to her desk to write a response to Violie.

Dear V,

I'm sure I don't have to tell you that removing E from the equation altogether would solve quite a few problems, and I prefer not to leave anything to chance. It's your choice to make, though.

As for my sister, let me know the moment she returns from her journey, or if you hear any word of her. Similarly, I will let you know if she reveals Leopold's location to my mother, though I worry there will be nothing to be done if she has.

I know S loved him, but there is no saving a fool from himself, I'm afraid.

Your friend,

B

After finishing the letter, Beatriz codes it and folds it into a small square, slips it into her pocket, and starts back out her door, giving the guards standing on either side of her doorway a bright smile.

"I'm afraid I lost a bracelet," she tells Alban. "I know I had it when I left my cousin's, but it must have dropped somewhere between there and here."

And so Alban and the other guard follow Beatriz as she makes her way through the palace hallway again, pretending to look at the floor but letting her eyes dart up to search the faces of the courtiers and servants bustling by, looking for Ambrose. She finds him standing beside a window and makes eye contact with him. He gives a small nod.

"Oh, here it is," Beatriz says, unclasping the bracelet she's still wearing and crouching down, pretending to pick it up, her other hand going to her pocket where the letter is. As she stands up, Ambrose brushes past her, taking the letter, while she distracts the guards by swinging the bracelet in front of their faces.

When all else fails, she thinks, never underestimate the power of a very shiny distraction.

"Now I'm exhausted," she says, faking a yawn. "I'd like to return to my rooms, please."

The guards escort Beatriz to her rooms once again, trailing behind her and not seeing the satisfied smirk she wears.

"Today," Nigellus tells Beatriz at her next lesson in his laboratory, "we are going to pinpoint the prime of your power."

Beatriz frowns, eyeing the instruments he's set up on the worktable between them. A dozen vials of stardust; a collection of beakers that contain liquids in a rainbow of hues; a potted rosebush, its leaves wilted and buds closed tight; and perhaps most perplexingly, a sheaf of blank parchment and a pen.

"The prime?" she echoes.

Nigellus tilts his head, his silver eyes scanning her face as if looking for hidden answers to questions he hasn't yet asked. "Empyreas can pull stars from the sky, but most go their entire lives doing so intentionally just once, if ever. There are other gifts that only we can wield, though."

Beatriz nods. "Like your gizmos," she says, thinking of the bracelets he made for her and her sisters, each containing a wish stronger than stardust.

Nigellus's nostrils flare. "My gizmos," he repeats, voice dripping with derision. "I prefer experiments. Or *apparati.* *Instruments,* even."

"Gadgets," Beatriz says, just to needle him. She's rewarded by seeing his mouth twisting in a grimace.

"Are you quite done?" he asks.

Beatriz can't stifle a snort of laughter. "The other gifts," she says. "Like prophecy? And amplification?"

Both of those she's read about—empyreas with the gift of foresight are rare, but she's thumbed through books of their prophecies in the library. The most recent volume is a century old. Amplification, on the other hand . . .

"Amplification is the most common," Nigellus says, as if reading her thoughts. "So, we'll begin there."

He picks up a vial of stardust and passes it to Beatriz, who turns the vial over in her hands, and he gestures to the wilted rosebush. "Stardust alone should be enough for you to wish it healthy again," he says. "But if you have an inclination toward amplification, the wish should be so strong that the flowers bloom as well."

Beatriz nods, her brow furrowed. She uncorks the vial of stardust and sprinkles it on the back of her hand. She turns her focus to the rosebush. "I wish this plant were healed and thriving," she says.

Nigellus gives a quick nod of approval at her wording, but his eyes are locked on the roses. Beatriz watches too, her breath bated, as the leaves shift from brown to green, unfurling where they'd shriveled. The whole plant straightens, growing several inches taller in the process. But the flowers remain tightly closed.

"Hmmm," Nigellus says.

Beatriz's mouth twists, but she tells herself it's a good thing—she doesn't have the most common prime. She has something rarer, it just needs to be discovered what.

"Perhaps you're an alchemist, like me," Nigellus says, though his voice is full of doubt. He passes her a rag to wipe the stardust off her hand, and when that's done, he sets another vial of stardust in a holder that keeps it upright just before her, and he hands her a vial filled with amber liquid.

"Pine resin," he says, eyes on Beatriz as she turns the vial this way and that, watching the slow trickle of the resin from one end of the vial to the other. "On its own, it's flammable. You're going to add the stardust to it and use a wish to transform it into a flame, without the use of a spark."

"Won't a wish with stardust be enough to light it?" she asks. Nigellus shakes his head. "Not without an alchemy gift."

Beatriz concentrates on the vial of pine resin as she slowly pours it into the stardust, keeping a careful distance as she watches them mix. "I wish this pine resin would catch fire." She braces herself for a pop of flame, but it never comes.

"Hmmm," Nigellus says again, and this time, disappointment slithers through Beatriz and takes root.

"Pick up the pen and paper," Nigellus instructs her. He crosses to the side of the room where a rope and pulley hang. He pulls the rope and with a clatter, the roof opens up, allowing the stars to shine down on them. Beatriz takes a second to scan the sky, noting the presence of the Hero's Heart, the Lost Voyager, and the Clouded Sun overhead. Nigellus returns to the table and hands her another vial of stardust. "We'll try for prophecy now," he says when she takes it.

"Spread it on your hand again, but this time do not voice a wish. Instead, feel the stars above, soak in their light, and then write whatever comes to mind, even if it doesn't make sense."

Beatriz gives him a skeptical look but does as he says, spreading the stardust over the back of her hand and bringing the tip of her pen to the paper. When she closes her eyes, she can feel the stars on her skin, shimmering and dancing like a gentle gust of wind. But try as she might to listen, no words come to mind. Her pen remains immobile on the paper. After what feels like an eternity, she glances up at Nigellus, who is watching her with a deep frown.

"Don't you dare *hmmm* again," she tells him, setting the pen down and reaching for the rag to wipe the stardust off her hand.

"Every empyrea has a prime gift," he assures her. "Those are the three most common, but there are others that aren't as easy to test for."

"Like?" Beatriz asks.

Nigellus thinks for a moment. "I've read about empyreas who could summon specific constellations into the sky, essentially altering fate," he offers after a moment. "There hasn't been one in centuries, but that's a possibility."

"Or it was only ever a myth," Beatriz points out.

Nigellus continues, ignoring her. "There have also been rumors of empyreas who can sense coming starshowers, able to pinpoint exactly when and where they will occur, but of course, we won't be able to test for that yet either."

Beatriz hears the disappointment in his voice, feels it flooding her own veins. She feels like she's failed. Much as Nigellus might insist that all empyreas have a prime gift, Beatriz doubts she does. And if she doesn't, what good is she? She can't pull stars down from the sky without dire consequences, so what good is her magic at all?

She looks up at the sky, watching as the Hero's Heart rolls out of the east. The Queen's Chalice appears from the south, and Beatriz's stomach clenches as she remembers the star she took from the constellation back in the Sororia. Guilt still nags at her over that, though she wouldn't be standing here now if she hadn't done it. Neither would Pasquale. She can't regret it, but she isn't proud of it either.

As her eyes scan the constellation, she frowns. Something isn't right, she realizes. She hurries toward Nigellus's telescope.

"Beatriz?" Nigellus asks, but she ignores him, pointing the telescope at the Queen's Chalice and fiddling with the dials on the side until she has a close-up view of the constellation, and all of the stars that make it up. Including one star at its center that shouldn't be there.

"It's back," she breathes, forcing herself to straighten up and step aside so that Nigellus can see as well. "The star I pulled down, the one I wished on. It's back. It's small, dim, but it's there."

Daphne

When Daphne wakes up in the summer castle on the second day, it takes a moment for her to remember why she's there, just as it did the day before. She stares up at the stone ceiling, the events of the past few days trickling back to her—her mother's instructions to find Gideon and Reid before Bairre and kill them, her realization that Levi the servant is King Leopold, the understanding that she'll have to kill him, too, in order for her mother's plans to work. For her plans to work, she reminds herself.

It doesn't bring her any peace.

The sun is streaming through the window near her bed, telling Daphne that she's already slept later than she should have, but all she wants to do is pull the covers over her head, bury her face in a pillow, and shut out the world, her mother included.

I need your help, Daph. The words from Sophronia's last letter echo through her mind, as clearly as if Sophronia had spoken them aloud. *You must have seen how wrong she is now, how wrong we are to do her bidding.*

When Daphne first received that letter, she thought her

sister was being ridiculous. Of course their mother wasn't wrong, hadn't asked anything of them that wasn't for the betterment of Vesteria. Daphne did believe that with all her heart, most of her believes it still. But there is another part— just a sliver of her—that wonders if Sophronia might have been right, if what the empress is asking her to do is wrong, if she is wrong for going along with it.

No, she thinks, sitting up in bed and shaking her head, forcing herself awake. No, her mother said that as long as the House of Bayard continued to live, it put her and her family's lives at risk. It doesn't matter that Reid and Gideon are innocent, it doesn't matter that Leopold truly loved Sophronia, none of that matters. They are a threat, whether they mean to be or not, and Daphne can't lose anyone else she loves.

Despite the fire burning in the fireplace, the room is chilly, and Daphne changes from her nightgown into a plain wool dress quickly, without bothering to call for help. She wraps herself in her warmest wool cloak and dons thick socks and boots. She passes a servant girl carrying a tray set with a cup of steaming tea to Cliona's room and stops her to ask where Bairre is. The servant directs her to the stables on the west side of the castle's grounds, so Daphne heads there. She doesn't have to search for him for long—Bairre is standing just inside the stable doors, talking with two young stableboys.

"You're sure?" Bairre asks them, looking from one boy to the other with a serious expression.

"Yes, Your Highness," one boy says. Daphne would guess that he's around thirteen, with a wildly freckled face and a mess of sandy-brown hair. "I swear on the stars, that's what happened."

"What happened?" Daphne asks as she approaches.

Bairre turns toward her, and despite the discomfort of their conversation the day before, his eyes brighten. "Daphne, the princes—they're nearby."

"Oh?" Daphne asks, unsure whether it's thrill or dread prickling at her skin at the news. She doesn't know if she wants an answer.

Bairre misreads the conflicting emotions on her face as skepticism. "I'm serious, it's a real lead," he says before looking back at the boys. "Tell her."

The other boy, who looks younger than the first, with darker hair and ruddy cheeks, turns to Daphne with animated eyes. "There's a group of men camping in the forest. Some of them have strange accents."

Daphne glances at Bairre. It may be a lead, but it's one she needs to follow without him, which means convincing him it isn't worth looking into. "That doesn't mean anything," she says, shrugging. "We're near the sea—plenty of travelers come and go, I'd imagine. Did you see any boys with them, near your age?"

"No, no one has," the younger boy says.

"You see?" Daphne says to Bairre. "There's no indication that it's anything other than—"

"Tell her about the coats," Bairre interrupts.

"The coats?" Daphne asks.

"Oh, the coats," the older boy says eagerly. "Well, my nan's neighbor's cousin's friend owns a shop in town and she said that one of the men came in asking for two coats that would fit boys around twelve and fourteen."

"Twelve and fourteen?" Daphne asks, her heartbeat picking up. "You're sure?"

"Yes, Your Highness," the older boy says. "I remember because I'm thirteen now, but big for my age, and my mother brought in my old coat to sell to them. She said they paid more than the coat was worth, but they seemed desperate."

Daphne and Bairre exchange a look. Gideon and Reid were wearing coats when they vanished, but they weren't nearly sturdy enough for the weather this far northeast, especially if they're camping outside.

"Thank you," Bairre says, reaching into his pocket to produce an aster coin for each boy. "Now, could you saddle up the horses?"

The boys take the coins quickly and scurry off toward the stables. Daphne watches them go, her mind scrabbling for a plan.

"It's likely nothing," she says to Bairre, though she has difficulty sounding convincing, even to her own ears.

"And if it isn't?" Bairre asks, shaking his head. "I have a good feeling about this, Daphne. And I'd like for you to come along. I could use your help here."

Her help rescuing Gideon and Reid, not killing them. She swallows down a protest. If her mother were here, she would tell Daphne to go along with Bairre, to use his lead and his tracking skills, and then do what needs to be done. It will be easy enough to lose him in the forest, to find the princes on her own. She has her daggers on her—it will be easy enough to slit their throats. They won't see her as a threat until it's too late. She'll make it quick and painless. There's no need for them to suffer. And when it's done, she'll scream and act like she found them dead already, at the hands of whoever kidnapped them. Bairre will never suspect her. He *can't* suspect her.

That is what her mother would tell her to do, so even though the thought turns her stomach, that is what she'll do.

"I'm ready to go when you are," she tells him, forcing a smile that feels like the biggest lie she's told him.

"Brilliant," he says, returning her smile. "But I'm not sure what we'll be walking into, so I sent a page inside to tell the others to get ready just before you came out."

Daphne does a quick mental tally—it will be more difficult to find the boys on her own if Cliona, Haimish, and Rufus are there as well.

"Does that include the servant and the guards?" she asks.

Bairre gives her a look. "Levi, Niels, and Evain," he says. "And yes—helpful as the stableboys were, neither knew how many men were in the encampment. Better safe than sorry, particularly if there are children's lives at stake."

"Of course," Daphne says, her stomach knotting up further.

It takes a little over an hour to reach the edge of the Trevail Forest, and Bairre leads their party farther north than where their group exited the forest the day before, explaining that the stableboys told him the encampment was close to the Tack River.

"It'll be better to go on foot, to avoid being overheard,"

Bairre says, pulling his horse to a stop and dismounting. Daphne and the others follow his lead.

"Levi, Niels, Evain, you three head around the north side, the rest of us will come at them from the south. Everyone fan out to cover as much ground as possible," he says. "If there's any sign of the boys, keeping them safe is the first priority. Do not attack if you're outnumbered, note the location and get help first. Only kill when absolutely necessary—I have questions that need answering."

The others nod, and Daphne can't help but be impressed by the authority with which Bairre gives commands. Since he begrudgingly took up the role of prince after Cillian's death, he's seemed uninterested in anything to do with ruling, though now Daphne knows that is at least in part because of his alignment with the rebels, but seeing him now, like this, she realizes that whether or not he ever wears a crown, he has the makings of a strong leader.

They find a tall oak tree to tie the horses to, then go their separate ways. As soon as Daphne has put enough distance between herself and the others, she draws her daggers, holding one in each hand as she proceeds, searching for any sign of human life in the woods. She keeps her steps quiet and her movements quick—if the princes are, in fact, nearby, she needs to find them first.

As she walks, she idly twirls the daggers in her hands— a nervous habit, she realizes, though she tells herself there is nothing to be nervous about. She knows what she has to do, and it will hardly be the first time she's killed some- one. Everything she knows about Gideon and Reid tells her that killing them won't even present a challenge. But in the deathly quiet of the woods, Sophronia's voice in Daphne's head is getting louder.

You must have seen how wrong she is now, how wrong we are to do her bidding.

Daphne is so caught up in the voice that she isn't sure anymore if she's been walking for minutes or hours, though the position of the sun in the sky peeking through the canopy of trees tells her it can't have been too long. Thirty minutes? Forty-five?

"Gideon, stop." A voice speaking Temarinian cuts through her thoughts, and she goes still, thrill and dread doing battle in her again once more. She knows that voice. Reid. They're here. And even more surprising . . . Reid doesn't sound afraid or upset, he sounds like he's barely holding back laughter.

"Hush now, both of you," another voice says, also in Temarinian without any trace of another accent. The voice is male and unrecognizable, but not unfriendly.

Daphne creeps closer, holstering her daggers and reaching instead for her bow, drawing an arrow as she crests a ridge of snow, keeping low to avoid being spotted.

She takes in the scene before her—a small campsite with three tents and the ashes of a dead fire. Gideon and Reid are on the far side of the camp from where Daphne is hiding, lobbing snowballs at each other, while a young man sits on a boulder, his face in profile. Daphne can see enough to note that he's handsome, but his expression is twisted and surly. Daphne trains her arrow on him—she'll need to eliminate him before the boys, but if she shoots now, Gideon and Reid will scream, alerting the rest of Daphne's party to their whereabouts, and she can't have that.

"How much longer are we going to stay here, Ansel?" Gideon asks, stopping the snowball fight to approach the man.

Ansel. The name triggers a vague memory for Daphne, but she can't remember where she knows it from.

"Another day, at least," he says, shaking his head. "The weather is keeping all of the ships docked for now. No one wants to risk crossing the Whistall Sea in anything but ideal conditions."

Gideon lets out a loud sigh. "But Leopold—"

"Your brother won't want you getting caught in a whirlpool—he can wait a few days longer," Ansel says.

Daphne's skin prickles as she processes the information—Ansel, whoever he is, is lying to Gideon and Reid, promising them that he's taking them to Leopold. But why would they believe him?

Eugenia mentioned an Ansel, she remembers. It was the name of the boy Violie was supposed to have been conspiring with, who led the riot in Kavelle. The realization causes anger to spark, but that doesn't make sense—why would Gideon and Reid trust him?

"Leo!" Reid's voice causes all attention to snap to him, then to the figure coming into the clearing from the opposite side of the woods. Levi, or rather, Leopold. One and the same. Daphne moves her arrow to him, then back to Ansel. After a second of internal debate, she keeps it there.

"Get behind me, both of you," Leopold snaps, his eyes trained on Ansel and the sword in his hands held in a white-knuckled grip.

Wide-eyed, Reid does as he says, but before Gideon can

do the same, Ansel grabs him, holding him as a shield and pressing the blade of a dagger to the boy's neck.

Daphne could solve all of this with a few arrows—one to Ansel, who would cut Gideon's throat as he died, then one to Leopold's throat, then finally Reid's. She knows her aim well enough to know that she'll make the shots, but she can't fire three arrows before someone screams, and when the rest of the party arrives to find her arrows buried in them, Daphne won't be able to answer those questions.

She lets out a whisper of a curse. There is nothing to do but wait, for now, and watch.

"You should be dead," Ansel says to Leopold, the words harsh and biting. "If that bitch hadn't—"

"Sophronia was smarter than you," Leopold interrupts. At the sound of her sister's name, Daphne's hold on the bow tightens.

"Leo, help," Gideon says, his voice coming out a whimper. Even from a distance, Daphne can see Ansel's blade pressing into the skin of Gideon's neck—not yet drawing blood but close.

"Let him go, Ansel," Leopold says, the words coming out level.

"Don't think I will, no," Ansel replies, taking a step backward, then another, and pulling Gideon with him. "I'm going to leave, with Gideon."

"Where are you taking him?" Leopold asks, and it strikes Daphne as a profoundly ridiculous question, until she realizes why he's asking it. Leopold's eyes flick toward her for just an instant. He knows she's there, and he's buying her time.

"My employer is paying me well to keep that quiet," Ansel replies.

"The empress, you mean?" Leopold asks, and Daphne swallows.

No. That can't be. Not because her mother isn't capable of kidnapping the princes, but because she ordered Daphne to kill them.

"The empress and I parted ways when she sent her men to kill me after I did exactly what she told me to," Ansel says.

"Kill Sophie, you mean," Leopold says.

Daphne's blood turns to ice and she realizes exactly what Leopold is doing—not just trying to buy time but trying to turn her against her mother. As if she would trust the words of this stranger.

"Sophie," Ansel says, the name dripping with derision. "Would you like to hear her last words? What she said after you abandoned her—"

"I didn't," Leopold snaps, but Ansel ignores him.

"She sobbed for days, absolutely heartbroken. It very nearly made me pity her," he says.

Daphne is so absorbed in the words, in the sheer wrongness of them, that she almost doesn't notice Ansel's free hand behind his back, pulling another dagger from the scabbard at his hip. The way he's holding Gideon means that Leopold doesn't see the movement at all, doesn't realize that Ansel is lifting his hand to throw it—

Daphne releases the arrow before she can think better of it and it whistles through the air, just past Gideon's head, before embedding itself in Ansel's neck.

Gideon screams, Reid screams, but Leopold and Daphne

simply watch as Ansel crumples to the ground, dying with nothing more than a gurgle.

And then Leopold looks at her and Daphne looks back, but there is no time to speak because already she can hear approaching footsteps from several different directions. Daphne clambers over the snowbank and rushes to get to him first.

"You'll stay Levi the servant awhile longer," she tells him before looking at Gideon and Reid, both shaken up from the ordeal. "You must pretend not to know him, all right? For just a little while."

They nod, just as Bairre, Cliona, and Rufus enter the clearing.

"What happened?" Bairre asks, his eyes seeming to brush over every inch of Daphne, searching for injury, before he takes in the rest of the scene—Gideon and Reid alive and well, the dead man with Daphne's arrow in his throat.

"Levi distracted him, and I took my shot," she says, shrugging as if it were that simple, though she supposes, technically, it is the truth.

"Well done," Bairre says, nodding at her, then at Leopold, before looking at the boys. "Let's get you two back to the castle and get word to your mother—she's been worrying herself sick."

At that, Daphne's and Leopold's eyes meet once again and she knows that the last thing they need is for Eugenia to be kept informed.

As they make their way out of the woods once more, Daphne realizes how much simpler things would have been if she'd let Ansel throw the dagger at Leopold before killing him. Leopold would have died, and if she'd aimed right, Ansel could have had time to kill Gideon before he'd gone too, leaving only Reid left for Daphne to kill. But she can't help but hear the exchange between Leopold and Ansel again and again in her mind.

Maybe she's made things more difficult for herself, but now, at least, Leopold will live long enough to answer her questions.

Daphne

That night, Daphne lets herself into Leopold's room at the castle, mildly disappointed that the door is unlocked and her picking skills are unrequired. She hurried back to her room from the celebratory dinner, letting a maid help her ready for bed before sneaking out again in order to arrive in Leopold's room before he did, and takes the opportunity to give the room a quick search, looking for letters or anything else that will serve her purpose. But she finds nothing more than a change of clothing, so she sits down on the edge of his narrow bed to wait for him.

Moments later, the door opens and he steps inside, stopping short when he sees her.

For a moment they only stare at each other, and Daphne takes another opportunity to search his face, looking for exactly what Sophronia found so enchanting that she turned her back on her family. He's handsome enough, Daphne can admit that, but she simply doesn't understand it.

"I'm not sure what to call you anymore," he says after a moment, closing the door behind him. "I feel like a fool calling you Your Highness still, when you know who I am." He pauses, but when Daphne doesn't fill the silence, he continues. "Sophie talked about you so much, I almost want to call you Daph."

Daphne can't stop herself from flinching. "Don't," she says, her voice tight. "Daphne will suffice."

"Daphne, then," Leopold says, nodding. "I owe you a thank-you, for saving me, and my brothers."

The words twist in Daphne's gut—she didn't save them, not really, she only drew out the inevitable.

"It must have been a shock for you," he says. "Finding out who I am."

At that, Daphne barks out a laugh. "Oh, I knew almost immediately," she says. "But I confess, I wasn't sure what to do with the information, and I didn't want you to run if you suspected I recognized you."

"Should I run now?" he asks. His eyes are wary. He reminds Daphne of a caged animal, seeking an escape. She could be honest with him, tell him that if he ran, he'd have to leave his brothers behind or risk Bairre following him. He found them once, he could find them again, and Leopold is a stranger in Friv. It would be true, and it would likely work to keep him here, close enough, but Daphne decides on a softer approach. She bites her lip the way Sophronia used to and tries to appear uneasy.

"You were traveling with that servant girl before, weren't you?" she asks. "Violie?"

Leopold frowns but gives a quick nod.

"She took me by surprise," Daphne says. She's planned this speech out during the last few hours, but still the words taste bitter in her mouth. She forces herself to say them anyway. "If she'd just given me a chance to understand what she was saying—imagine, someone telling you your mother murdered your sister. Would you believe them straight-away?"

Something flickers in Leopold's expression, but it's gone before Daphne can name it. She carries on.

"But the truth is, Sophronia didn't trust our mother toward the end of her life. She told me as much and I didn't believe her." She pauses, taking a deep breath. "Whatever you may think of me, I loved my sister very much, and I miss her every day." That much, at least, is the truth. "And if my mother did have anything to do with her death, I'd like to see her answer for it."

A long moment stretches between them in silence, and Daphne worries that she's overplayed her hand, that she isn't as good an actress as she thought, that he doesn't believe her loyalties have shifted. Finally, though, Leopold softens.

"Sophie didn't believe it either, at first," he says quietly, and Daphne stiffens.

"What do you mean?" she asks.

"Ansel was the one who told her, actually. You heard him admit that he worked for your mother," he says.

Daphne doesn't deny it, but what she heard from Ansel wasn't exactly a confession. Just because he worked for her mother at one point didn't mean she was behind Sophronia's death. It was far more likely that Ansel had double-crossed the empress.

Leopold continues. "I suppose she knew at that point that her mother was working with the revolutionaries, that she'd orchestrated the plot to have her—have us—killed, but she believed it was reactionary. She believed that it was because she'd failed in your mother's eyes, that she'd betrayed her orders. She thought it was a punishment."

Daphne suddenly has to remind herself to breathe. Their mother is not a forgiving woman, she has no illusions about that. Hearing it laid out in this manner, Daphne can almost believe her mother is capable of having killed Sophronia. If she believed Sophronia was a threat to her plans, would she have done it? Daphne wants to say no, but the truth of it is, she doesn't know.

"Was it a punishment?" she asks.

Leopold gazes at her and for a moment, Daphne feels like he sees every secret she's ever kept. He looks at her with pity.

"No," he says. "Ansel said that killing Sophronia was always your mother's plan, from the very beginning. That everything Sophie had done, your mother had expected. That it was always going to end just as it did—well, nearly. Your mother wanted me dead as well. Sophie did manage to surprise her that once, I suppose, using her wish to save my life."

Daphne's fingers fly to her own wish, hanging from her wrist. There's one question answered, at least, though she doesn't feel any better knowing that information. It just makes her miss her sister more.

"Beatriz confirmed it, when our paths crossed," he says, jerking Daphne out of her thoughts.

She frowns. "Beatriz confirmed what?"

"That your mother killed Sophie intentionally. She said she'd tried to kill Beatriz as well, but there were complications in Cellaria."

Daphne can't help but snort. "I wouldn't take Beatriz too seriously—she's always been the dramatic one of us. It's possible she's seeing murder plots everywhere, especially after Sophie was killed."

"I'm not sure about that," Leopold says, and Daphne gets the feeling he is being delicate with her, handling her like a hollowed-out eggshell. She detests it. "When we met Beatriz, she was traveling with Nigellus. He was the one who revealed the empress's plots to her."

Daphne's stomach drops. "Nigellus?" she asks. "You're sure?"

"Positive," he says. "That's why we came to Friv—not just because it's the only place I can be safe but . . . well . . ." He trails off, struggling to find his words. "I think it's what Sophie would have wanted. For us to warn you and Beatriz, to protect you if we could."

Daphne doesn't know whether to laugh or sob at that. She doubts she is in any kind of danger, at least not from her mother, but she knows, too, that he's right about Sophronia. Even with her life in danger, she was thinking about others: Leopold, and her, and Beatriz too.

For the first time since hearing of Sophronia's death, the truth of it hits Daphne square in the chest. She lifts a hand to her mouth, as if she can keep her emotions in that way, but she doesn't realize she's crying until Leopold's hand comes to rest on her shoulder. When she looks up at him, that awful pity is back on his face, along with an understanding, which Daphne hates even more.

Leopold doesn't understand her. They aren't the same. No matter what he might believe, he didn't love Sophronia, not really, not the way Daphne did. If he had, he wouldn't have let her die.

But then, as soon as she thinks that, she hears Sophronia's letter again in her mind, read in her voice. *I need your help, Daph.*

She shrugs Leopold's hand off and takes a step back. "I'm fine," she says, her voice coming out harsher than she intended. She forces herself to soften, at least on the surface. "I'm fine," she repeats. "It's just . . . difficult to talk about her still. And difficult to imagine that what you're saying is true."

Leopold nods, making no move toward her again. Instead, he clasps his hands behind his back, his expression tense. "Strange as it is, I do understand to an extent," he says. "My mother wants me dead too."

Daphne looks at him, not quite surprised given what Violie said about Eugenia and what she herself witnessed in the way the woman spoke of Leopold.

"I didn't believe it at first either," he continues. "But I suppose I was faced with the proof of it much quicker than you."

Unease seeps through Daphne's veins as she forces herself to nod. Even pretending to go against her mother makes her feel ill, though she's sure if the empress were here she would encourage Daphne's deception, and the endgame it ensures.

Just now, though, she doesn't want to be around Leopold for another moment, not with the ghost of Sophronia between them, or this sham of an understanding he thinks they've forged. It's too much, and suddenly Daphne feels exhausted by it, by all of the other deceptions as well. Suddenly, she would give anything in the world to have Sophronia back, for just a few moments.

"He was lying, you know," she blurts out before she can stop herself.

"Who?" Leopold asks.

"Ansel," she tells him. "When he said that after you left her, she sobbed for days, heartbroken."

He doesn't reply, but Daphne can see the doubt in his eyes, the guilt lingering there. She owes Leopold nothing, certainly not grace, but she knows that Sophronia would want him to know this at least.

"I spoke to her," she tells him. "Frivian stardust can be stronger than the regular kind, it can allow star-touched people to speak to one another. That day, the day she . . . I used it to speak with her and Beatriz. She wasn't heartbroken, and she wasn't crying. She told Beatriz and me to look out for you, to keep you safe. In her last moments, she wasn't upset with you for leaving her, she was relieved that you had gotten away."

Leopold doesn't speak for a moment, but she can see him absorb her words. "Thank you, Daphne," he says. "I'd hoped Sophie was right about you."

Those words haunt Daphne as she leaves Leopold's room. She just makes it to the stairway before she can't hold her tears back anymore. She grips the banister tightly with one hand while the other rises to her lips as if she can shove the sobs back down her throat, but to no avail. The sobs wrack her body, almost painfully, but worse still is the shame that burns through her. She feels disgustingly weak, crying like a child. She knows her mother would be so disappointed to see her now, and that thought only makes her sob harder.

A hand comes down on her shoulder and she whirls around, prepared to find herself face to face once again with Leopold and that hateful pity in his eyes, but instead she finds Bairre.

Rather than pull away, she turns toward him, pressing her face into his shoulder and wrapping her arms around his neck as if by holding him tight enough, she can disappear into him, can cease to exist altogether.

She feels his surprise, but his arms come around her all the same, one hand rubbing small circles between her shoulder blades.

Mercifully, he says nothing—not questions or words of comfort or empty platitudes. He just holds her and lets her cry.

When she has no tears left, she tentatively steps out of his embrace, wiping at her eyes.

"Levi is King Leopold," she says, trying to get back to the matter at hand rather than her own histrionics. She'd planned on telling him, though she'd hoped to be more composed.

Bairre looks surprised at the news, if not entirely shocked. She supposes it makes sense to him—Leopold's accent was hideous, and it was difficult to discount how attached Gideon and Reid were to him after their rescue. Bairre must have known something was amiss, even if he didn't know what it was.

"Right now, I don't care about Leopold," Bairre says before shaking his head. "I mean, I do, but are you—"

"I'm fine," she says, though the words are a palpable lie and she knows Bairre doesn't believe her. She doesn't believe herself. Though she can't cry anymore, she feels thoroughly wrung out, like the slightest breeze could shatter her. She looks up at Bairre, relieved to find that he at least doesn't look at her with pity, or like he understands her. It is almost worse, though, because he looks at her like the fact that she is hurting hurts him.

"Does it get easier?" she asks him.

He doesn't ask what she means. "No," he says. "Can I walk you back to your room?"

Daphne should say yes. She should let him walk her back to her room, say good night, and go to bed, alone. She should wake up tomorrow and forget that this conversation ever happened, this one moment of weakness banished to the back of her mind forever. She should forget the way it felt when he held her, the way she felt safe. Not weak, even as she was falling apart. She should close the door between them and remind herself that she is perfectly fine on her own— better on her own.

Instead, she shakes her head. "I don't want to be alone," she tells him quietly. "Can I . . . can I stay with you?"

Asking the question feels like being ripped open before vultures. For an awful moment, she worries that he will say no, that he will tell her he doesn't want to be with her for another moment, that she has shown herself now to be too open, too emotional, too wanting. That what- ever fragile thing that once existed between them has been slaughtered, murdered by the lies and secrets that have amassed between them.

It is terrifying, she realizes, to need someone, even for a moment. Her mother was right, it is better to need no one at all.

Instead of answering, though, he takes her hand in his and leads her down the spiral staircase, away from the servants' corridor and into the royal wing. Instead of making the left that would take them to her room, he makes a right and brings her to his.

In many ways, his room is a replica of her own, with a large bed piled with furs, a roaring fireplace, heavy velvet curtains covering the windows, but his room is done in rich navy blue instead of the shades of lavender that make up her own room. When he closes the door behind her, he stands awkwardly, watching her with wary eyes, like he isn't sure what to expect of her.

Her fingers go to the ribbon that ties her cloak around her neck and she shrugs it off, leaving her in just her nightgown. She goes to his bed and crawls beneath the covers, turning on her side and watching him, but he doesn't move toward her or away.

"I'm not stealing your bed from you," she tells him. "It's hardly the first time we shared."

"That was different," he says. "You were poisoned."

"It was nice," she tells him. "Not the poison," she adds quickly with a small smile. "But being held. It was nice to be held by you."

He exhales but doesn't speak, so Daphne continues.

"It feels like we were different people then, doesn't it?" she asks. "We were, I suppose. All dressed up in lies."

"It wasn't all lies, though," he says softly.

"You called me lightning," she says. *Terrifying and beautiful and dangerous and bright all at once.* I suppose I'm more terrifying and dangerous than bright and beautiful now."

For a moment, he doesn't speak, but finally he shakes his head. "You're still all of it," he says before pausing. "Daphne . . ."

She doesn't know what he is going to say, but she knows she doesn't want to hear it.

"Please, just hold me," she says before he can get the words out.

His shoulders slump forward, but after a second he nods, coming around to the other side of the bed and climbing in beside her, wrapping an arm around her waist. She feels herself soften in his hold, her eyes closing. She focuses on the rhythm of his heart beating, her own slowing to match it.

"Leopold was hiding who he is because he's convinced that my mother is responsible for killing Sophie and he didn't know if he could trust me," she says into the silence. She hopes that saying the words out loud will make them sound as ridiculous as they do in her mind, but it doesn't. And in the silence that follows, she hears him considering them, weighing them as if they could possibly be taken seriously.

"It can't be true, obviously," she says. "But I told him I believed it in order to earn his trust."

"Hmmm," Bairre says, the sound a rumble in his chest that Daphne feels more than hears.

"It isn't the truth," she repeats.

"You know her better than I do," he says after a moment. "Is that what upset you so much?"

She frowns, considering the question. "Not only that. It was just everything—hearing him talk about Sophie, how she wanted him to find me before my mother tried to kill me, too. To protect me, as if that's necessary."

"Well, someone has tried three times now to have you killed," he points out. She hears his breath catch. "Daphne . . ."

"It wasn't my mother," she says quickly. "She loves me. She *needs* me."

He doesn't answer, and Daphne finds that she's grateful for it. After a few moments, his breathing turns steady, and Daphne joins him in sleep soon after.

Violie

Violie rides straight to Lake Olveen, stopping only in short bursts to allow the horse she stole from the castle stables to rest and eat. All the while, guilt threatens to drown her. She promised Sophronia she would keep Leopold safe, and instead she walked him and his brothers straight into danger.

Beatriz was right—Daphne can't be trusted, can't be persuaded, can't be reasoned with. If she could go back now, Violie wouldn't let Leopold go off with Prince Bairre and the others. She would insist that he stay in Eldevale, where Violie could keep a close watch on him, protect him from Daphne. If she had . . .

But every time she reaches that thought, she knows the truth. If she had, Leopold wouldn't have listened to her, and short of keeping him physically restrained, drugging him with Daphne's poisoned ring every few hours, there was nothing she could have done to stop him.

Of course, she *could* have resorted to using the ring. He wouldn't be happy with her, but at least he would be safe.

And his brothers? The thought makes Violie's stomach lurch, but they were never her responsibility. Only Leopold is.

When the spires of the summer castle rise into view over the treetops, Violie urges her horse to go faster—part of her sure that she is already too late, that she will arrive to find him dead and Daphne's hands bloodied. If that's the case, Violie won't bother waiting to hear from Beatriz—she'll kill Daphne herself.

Getting into the castle is easy for Violie—there are even fewer guards here than at the Eldevale castle, and that was already far laxer security than Violie is used to from Bessemia and Temarin. Violie wastes no time finding Daphne's room, deciding that that will be quicker than searching every room in the servants' quarters looking for Leopold, but when she opens the door and slips inside, she finds it empty, the bed still pristinely made and a low fire burning in the fireplace. She doesn't know where Daphne could possibly be at this time of night, but she wastes no time in combing through the room. It's quicker here than at the castle in Eldevale because Daphne's belongings are largely restricted to a trunk, which Violie manages to sift through in a matter of minutes, stopping when she finds a folded piece of parchment tucked between the pages of a book of poetry.

She unfolds it, her heart plummeting further as she reads.

Dear Mama,

The trip to Lake Olveen has been dreadful, but I was pleasantly surprised to find an old friend among our party, one we'd believed dead. I'll give him your regards, and Sophronia's. I'll do the same should I meet with any other familiar faces.

Your dutiful daughter,
Daphne

No, no, no, Violie thinks, crumpling the letter in her hand. She's too late after all. She's failed Sophronia in the only thing she asked of her.

The door behind Violie opens and she whirls to see Daphne standing in the doorway in her white nightgown with a cloak folded over her arm. Her braided hair is mostly undone, and she looks exhausted, her silver eyes bloodshot. Those eyes widen as she takes in Violie, the letter she's holding crumpled in her hand, the open trunk behind her.

"You," she snaps, closing the door behind her, though she doesn't move to attack. She's clever enough to realize that unarmed, dressed only in a nightgown, she's in no position for a fight, but then cleverness has never been something Daphne lacks.

Violie holds up the letter. "You killed him?" she asks, but she doesn't need an answer and she doesn't wait for one. "Sophronia trusted you, she believed you would do what was right, and you killed him. I hope she haunts you from the stars forever for this."

"He's not . . ." Daphne trails off, the weight of Violie's words hitting her. She squares her shoulders, masking the flash of true fear that flashed across her face for just the barest instant. "I didn't kill him."

Violie can't let herself believe that, not without proof, but a small spark of hope lights in her chest. "And his brothers?"

347

she asks, digging into the pocket of her cloak to produce the other letter. "Did you kill them yet?"

Daphne's eyes are cold as they move between the two letters in Violie's hands. "I would really appreciate it if you didn't go through my personal things. It isn't very good manners, is it?"

"And murder is?" Violie asks, barking out a laugh.

"I haven't murdered anyone," Daphne says, rolling her eyes. "At least not in a way that couldn't be considered self-defense, though I'm tempted to break that streak with you."

"Oh, if you managed to kill me I can assure you it would be in self-defense," Violie retorts.

It's gone too quickly to be sure, but Violie thinks Daphne might have smiled at that.

"Regardless," she says. "Leopold is alive and well. I know who he is, he knows I know, and together, we just rescued his brothers and killed their kidnapper. I believe you knew him—Ansel?"

Violie feels the blood drain from her face. "Ansel is here?"

"Was," Daphne says, shrugging. "Eugenia mentioned the two of you were . . . involved."

At that, Violie can't help but snort. "Yes, I'm sure she told you the truth of it, with no thought to casting blame and suspicion from herself and onto me."

"Did I say I believed her?" Daphne asks. When Violie stays quiet, she continues. "But we both know that the best lies contain shades of truth."

Violie flinches. "Fine, we were involved, close to a year ago. When I first arrived in Temarin and long before your sister did. It was short-lived, and when I had to choose between my loyalty to him and my loyalty to Sophie, it was so easy it barely counts as a choice at all. Eugenia, though? They were in league, brought together by your mother."

Violie watches as those words land, waits for the instant denial and rejection to follow, like they did the first time they had this conversation.

"Do you . . . believe me?" Violie asks, not quite daring to hope it's true.

"No," Daphne snaps, but the venom she injects the word with isn't quite strong enough to mask the uncertainty there.

Violie looks at Daphne, truly looks at her, beyond the exhaustion lining her face and the bloodshot eyes and the mussed hair and the fact that she wasn't in her own bed at this hour. Once she starts looking, it's impossible not to see the cracks on her surface spidering larger and larger with every passing moment—the red eyes, the wan complexion, the brittleness in her face.

Of all the things Violie expected to find when she arrived here, a broken Daphne was not one of them.

"But you don't *not* believe me," Violie says, her voice softening.

Daphne's throat works and she glances away. "I don't not believe you," she says softly, her voice cracking on the last syllable.

Violie wants to push her further—how is it possible that Daphne can't see all of the evidence in front of her? How can she still not believe that her mother killed Sophronia, that she intends to kill Daphne and Beatriz, too? It is so painfully obvious to Violie, and Leopold said that Sophronia accepted the truth easily enough. It's frustrating, to have to convince Daphne of the truth, like having to explain to a child that the sky is blue when they want to insist that it's red.

But Daphne isn't Sophronia. Even if they grew up in the same world, with the same mother, their relationships with her are different. Sophronia was acquainted with the worst in her mother, she'd seen her as a villain practically her whole life, as someone to be feared. Beatriz, on the other hand, saw the empress as a force to rebel against, if for no other reason than the joy of it. She, too, had been ready to see the truth.

But Daphne? Daphne isn't like her sisters. Violie knew that before she even met the girl in front of her. Daphne doesn't fear her mother; she fears disappointing her. She craves her approval, and her love, which is always just out of reach.

Calling her a fool won't help anyone, not Daphne and not Violie, no matter how desperately Violie might wish to give her a good shake.

Instead, she clears her throat. "Leopold and his brothers are safe?" she asks.

Daphne's eyes cut back to her and she gives a sharp nod. "They're safe," she confirms, though something in her voice sounds to Violie's ears like a question. Daphne must read the skepticism in her face, because she rolls her eyes.

"You can ask him yourself in the morning," she says. "But we're keeping his identity a secret for now, so he's still in the servants' quarters. I'll have you set up there as well— I'll claim I simply couldn't do without a lady's maid and sent for one. Most people will believe it of me easily enough."

Violie nods. It's a good idea—Violie believes that Daphne hasn't hurt Leopold or his brothers yet, but she isn't sure that will remain the case. If she can stay close, to keep watch over him and to keep working on swaying Daphne, she'll do it.

"Who knows the truth about him?" Violie asks.

"You, me, and Bairre," Daphne says, and the last name surprises Violie—as does the glimpse of vulnerability from Daphne when she says his name. Violie notes again that Daphne was not in her own bed tonight. Is it possible that Daphne is more like Sophronia than she thought, developing feelings for the prince she's destined to destroy? "Cliona suspects he isn't who he seems," Daphne adds.

"Cliona?" Violie asks.

"Lady Cliona," Daphne corrects. "A . . . friend. Of Bairre's, and Cillian's before he . . . ," she adds hastily.

"Do you trust her?" Violie asks.

Daphne snorts. "More than I should," she says. "But you certainly shouldn't."

Violie follows Daphne through the winding halls of the summer castle, though she barely seems to know her way. She points out Leopold's bedroom door and doesn't appear offended when Violie opens it, poking her head inside just far enough to see the vague shape of him, asleep in bed, the moonlight pouring through the window just strong enough for her to make out his features. When Violie closes the door again, she gives Daphne a nod.

"You look like you've seen the stars go dark," Daphne tells her. During their brief walk, she's managed to pull herself together, but Violie can still see the seams and knows it is only a matter of time before they split open again. It makes her dangerous.

"The stars go dark?" Violie asks.

"A Frivian expression," she says, shrugging. "I don't fully understand it, but they use it for many different things. I gather it means the end of the world."

"And to think, in Bessemia we just called it looking a mess," Violie says, running a hand through her hair and catching it in a knot of tangles.

"Most of the servants' rooms are empty," Daphne tells her. "I believe the only ones in use are at this end of the hall. Help yourself to a free one, and there should be spare clothing in the laundry room, down and to the left," she adds, motioning down the stone hallway.

Violie nods, feeling uncertain. Just an hour ago, she was ready to tear Daphne limb from limb, and now . . . well, it still may come to that, but not tonight.

"Thank you," she says, and Daphne walks away without a backward glance, heading up the stairs and out of sight.

Violie finds the laundry room and a nightgown and a maid's dress in roughly her size before locating a room with the door open and no one inside. She claims it as her own, changing into the nightgown and splashing her face with water from the basin in the corner. But as much as she would love to sleep, she needs to speak with Leopold first. She rifles through her cloak, looking for the letters to show him proof that at least a few days prior, Daphne was set to kill him, but the letters are gone.

A harsh laugh forces past her throat. Of course Daphne

stole them back. It doesn't matter, though. If Leopold truly wants to believe Daphne over Violie, there's no use even trying to save him, though Violie doesn't think it'll come to that.

She lets herself into his room and closes the door behind her, making no effort to be quiet. During their travels, she learned he was a light sleeper, accustomed to a soft bed, warm blankets, and total silence. Sure enough, his eyes snap open and for a moment he just stares at her, blinking like he thinks he might be dreaming.

"Violie?" he asks, his voice coming out rough and laced with sleep.

Violie lets out a breath. Even when she caught a glimpse of him sleeping earlier, she still worried, but here he is—alive. Now she just has to keep it that way.

"Daphne was planning on killing you, and your brothers," she tells him, watching as he sits up, shaking his head as though to clear the sleep from it.

"My brothers?" he asks, dazed.

"I heard you found them," she says. "Ansel was behind it?" She still can't wrap her mind around that. Not because she doesn't think Ansel capable of kidnapping and potentially hurting Gideon and Reid, but because she doesn't know what he had to gain by doing it.

"Give me a minute, here," Leopold says, swinging his legs over the side of the narrow bed. "Daphne wanted to kill us? Why—" He breaks off, then continues. "Foolish question, I suppose. Empress's orders?"

Violie nods. "I found the letter she sent in Daphne's rooms back at Eldevale Castle and came as quickly as I could, but she says she's had an epiphany and changed her mind. We're close enough to the eastern coast—it would be an easy thing to get on a ship now, with your brothers, and sail beyond the empress's reach."

Leopold straightens up. "You don't believe Daphne?" he asks.

"I don't trust her," Violie corrects. "She's . . . broken."

Leopold doesn't say anything right away, but his expression is conflicted. "Sophronia believed she could be trusted," he says after a moment. "That in time, she could be reasoned with."

Violie shakes her head. "I think . . . I think reason is beginning to win out—deep down, I think she does know the truth. But the empress has buried her claws deep in Daphne. I don't think she can extricate herself from that grip without tearing herself apart."

Leopold absorbs this, his dark blue eyes pensive. "Sophie believed she could—I'm not saying she's right," he adds quickly when Violie opens her mouth to argue. "But if there's a chance . . . I have to see it through."

"Even if it puts your life at stake?" Violie asks, unable to keep a laugh from escaping. She's thought Sophronia naïve, but Leopold's naïveté is truly breathtaking. "She has orders to kill you. And your brothers."

Leopold nods. "And I'm willing to risk my life, but not theirs. Which is why I need to ask you a favor."

Violie's stomach knots. She knows what he is thinking before he asks it of her, knows too that he's right. Leopold has managed to get further with Daphne than anyone else has yet; if there is a chance for anyone to convince her to stand against the empress, it isn't Violie, it's him. But still, Violie promised Sophronia that she would protect him, and he is making it impossible to keep that promise.

"Bring Gideon and Reid to the Silvan Isles. Get them to safety with Lord Savelle—I trust him to keep them safe, and no one will be looking for them there. Everyone will assume Ansel had accomplices, that they kidnapped them back and took them east, no one will think to look west."

Violie knows he's right, but she doesn't want him to be. She can't keep him safe from Daphne if she's hundreds of miles away.

"Please, Violie," he says, his voice low.

The last thing Violie wants to do is break her promise to Sophronia, but she also knows that if Sophronia were here now, she would agree with him.

"Fine," she says. "We'll discuss it more in the morning."

Leopold nods, relief washing over his expression. "Thank you," he says.

Beatriz

In the two days since Beatriz saw the star she pulled down from the sky reappear, she hasn't been able to stop thinking about what it means. As soon as Nigellus saw it, he went a shade paler and shooed her out of his laboratory, muttering under his breath about miracles and impossibilities. But hadn't Nigellus said it himself? Many things seem impossible, until they are done. And whatever Beatriz has done, she's seen the reappeared star with her own eyes. It isn't impossible.

She's been anxiously waiting a summons for another lesson, but so far none has come. She hasn't seen Nigellus at court, either, though his absence isn't odd enough that anyone else seems to notice it.

When her mother sends an invitation to her and Pasquale to join her in her rose garden, Beatriz is almost relieved to have something else to focus on. She knows that for her to step into battle with her mother, her mind will need to be clear of everything else, even miracles.

"She will try to break you," she warns Pasquale under her breath as they make their way down the hall, guards trailing behind them. "She'll view you as a weak entry point."

"Compared to you, I'm not sure that isn't exactly what I am," he mutters.

"You'll be fine," Beatriz says, trying to sound more confident than she is. "And when in doubt, stay quiet."

Pasquale nods, but Beatriz notices he looks a little green. She catches his hand and squeezes it. "We'll get through this," she says. "And visit Gisella again tonight to see if she's changed her mind."

He glances sideways at her, brow furrowed. "And you haven't?" he asks. "You're still intent on . . ." He trails off, and wisely so. They're speaking quietly enough that the guards won't be able to hear them, but when discussing regicide, one can't be too careful.

"I don't see another choice," Beatriz says. "Do you disagree?"

Pasquale's moral compass should be the least of her concerns, but Beatriz finds herself holding her breath and waiting for his answer. She knows she will proceed no matter what, but she wants his blessing nonetheless.

"No," he says after a moment. He glances over his shoulder at the guards before turning back to her. "What Gisella and Nicolo did . . . ," he starts. "How many lives would have been saved if I'd had the strength to do it earlier? No, I don't disagree at all, Beatriz. More than that, I want to help you, however I can."

Beatriz nods, struggling to hide how much his words mean to her. Before she can answer, they arrive at the door that leads to her mother's rose garden. A waiting servant opens it and gestures them through, bowing as they pass.

As they step into the fragrant garden, surrounded by

roses of every color imaginable, it takes Beatriz a moment to find her mother, perched beside a bush of roses the color of fresh lemons, though a few petals are browning. As Beatriz and Pasquale approach, the empress takes a pair of shears and snips off the head of one of the dying roses, sending it rolling away till it comes to a stop at Beatriz's feet. Beatriz's stomach turns, and she can't shake the thought of Sophronia's head being severed just like that. Every bit as much her mother's doing.

The empress sees them, her dark brown eyes sweeping over first Pasquale, then Beatriz, as she rocks back onto her heels to stand, drawing herself up to her full height.

"You're late," she says.

"Are we?" Beatriz replies, tilting her head. "Your invitation was quite last-minute, Mother. We came as soon as we were able."

The empress's nostrils flare, but without a word she turns and starts down the path, leaving Beatriz and Pasquale no choice but to trail after her. The guards, Beatriz notes, stay where they are.

The empress wants privacy, Beatriz thinks, watching her mother's back. Though whether she wants to keep prying ears away from their conversation or private eyes off something more sinister, she isn't sure. There have been plenty of times the empress has brought Beatriz and her sisters to some secluded corner in order to inflict some sort of lesson on them. Once, in this very garden, Beatriz, Daphne, and Sophronia found themselves set upon suddenly by five attackers, leaving Sophronia with a broken arm and Beatriz with fractured ribs. Only Daphne escaped unscathed, and only because she was the only one of them who'd remembered to carry her dagger.

But if the empress is hoping to repeat that incident, she will be disappointed. Beatriz learned her lesson well, and she carries not just one but two daggers—one on her forearm, the other on her thigh. She's made sure Pasquale is armed as well, with a dagger in his boot, though she doubts he would be able to wield it with any particular skill.

After a moment of walking, the empress stops short and turns toward them. She reaches into the pocket of her skirt and Beatriz stiffens—perhaps her mother has found out what they've been plotting and has decided to kill them before they can kill her. When the empress withdraws a letter rather than a weapon, Beatriz lets out a breath.

"King Nicolo has responded to your letter," she says, passing it to Beatriz.

The seal has been broken, which doesn't surprise Beatriz, though it sets her on edge. She can only imagine what Nicolo had to say about her, and she hopes he didn't say anything too damning. If her mother knows about Nicolo's proposal, that he would take Beatriz as his queen, Pasquale's life will be in danger. Marrying Beatriz to Nicolo would solve all of her mother's problems, if she knew it was an option.

"He's quite angry with you," her mother says, and once again, relief floods Beatriz.

"He usually is," Beatriz lies, making no move to read the letter. It can wait until she has a moment of privacy, and she doesn't want to appear too keen in front of her mother. "I assume there is something else. A letter doesn't require privacy—it doesn't even require a meeting."

The empress's nostrils flare again and her eyes dart between Beatriz and Pasquale. "Very well," she says. "I wished to inform you that Daphne's life is in danger."

On their sixth birthday, a traveling group of acrobats was brought in to perform for Beatriz and her sisters, and one of the acrobats made her way across a thin rope suspended far above the marble floors. Beatriz remembers holding her breath as she crossed, certain that any wobble might lead to her death.

Beatriz feels like that same acrobat now.

"How do you know?" she asks, widening her eyes. "Is Daphne all right?"

"Fine, as of now," the empress says. "I received word from one of my sources in Temarin that Sophronia had befriended a servant girl later linked to the rebellion that executed her."

Violie, Beatriz thinks, though she's careful not to show that realization on her face.

"I have reason to believe that same servant girl has made her way to Friv," her mother continues.

Beatriz frowns, as if this is news to her. "But why? A Temarinian servant girl surely has no interest in Friv, and I doubt she went to enjoy the weather," she says.

"I was confused about that myself," the empress admits, her brow furrowing. "But I've recently made a discovery—the girl in question isn't Temarinian at all. She's Bessemian, born and raised a mere mile outside the palace. I have every reason to believe she is part of some nefarious plot to kill not just Sophronia but you and Daphne as well."

It takes everything in Beatriz's power not to laugh at that. It's almost brilliant—Violie makes a spectacular scapegoat for all of her mother's sins. If she hadn't met the girl herself, if Nigellus hadn't told her that her mother aimed to kill all of her daughters, she might be tempted to believe it.

Ambrose's words come back to her as well and she realizes he was right. In telling Beatriz this, her mother is nudging her toward Friv even further, manipulating Beatriz's next move in a way that leaves no fingerprints. The only question is why.

"What would she have to gain by that?" Beatriz asks after a moment.

The empress is an excellent actress, Beatriz realizes as she watches her mother cast her gaze sideways and bite her lip, as if weighing whether or not to reveal information Beatriz is sure she's made up.

"I've received word that some of my enemies in Bessemia have been biding their time over the last decade, waiting until they could go after my daughters, when they were viewed as vulnerable. I believe they've been organizing and that this girl is one of them," she says.

Beatriz glances at Pasquale, who is absorbing everything in stoic silence. She knows that this show her mother is putting on is for his benefit as well, because the empress doesn't know how much Beatriz has told him.

"I do have good news, however," the empress continues, and there is a glimmer in her eye that makes Beatriz's stomach plummet.

"Oh?" she hears herself ask.

"While that villain remains at large, I've managed to capture one of her associates in Hapantoile, who I believe has been in contact with her."

Next to her, Beatriz feels Pasquale stiffen. Ambrose.

"Even more concerning, though, is that this boy appears to be Cellarian," the empress says, shaking her head, though Beatriz doesn't find her convincing. She can't be sure how much the empress knows about Ambrose, or his relationship with Pasquale, but if she hasn't sussed out the whole truth yet, it is only a matter of time before she does.

"Oh?" Beatriz asks, careful to keep her tone level. "That is concerning," she says.

"Yes, I believe it is a lucky thing that this boy didn't manage to have the two of you killed before you fled Cellaria, though, of course, I would imagine he followed you here to do just that! I have it on good authority that he followed you to a teahouse just two days ago. Did anyone approach you there?"

Beatriz is aware of her mother's eyes on her, reading every shift of her expression. Which is fine, Beatriz thinks. So long as the empress keeps watching her and doesn't look at Pasquale—he can't hide his feelings nearly as well as she can. He isn't cut out for this sort of questioning—he's worried about Ambrose, and if she isn't careful, he will say something foolish.

"No," Beatriz tells her, shrugging. "We weren't there for more than twenty minutes. There was a boy sitting near us, I remember that, but he kept to himself, reading a book."

"Hmm," the empress says, giving no indication whether or not she believes Beatriz. "Well, you were very lucky he didn't strike there, I suppose."

"Lucky indeed," Beatriz adds. She glances at Pasquale, who has gone quite pale, though that can be attributed to his alleged near-death experience with a rebel spy, she supposes. Still, she knows she needs to get him out of her mother's presence as quickly as possible. "You said the boy was in contact with this servant girl?" she asks, tilting her head and acting like her next question is only of mild interest to her. "How do you know? Did he have a letter on him?"

If he did have Beatriz's letter still, her mother will soon be able to decode it, and then she will know at least most of what Beatriz is hiding.

"Unfortunately not," the empress says, with such distaste that Beatriz is sure it's the truth. "The postmaster reported that a letter had arrived from Friv for the boy, but by the time he was apprehended, he didn't have it in his possession."

As much of a relief as that is, Beatriz wonders what, exactly, happened to the letter she gave him in return. She forces herself to smile. "Thank you for sharing this information, Mama," she says before glancing at Pasquale. "Oh, Pas, you look quite ill," she says, resting her hand on his arm. "I know this must have come as a shock to you—I'm shocked as well. Do you need anything else, Mother, or is it all right if we retire?"

The empress's eyes dart between them for a moment before she gives a quick nod and waves her hand in dismissal.

Pasquale manages to make it back to Beatriz's room before he falls apart—a feat Beatriz is impressed and surprised by—though as soon as they are safe behind closed doors, he collapses onto the sofa in her sitting room and drops his head into his hands.

Beatriz stares at him, unsure what to do. She wants to comfort him, but the fact that Ambrose has been arrested is her fault. Surely he won't want her comfort now.

"I'm sorry, Pas," she says after a moment. "I . . . I'm sorry."

He looks up at her, surprised. "It isn't your fault, Beatriz," he says slowly. "It's hers."

Beatriz shakes her head. "She's my mother, I know what she's capable of—"

"So did I, more or less," he says, running a hand through his hair. "And so did Ambrose, for that matter. We had every opportunity to go somewhere else, but even knowing the risks, we didn't."

Beatriz wants to argue, but she knows it won't go anywhere. "I don't know how much she knows," she says after a moment. "Whether she simply suspects him of conspiring with Violie, or if she's using him to catch us as well. I don't . . ." She pauses, swallowing. "My mother is always five steps ahead of me, even when I think I'm getting away with something. Perhaps she knows all of it—about your relationship with Ambrose, about my plotting against her, about us working with Violie."

For a few breaths, Pasquale doesn't say anything. "If she knew all of that," he says, "would she let us roam free like we are?"

Beatriz considers it. "She might give us the illusion of freedom," she admits. "Though I have to believe I would know if I were being followed—by more than the usual guards, at least."

"If she were having us followed, she would know about Gigi," Pasquale continues.

Beatriz nods slowly. "She can't," she says after a moment. "She could break Gigi quite easily if she knew we'd met with her that night. Gigi would spill all of our secrets if my mother offered her the right price. And if they'd had that conversation, we would be in the dungeon right beside her."

"And Ambrose," Pasquale adds.

Beatriz bites her lip. "She won't kill him," she says, and even though she is only mostly sure of that, she tries to sound certain. "Not right away, at least. And I swear to you, we will get him out, alive and well."

Pasquale looks at her for a long moment without speaking. "I believe you," he says before one corner of his mouth quirks up in a sad excuse for a smile. "We've managed a jailbreak once; I can only imagine the second attempt will go better."

"It will," Beatriz assures him. "This time, we'll be sure to trust the right people. Which is to say, we'll trust no one but each other."

Later, after Pasquale goes back to his own rooms, Beatriz fishes Nicolo's letter from her dress pocket, unfolds it, and sits down on the parlor sofa to read it, curling her legs up to her chest and propping the letter against her knees. She begins to read.

> Beatriz,
>
> My sister made her own mess, and I daresay she can clean it up for herself.
>
> Nicolo

Beatriz frowns, turning the letter over, sure there must be more to it, but the back is blank. A single sentence. She spent the better part of an hour crafting the perfect message to get under his skin, and he's managed to do the same to her with a single sentence. Nothing even about Beatriz herself, or Nicolo, no information about what he's doing, how he's doing.

It isn't until this moment that Beatriz realizes she wants to know those things. She gives herself a mental shake and folds the letter up, tucking it into the drawer of her desk.

Very well, she thinks—just because she got nothing from the letter itself doesn't mean it can't be of use to her. She wonders how Gisella will feel about him coldly leaving her to fend for herself.

Daphne

The next morning, Daphne is exhausted. After her run-in with Violie, she got little sleep, tossing and turn-ing in her bed while she replayed the conversations with her and with Leopold in her mind. She's even more exhausted thinking about speaking to them again today, knowing that they'll come prepared to chip away more of her mother's words, turning them into lies.

When she makes her way downstairs, to the dining hall, it's to find the rest of their party already awake, bundled up in wool and furs. Even Gideon and Reid are there, wearing cloaks several sizes too big for them—likely borrowed from Bairre, Rufus, or Haimish.

"Are you going ice-skating too, Daphne?" Gideon asks when he sees her.

Daphne gives a snort and crosses to the sideboard to pour herself a steaming cup of coffee. "I don't ice-skate," she tells him flatly.

"Come on, Daphne," Cliona says, shaking her head. "You'll have such fun."

Haimish snorts and Cliona elbows him. When Cliona notices Daphne's raised eyebrows, she shrugs.

"You should come," she says, firmer this time. "We all deserve a bit of rest and relaxation, don't we? After yesterday, you certainly deserve it."

Daphne opens her mouth to argue but quickly closes it. Ice-skating sounds like it wouldn't be much fun for anyone over the age of ten, but if she stays behind, that will only mean another conversation with Violie and Leopold, and ice-skating is certainly more fun than that. Her eyes drift to Bairre where he sits near the window, watching her warily. She left him last night while he was asleep, and she's sure she owes him a conversation as well. Will that be more or less painful than dealing with Violie and Leopold?

"Fine," she says, taking a long sip of her coffee and ignoring the scald of it on her tongue. "I suppose ice-skating it is."

Half an hour later, Daphne has changed into a warmer gown with thick stockings underneath and a heavy fur cape draped over her shoulders, but it isn't enough to prevent the bite of the frigid air as she and the others step outside. Bairre leads their party, Gideon and Reid keeping close to him, while Daphne lets herself fall toward the back of the group.

"I can't believe you've never ice-skated before, Daphne," Cliona says from beside her, linking her arm through Daphne's, which Daphne finds herself grateful for because she is unused to traipsing through snow this deep.

"I've never wrestled a bear, either, but that's another thing I never saw a point in," Daphne grumbles. Strapping blades onto her boots to glide over ice that may or may not crack beneath her weight isn't Daphne's idea of a good time, but if everyone else is doing it she doesn't want to appear cowardly.

"You're going to fall so much," Cliona says cheerfully. "Everyone does when they first try, so you mustn't get discouraged, and we brought a vial of stardust in case you truly hurt yourself. It will be funny to watch, though."

"I exist solely for your amusement," Daphne retorts.

Already, the winter chill is working its way into her bones and making her grumpy—a fact that Cliona doesn't seem at all bothered by. Instead she laughs.

"Our friend has been lying low since his show of heroics yesterday," Cliona comments, the words idle, but Daphne isn't fooled. She shrugs.

"I'm sure he's quite tired after all of that, and I can't quite blame him for wanting to stay safe and warm indoors after nearly dying."

"Hmmm," Cliona says, the sound noncommittal. "I have a theory," she announces.

"A theory?" Daphne asks, her gaze going to the back of Bairre's head, his chestnut curls hidden by the fur cap he wears pulled down over his ears. Disappointment makes her stomach sink. How quickly did he run and tattle to Cliona about Leopold's identity? She shouldn't feel betrayed—if anything, it should come as a relief; after all, Bairre has his loyalties, and Daphne has hers.

Except Daphne is no longer sure where her loyalties lie.

"I think he is in league with Queen Eugenia after all," Cliona says, jerking Daphne out of her thoughts. "Maybe he's an exiled Temarinian nobleman or something like that— you can see something noble in his bearing, can't you? She must have sent him because she didn't trust us."

It's more or less the same story Daphne spun a few days

before, but she's too relieved to be annoyed about that. Bairre didn't tell Cliona.

"Maybe," Daphne echoes.

Daphne told Cliona that she'd seen lakes before and there couldn't be anything different about Lake Olveen—after all, what is a lake but a large body of still water? It was difficult to imagine there was much variety in the phenomenon.

But as they approach the shore, Daphne realizes she was wrong. Well, not wrong, perhaps. Lake Olveen is indeed much like any other lake: more or less round, more or less large, and, she imagines, beneath the layer of ice more or less placid. There is nothing remarkable about the lake itself. What surrounds the lake, however, is enough to take Daphne's breath away.

Great snow-covered mountains rise up from the horizon on the lake's north side, the bright morning sunlight making them look like they're covered in a thick layer of stardust. Pine trees taller than Daphne has ever seen cluster on the lake's east coast, dusted in the same glittering snow. A meadow sits to the west, and though it is at quite a distance from where Daphne stands, she can make out clusters of red on the bushes there—berries.

And on the lake itself, a crowd of gathered townsfolk from young children to adults glide along the surface, stumbling and laughing and barely seeming to notice the cold at all.

It isn't anything like the lakes she's seen in Bessemia, Daphne thinks, taking in the scenery along with a deep breath of crisp mountain air.

"Come on," Bairre says, waiting for her to catch up to him. "I'll help you with your skates."

Daphne glances around for Cliona, but she's already abandoned her, throwing a snowball at the back of Haimish's head and laughing when he lunges after her, giving chase and laughing as well.

Daphne follows Bairre to a large flat stone on the edge of the lake and sits down on it while he digs into the knapsack he carries, drawing out two contraptions that look to Daphne like weapons, if she didn't know better.

Wordlessly, he sits down beside her and she turns toward him, lifting one booted foot into his lap. His hand reaches around her ankle to turn her foot so that he can attach the blade to the bottom of her shoe, tightening one strap around the ball of her foot, then the second around her heel, and wrapping it around her ankle.

It shouldn't feel intimate—not after she spent the night in his bed, going to sleep and waking up with his arms around her, but still Daphne feels herself blush.

"You didn't tell Cliona," she blurts out. "About Leopold, I mean."

Bairre finishes the first skate and moves on to the next, glancing up at her with a furrowed brow. "No," he says slowly. "I didn't tell Cliona, or anyone else for that matter."

Daphne doesn't answer right away, and they fall into silence as he finishes tying her second lace.

"Why not? I'm sure the information would be of use to the rebellion."

He shrugs. "I don't believe it's any of their business. He's a Temarinian king in hiding, who saved his brothers. That has nothing to do with the rebellion."

"They might disagree," she says.

"They're entitled to," he says. "But I made my decision, and keeping your confidence was more important than what essentially amounts to gossip."

Daphne doesn't know what to say to that, so she stays quiet and lets him help her to her feet, wobbly as she finds her balance on the skates. As he guides her toward the edge of the lake, she has to grip his arm tightly to keep from toppling over.

"Did you come out here often with Cillian?" she asks, hoping to change the subject.

He shakes his head. "No, we were mostly here in the summer, though there was once or twice when we traveled up in late fall or early spring, before the ice melted. There are other lakes closer to Eldevale we would skate on, though. We'd mostly race."

"And who won?" she asks.

"I did, usually," Bairre admits. "Though sometimes I let him win."

"I did the same with Sophie," Daphne says after a moment, memories filtering through her mind. "Not always with racing, but other things—with lessons and things like that." She doesn't elaborate on things like that and is sure that wherever his mind takes him, it's a far cry from sparring or shooting or any number of the things their mother pitted them against one another in, to make them stronger.

"Archery?" Bairre asks.

Daphne scoffs. "I'd never let her win at archery," she says. "Besides, Sophie had little interest in it. She preferred to spend her time in the kitchens, persuading the cook to teach her how to bake."

Bairre guides her onto the ice and she grips his arm tighter, her skates slipping and sliding beneath her, though she manages to stay upright, barely. When she glances up at him, embarrassed, he's just managing to hold back a laugh, though he keeps a steady grip on her, helping her balance.

"I feel as though I talk about her constantly," she says, shaking her head.

"You don't," he says. "And when you do talk about her, it's as part of a unit with you and Beatriz."

"Oh," she says, wondering if that's true. "Well, I suppose that is the danger of being triplets. People tend to see us as a unit, and it can be easy to do that yourself. Sophie was very different from me, though, and from Beatriz. I'm sure you'd have liked her."

Bairre doesn't answer for a second. He releases her arm and takes hold of her hands instead, skating backward to put as much distance between them as he can while still holding her hands.

"Now slowly—slowly—come toward me," he tells her.

Part of Daphne rebels at the tone he's taking—she is a perfectly capable girl. She can pick locks and fend off assassins and carry out plots to overthrow kings. She is more than capable of mastering a sport favored by children.

But as soon as she tries to move, her skates slip out from beneath her and she realizes her folly, falling toward him and grabbing his shoulders, tumbling them both onto the hard, cold ice, Bairre flat on his back and Daphne sprawled on top of him.

"Oof," Bairre says, his arms going around her waist to steady her.

"Oh, I'm sorry," Daphne says, struggling to get off him, but when she tries to stand up, her skates fail to find purchase and she falls on top of him again. "Oh no," she groans.

Bairre says nothing, but his whole body is shaking, his face buried in her shoulder.

"Bairre?" she asks, alarmed. She pulls back as far as she dares, worried she's hurting him, but when she can see his face clearly she realizes he's laughing at her.

"Some help you are," she says, shoving his shoulder.

"Sorry, sorry," he says, still laughing, but he manages to grip her elbows and lift her off him, helping them both get back to their feet. "I never thought I'd see the day you failed at anything," he admits.

Daphne shoots him a glare, though she's still clinging to his arm so tightly she's sure she'll leave bruises. She knows if she loosens her grip, she'll fall again. "I haven't failed," she says. "Just you wait, by the end of the day, I'll be a better skater than you are."

Bairre laughs. "You know, I don't doubt that."

As the day drags on, Daphne does manage to skate on her own, arms thrown wide for balance, though that is the extent of her skating skills. Even Gideon and Reid are, quite literally, skating circles around her. It's frustrating to see the others whirl by her, many executing twirls and jumps while she just barely manages to stay upright, feeling like a baby deer taking its first steps.

But despite that frustration, she is enjoying herself. After a few hours of skating, she doesn't even notice the cold anymore, especially after a village woman brings out a jug of hot cocoa for all of the skaters to partake in.

Daphne tries her first sip and decides there are a great number of miseries she would suffer for hot cocoa, cold weather the least among them.

It's only when she notices that the sun is close to setting that she realizes almost an entire day has gone by without her thinking about her mother or her sisters or all of the things she's meant to be doing. Nothing she's done today has furthered her mother's plots at all, and Daphne isn't sure she's ever gone this long with that being the case. All she has done for the last few hours is enjoy herself. What wasted time.

But it doesn't *feel* wasted.

Daphne is having so much fun, she almost doesn't notice Cliona slipping away, toward the edge of the woods where they meet the lake, but when she does, her eyes narrow. Where could she possibly be going? And not even Haimish follows her, when he's practically been her shadow since they left Eldevale. What's more, as Cliona slips away, Haimish appears to lose his balance on his skates, knocking over Bairre and Rufus in the process and thoroughly distracting everyone. Everyone except Daphne.

Mind made up, Daphne makes her way toward the edge of the forest, not as quick as she might be on foot, but quick enough.

"Daphne!" Haimish calls behind her, and in seconds, he's at her side. "Where are you hurrying off to?" he asks, and to anyone else, he might sound casual.

She cuts him a sideways look. "It's ungentlemanly to ask a lady why she's heading to the cover of woods, but suffice to say I'm dealing with a delicate personal situation. Kindly do us both a favor and leave it at that."

"The woods are dangerous," he says. "Surely you can hold it until we return to the castle."

"Are they?" she asks, glancing at him with raised eyebrows. "Well, I saw Cliona go this way—I'm sure with the same goal in mind. We should gather the others to find her, should she find herself in danger. Don't you think?"

Haimish glares at her, but he stops skating, allowing her to reach the edge of the lake on her own. She stumbles onto the ground, but she's steadier here than she was on the ice despite the blades still attached to her feet. She makes her way deeper into the woods, stopping short when she hears voices. Two distinctly familiar voices.

"I don't take orders from you," Cliona says, steel in her voice. Even though Daphne can't see the other girl, she can imagine her expression—chin raised in defiance, brown eyes bright with irritation, and a haughty lift to her brow.

"You take them from your father," the second voice says, and Daphne nearly loses her already precarious balance. Aurelia.

"My father would never order that," Cliona says, but even though Daphne can't see her face, she hears the doubt in Cliona's voice. "Gideon and Reid are children, and they've done nothing wrong."

Daphne feels as if a bucket of snow has been poured over her head.

"You're the one acting like a child, and you know perfectly

well that if your father were here, he'd say the same," Aurelia says coolly. "There's a reason you had to beg your father to let you be involved with rebellion matters. Are you really so keen to prove him right?"

Cliona doesn't speak for a moment. "Perhaps if I understood why," she says.

Aurelia laughs, the sound harsh. "The same reason we do anything, Cliona. For Friv. You've come too far to suddenly be squeamish. I'll be waiting tomorrow at midnight by the old clock tower. That should give you plenty of time to work out how to get them there."

There are footsteps—belonging to Aurelia, Daphne suspects, but Cliona's voice stops them short.

"And after I bring them to you?" Cliona asks. "What will happen to them?"

Aurelia lets out a long, beleaguered sigh. "Don't ask questions you don't want answers to, Cliona. Just follow your orders."

Daphne makes it back to the lake before Cliona, but since Haimish knew exactly what Daphne was up to in following her, Daphne isn't surprised when Cliona falls into step beside her as they walk back to the castle, the sun beginning to set over the forest.

"What you heard," Cliona begins without preamble, her voice curt. "It wasn't what it sounded like."

Daphne laughs. She can't help it. Cliona has never been a good liar, but she doesn't even bother trying to sound like she's telling the truth.

"Nothing about it is funny," Cliona snaps.

"Oh, I know that," Daphne manages to say through her laughter. But part of it *is* funny, she thinks. Here Cliona is, under similar orders to her own, and every bit as conflicted about them. She manages to smother her laughter and fixes the other girl with a frank look. "Are you going to do it?" she asks.

Cliona opens her mouth, and Daphne is sure whatever she is going to say will be a lie, but she closes it just as quickly. "I don't have a choice," she says. "He's my father. If he says it's what's best for the rebellion, it is. And she won't . . . she has nothing to gain by hurting them. She just wants to remove them from the game board before they cause . . . complications."

Cliona doesn't believe that, no more than Daphne believed that her mother was ordering her to kill Gideon and Reid to protect their family. She wanted to believe it. Desperately, in fact, but she's always known the truth. Just as she's always known that she couldn't go through with it. Even if it's taken her until now, until she's seen Cliona just as conflicted, for her to admit it to herself.

She sighs. "I have an idea," she says slowly. "But I need to know I can trust you. And I need you to trust me in turn."

Cliona looks at her for a long moment, her expression inscrutable. "If we don't trust each other by now, Daphne, I don't know how we ever can."

Daphne doesn't speak for a moment. "Tell me the truth about Aurelia," she says. "And I'll tell you the truth about Levi."

Violie

While most of the household is at the lake ice-skating, Violie takes the opportunity to sneak once more into Daphne's bedchamber, though this time Leopold is at her heels.

"You're going to get caught," he whispers.

She glances at him over her shoulder as she makes her way to Daphne's wardrobe, lifting a single eyebrow. "I have yet to, accidentally at least," she says primly. "Close the door, but don't lock it," she adds, relieved when he does as she asks.

"Why not lock it?" he asks.

"A locked door is suspicious," she explains.

"As opposed to someone simply walking in and finding us here?" he asks.

"If someone walks in and finds us here, we'll just convince them we snuck in here for unsuspicious reasons," she tells him, finding Daphne's cosmetics case and lugging it out. When she glances up at Leopold, his brow is furrowed in confusion she can't help but laugh at. Sometimes, it's difficult to remember just how sheltered a life he's led.

"We would hardly be the first servants to slip away to an empty bedroom for a little . . . privacy," she says.

Recognition dawns on Leopold's face for a second before his cheeks flush and he drops his gaze.

"No one does that," he says.

"Plenty of people do that," she says, laughing. "Most people wouldn't be bold enough to try the princess's bedchamber, but it would be more believable than the alternative."

She opens the lid of the cosmetics case and begins removing vials and powders, sorting them into two piles.

"Which is . . . stealing lip paint?" Leopold asks, watching her.

She glances up at him. "Sophronia had the same set," she says, motioning to the one pile. "These are cosmetics." She gestures to the other. "These are poisons."

He stares at her for a moment. "Poisons," he says slowly. "Sophie kept poison alongside her cosmetics?"

"She never used it, as far as I'm aware, but I'm sure the empress would have preferred it if she had," Violie says. "Daphne, though, isn't quite so precious about it."

She finishes sorting through everything in the cosmetics case, including all of the vials and tubes she finds in the hidden compartment at the bottom.

"Can you get the jewelry case out of the wardrobe?" she asks as she begins to put the ordinary cosmetics back in their place, jamming the poisons into the pockets of her apron.

Leopold lifts his eyebrows but does as she asks, dragging the jewelry box out and taking the liberty of opening the lid.

"Are these poisonous as well?" he asks warily.

Violie stands up, moving toward him and peering over his shoulder. "That is," she says, pointing to a heavy gold pendant necklace in the shape of the Hermit's Cane constellation. He lifts it, looking at it closely before passing it to her. She shows him how the top of the pendant unscrews.

"It's only sleeping powder," she says, shrugging. "But I'm not taking any chances."

She pockets the necklace as well before crouching next to Leopold. She sifts through the rest of Daphne's jewelry, pulling out a cuff bracelet that hides a small dagger, a heavy ring that emits a cloud of noxious gas when two of its stones are pressed at once, and a moon-shaped diamond brooch that Violie decides is too ugly not to contain some hidden and dangerous facet.

That done, they pack away the rest of the jewelry and Leopold puts the boxes back in the wardrobe, just as they were before.

"Do you think I'm safe from her now?" Leopold asks.

Violie snorts. "Stars, no," she says. "Daphne could kill you with her bare hands, Leo. She could fashion a weapon out of practically anything in this or any room, and I've heard she's even more skilled at crafting poisons of her own. If she decides to kill you, you stand the same chance of surviving as you would trekking across Friv in winter in the nude. But I'm not inclined to make killing you any easier for her."

Leopold blinks. "Are you trying to scare me?" he asks.

Violie rolls her eyes. "You're the one insisting on sending me, the only one who actually can hold my own against her, away and remaining alone in the company of a princess who seems to constantly vacillate between wanting to kill you and not," she points out.

For a moment, Leopold doesn't speak. "You are the only one who stands a chance against her," he says slowly. "Which is why I need you to go with my brothers."

Violie knows there is no talking him out of the decision, but she can't help letting out a huff. She understands what he's saying, why he's asking it of her, but it doesn't make it any easier for her to agree.

"You're sure you trust your brothers under my watch?" she asks him. "I might introduce them to some questionable characters in a tavern. Teach them how to cheat at dice. Show them the best methods for pickpocketing."

She means the words as a joke, but Leopold fixes her with a serious look.

"Just get them to Lord Savelle alive," he says. "That's all I ask."

Violie hesitates a second before nodding. "All right," she says. "Talk to them tonight, let them know to expect me— the last thing I need is for them to believe they're being kidnapped again. We'll leave at midnight."

That evening, when Daphne, Prince Bairre, Gideon, Reid, and the others arrive back at the castle, something is wrong. Violie notices it as soon as she catches a glimpse of Daphne walking into the banquet hall, where Violie is wiping down the long wood table. Daphne's head is bent low toward the only other girl in the party—Cliona, Daphne said her name was. Both of them wear somber expressions, and it's unclear to Violie whether they are quarreling or conspiring.

Either one is a concern.

Daphne glances up, her eyes colliding with Violie's, and Violie ducks her head, knowing now is not the right time for a conversation, but Daphne surprises her by saying her name, the sound ringing like a bell in the quiet room.

Violie looks up, blinking. Her eyes dart to Cliona, who is eyeing her warily, as if she is sizing her up. Violie decides to play things safely.

"Yes, Your Highness?" she asks, maintaining her Frivian accent.

Cliona laughs. "I must say, your accent is much better than Levi's . . . or rather, King Leopold's?" she says.

Violie's hands ball into fists at her sides. "You told her?" she asks Daphne through clenched teeth.

"You'll thank me for it if you give me a moment to explain," Daphne says, her voice level.

"You said not to trust her," Violie points out.

"Ouch," Cliona says, though she doesn't actually sound wounded, more amused.

Daphne doesn't deny it. "In some things, we are on the same side," she says carefully. "And in this, we're on your side."

"In what, exactly?" Violie asks.

Daphne glances sideways at Cliona before looking back at Violie. "The east wing of the castle is closed off. Meet us there."

"There's a sitting room on the first floor," Cliona supplies. "Up the stairs from the servants' quarters, third door on your right."

Daphne nods. "Right. Bring Leopold."

"Will it be just you?" Violie asks warily. "What about Bairre?"

Daphne and Cliona exchange a loaded look that Violie can't begin to decipher.

"Not Bairre," Daphne finally says, the words heavy. "Not yet."

Violie finds Leopold and together they follow Cliona's directions to the parlor in the east wing. When they enter, it's to find the windows boarded up, the fireplace cold, and sheets covering the furniture. Daphne and Cliona are already there, standing side by side, both still wearing their heavy coats from their earlier journey to the lake. When Violie closes the door behind her, Cliona takes a moment to look Leopold over.

"Should I bow, Your Majesty?" she asks, the question dry.

Leopold, to his credit, isn't ruffled. "I wouldn't dream of telling a lady what to do," he says in his natural accent.

Cliona laughs, the sound loud before Daphne elbows her and lifts a finger to her lips.

"Oh, but I like him," Cliona tells her, shaking her head.

"The feeling won't be mutual if you assist in kidnapping his brothers," Daphne says.

And just like that, any element of levity in the room evaporates.

"And here I thought that was your assignment," Violie says, looking at Daphne.

"My assignment was to murder them," she says plainly. "And you," she adds, nodding at Leopold. "But as it happens, Cliona is every bit as . . . ambivalent as I am."

"*Ambivalent* is not the word I would prefer you use in this context," Leopold says, his words coming out a growl.

"If you'd rather I lie to you, I'll keep that in mind for the future," Daphne retorts. "But I told Violie we had the same goal, at least in this, and I meant it." She glances at Cliona, then back at Leopold. "Neither of us wants to do harm to innocent children."

It isn't the first time Violie has heard Gideon and Reid referred to as children, but the description always unsettles her. They're twelve and fourteen. When Violie was their age, she was already in the employ of the empress—she hardly felt like an innocent child to be protected at all costs. She can't imagine Daphne did at their age either. Still, she isn't about to question the line Daphne has decided she is unwilling to cross. She's just glad it exists at all.

Violie fights not to look at Leopold, though she's sure he's thinking the same thing she is—that if their plan goes off as scheduled tonight, Gideon and Reid will be out of Daphne's and Cliona's reach.

A soft knock sounds at the parlor door and Violie feels herself stiffen, but Cliona and Daphne don't appear surprised.

"Come in, Rufus," Daphne says.

The door opens and a tall boy with lanky limbs and an overgrown mess of red hair enters. His broad, handsome face and easy smile are familiar to Violie—he's a friend of Bairre's, she remembers, having seen him around the summer castle earlier in the day.

"I was summoned," he says, closing the door behind him.

"Rufus," Daphne says, "has no ties to my mother, no ties to the rebellion in Friv, isn't that right, Rufus?"

Rufus looks perplexed, like he's vastly misread the situation he just stepped into. "I . . . uh . . . yes, that's right."

"And you have no reason at all to wish harm on Gideon and Reid," Cliona continues.

"Why in the name of the stars would I? What, exactly, is going on—"

"It's settled, then," Daphne says, giving him a beaming smile. "You will escort the boys back to your family's estate—it's far enough from Eldevale that no one will think to look there."

"And if they do," Cliona adds, "you can say they're orphaned children of one of your servants whom you've taken in as wards."

Rufus doesn't say anything for a moment. "I'm very confused," he says finally. "But if the safety of Gideon and Reid is an issue, they are, of course, welcome at Cadringal House."

"That won't be necessary," Leopold interrupts.

Rufus gapes at him. "Levi, your accent—"

"Is not important right now, Rufus," Daphne cuts in smoothly.

"I beg to differ," Rufus says. "If the four of you don't tell me what, exactly, is going on, I'll walk out that door this second."

For a moment, no one moves, but finally, Daphne lets out a sigh. "Fine," she says, nodding toward Leopold. "Tell him whatever you see fit," she says.

Leopold looks wary. "Really?" he asks, glancing to Violie for confirmation.

"You trust him?" Violie asks Daphne.

Daphne holds her gaze. "In this, yes," she says. "Because

Rufus owes me for my kindness to his own sister. Isn't that right, Rufus?"

Rufus hesitates. "That's right," he says.

Violie looks toward Leopold and nods. Leopold shakes his head before turning back to Rufus and giving him an abridged version of the truth—his true name and title, the identity of his brothers, and the fact that Eugenia was behind the plot to kill him, hence his need to remain hidden.

"I'm not keen on sending my brothers back into her care, for obvious reasons," Leopold says. "But I won't send them to a stranger, either. No offense."

"There's no other choice," Daphne says.

"There is, actually," Violie inserts. "Leopold is right—and what's more, frankly we have no reason to trust you to know where they're being sent. If you change your mind—"

"We won't," Cliona says, sounding offended at the thought.

"You'll pardon me for not taking you at your word," Violie retorts, gratified when Cliona doesn't have a comeback to that. "I have an alternate plan," she says. "Rufus and I will take the princes to a destination Leopold and I have already agreed to."

Daphne looks surprised at that, but Violie laughs.

"You didn't really think we were going to let them stay under your care," she says.

Daphne's jaw tightens, but after a moment and a glance toward Cliona, she nods.

"Very well," she says. "Rufus, that's all. I'll send a note when it's time."

Rufus glances around the room once more, his gaze furtive. "I take it I don't get any more questions?" he asks.

"You don't," Daphne says. "But after this, I'll consider us even for Zenia."

Rufus looks like he wants to argue, but finally he nods. "Fine, then," he says before ducking out of the room.

When he's gone, Daphne looks at Cliona. "And which of us is going to tell Bairre that his mother was responsible for kidnapping the boys he was so determined to rescue?" she asks.

Cliona winces. "I still don't believe it was the rebellion," she says. When Daphne opens her mouth, looking ready to argue, Cliona shakes her head. "I know, I know, but I need to speak to my father about it. She may have been working on her own."

"The Frivian rebellion kidnapped Gideon and Reid?" Leopold asks, frowning.

What's more, if Violie read that conversation correctly, Cliona is part of the rebellion. Remembering how the empress used the Temarinian revolutionaries to suit her purpose, it raises her suspicions.

"It would appear so," Daphne says to Leopold before pausing. "I expected you to insist on traveling with them," she says. "Not Violie."

Leopold glances at Violie and shrugs. "Would you have let me?" he asks her.

Daphne's lips purse, but rather than answer, she shrugs and turns to Violie. "You'll leave tonight. When Bairre realizes, Cliona and I will tell him the truth and he won't follow. Take them wherever you see fit."

Without another word, Daphne brushes past Violie and Leopold and out of the room, Cliona at her heels.

That night, Violie goes with Leopold to the room his brothers are staying in, finding Gideon and Reid already in their nightclothes, though they aren't asleep. Gideon is reading a book of Frivian folklore in his bed while Reid sits cross-legged on the floor by the fire, surrounded by half a dozen pieces of paper scribbled with drawings Violie can't quite make out.

Gideon notices Leopold first, closing his book and sitting up straighter, blue eyes bright.

"Leopold!" he says, which draws Reid's attention as well.

Leopold lifts his finger to his lips to signal for them to keep their voices low as Violie closes the door. Then he sits at the edge of Gideon's bed and gestures for Reid to come closer. Violie hangs back, watching and listening as he explains to Gideon and Reid that they'll be leaving the castle tonight—without him.

"Are we going back to Mother?" Reid asks, frowning.

Over his head, Leopold gives Violie a strained look, and she can't bring herself to envy him his position. As far as Gideon and Reid know, their mother is just that—the woman who dried their tears and tucked them into bed, the one who told stories and sang lullabies.

"No, that isn't safe," Leopold says, rather than try to explain why that is. "You're going to go with Violie," he adds, nodding to her.

Both boys turn to look at her.

"I know you," Reid says, frowning. "You were at the palace, in Kavelle."

Violie opens her mouth to answer, but Leopold gets there first.

"Violie was a friend of Sophie's," he says. "She's going to take you to another friend—Lord Savelle."

The name doesn't seem to spark any recognition in them, but Violie supposes that they would have been very young the last time Lord Savelle was in the Temarinian court, if they crossed paths at all.

"He lives in the Silvan Isles," Leopold continues. "I'm very jealous—you'll certainly have much better weather than I'll have here."

Violie hears the forced lightness in his voice, and she knows that despite how insistent he was on this path, saying goodbye to his brothers again is difficult for him.

"You don't have to be jealous if you come too," Gideon says.

"I can't, Gid," Leopold says, shaking his head. "I told Sophie I would help Daphne, and I have to see that through. But when it's safe, we'll see one another again. I promise."

Violie averts her eyes as Leopold hugs both his brothers, speaking low words to them that aren't meant for her ears. Then he tells them to change into the warmest clothes they have. There is nothing to pack, since they arrived with nothing, and Violie assumes Rufus will be well funded for this trip and able to purchase whatever they need.

Leopold and Violie step out into the hall while Gideon and Reid change, but Leopold remains silent.

"Leo . . . ," Violie starts, unsure what to say. She knows

better than to promise him he'll see his brothers again some-day, but she wants to nonetheless.

"Please don't try to convince me to go with them," he says, his voice quiet. "I'm already close to agreeing, but I can't."

"No," Violie agrees. "You're right—you have the best chance of fully swaying Daphne. She's already almost there. I don't think she'd let your brothers go if she weren't."

Leopold laughs, but the sound is hard-edged. "She's letting them go because she doesn't trust herself not to kill them," he says. "And because she doesn't want to risk Cliona's morals being weaker than hers."

He's right, Violie knows he's right, but she can't help but think that two weeks ago, Leopold wouldn't have seen that truth.

"I'll keep them safe, Leopold," she tells him, her voice soft. She reaches out to him, her hand landing on his shoulder, giving it a squeeze. "I promise you that."

Leopold looks at her, his dark blue eyes nearly glowing in the dark. "Thank you, Violie," he says. "I wouldn't trust them with anyone else."

When Gideon and Reid emerge from their room, dressed in the heavy cloaks and boots, they say their goodbyes to Leopold before letting Violie lead them out of the palace, to the stables where Rufus is already waiting, four horses saddled and ready to go.

Beatriz

Beatriz has too much to occupy her thoughts to spare many for Nicolo, or so she tells herself. She has the power to bring stars down from the sky, and one somehow reappeared! She still hasn't heard from Nigellus! She is preparing to attempt regicide and matricide! She has to find a way to rescue her husband's paramour from the dungeon! Nicolo shouldn't warrant a space in her thoughts, but instead, he's begun to sneak into her mind so often she begins to doubt he ever left it.

Whether he intended it or not, his short letter wedged its way beneath her skin, and the only thing that annoys her more than that single line is the fact that she is still thinking about it.

As she watches the sunset out her bedroom window and the stars flicker awake in the ink-dark sky, a shiver runs down her spine. There it is—that feeling that she felt twice before in Cellaria but didn't understand. Now she knows it's the stars, calling to her to use her magic. Summons or not, she needs to speak to Nigellus.

Beatriz is even more aware of her surroundings than usual as she makes her way to Nigellus's laboratory near midnight. After Ambrose's arrest, she's been particularly uneasy, wondering how much her mother knows about him, or his connection to her and Pasquale. She takes a longer route, making use of several hidden passageways she, Sophronia, and Daphne discovered as children. She rounds corners, then stops short, listening for any sound or shadow, but none appear. No one is following her, she realizes, and somehow, that knowledge makes her even more anxious.

When she finally pushes open the door to Nigellus's laboratory, she's confronted with a mess. Where before, the worktables and desk were kept clear of everything but the equipment and whatever text he had out at that moment, now the equipment has been shoved to the side and every inch of space is covered with open books—more than Beatriz can count. As she steps into the room, she realizes they're even spread out on the floor, all open to different pages.

She catches sight of an illustration in one and recognizes it as the same image he showed her before, of what the sky looked like eons ago. She steps over the books, careful not to muss them, and looks around for any sign of Nigellus himself.

Beatriz finds him beneath the worktable, fast asleep. When she nudges his leg with the toe of her boot, he jerks awake, sitting upright so fast he bangs his head on the underside of the table.

"Ow," he mutters, bringing a hand to his head while he blinks, eyes adjusting to the low light until he sees Beatriz. He frowns.

"What are you doing here?" he asks, scrambling to stand. "I didn't send for you."

"It's been two days without word and I was beginning to

worry," Beatriz tells him, glancing around the room again. "Have you been here this whole time?" she asks.

"No," he says before pausing. "Yes, maybe," he adds, frowning. "I've found no mention, in eons of texts, of an empyrea who can put stars back into the sky."

"Is . . . that what I did?" Beatriz asks. The star she pulled down from the Queen's Chalice reappeared, but then so did the star Nigellus pulled down to create Sophronia, and she didn't have anything to do with that. "You might have made a mistake about the star I pulled down in Cellaria. What with Sophie's star reappearing, perhaps something larger is happening with the stars."

"Sophronia's star reappeared because she died," Nigellus says. "No other stars I've pulled down have come back. But you . . . it isn't only the Queen's Chalice that's altered, it's the Stinging Bee and the Wandering Wheel. Both constellations have reappeared in the last two days, neither missing the star you took."

Beatriz stares at him, processing his words. "You think I did that?" she asks. "Surely I would know."

"You didn't know you were pulling stars down in the first place," he reminds her. "It's hardly surprising you would be just as ignorant about putting them back."

The word *ignorant* digs at Beatriz, though she has to admit she *is* ignorant about star magic, at least compared to Nigellus.

"If I can put the stars back in the sky after wishing on them, isn't that good news?" she asks. "You showed me how few stars are left in the sky—if I can bring them back . . ."

"I've been studying the stars all my life, Princess. If there is one thing they've taught me, it's that magic always has a cost. Just because we don't know what that cost is yet doesn't mean it doesn't exist. So no, I'm not inclined to celebrate this revelation yet, and you shouldn't be either."

"Well, perhaps if I do it again, we could get more information," she offers. "I feel the stars calling me to."

At that, Nigellus frowns. "Calling you to what?"

Beatriz shrugs. "You know how it is, I'm sure . . . it feels like the stars are dancing on my skin, pulling at me. It only ever goes away when I make a wish."

Nigellus stares at her blankly for a moment before shaking his head. "You didn't mention that before."

"I didn't think it was relevant," she says. "And it took me ages to put it together—as I told you, the two times I wished on stars in Cellaria, I didn't realize what I was doing, but before each of those incidents, I felt that same pull. I thought it was insomnia at first."

"And . . . you feel that now?" he asks, frown deepening.

Beatriz nods. "You've never experienced it?" she asks. When Nigellus shakes his head, she bites her lip. "I assumed it was a normal thing, or at least normal for empyreas."

"Well, whatever pull you feel, you'll have to resist it. Using your power when we understand so little of it is dangerous."

Beatriz laughs. "If what you're saying is true, I can make wishes without killing stars," she says. "Why are you so determined to find doom and gloom in everything? Surely this is a miracle."

"Perhaps," he allows. "But there simply isn't enough information to know what it is yet. And that's another thing—did you, in fact, bring the star back? Or did you birth a new star to take its place?"

Beatriz hadn't considered that, but surely she couldn't birth a star by accident. "Does it matter?" she asks. "The star is there, in the same place it was before."

"Of course it matters!" Nigellus snaps, and Beatriz takes a step back from him.

She isn't afraid of Nigellus, not really, but she's known the man her entire life and he's always been a calm and aloof presence. Seeing him so unraveled is disconcerting. He takes a deep breath, closing his eyes and tilting his face toward the stars shining down through the open roof.

"I need more time, Princess Beatriz," he says finally. "I've written to other empyreas to see if they know any more than I do, but it will take time to find answers. Until then, you need to exercise patience and caution—two things I know don't come easily to you, but if you're going to survive as an empyrea, you'll need to learn both."

With her lesson cut short and the stars making her even more restless than usual, Beatriz makes her way down to the dungeon, using a vial of stardust she swiped on her way out of Nigellus's laboratory to render herself invisible. Weak as stardust is, it only lasts a few minutes, but that's time enough for her to make it down the halls and stairways until she reaches the deserted dungeon.

Gisella's cell is separate from the others, secluded in a separate wing of the dungeon reserved for foreign dignitaries, but rather than going there first, Beatriz makes her way down the main cellblock, half full of common prisoners who glance at her as she passes but don't speak.

She finds Ambrose in the last cell, dressed in soiled rags, with a dirt-smudged face, but other than that no worse for wear. She lets out a breath, stopping in front of the bars and leaning against them. When he looks up and sees her, he jumps to his feet.

"Triz," he says softly, as aware as she is of the prisoners in nearby cells who might be eavesdropping.

"Ambrose," she replies. "Are you all right? Have you been hurt?"

"I'm fine," he assures her. "I'd just left your letter at the Crimson Petal—they promised they'd send it out with their mail."

"The Crimson Petal?" she asks, frowning. "The brothel?"

At the word, Ambrose's cheeks stain red, evident even in the dim lighting. "I've been checking in on Violie's mother as often as I can," he explains. "How is Pasquale?" he asks.

"Worried, but he's putting on a brave face," she says. "I thought about bringing him, but I'm not sure he could handle it."

"No," Ambrose says, grimacing. "I don't want him to see me like this."

"I'll need a few days," Beatriz tells him. "But I will get you out of here, I swear it."

She considers going against Nigellus's call for caution and patience and making her way to the nearest window to wish Ambrose free, but she knows that would only make matters worse for all of them. If her mother found out Ambrose is working with her, and more than that, that Beatriz is an empyrea, it would tangle them all in a far more dangerous web. And then there's the matter of where, exactly,

Ambrose would be safe. She tells herself that the dungeon is the safest place for him right now.

"I know you will," Ambrose says, and the confidence in his voice twists at Beatriz's heart.

"I don't think my mother knows about the connection between you and Pasquale—though I can't be sure," she tells him. "But she does believe you're in league with Violie. I'd imagine she'll have you questioned."

Fear flickers in Ambrose's eyes. "Tortured?" he asks.

Beatriz hesitates. "I don't know," she admits. "But if it comes to that, place all of the blame on me, all right?"

Ambrose frowns. "Triz . . ."

"All of it," she says. "It's what my mother will want to hear, so she'll be quick to believe it. I won't lie, you and Pas might still end up caught in the crossfire, but at least I'll take the brunt of the blame. As I should," she adds quickly when he opens his mouth to argue. "This was my idea, you followed me here."

"By choice, not force," Ambrose says, not so different from what Pasquale said, but Beatriz still doesn't fully believe it.

"Promise me," she says. "If you need to blame someone, blame me." She pauses. "And if that happens, I will find a way to keep us all safe." Even if Nigellus does think her reckless for using her magic, she knows she wouldn't hesitate to protect herself, Pasquale, and Ambrose if she needs to.

"If I need to," he says carefully. "But I won't. I'm stronger than you seem to think."

Beatriz gives him a reassuring smile. She knows he believes that, but he also hasn't yet met her mother.

When Beatriz makes it to the other side of the dungeon, where Gisella's isolated cell is located, she's mildly annoyed to find Gisella peacefully asleep, curled up on the narrow cot with her back to Beatriz and a threadbare blanket pulled up over her reedy frame.

Beatriz clears her throat, but Gisella doesn't stir.

"Gisella," she says, as loud as she dares. The nearest guards are at the entrance to the dungeon, a good fifty feet down the winding hallways, but she isn't keen on taking chances.

Gisella doesn't move for a few seconds, but before Beatriz can try again, she rolls over toward her, fixing Beatriz with a hooded stare, half asleep and fully annoyed.

"Do you know how difficult it is to fall asleep in this place?" she asks, sitting up slowly. "I'd finally managed to get comfortable on this bed of stones."

Beatriz has never spent time in the dungeon, but she doesn't think Gisella is exaggerating. The mattress looks hard even from a distance, and a winter chill has worked its way past the stone walls, with no fire to drive it off. A twinge of pity nags at Beatriz, but she pushes it aside. She'd still prefer this dungeon to the Sororia.

Reaching into the pocket of her cloak, she draws out Nicolo's letter and passes it through the bars. "A letter from Nico," she says when Gisella eyes it warily.

That wakes Gisella up, and she launches herself out of bed and across the cell, grabbing the letter and unfolding it.

Beatriz watches, feeling smug as Gisella's eyes scan the letter, hope giving way to fury when she reads the single sentence.

"Is this a joke?" she demands.

Beatriz shrugs. "If it is, the humor is lost on me," she says. "Though I'm sure he has his hands full trying to keep his throne."

"The throne I secured for him," Gisella seethes. "He would still be holding a wine goblet for a mad king if it weren't for me."

"Perhaps he might prefer that," Beatriz points out, remembering the last time she saw Nicolo, drunk and miserable and freshly crowned.

If she weren't still half asleep, Gisella might be able to mask the expression that flits over her face—the slight roll of her eyes, the tired sigh.

"Did he tell you that?" Beatriz asks, tilting her head. Pieces begin to fall into place. "Let me guess," she says, folding her arms across her chest. "You argued after Pas and I were sent to the mountains, he said the same sorts of things. He was furious with you. Sending you to Bessemia as a messenger wasn't an honor for you, it was a punishment."

Gisella's jaw clenches, as if she's trying to keep the truth inside. "He needed space," she says after a moment. "But I didn't think . . ." She trails off, glancing away. "He's an ungrateful bastard," she snaps, crumpling the letter and throwing it toward Beatriz. It lands on the floor, rolling past the bars and stopping at Beatriz's feet.

"Unfortunately, that's only half true, or he wouldn't be king," Beatriz says.

Gisella laughs, the sound more bitter than mirthful. She

sits back down on her cot and looks up at Beatriz, her brow furrowed. "He isn't wrong, though, is he?" she asks. "I can clean this mess up myself, especially since you gave me a broom."

Beatriz eyes her warily. Gisella is backed into a corner, beaten down, with no options, but still Beatriz doesn't trust her. She can't. But she needs her, so she has to at least pretend.

"You'll help me, then?" she asks.

Gisella nods slowly, her gaze far away. "I can't very well brew a poison in here, can I?"

"You don't need to," Beatriz says. "Tell me how to mix it and I'll do it myself."

Gisella makes a noise in the back of her throat. "And I'm supposed to take your word that you'll get me out of here once I give you what you want?"

Beatriz smirks. "Of the two of us, I have more reason not to trust you than you have not to trust me," she says.

"I disagree," Gisella says, raising an eyebrow. "You're angry with me. You want revenge. At least you know exactly what I'm capable of, but I don't think I can say the same of you."

Beatriz never thought Gisella a fool, and even now she has to admit she has a point.

"I'm not angry with you," she tells her. "And I've gotten my revenge. Everything I told you would come to pass has— you're out of power and your own twin wants nothing to do with you. My revenge is complete, and I didn't even have to lift a finger to achieve it." Gisella flinches but doesn't deny it. After a few seconds, Beatriz sighs. "Fine, then. What would you suggest, since neither of us can trust the other?"

Gisella purses her lips. "I'll give you almost all of the recipe now, save one ingredient. Once you've upheld your end of our bargain, I'll give you the other."

Beatriz shakes her head. "You'll be halfway back to Cellaria before I discover your 'poison' is nothing but rat piss." She pauses, deciding to hew close to the truth without giving Gisella any information that can be held against her later. "Ambrose was arrested yesterday," she says.

Gisella's eyebrows shoot up. "Ambrose is here?"

Beatriz nods. "At the other end of the dungeon," she says. "It's a misunderstanding, but not one I'm able to clear up. My mother is planning on sending Pasquale and me back to Cellaria in a few days with an army at our backs in order to reclaim the throne from Nicolo. I'd like to administer this poison as we leave, getting Ambrose out as we go, and you along with him."

"So you can take me back to Cellaria as a hostage?" Gisella asks.

Beatriz has no intention of ever going back to Cellaria, but she isn't about to tell Gisella her true plans. She shrugs. "Where you go when you're out is up to you, though I'm not sure where else you would go but Cellaria."

Gisella considers this for a moment. "If I give you the entire poison recipe before I'm sure you'll follow through on your end, I bear the entirety of the risk," she says.

"Am I supposed to care?" Beatriz asks, laughing. "In case you haven't realized, I hold all the power here. You're in a cell, and there are other poison masters in Bessemia I can find."

"And yet you're here," Gisella counters. "Bargaining with me."

Beatriz clenches her jaw but doesn't deny it. She could find another poison master, but not without her mother finding out.

"You can trust me or not," Beatriz says after a moment. "Of the two of us, you have infinitely more to lose and gain."

She turns away from Gisella and starts back down the hall. She makes it three steps before Gisella speaks.

"Wait," she says, her voice heavy with defeat. "You have a deal."

Beatriz grins, turning back to face Gisella. "I thought you'd see it my way. The poison needs to be tactile, not oral. The target is too paranoid about poisons in their food or drink. And it needs to look like an accident."

Gisella nods, brow furrowed. "I have an idea, but I'll need time to think it through."

"I'll be back tomorrow," Beatriz tells her before turning again and leaving Gisella alone in the dark.

Whatever pull you feel, you'll have to resist it, Nigellus told Beatriz, but as she lies in her bed after returning from the dungeon, watching the hands of the tall grandfather clock in the corner move from one in the morning to two, Beatriz realizes that is easier said than done. It isn't just an itch that grows stronger the more she thinks about it until it consumes her, it's as if her entire body is covered in those itches. It's as if she herself is nothing *but* itches.

No matter how she tosses and turns, she can't sleep, and by the time the clock strikes three, she's given up trying. She throws off the covers and climbs out of bed, crossing to a large window and pushing open the glass to let the night air wash over her. She closes her eyes, feeling the stars on her skin, a divine sort of torture.

What if she did make a wish? Nigellus told her not to, but he himself admitted he doesn't know anything about her power or what she is capable of. But the stars know, don't they? They urged Nigellus to create her, to make her an empyrea. And now they are urging her to use her magic. Surely it would be wrong to disobey them. Wouldn't it?

Her mind all but made up, she opens her eyes and searches the skies, watching as constellations roll into and out of view.

The Dancing Bear for frivolity.

The Dazzling Sun for enlightenment.

The Glittering Diamond for strength.

Her eyes catch on one constellation as it creeps in from the south—from Cellaria, she realizes: the Stinging Bee. When she looks carefully, she can see the star she wished on weeks ago just before Nicolo kissed her in a dark corridor. Even thinking about it kindles her anger, not just toward Nicolo but toward herself for being foolish enough to trust him.

Though here, with no one but the stars to judge her, she can admit that it isn't only anger she feels but heartbreak. Oh, she never imagined herself in love with Nicolo, but she did care for him, not just as a friend or an accomplice in her schemes, and it didn't only anger her when he betrayed her— it hurt her. Even admitting that to herself is mortifying. The empress raised Beatriz and her sisters to be too strong to be hurt, to be invulnerable—to everyone but her, at least.

The fact that Nicolo managed to hurt Beatriz, even if only emotionally, feels like a failure.

At least before, when she remembered how heartbroken Nicolo was, it felt like they were even, in a way. He hurt her, she hurt him. But now, she is still here, with Nicolo never far from her thoughts, and according to his letter, he doesn't seem to be thinking about her at all.

That hurts. But as the Stinging Bee arcs overhead, an idea occurs to Beatriz.

Her eyes seek out a star at the tip of the bee's stinger and she focuses on it.

"I wish I could see and speak to King Nicolo," she says, the words coming out quiet but firm.

She blinks and when her eyes open again, she is no longer in her room. Instead, she finds herself back in the Cellarian palace, walking through a dark hall lit by dying sconces. But no, she realizes—the air in Cellaria was warmer, so humid it felt heavy on your skin. Beatriz doesn't feel that, and when she takes a deep breath, she can still smell the roses from her mother's garden. She can still feel the cool stone window ledge against her palms.

Physically, at least, she is still in Bessemia. But part of her isn't. Part of her is in Cellaria, in the palace she never imagined she would see again.

"It's late, Your Majesty. Perhaps you should rest," a voice says, drawing Beatriz to an open door at the end of the hall—one she recognizes belatedly as the throne room. When she steps through, she notes that the room is nearly empty, with only one man standing before the great golden throne and

Nicolo perched atop it, slumped down, crown askew over his pale blond hair, and a goblet in hand. Though she can't see the contents, the glazed look in Nicolo's eyes makes her suspect it's wine, or something stronger.

Beatriz doesn't know what the rules of her wish are here, but when Nicolo's eyes snap to her, she at least knows he can see her.

"Beatriz," he says, his voice coming out hoarse.

Bewildered, the other man turns toward her and she recognizes him as Lord Halvario, who was a member of King Cesare's council. His eyes glide right past her and Beatriz smiles, realizing Nicolo is the only one who can see her.

"Er . . . Your Majesty?" Lord Halvario asks, looking perplexed as he turns back to Nicolo.

"He can't see me," Beatriz says, not even trying to keep the glee from her voice as she steps farther into the room, crossing to stand just in front of Lord Halvario. She leans in close, but he doesn't so much as flinch. Beatriz glances back at Nicolo, who continues to look at her like he is seeing a ghost.

"That'll be all, Hal," Nicolo says. "Close the door behind you."

With a hasty bow and a bemused last look at Nicolo, Lord Halvario does as instructed. When the door closes firmly behind him, Beatriz clicks her tongue.

"Oh, Nico, by breakfast they'll be saying you're mad, and you know what Cellaria does to mad kings," she says.

"How are you here?" Nicolo asks, rising to his feet and coming toward her, but Beatriz holds her ground. Even if she were physically in Cellaria, she doesn't think Nicolo would actually harm her.

"Magic," she tells him, enjoying how unnerved he is. "Tell me, does that make you a heretic too? Though I suppose the magic is using you, rather than you using the magic."

He sinks back onto his throne and takes another gulp from his goblet. "Or perhaps I truly am going mad," he mutters.

Rather than reassure him, Beatriz shrugs. "It is in your bloodline, I suppose," she muses. "Though at least you know Gisella isn't poisoning your wine."

For a moment he only looks at her, before he finally speaks. "How is she?" he asks, his voice barely above a whisper.

So he *does* believe Beatriz is real, she thinks. "As I said in my letter, she's more comfortable than I was in the Sororia."

Nicolo frowns, his forehead creasing so deeply that Beatriz is reminded of how he looked when she used cosmetics to disguise him as an older man when they rescued Lord Savelle.

"Your letter?" he asks. "The only letter I received was from your mother."

A laugh forces its way past her lips before her brain can catch up. Even when it does, though, she can't bring herself to be surprised. Her mother is trying to manipulate her— manipulate them both—and Beatriz has been fool enough to let her succeed.

"What did my mother say, exactly?" she asks him.

Nicolo doesn't answer, though. He leans back in his throne, dark brown eyes on Beatriz, suddenly appraising.

"What did your letter say?" he asks.

Beatriz's mind works quickly—she's underestimated Nicolo before, and that isn't a mistake she'll make again. Even without Gisella at his side, he's dangerous. But if

Beatriz ever did see the truth about Nicolo, it was the side she saw when he was crouched outside her bedroom window, drunk and desperate. She can use that, but she has to be careful. For all that she knows how to read Nicolo, he has always had a knack for reading her, too.

She stays as close to the truth as possible.

"I offered to write you, to tell you about Gisella, though of course I knew that my mother would read the letter before I sent it, along with plenty of others before it reached your hands, I'm sure. I didn't say everything I wished to. I had to keep it simple—that Gisella was in Bessemia, she arrived mere days after Pas and me—he's safe too, in case you were wondering."

"I was," Nicolo says. "He's my cousin—and my friend. He was, at least."

Beatriz forces herself to tamp down her anger, even though she'd like nothing more than to tell him exactly what his friendship did to Pasquale, the shape he was in when he got free of the Fraternia.

"He's safe," she says instead. "Though I daresay he no longer considers you friend or family. I mentioned that in my letter as well."

"Was that all?" Nicolo asks, like he knows the answer, and Beatriz is struck anew by how well he understands her.

"There might have been a barb or two," she says.

"Come now, Beatriz," he says with a slow smile. "I'm sure you remember exactly what they were. Tell me."

Very well, Beatriz thinks, *if he really wishes to know*—it was satisfying enough to write them, but she will find far more pleasure by saying them to his face. "I simply reminded you of the last time we spoke; I told you I'd carry the memory of you as I last saw you, drunk, desperate, and disappointed, to bring me joy in my darkest hours, but seeing Gisella dragged away in chains might have supplanted it."

Nicolo considers this for a moment, taking another sip of his wine. "And?" he asks after a moment. "Has it?"

Beatriz allows her smug smile to falter just slightly, an illusion of vulnerability that Nicolo is no doubt searching for. "I have a large imagination, I can assure you—it's plenty big enough to hold the memories of both of you miserable."

He laughs. "I'd wager, Beatriz, that I'm in your thoughts just as often as you're in mine."

Beatriz allows those words to warm her only long enough for Nicolo to see it on her face, but not a second longer.

"Now it's your turn, Nico," she says. "What did my mother say to you?"

Nicolo takes a long sip of wine, and for a moment, Beatriz wonders if he'll answer her at all. After what feels like ages, he speaks again.

"She wished for me to know that Bessemia's loyalty was to you and your husband," he says, shrugging. "And that Gisella would be treated as a hostage until you were once more seated on Cellaria's throne."

Beatriz remembers playing Confessions and Bluffs with Nicolo, Gisella, Pasquale, and Ambrose, how she knew when Nicolo was lying, just as he knew when she was lying. At the time, feeling so evenly matched only made her more infatuated, but now it makes her wary.

She knows that every word Nicolo has just spoken is

true, as surely as she knows it isn't the entire truth. She also suspects he knows the same about what she's said.

"And what you replied to my mother?" she asks. "I must say, Gisella was quite put out by the message she believed came from you."

"What message was that?" he asks.

"You—or rather someone—said she was capable of cleaning up her own mess," Beatriz says.

Nicolo laughs. "True as that may be, it was only half my message."

"And the other half?" Beatriz presses.

Nicolo doesn't answer. Instead he rises to his feet, setting his wine goblet down on the arm of his throne and stepping down off the dais. He stops just in front of her, so close that if they were truly in the same room, she would surely feel his breath against her cheek. So close she could reach out to curl her fingers through his pale blond hair—or wrap her hands around his throat and squeeze.

"If I just told you . . . ," he says, his voice low in her ear. Goose bumps rise on her arms and she hopes he doesn't notice them, doesn't see how much he affects her still. ". . . what fun would that be?"

Beatriz opens her mouth to respond, but in the space of a single blink, she finds herself back in her bedroom in the Bessemian palace, her head spinning and hands clutching the windowsill in a white-knuckled grip. There, piled on the stone sill between her hands, is roughly a tablespoon of stardust.

She stumbles away from the window, dizzy, and steadies herself against the side of her desk, gripping the wooden edge with both hands. Bile rises in her throat and she forces herself to take deep breaths to calm her riotous stomach.

It will pass, she knows it will pass, and then she'll sleep for an eternity. This is how magic affects the body, but in the moment she feels like she's dying. She knows she should gather the stardust, find a vial for it and save it for another day, another wish, but she doesn't have the strength to do that. Which leaves her with two options—leave the stardust there to be discovered in the morning, alerting the servants and therefore her mother to what she is, or get rid of it. It isn't much of a choice at all. Beatriz stumbles back toward the windowsill and brushes the stardust away with her hand, watching the glittering dust fall into the darkness below.

That done, she takes a step toward her bed, then another, her legs shaky beneath her, but eventually she makes it there and crawls beneath the covers, sleep already pulling at her mind. Just before it drags her under completely, there's a tickle in her throat and she sits up, coughing violently into the sleeve of her white nightgown. When she looks down, she blinks, as if she might still be hallucinating, but she isn't.

The sleeve of her nightgown is now speckled in blood. Her head spins once more and then everything goes dark.

Daphne

"You did what?" Bairre asks the next morning when Daphne and Cliona corner him in his bedchamber before breakfast, before he learns from anyone else that Gideon and Reid are gone.

Daphne and Cliona agreed on how to handle him, though neither of them was keen to explain to him that his mother ordered Cliona to kidnap Gideon and Reid. Daphne managed to convince Cliona that there was no point in telling him about her own mother's orders, though as usual with Cliona, Daphne wonders what she'll have to pay for that favor. Whatever it is, though, it will be worth hiding the truth from Bairre a little bit longer.

"It was the only way to protect them," Daphne says levelly.

"Protect them from who?" he asks, looking between Daphne and Cliona, bewildered. He woke up mere moments ago and his brown hair is a mess, pieces sticking up at strange angles.

"Your mother," Cliona says.

Daphne shoots her a glare—saying it so plainly was not the plan.

"What?" Cliona asks her. "You certainly weren't going to say it."

Loath as Daphne is to admit it, she's right. Part of Daphne is grateful that Cliona has taken responsibility for saying the words.

"You're both mad," Bairre says, shaking his head.

"Are we?" Daphne asks. "Both of us suffering from the same delusion? Is that more believable to you?"

"Frankly, yes," Bairre snaps, running his hands through his hair and taking a deep breath. "I didn't . . . I didn't mean that. But it must be a misunderstanding."

"Cliona had the conversation with her. I overheard it. Do you believe either one of us unintelligent enough to misunderstand that, let alone both?"

Bairre's mouth tightens. "But why?" he asks.

"That, I don't know," Cliona admits. "She said it was my father's orders, but I have difficulty believing that."

"It would make the most sense, though," Daphne points out, unable to help herself, even as Cliona glares daggers at her. "Well, it would," she says. "As far as he and the rest of the rebellion know, Gideon is the rightful heir to the Temarinian throne, and Reid next in line. There are plenty of reasons a rebel faction would want them in their grasp—not the least of which would be blackmail for sorely needed funds."

"We do not sorely need funds," Cliona snaps.

Daphne doesn't dignify that with more than an eye roll. "Regardless," she says, "the safest place for them is far away from here, so that is where Rufus and Violie are taking them."

"Where, exactly?" Bairre asks.

Daphne and Cliona exchange a glance.

"It seemed best that we didn't know," she says.

Bairre frowns. "Cliona, I understand keeping it from. But you don't know either?"

Daphne clenches her jaw. "No," she says.

"Why would they keep that from you?" he asks.

"It seemed prudent to limit the people who know," she says, though to her own ears it rings false. But she can't very well tell him that Cliona was the lesser threat to Gideon and Reid.

For an eternity of a moment, Bairre doesn't say anything, and Daphne worries that he'll go ahead and chase after Gideon and Reid anyway. She doesn't think she could stop him if he did, only hope he went east instead of west. But eventually, he sighs.

"You're sure about this?" he asks.

"It was the best move we had," Cliona says. "And you trust Rufus."

"I trust Rufus," he agrees, but his eyes are heavy on Daphne and she hears the words he doesn't say. *But I don't trust you.*

She can hardly fault him for that, can she? But it stings all the same.

That night, the northern lights finally show themselves. When a scout arrives with the news after dinner, Daphne, Bairre, Cliona, Haimish, and Leopold walk down to the edge of Lake Olveen.

Everyone in their party knows Leopold's identity now.

Daphne guesses that Cliona told Haimish at the earliest opportunity. As long as the truth stays among them, it won't cause any issues, though as soon as Daphne begins to think that, she stops herself short.

Just because she's decided to go against her mother in regard to Gideon and Reid doesn't mean she can avoid killing Leopold. Unlike his brothers, Daphne better understands the threat he poses to her mother and their grip on Vesteria. Unlike his brothers, Leopold isn't an innocent in Daphne's eyes.

Now that Violie has gone, there is nothing stopping Daphne from killing Leopold this very night.

Unaware of the turn her thoughts have taken, Leopold meets her stare and gives her a small smile, which she tries her best to return before Bairre clears his throat, diverting her attention.

Bairre holds Cillian's urn—regal and understated as Daphne has heard Cillian himself was—while Haimish and Leopold use picks to break a hole in the thick ice that covers the lake. Daphne and Cliona wait onshore, bundled in furs and clutching mugs of hot mulled wine.

They haven't talked since this morning, but the weight of unspoken words is heavy between them. Cliona knows that Daphne wasn't completely honest with Bairre—she must suspect, too, that Daphne isn't being entirely honest with her—but she doesn't press her on it. Not yet, at least. And Daphne is grateful for that.

Soon, Cliona and Bairre and everyone else will know the truth about her, the full extent of her mother's plots. She has always known that they won't forgive her for it, but more and more she wonders if she will be able to forgive herself.

Daphne's gaze lowers and she watches Bairre holding his brother's urn, his hands shaking in a way that she doubts is due to the frigid cold. She's struck by the desire to hold him so closely that their twin shattered hearts would melt into one.

You sound like Beatriz, she thinks, giving herself a mental shake.

"Stars above!" Leopold exclaims. Daphne follows his gaze up to the sky, her breath catching at the sight of neon greens, violets, and turquoises streaking across the star-littered sky. As Daphne watches, mouth agape, the colors ripple and spread across the sky like drops of ink in water.

She's seen paintings of the northern lights before, but she isn't prepared for the experience of seeing them with her own eyes. Looking at a painting doesn't compare—this is more akin to stepping inside a work of art. Daphne could search for centuries for the words to describe it, but she would still fall short. She understands how this sight could spawn stories that transcend reality; standing beneath the stars and the lights and the wide, Frivian sky, anything suddenly seems possible, even fairy tales and folklore.

The moment shifts as soon as Bairre clears his throat, and she forces her gaze away from the sky and to him. He has his back to her, facing the lake and the hole in the ice Haimish and Leopold created.

"Cillian, you were the best brother I could have asked for," he says, and though his voice is soft, his words carry on the wind. "When you were alive, I felt like I was forever in your shadow. In most everything, you were smarter, stronger, braver, better than me. There were times I even resented you for that. And now, I would give anything to have you back, no matter how insufferable you could be. But not a day goes by that I don't feel your presence, guiding me." He pauses, taking a deep breath. "I hope you understand what I'm doing, even if you don't agree with it. I hope that one day, you'll forgive me for it."

Daphne swallows, her throat suddenly thick. Bairre told her that Cillian never knew about his work with the rebellion. He said he thought that with time, Cillian would have understood it, but they never had that chance. She understands, suddenly, the power that comes in talking to the dead during a starjourn, even if the dead don't talk back.

She wishes she could ask Sophronia's forgiveness.

"May the stars guide you home, to the rest you deserve among them," Bairre says, the traditional Frivian mourning words.

Daphne and the others echo the words, just as Bairre turns Cillian's urn upside down, the ashes spilling into Lake Olveen.

A moment of silence stretches on around them and Daphne turns her face back up to the stars, searching the constellations for some sort of meaning.

The Lonely Heart catches her eye, flitting into the sky from the south—one of the birth constellations she shares with Beatriz and Sophronia.

The Lonely Heart indicates sacrifice and suffering. An inauspicious sign to be born under, to be sure, but one Daphne has never felt as much as this night. Dread pools in her stomach; how much more suffering can she endure?

The smell of warm sugar and roses fills the air and Daphne breathes in deeply. Sophie. If she closes her eyes, she can pretend Sophronia is standing beside her. Even that smell is hers—a blend of the rose soap she used and the sugary scent that clung to her after her excursions to the kitchens.

If Daphne focuses, she can hear Sophronia's laugh, hear her voice echo in her mind. *I love you all the way to the stars.*

She can even feel Sophronia's arms around her. She remembers all the nights Sophronia would wake up with nightmares, sometimes crawling into Daphne's bed for comfort, sometimes Beatriz's, sometimes all three of them piling into one bed and staying up for hours whispering and giggling together until the sun lightened the sky outside.

She feels the tears on her cheeks before she realizes she's crying. When she opens her eyes, the northern lights are brighter than they were before—so bright it no longer feels like night. So bright they blind Daphne momentarily.

When her eyes adjust, everything around her has gone dark and Sophronia stands before her, wearing the same pale yellow gown she wore the last time Daphne saw her, but Daphne has never seen her sister stand so straight, never seen such conviction in her eyes.

"I'm dreaming," Daphne says when she finds her voice.

Sophronia smiles, and the sight of it threatens to buckle Daphne's knees.

"Oh, Daph," she says, and the sound of her sister's voice, the way she says her name, is what finally breaks her. Daphne shatters into countless pieces, so many that she feels she will never be whole again, but then she feels Sophronia's arms come around her, rebuilding her, and she buries her face in her shoulder, great sobs wracking her body. She's overwhelmed by the scent of warm sugar and roses.

"I'm so sorry, Sophie," Daphne manages to get out between sobs.

"I know," Sophronia says. When Daphne's cries calm, Sophronia pulls away, holding Daphne at arm's length to look at her. And there it is again, the steel in Sophronia's silver gaze that Daphne has never seen before. "But it isn't enough to be sorry."

Daphne swallows. "Is this the part where you tell me the truth?" she asks. "About what truly happened to you?"

Daphne wants to hear it but she doesn't. She finds that she's holding her breath, waiting for Sophronia's answer, but her sister only smiles, reaching her hands up to brush away Daphne's tears.

"You know what truly happened to me, Daphne," she says, her voice low.

Daphne shakes her head, but she can't form words.

"You've always known," she continues.

Before Daphne can think of how to reply, Sophronia leans toward her and kisses her cheek, her lips like ice against Daphne's skin.

"Give Beatriz my love," she says. "Tell Violie her debt is paid. And tell Leopold . . ." Sophronia's smile turns sad. "Tell him I forgive him, and I hope he can forgive me in turn."

"He's a fool," Daphne says, her voice coming out rough with tears.

"He's brave," Sophronia corrects. "It takes bravery to open one's eyes and refuse to close them again, even when it would be so much easier to."

Daphne swallows back a protest and forces herself to nod. She feels the goodbye hanging in the air, knows this—whatever it is—won't last forever, but she would give just about anything for five more minutes. Sophronia takes Daphne's hands in hers and squeezes them tightly.

"We need you to be brave now too, Daphne," Sophronia says.

This time, when Sophronia wraps her arms around Daphne, the embrace is like smoke on Daphne's skin, swallowing her up into darkness.

Daphne comes to, still standing beneath the northern lights. As far as she can tell, only seconds have passed, but every part of her feels fundamentally altered. More than that, she feels broken open, raw and vulnerable. And this time, Sophronia isn't here to put her back together.

She doesn't understand what happened, how speaking to Sophronia, feeling her touch, was possible, but she knows that whatever it was, it was real. She was real.

Daphne wishes her sister had simply told her the truth, but she knows Sophronia was right—she doesn't really need her to. Daphne knows the truth; she always has. It doesn't mean she knows what to do with the revelation—it isn't as simple as washing her hands of her mother, appealing as that idea feels in the moment. There are too many strings tying them together, too much of Daphne's identity wrapped up in her and the role she's been born to fill. But she does know one thing.

Shaking slightly, she closes the distance between herself and Leopold, coming to stand at his side.

"You should follow your brothers in the morning," she says, not looking at him. "Take them somewhere far away."

For a moment, Leopold doesn't respond, but when he speaks his voice is hoarse. "No. I'm not running."

It occurs to Daphne that both she and Sophronia were right about him—he's a very brave fool, but a fool all the same. "Sophie gave her life to save yours. And you owe it to her to do something good with it."

Again, he falls silent for a moment.

"I think running would be a waste of her sacrifice," he says. "She didn't just sacrifice herself for me, you know."

Daphne frowns. "What is that supposed to mean?"

"If Sophie and I had died together," he says, "you and Beatriz would have been none the wiser. You would have thought that Sophie had failed, in some way, that her execution was a blunder."

Daphne wants to argue that, but she knows he's right. It would have been easy to believe that was the case. She would have blamed Sophronia for her own failure, for her own death, and she would have blamed Temarin as well. It would have been easy, certainly easier than blaming her mother.

"Beatriz learned the truth from Nigellus, which was a happy twist of fate, but if Sophronia hadn't given her life, yours would be forfeit as well. She sacrificed herself for *you*, Daphne. You and Beatriz."

Daphne reaches up to wipe away the tears gathering in her eyes. It doesn't make her thankful for Sophronia's choice—if anything, she understands it even less than her sacrificing herself for Leopold alone. The world isn't a better place with Daphne in it, not like it was with Sophronia. It wasn't an even trade.

"The best way to honor the sacrifice Sophie made isn't for me to stay safe," Leopold says. "It's to help you in any way that I can. It's to keep you alive, and to make your mother pay."

Make your mother pay. The words echo in Daphne's mind, but she can't conceptualize them. In her mind, her mother is infallible. Trying to hold her accountable for Sophronia's death is a fool's errand. She wouldn't even know where to begin, and the idea of acting against the empress still leaves her feeling nauseated. *We need you to be brave now too, Daphne.*

"Tell me the truth," Daphne says to him. "Tell me exactly what happened to Sophronia."

Daphne falls asleep thinking about what Leopold told her of Sophronia's final days—how she decided to go against their mother's plans for Temarin, helping to begin righting their economy and showing Leopold how to be a better ruler, how she made an enemy in Leopold's mother, Queen Eugenia—how crossing her eventually cost Sophronia her life.

It doesn't sound like the sister Daphne knew. In the sixteen years Daphne spent with Sophronia, she never saw her go against their mother in anything—that was Beatriz, who seemed to enjoy rebelling for the sheer sake of it. Sophronia had always been every bit as obedient as Daphne, or at least she'd tried to be. Sophronia had disappointed their mother often, but never by choice.

Not until Temarin.

We need you to be brave now too, Daphne.

The words echo in her mind, but whenever she thinks about striking out at her mother directly—telling Bairre the truth about her plots, aligning herself fully with the rebels, even reaching out to Beatriz to tell her she believes her, that they're on the same side—she feels sick to her stomach.

When Daphne wakes up the next morning, she doesn't get out of bed right away. Instead, she stares up at the velvet canopy hanging over her and she realizes that there is someone else she can strike at, a blow she can see delivered without so much as a shred of guilt. Someone who can pay for their part in Sophronia's death.

Daphne forces herself out of bed and makes her way to her wardrobe, searching through the three cloaks hanging there until she finds the vial of stardust tucked away in a hidden pocket. She carries it with her as she returns to bed, sitting cross-legged on the coverlet. With a steadying breath, she rolls up the sleeve of her nightgown and uncorks the bottle of stardust, tipping it onto the back of her hand.

She makes her wish.

Violie

"Violie."

Violie nearly falls out of her saddle at the murmur of Daphne's voice. Her head whips around, eyes searching the woods around her, but there is no one there apart from Gideon, Reid, and Rufus all astride their own horses. Rufus looks at her with raised eyebrows.

In the day since they left the summer castle, there hasn't been much time for talking. They stayed overnight at an inn, but by the time they arrived, all four of them were so exhausted they barely managed a few words to the innkeeper to arrange their rooms, let alone to one another. Still, Rufus has been nothing but kind to her, and Gideon and Reid like him much better than they like her—not a difficult feat considering how quick Rufus is to smile and joke with them, while Violie is too distracted thinking about Leopold and the mess she left him in.

Now, she shakes her head, offering him an embarrassed smile. "Sorry, I think I nearly fell asleep in the saddle."

"Violie."

This time it's unmistakable—Daphne's voice, in her head. She frowns.

"Daphne?" she thinks. She didn't get much sleep at the inn before it was time to be on their way again—perhaps she's hallucinating.

"Yes, it's me. Stardust can allow people who are star-touched to communicate, but we don't have long."

"Leopold—" Violie says in her mind, her heartbeat picking up.

"He's fine," Daphne says, impatience clear in her voice.

She launches into a story about the northern lights, about speaking to Sophronia and finally letting herself believe the truth about her mother and the circumstances of her sister's death.

"Leopold told me everything," she finishes. "And I listened."

It feels like a trap, but Violie can't see the shape of it yet.

"Sophie said to tell you that your debt was forgiven, that you've paid it back."

Violie pulls her horse to a stop, ignoring the confused looks from Rufus, Gideon, and Reid.

"I've no idea what she meant by that, but there it is. Whatever you're doing because you think you owe her something, she's given you permission to stop."

For a moment, Violie doesn't know what to say. "Is this some sort of ploy?" she asks. "Do you think I'll simply abandon Gideon and Reid to you because you mention her name?"

"No," Daphne says, though she doesn't sound offended by the idea. "But you and I are more alike than we want to admit, and I think there's something you'd rather be doing than nannying."

Violie glances at Gideon and Reid, who are watching her uncertainly.

"I'm not telling you to do anything," Daphne continues when Violie doesn't say anything. "But Rufus is a good person, Gideon and Reid will be safe with him, if you decide you have other matters to attend to back in Eldevale."

That is when Violie knows exactly what Daphne is talking around—the only thing of interest to Violie in Eldevale is Eugenia. If Leopold told Daphne about the circumstances of Sophronia's death, she knows the part Eugenia played in it.

"I'm not your assassin," Violie says. "If you want Eugenia dead, do it yourself."

"Oh, I will," Daphne says. "But I wanted to offer her to you first. Consider it a gesture of peace, from me to you."

Violie feels her jaw tighten. Killing Eugenia herself shouldn't be such an appealing thought, but it is. And besides, she already has Daphne's collection of weapons and poisons at her disposal. Still . . .

"If you really intend it as a gesture of peace, don't treat me like a fool. There's a reason you don't want to do it, and I doubt it's because you're squeamish."

For a moment, Daphne doesn't speak. "I believe you about my mother," she says. "But it is in all of our best interests if my mother doesn't know that. If she thinks I've had anything to do with killing Eugenia, she might begin to suspect my loyalties have shifted."

But if Violie does it, while Daphne is away from the castle, she will be blameless. Violie knows it's a compelling argument, but it's no reason to rush.

"I'll return to Eldevale after seeing the princes to their destination," she says.

"We're heading back to Eldevale tomorrow morning," Daphne says. "I may not know where your destination is, but I doubt it's close enough that we won't return before you."

She's right—the Silvan Isles will take her an extra two days from Eldevale—more, depending on the ship's schedules and how long it takes to locate Lord Savelle.

Violie curses, only realizing she's done so out loud when Rufus raises his eyebrows again.

"Fine," Violie says. "You should know I've taken the poisons from your cases—any one in particular you'd recommend?"

Daphne is quiet for a moment, but when she speaks again, Violie can hear the irritation in her voice. "The translucent powder in the case with the rubies. She'll only need to inhale it, but you'd be wise not to."

"I know what septin mist is," Violie tells her, resisting the urge to roll her eyes.

"Then you know how to use it," Daphne replies.

The connection snaps, like a scissors taken to a taut piece of string. Violie blinks, looking between Rufus, Gideon, and Reid, all of whom are watching her like she's gone mad. Violie is half certain she has.

"There's been a change of plans," she tells them.

Beatriz

Beatriz wakes with full sun streaming through her bedroom window, and the grandfather clock in the corner informs her it's nearly noon, though the pounding in her head is so strong she rolls over and buries her face in her pillow, hoping to sleep awhile longer. As she does, though, she catches sight of the sleeve of her nightgown—stark white, splotched with dark red, nearly brown. Beatriz knows better than most what dried blood looks like and as she bolts upright, sending another round of fireworks off in her head, the events of last night come back to her: making that foolish wish, talking to Nicolo, seeing his face, and then coughing blood.

Did he do something to her? Surely that isn't possible—she hasn't truly been in Cellaria, and what Nicolo knows about magic couldn't fill a mouse's teacup. No, it must have been her, she realizes, her stomach sinking.

Beatriz stares at the blood-splattered nightgown sleeve for a moment, her mind spinning so quickly that her headache becomes an easy thing to ignore.

Magic has a cost, Nigellus warned her as much. Perhaps this is an escalation of her usual illness after making a wish.

The thought has a touch of truth to it, but not quite enough to put her at ease. She coughed blood, after all. That is a far cry from a headache and fatigue.

"Apologies, Your Highness." A muted female voice comes through the wall that separates Beatriz's room from the sitting room she shared with her sisters. Beatriz recognizes it as one of her lady's maids. "Princess Beatriz hasn't woken yet."

"It's nearly noon," another voice says. Pasquale. She pushes off the covers and climbs out of bed on unsteady legs.

"I'm awake," she calls out. "Come in, Pas!"

Seconds later, the door to her bedroom opens and Pasquale comes in. "You slept late. Long night?" he asks before his eyes drop to the blood on her nightgown sleeve and he stops short before hastily closing the door behind him.

"Beatriz . . . ," he says slowly, his voice low.

"I'm fine," she tells him, forcing a bright smile, though she doesn't know if that's the truth. As quickly as she can, she tells him about the events of last night, from her canceled lesson with Nigellus, to visiting Ambrose and Gisella in the dungeon, to making the wish to speak to Nicolo and the conversation that followed.

"And the last thing I remember is coughing, noticing the blood, and then I must have passed out," Beatriz says, shaking her head. Seeing the concern in Pasquale's soft, hazel eyes, she reaches out to take his hand. "I feel fine now," she assures him, which isn't the whole truth, but he doesn't need to know about the headache.

"Even still," Pasquale says. "Coughing blood is not something to take lightly. I'll call a physician."

He starts to move toward the door, but Beatriz, still holding his hand, pulls him back. "No," she says. "If it's related to the magic, a physician won't be able to do anything more than tattle to my mother. I need to speak to Nigellus, but I can't do that at this hour without rousing suspicions either."

"I'll go," Pasquale offers, just as Beatriz knew and hoped that he would.

"Thank you," she says, crossing toward her desk and withdrawing a paper and pen. "I'll write down exactly what happened, and while you're speaking with him, I'll distract my mother."

Before they left Bessemia, Beatriz and her sisters would regularly sit in on their mother's council meetings—Daphne paying rapt attention, Sophronia taking notes with a permanent furrow between her brows, and Beatriz only half listening while her mind wandered to more interesting topics. Sometimes she even managed to sneak in a book of poetry, hiding it in her lap.

Today, though, Beatriz is not expected at her mother's weekly council meeting, and by the look the empress gives her when she enters the council chamber five minutes late, she isn't welcome, either. But if Beatriz makes herself a target of her mother's ire, it allows Pasquale enough freedom to carry her message to Nigellus.

It occurs to Beatriz that making herself a target for her mother in order to protect someone else isn't an unfamiliar concept to her. She did it often with Sophronia. The thought is a sudden stab of grief.

Beatriz ignores her mother's glare, flashing a smile at the

other council members gathered around the great marble table with her mother at its head—Madame Renoire, who runs the country's treasury; the Duke of Allevue, who represents the nobility; Mother Ippoline, the head of a nearby Sororia, to represent spiritual interests; and General Urden, who advises on military matters. Other advisors sometimes attend these meetings to discuss commerce or agriculture, but these are the four faces Beatriz is most familiar with and they mirror her smile, if somewhat warily.

"I hope you don't mind, Mama," Beatriz says, returning her gaze to the empress and widening her smile. "I assumed there would be some discussion of Cellaria and I'd like to be kept informed."

Her mother smiles back, though Beatriz suspects she is the only one to see the ice in it.

"Of course, my dear," the empress says. "Though I'm surprised you didn't bring Prince Pasquale with you."

"Would you like me to fetch him?" Beatriz asks, and though she knows what her mother's answer will be, she still finds herself holding her breath.

"No," the empress says after a brief hesitation. "Sit, then, Beatriz. You're late as it is and we have much to get through."

Beatriz inclines her head toward her mother before sinking into an empty chair beside Mother Ippoline.

"As I was saying, Your Majesty," General Urden continues. A short, stout man with a shining bald head, he has always reminded Beatriz of an illustration she once saw of a walrus, though that might be mostly attributed to his spectacular yellow mustache. "The situation in Temarin has grown somewhat precarious."

"Our hold on Temarin was secure, as I last heard," the empress says, turning her gaze to General Urden. Even the general, who doubtless saw all sorts of horrors during the Celestian War, withers beneath the empress's gaze.

"It was—it *is,* but I've received word from some of my men that there have been spots of rebellion cropping up over the last few days," he says.

The empress blinks slowly. "What in the name of the stars do they have to rebel against?" she asks. "Are they not grateful that Bessemia stepped in when we did?"

"Many are," the general is quick to assure her. "But there are some who believe King Leopold survives and call for his reinstatement."

The empress's mouth purses. "There has been no word of King Leopold since Sophronia was executed; it is difficult to imagine a scenario where he is still alive."

"Logical as that assumption might be, Your Majesty, the people of Temarin hold out hope for a Temarinian king to lead them, and many are openly resentful of your leadership," General Urden says.

"I see," the empress says, though those two syllables carry an ocean of venom. "Can these rebellions simply be stamped out?" she asks. "From my understanding, Leopold had few supporters when he was alive and reigning—I can't imagine there are too many hoping for his return."

"While you are correct, Your Majesty, Temarinian pride runs deep," General Urden says.

"The Temarinian people prefer a dead, incompetent king to our illustrious empress?" Beatriz asks, widening her eyes. The rest of the council might think her truly confused, but her mother knows her well enough to detect the sarcasm in her voice. Her eyes narrow at Beatriz.

"You are welcome to stay, Beatriz, but your commentary isn't wanted or needed."

"Of course, Mother," Beatriz says. "It's only . . . one must . . . wonder, I suppose."

"Must one?" the empress asks, and Beatriz knows that if they were alone in this room, her mother would eviscerate her, but there is power in an audience. Retribution will be coming in some roundabout way, but Beatriz tells herself it will be worth it to knock her mother off-balance and plant just a few seeds of doubt in the minds of her council.

"Well," Beatriz says placidly, "perhaps we ought to put some effort into finding the missing princes. Surely it doesn't look good, even to our allies, that you are seizing a throne that rightfully belongs to mysteriously kidnapped children." She pauses. "Allowing for the assumption that King Leopold is dead, of course," she adds as an afterthought.

The empress's pinched face gives way to a smile that twists Beatriz's stomach. It's a smile of triumph, which means Beatriz made a misstep, she just doesn't know what it is.

"In that, at least, we agree, Beatriz," the empress says, turning back to her council. "As it happens, I received word from some of my spies in Friv about where the kidnappers were taking the princes and sent soldiers to intercept them. The spies sent word ahead that the boys are safe and sound, though as the rest of his family is dead, as far as any of us knows, Gideon will need a regent to rule in his stead until he comes of age."

Beatriz struggles not to frown even as she tries to make

sense of her mother's new plot. A plot that appears to sever her relationship with Eugenia—and possibly sever more than that, knowing her mother. Beatriz will have to figure out how to get a letter to Violie as soon as possible.

"I know that Pasquale is the boys' cousin, and their closest living relative, but he seems to have his hands full at the moment with his own country," her mother continues. "I know that my relationship to them was only through our dear Sophronia, but in her honor, I feel obliged to help guide this new King Gideon for as long as he has need of me."

For a moment, all Beatriz can do is stare at her mother, trying to understand the rules of this new game she's playing. Was she responsible for kidnapping the princes in the first place, all to arrange this? Beatriz would assume so, if not for the fact that she could have had them here far quicker. Perhaps there is some truth to the story she's spinning. When the tense silence between them stretches on too long, General Urden clears his throat.

"Very good, Your Majesty," he says. "It would be better to have a solid ally in an independent Temarin than for you to rule over a country that is eating itself alive."

The empress inclines her head toward the general, but her mouth has gone back to appearing pinched, which gives Beatriz some comfort, though she can't keep her mind from spinning. She is staring at a puzzle with half the pieces missing, and she can't quite make out the shape of it.

"Now, in regard to Cellaria, we've received some interesting news from our spies," General Urden says, shuffling the papers in front of him. "There have been whispers of a coup to overthrow King Nicolo, led by another of Prince Pasquale's cousins—a Duke of Ribel."

Beatriz frowns. She didn't meet the Duke of Ribel during her time in Cellaria—she knew him by name, but he hadn't set foot in court. As Beatriz understood it, he and King Cesare didn't get along, and the duke rightly believed his best chance of keeping his head was to stay in his summer manor on Cellaria's western coast.

"The Duke of Ribel has courted favor with other noble families who were outcast during Cesare's reign. It's understood that he is far more popular a choice for king than King Nicolo, who has enemies aplenty in his own circle."

The empress turns toward Beatriz with raised eyebrows. "Well, Beatriz?" she asks. "In this, your opinions might just be of use."

Beatriz resists the urge to glower at her mother.

"Nicolo and his sister spent far too much time trying to claim the throne, not nearly enough time understanding how to keep it," Beatriz says, choosing her words carefully. She thinks about Nicolo as she saw him last night, drunk and reckless but by no means defeated. He has something up his sleeve, Beatriz is sure of it, and she won't underestimate him again, but the empress certainly can. "If Gisella were at his side, I would caution against underestimating them, but divided from her, he won't stand a chance against Ribel."

"Good," the empress says. "And, of course, the chaos around this infighting will make it all the easier to put you and Pasquale on your rightful throne, if you can manage it."

Beatriz stares at her mother. So they're still keeping up this pretense, that Beatriz and Pasquale will waltz back into Cellaria and onto their thrones, despite the fact that no one in Cellaria seems to want them there.

On Cellarian soil, by Cellarian hands, Nigellus said. Having a Cellarian kill Beatriz in Cellaria is the only way the spell Nigellus cast upon her birth will come true. But Beatriz isn't about to give her mother that opportunity.

"How many troops can you spare to accompany us?" Beatriz asks—not of her mother but of General Urden.

Still, the general's eyes flicker toward the empress before he answers. "The empress has assured me that five hundred men will be sufficient," he says carefully.

Beatriz stifles a laugh. "I see," she manages to say with a straight face. "And tell me, General, do you have any reports on the number of troops Nicolo and the duke have at their disposal?"

The general opens his mouth to answer, but the empress gets there first.

"Surely that shouldn't matter," she says with a smooth smile. "You are the rightful King and Queen of Cellaria, and if this business in Temarin has shown us anything, it's that loyalty to the royal line always wins out. Do you believe yourself less deserving of loyalty than two boys who have barely entered adolescence?"

It's a trick question—there is no comparing Beatriz and Pasquale to Leopold's brothers. But the empress knows this, and so does everyone else in the room, Beatriz is sure. And it doesn't change the empress's mind.

"I believe we can manage," Beatriz says through clenched teeth.

"I'm sure you can," the empress counters. "After all, have I not raised you to move mountains, my dear? What trouble, then, is an anthill?"

For one thing, Beatriz thinks as the subject shifts to import taxes on Cellarian silk, ants bite. Mountains don't.

When the meeting eventually dwindles to a close and the council members hurry to say their goodbyes to the empress, Mother Ippoline lingers beside Beatriz, offering her a small smile that Beatriz uncertainly returns. There has always been something discomfiting about Mother Ippoline—a constant cloud of disapproval that hangs over the older woman, and has ever since Beatriz can remember. Seeing her smile, small a thing as it might be, is as strange to Beatriz as hearing a cat bark.

"I heard about your unfortunate experience at that Sororia in Cellaria, Princess Beatriz," Mother Ippoline murmurs. "I'm sure it's left you with a terrible impression of Sororias. You've never visited mine, have you?"

"I haven't, Mother," Beatriz says, working to hide how little the idea appeals to her. If Beatriz never sees another Sororia again, she'll die happy.

"You should remedy that," Mother Ippoline says. "I would love to show you how different our Bessemian Sororias are from where you were kept—for one thing, everyone within our walls chooses to be there."

"Oh, I know, Mother Ippoline," Beatriz assures her. "While I haven't been to your Sororia, I've met several Sisters who lived there and they all spoke very highly of the place, and of you. But I'm afraid my mother keeps me quite busy here. I'm not sure I'll have the time before returning to Cellaria."

Mother Ippoline's gaze flickers to the empress, and Beatriz's follows. Her mother is deep in conversation with General Urden.

"I hope you will make time, Princess," Mother Ippoline says. "There is someone there who is keen to make your acquaintance."

Beatriz looks at Mother Ippoline, unable to suppress a frown. Who at a Sororia could possibly seek her out? Before Beatriz can ask as much, Mother Ippoline rises to her feet.

"Should you find time in your schedule, it would be best for all of us if your mother didn't know of your visit," she tells Beatriz before curtsying and making her way to where the other councilors are gathered around the empress.

Beatriz watches her go, unable to make sense of her words but knowing one thing: she'll be setting foot in another Sororia after all.

When Beatriz returns to her rooms, Pasquale is already waiting in the sitting room, pacing in front of the fireplace decorated with the birth constellations of Beatriz and her sisters. When she enters, he stops, and the way he looks at her tells Beatriz he doesn't have good news.

"I take it coughing blood after making a wish is not a good

thing," she says, keeping her voice light to try to alleviate the tension in his brow—something else she used to do for Sophronia, she remembers before pushing that thought away.

"Nigellus didn't seem to think so," he says, wringing his hands. "He . . . said you shouldn't have made a wish after he explicitly told you not to."

Beatriz rolls her eyes, collapsing onto the sofa. "I'm sure he said far more harsh things than that, but it's kind of you to soften them."

One corner of Pasquale's mouth lifts, just a fraction, for just an instant, but that feels like a triumph for Beatriz. "He said he didn't know the stars cursed you to be a fool as well as an empyrea," he says.

"That sounds more like Nigellus," Beatriz says before sighing. "I'll have to find a way to sneak off to see him again tonight. It won't be easy, but "

"Actually," Pasquale cuts in, "he explicitly said not to come tonight. Apparently your mother has need of him."

Beatriz frowns, sitting up straighter. "Has need of him how?"

Pasquale surprises her by giving a snort of laughter, and Beatriz shakes her head.

"Right. Of course he didn't tell you." She pauses. "Well, surely my incident can't be all that serious. If it were . . . if I were . . ."

"Dying?" Pasquale supplies.

Beatriz nods. "I mean, surely that would take precedence over whatever my mother has need of."

Pasquale doesn't reply, but she hears the doubt in his silence, feels it in her own bones. Surely Nigellus would care if she were dying, wouldn't he? If only because she would be a mystery unsolved and he couldn't abide that.

"I'm not dying," she tells Pasquale firmly. "I feel fine now—it was a fluke, nothing more."

She can tell Pasquale still doesn't completely believe her, so she tells him about Mother Ippoline to distract him.

"What could she want?" he asks when she's done, his brow furrowed.

"I don't know, but if I'm not seeing Nigellus tonight, my schedule just cleared, and I intend to find out. Would you like to join me?" she asks.

Pasquale's smile becomes a little more genuine. "Do you even have to ask?"

Beatriz and Pasquale sneak out of the palace the same way Beatriz and her sisters used to—by dressing in servants' clothes stolen from the laundry, and Beatriz hides her auburn hair beneath a kerchief. They wait until the guards outside her room rotate at dusk before slipping out.

"Princess Beatriz and Prince Pasquale are resting," she tells one of the guards, careful to keep her face lowered, taking advantage of the shadows that have already begun creeping into the darkening hallway.

The guards seem to accept this readily enough, and from there, it's easy for Beatriz and Pasquale to slip out of the palace and into the city surrounding it. Pasquale finds a carriage for hire and Beatriz tells the driver to take them to Saint Elstrid's Sororia—a place she knows by name but has never seen in person. When they arrive, Beatriz gives the carriage driver two gold aster coins and asks him to wait, promising him a third if he does.

As they approach the Sororia, Beatriz looks up at the large white stone edifice, gleaming silver in the twilight. Before they reach the wooden door, it opens and Mother Ippoline steps out, looking much the same as she did when Beatriz saw her earlier in the day.

"You didn't waste time," she comments to Beatriz, her narrowed blue eyes darting toward Pasquale. "And you brought company."

"Surely the stars wouldn't wish me to keep secrets from my husband, Mother," Beatriz says, injecting her voice with sugar.

Mother Ippoline gives a *harrumph* and ushers them both inside, closing the heavy door behind them. "This way," she says, leading them down a dark and winding hallway, lit only by a few sconces.

Beatriz takes the opportunity to survey the Sororia—how different it is in some ways from the Cellarian Sororia she was imprisoned in, and how similar in other ways. It is just as sparsely decorated, just as severe, but here there is some warmth—plush rugs that line the stone halls, a tapestry showing a dozen constellations on one wall. The biggest difference, though, is the glass ceiling that reveals the stars flickering to life overhead. In the Cellarian Sororia, at least the parts Beatriz was restricted to, there was no sign of the stars at all.

"Are you all right?" Pasquale asks, his voice hushed.

"Fine," Beatriz whispers back, giving him a small smile. And it's the truth, she realizes. This isn't the Cellarian

Sororia in many ways, but chief among them is the fact that she will be able to walk out its doors whenever she chooses.

Mother Ippoline stops in front of a wooden door and opens it, ushering Beatriz and Pasquale into what appears to be a small chapel, set with five rows of pews, an altar, and the open sky above. One figure is kneeling at the front, lighting small candles.

"Sister Heloise," Mother Ippoline says. "Your guest has arrived."

The woman turns toward them. She must be near sixty, with lined skin, bright green eyes, and a few gray curls springing out from beneath her headdress. When her gaze moves over Beatriz, she blinks as if she is seeing a ghost. She turns her attention to Mother Ippoline.

"Thank you, Mother," she says, her voice coming out soft but marked by the polished accent of a Bessemian courtier. She rises to her feet gracefully.

"You don't have long," Mother Ippoline says. "If the empress finds out about this—"

"The empress doesn't scare me, Mother," Sister Heloise says. "And she shouldn't scare you, either."

Mother Ippoline sets her jaw but doesn't reply. Instead, she inclines her head and ducks out of the room, closing the door behind her.

Silence stretches out in the chapel, and Beatriz doesn't know what to do with it. She doesn't know who this woman is, or why she's been summoned here, or how Sister Heloise knows her mother. Before she can ask any of those questions, though, the woman speaks, approaching her.

"You have a bit of your father in you," she says, her eyes scanning Beatriz's face like she is searching for something.

Whatever she might have said, Beatriz wasn't prepared for that, and she stumbles back a step in surprise. In sixteen years, she can't remember anyone comparing her to her father, or speaking much of him at all. Most days, it felt as if the empress created her from whole cloth.

"It's the nose," Sister Heloise continues when Beatriz doesn't reply. "I wonder . . . might I see your hair?"

Beatriz and Pasquale exchange a look and he shrugs. Beatriz reaches up to unwind the kerchief she tied around her head, letting her auburn hair fall down around her shoulders, earning a smile from the woman.

"Ah yes," Sister Heloise says. "I'd heard you got his hair. Of course, everything else is hers as far as I can tell."

Hers. The empress's.

"Who are you?" Beatriz asks.

"Sister Heloise," the woman says with a wry smile. "But before I took that name, I was Empress Seline."

Empress Seline. The name slides through Beatriz's mind and out again, catching on no memories. Sister Heloise must notice the blank expression on her face, because she smiles.

"You truly don't know me," she says, sounding more amused than offended.

Beside her, Pasquale clears his throat. "Seline was the name of Emperor Aristede's first wife," he says.

Rather than jog Beatriz's memory, that only confuses her more. "I thought my father's first wife was dead." And on top of that, it only strikes her now as strange that she didn't know the former empress's name. She never heard it spoken in the Bessemian court, heard few references to the former empress at all, except when absolutely necessary.

Though she only needs a few seconds of thought before she understands why the woman standing before her has been so thoroughly erased. Sister Heloise or Empress Seline or whoever she may be sees the understanding in her eyes and smiles.

"Your mother hated me," she says, shrugging. "I won't lie and tell you I didn't hate her in turn, that I was some paragon of virtue while she took everything from me. But . . . well . . . you of all people should know that your mother makes a formidable opponent."

Beatriz doesn't know what to say to that. "You said I looked like my father," she says instead. "Did you love him?"

To that, Sister Heloise laughs. "You don't strike me as a naïve person, Princess Beatriz. I'm sure you understand perfectly well what royal marriages are made of." Her eyes flick toward Pasquale and back to Beatriz and she raises her eyebrows. "Unless you truly are that naïve?"

Beatriz doesn't flinch. Instead, she holds Sister Heloise's gaze. "I'm not naïve," she says. "But if you believe I wouldn't burn the world down to keep Pasquale safe—"

"Triz," Pasquale says softly.

"It's quite all right," Sister Heloise says. "It's more than I ever felt for Aristede, I'll admit, but I did care for him in my way. For a while, he cared for me, too."

"Until my mother came along," Beatriz says.

"Stars, no," Sister Heloise scoffs. "No, I lost count of

the women who came before your mother. But I won't bore you with the details of my failed marriage. I asked Mother Ippoline to bring you here because you are in grave danger, and your sister, too."

"Daphne?" Beatriz asks. "What danger?"

Sister Heloise takes a steadying breath. "I know you will find this difficult to believe, but your mother created you and your sisters from a wish to take over the continent—and to do that, she'll have to kill you. Sophronia was the first, but you and Daphne—"

She breaks off when Beatriz starts laughing.

"I assure you, this isn't a jest," Sister Heloise says coolly.

"Oh, I know it isn't," Beatriz says when she catches her breath. "I'm very aware of just how serious it is."

Pasquale places a hand on her arm and speaks. "What she means to say is that we know about Empress Margaraux's plans."

"You know," Sister Heloise says slowly. "You know? Then what in the name of the stars are you doing here still? You should leave Bessemia as soon as you're able! Run to Friv, fetch your sister, and then flee even farther."

"To where?" Beatriz asks with another laugh, harsher this time. "To a Sororia? Like you?"

"I'm alive," Sister Heloise says. "And if I hadn't surrendered, if I'd refused to go peacefully, I can assure you I wouldn't be."

"And that might have worked well for you, but I'm not a coward," Beatriz snaps.

For a moment, Sister Heloise just looks at her. When

she finally speaks again, her voice has softened. "You're so young," she says, shaking her head. "And there is so much you don't understand."

That raises Beatriz's hackles more than anything else the woman has said. "I understand enough. She murdered my sister, and if someone doesn't stop her, she'll murder the other one too. And if I run she won't simply give up. She'll do whatever she can—hurt whoever she can—to reach me, to kill me."

That renders Sister Heloise silent, and Pasquale's grip on Beatriz's arm tightens. Beatriz continues, speaking through gritted teeth.

"My mother is a monster. If that is all you sought to tell me, I can assure you, I've known as much my entire life." Beatriz turns to go, shrugging off Pasquale's arm, but she doesn't take three steps before Sister Heloise's voice stops her.

"Wait," she says, and though the word is quiet, Beatriz feels it wrap around her, forcing her to heed it.

"Do you intend to kill her?"

In the silence of the chapel, the words seem loud, and Beatriz can't help but cast a wary eye around, as if expecting someone to overhear, but it is only her, Pasquale, and Sister Heloise.

"If I did," she says carefully, "I'd hardly say as much to you, in a chapel of all places." She casts a meaningful gaze at the stars watching overhead. She notes the presence of the Swan's Flight, the Ship in a Storm, the Worm in the Apple.

"If you were," Sister Heloise says, matching Beatriz's tone, "the stars would hardly fault you for it. Nor would I."

"I'll rest easy, knowing that," Beatriz says, her voice

dripping with sarcasm, but that doesn't seem to affect Sister Heloise. She's quiet for a moment, but Beatriz sees her thoughts turning. She crosses toward Beatriz and Pasquale, stopping mere inches away and dropping her voice to a whisper.

"There is an escape tunnel from the emperor's chambers—I'd imagine that is where your mother has taken up residence?"

Beatriz frowns and gives a quick nod. "I wasn't aware of an escape tunnel," she says. She knows about plenty of other secret passages in the castle, but not that one.

"I daresay the number of people in the world who do can be counted on one hand with fingers to spare," Sister Heloise says. "It's there in case the palace ever comes under siege—the tunnel leads to a safe house in the woods outside Hapantoile."

Beatriz's mind is a whirl of possibilities. "Tell me everything you know about this tunnel," she says.

Daphne

D aphne and the others begin the journey back to Eldevale the morning after Daphne spoke with Violie,
and the trip seems to pass quicker than it did on the
way out. As Daphne rides through the woods, she realizes
that she's actually enjoyed her time away from the castle far
more than she believed she would, and as she looks around
the barren trees with their branches draped in glittering
snow, the Tack Mountains on the northern horizon, the way
the stars are so much brighter out here, with so many more
of them visible, she realizes that she no longer thinks of Friv
as the ugly, frigid wasteland she believed it to be when she
arrived here from Bessemia.

She thinks it might actually be beautiful, in its own way.
She thinks she might be sad when the day comes for her to
leave.

The thought catches her by surprise. The future has always been set in stone for her, but that's no longer the case.
It occurs to her suddenly that her future might not lie in Bessemia at all, tucked back safely beneath her mother's wing.
Her future could take her anywhere. It could even keep her
here, in Friv.

Once, that idea would have horrified her.

Now, looking around not just at the winter wonderland of a forest but at Bairre, Cliona, and the others, she doesn't feel horrified. She still feels homesick for Bessemia, for her sisters, even for her mother, despite everything, but she thinks that if she were back in Bessemia now, she might just feel even more homesick for Friv.

At the inn they stop at midway between Lake Olveen and Eldevale, Daphne takes the liberty of going to Bairre's room instead of her own, sitting at the foot of his bed and waiting for him to arrive after he tends to the horses and makes sure that everyone else is settled. When he eventually walks through the door, he stops short at the sight of her. The moment hangs tense between them and Daphne expects that if she lets him, he'll turn around and walk out that door again, preferring to sleep in the stable rather than speak with her after she went behind his back with Cliona.

She decides not to let him.

"My mother raised my sisters and me to marry the princes of Vesteria, but that wasn't our only goal," she blurts out.

Bairre hesitates a second longer. This isn't anything he doesn't already know, but hearing the words from her mouth seems to stun him. Finally, he closes the door and steps into the room, waiting for her to continue.

In her mind, she hears her mother call her a fool, feels her disappointment all the way from Bessemia. She wishes it didn't still steal her breath, the knowledge that she is letting her mother down, but it does. It doesn't, however, last.

"We were instructed not just in diplomacy and the language and culture of our future countries but in the princes we would marry themselves, and in skills that would help us bring them and their countries to ruin so that our mother could claim them for her own."

That shocks him. She can practically see his mind whirling, putting together everything he knows about what happened in Temarin, squaring it with everything he knows about her, everything he knows she's done since arriving in Friv. He drops his gaze from hers, but instead of walking out, he moves farther into the room, sitting in the worn armchair near the fire. He doesn't look at her, but she knows he's listening.

"I knew all about Cillian," she continues, the words coming quick now, like the rush of a river when a dam is broken. "I learned archery because I knew he liked archery, I read poetry because he liked poetry—much as I hated it myself. You said once that he was mad about me, just through the letters I sent him. That wasn't an accident, Bairre. My mother had spies in your court, telling me everything I needed to know to make him mad about me. I knew he was a kind person, and I knew just how to use that kindness against him."

She hates saying the words, as much as she hates the flash of disgust on Bairre's face when she says them, but she feels freer, too, laying her secrets out before him.

"And then I came here and you . . . you made everything more complicated because you weren't Cillian, and I had no idea how to control you, how to destroy you. And, on top of that, the wedding kept getting—*keeps* getting postponed.

All my mother's plans, seventeen years in the making, and I keep failing."

"Did you fail?" he asks, the first words he's spoken since he entered the room. "My father's seal—you did steal it somehow."

Daphne nods. "He has a duplicate, made with stardust Cliona gave me," she says. "I sent the real one to Temarin, to Sophie, who was supposed to use it to forge a letter from your father, offering his support to Leopold in a war between Temarin and Cellaria."

More gears turn in Bairre's mind. "That forgery never happened," he says.

Daphne's throat tightens, but she doesn't let herself cry. Not because she's afraid to or embarrassed to but because she knows if she does, Bairre will comfort her, and she doesn't want that. This isn't about her comfort. She swallows and forces herself to continue.

"Sophie changed her mind," she says. "She wrote a letter to me, telling me as much, begging me to stand with her because our mother's plan was wrong. I couldn't hear it, didn't believe it. I was so angry with her, Bairre, for not being able to do the one thing she'd been born to do, the one thing we needed her to do. I didn't . . ." She breaks off, tears blurring her vision, but she blinks them away. "I didn't know where that would lead."

Bairre is quiet for a moment. "You said that Leopold believed your mother was responsible for Sophronia's death," he says. "Did she kill Sophronia for disobeying her?"

Daphne laughs, but there is no mirth in the sound. "No,

as it turns out," she says. "My mother orchestrated her death because that was always her plan. To kill Sophronia in order to claim Temarin, to kill Beatriz in order to claim Cellaria . . ."

"To kill you in order to claim Friv," he finishes.

Daphne manages a jerky nod.

"The assassins," he says slowly. "Was your mother behind that?"

It isn't until he says the words that Daphne considers that idea. Could her mother have hired them? Daphne hadn't had much of a chance to do anything in Friv yet, but maybe Cillian's death had made the empress skittish. Maybe she already counted Daphne as a failure by then, and it was easier to kill her quickly and take Friv by force as retribution.

"I don't know," Daphne admits. "But it's certainly possible."

"Why are you telling me this now, Daphne?" Bairre asks, and the way he says her name revives just a small spark of hope. He can't hate her and say her name that way, but then, she isn't done yet.

"I insisted on coming on this trip because my mother sent me a letter—well, two letters. The first was vague, but her meaning was clear to me: that if Leopold found his way to me, I would kill him. His being alive is a threat to her rule, after all. Keeping him alive was Sophronia's final strike against her, and a good one. I didn't know where he was exactly, but I knew he was near—Violie had visited me, and she told me as much, though she was wise enough not to trust me with more information. The second letter came after the princes had been kidnapped. She said she had reason to believe they were near Lake Olveen, and that I should find them and . . . well, the words she used were that the only way to protect myself, Beatriz, and her was for the princes to disappear altogether. She told me to leave nothing to chance, that I should take care of them how I saw fit, though she recommended a poison that would be 'merciful.' "

"Stars above, Daphne!" he exclaims, raking a hand through his hair. "You insisted on coming on Cillian's star-journ for the opportunity to murder children?"

"I didn't do it," she replies, though to her own ears it's a hollow defense. "Obviously. I changed my mind."

"The fact that your mind needed changing—"

"I know," Daphne interrupts, wincing. "I won't defend it, I can't. And I can't tell you that if things had unfolded differently, I wouldn't have done it. I wish I could, Bairre. But my mother . . . I've never known how to say no to her. She's never presented it as an option."

"Your sister did," he points out.

"Both my sisters did," Daphne corrects, thinking about Beatriz, the last letter she sent, warning her as plainly as she could, though Daphne had dismissed her as being dramatic. "And I should have much earlier, but I am now. It's why I sent Gideon and Reid to safety, where I don't even know their location. It's why Leopold is still alive and well, though I've had plenty of opportunities to fix that. I don't want to follow her orders anymore, Bairre."

Bairre finally looks at her, but his expression is inscrutable. He's still here, though, which is more than Daphne dared to hope for. He's still listening to her.

"Then what do you want?" he asks.

A handful of answers flit through her mind. *I want you. I want to see Beatriz again. I want vengeance for Sophronia's death.* All of them are true, but none of them are the whole truth. She settles on the truest answer she can give him.

"I don't know." The words come out quiet, barely audible even in the otherwise silent room.

Bairre nods slowly before finally getting to his feet and crossing to the door. He opens it. "Get some sleep, Daphne. We're leaving at first light."

Daphne stares at him for a moment, unsure what to make of her dismissal, though his use of *we* makes her feel slightly optimistic. He isn't tossing her out now, banishing her from Friv or having her arrested on any number of charges. But when she gets to her feet and walks past him out the door, he takes a step back to avoid even brushing against her, as if she is poison personified, and somehow that one small gesture hurts her worse than any angry words could have.

Despite Bairre's advice, when Daphne returns to her room, she can't sleep. Cliona's bed is empty—a fact that doesn't quite surprise Daphne. She'd wager she's with Haimish, which Daphne is grateful for because she doesn't know how to be around another person just now.

Instead of sleeping, she finds a blank piece of parchment and a quill and inkpot in her trunk, bringing them to the desk and sitting down. She stares at the blank sheet of paper for what feels like eons, Bairre's words echoing in her head. *Then what do you want?*

It isn't quite midnight, and the voices of other patrons

still filter up the stairs to her, but she tries to ignore them and focus on what to say to Beatriz. She picks up her quill, dips it into the inkwell, hovers it over the paper for a moment, then sets it down again. The process repeats more times than she can count, but even as the voices downstairs quiet and the inn around her falls asleep, words still don't come.

It isn't that there is a lack of things she should say to her sister, but putting them on paper feels like an impossible task. She closes her eyes and drops her head into her hands. After a long moment, she straightens up. There are indeed many things she should say to her sister, but she sets them aside. What does she want to say to Beatriz?

Dear Triz,

Do you remember our tenth birthday? We were dressed in those hideous matching dresses with the enormous blue bows at the backs? We were arguing, of course, though I don't remember what that particular quarrel was about. Something ridiculous, I'm sure, though at the time I know it seemed of dire importance.

We were standing there, at that elaborate ball Mama threw for us, standing side by side and pointedly not speaking. Neither of us noticed Sophronia, tying the bows of our dresses together, until we tried to move and fell on top of each other into a pile of white chiffon. I can still hear Sophronia's laughter, and still see Mama's furious expression. Her face turned puce underneath all of her creams and powders.

You and I laughed too. It was impossible not to, with Sophie there.

Sophie was always the ribbon that tied us together—sometimes it felt like she was the only tie we had. I know a part of you must hate me for failing her, but please know that is not a mistake I intend to make twice.

There is another ribbon tying us together, though. Mama. Though now I believe—like you and Sophie—that ribbon is a noose. In Sophie's last letter to me, she said that if the three of us went against Mama together, we could stand a chance of outsmarting her. I'm sorry that we'll never know if there was truth to that, but I am by your side now, and the stars themselves couldn't move me.

Come to Friv. Please.
Daphne

Violie

iolie parts ways with Rufus and the princes just outside Eldevale, making her way to the castle as they
head westward toward the Silvan Isles. There is little
fanfare when it comes to goodbyes, but Rufus does tell her
to be careful with a kind of gravity that makes her wonder
if beneath his easygoing facade, he is more perceptive than
anyone gives him credit for.

Once Violie returns the horse to the stables, she makes
her way into the castle. There are no clocks around to
tell her the exact time, but she can guess by how deserted the
halls are that it's well after midnight but before dawn—no
time to waste. She ducks around a corner and hides behind
a marble bust of a Frivian man with a long beard, digging
into her rucksack and withdrawing the powder case Daphne
mentioned—studded with rubies.

This will be easy, she tells herself. All she has to do is get
Eugenia to inhale with the powder below her nose.

And it is easy to make her way down the deserted castle
hallways, not another soul in sight. Easy to get into Queen
Eugenia's sitting room, then her bedroom without anyone
noticing her. As Violie finds herself standing at the foot of

the dowager queen's bed while she sleeps on, oblivious, it strikes Violie as ludicrous that killing a queen is this easy. Surely it should be more difficult. Part of her *wants* it to be more difficult.

The poison powder will act quickly. It's entirely possible Eugenia won't wake up at all. She will simply die in her sleep, easily and painlessly. Violie closes her eyes and sees Sophronia led out to the executioner's block, sees the guillotine fall, sees her friend's head leave her body.

That, too, was a quick death, she supposes, though it doesn't make her hate Eugenia any less. Using the poison powder feels like a kindness Eugenia doesn't deserve. It would be far more satisfying for Violie to wrap her hands around Eugenia's throat, to see her eyes fly open. Violie wants Eugenia to see her, to know what is happening, why death has come to her now. She wants Eugenia to know that she is the one killing her.

The thought surprises Violie. The previous times she's killed have been unemotional affairs. She has killed out of necessity, her victims more obstacles than enemies. It has felt almost clinical.

There is nothing clinical about this, though, she thinks, watching the steady rise and fall of Eugenia's chest.

She brings her cloak up to cover her nose and mouth as a precaution before withdrawing the powder jar from her pocket and unscrewing the lid as she moves to stand beside Eugenia's bed.

Eugenia is asleep on her back, the covers pulled up to her chin and her dark brown hair in a long braid. She looks younger than Violie has ever seen her, but she knows that the illusion of innocence is just that—an illusion. She will not hesitate, she tells herself. She extends the powder jar, holding it just beneath Eugenia's nose and waiting for her to inhale.

When she does, several things happen, almost at once.

Eugenia jerks awake, sitting up straight and knocking the jar out of Violie's hand.

Powder flies, much of it landing on Eugenia, but enough of it dispersing through the air that Violie holds her breath, pressing her cloak harder to her nose and mouth.

Then Eugenia's scream pierces the air and suddenly, Violie gets her wish—Eugenia looks at her, recognizes her, and in other circumstances, Violie would relish the fear that flashes in the woman's eyes, but not now. Now she needs to get out.

"What did you do?" Eugenia demands, coughing, her hand reaching out to grab Violie's arm in a viselike grip.

Violie twists out of it, but already her head is spinning from the lack of oxygen, making her feel dizzy. She cannot allow herself to breathe, not in this room with poison now all around her.

Dimly aware of Eugenia coughing behind her, Violie has nearly made it to the door when it is thrown open, hitting Violie in the face and sending her backward, the cloak falling from around her face as Genevieve bursts in, taking in the scene with wide eyes.

It is the last thing Violie sees before everything goes black.

Beatriz

The day after her visit to Saint Elstrid's Sororia, Beatriz can't put her conversation with Sister Heloise out of her mind. What the woman said about her mother—and even more surprising in some ways, her father—nags at Beatriz's thoughts. And when she isn't thinking about that, she's dreading her lesson with Nigellus tonight, terrified of what he will tell her, what she fears she already knows.

Pasquale hasn't been of much help, though she'd never tell him as much. He's trying, but his instinct is to see the good in the situation.

"The stars gave you a gift, Triz," he said that morning over breakfast when Beatriz confessed her fears to him. "They would never be so cruel as to make that gift a poison. What happened was a . . . misunderstanding. Or, perhaps, a coincidence."

"A coincidence?" Beatriz asked skeptically.

He raised his eyebrows as he took a sip of his coffee. "I can think of several people in this palace who have more reason to want you dead than the stars. We can't rule out the possibility that your sudden illness wasn't caused by your wish at all."

The thought hadn't occurred to Beatriz, but it doesn't hold water. If her mother wanted her dead, she would be, and even if Gisella had the power to poison her from her cell, she's smart enough to know that Beatriz is her best shot at freedom. She didn't tell Pasquale that, though. It was kinder to let him keep his comforting story until they had a real answer.

But Pasquale wasn't finished speaking. He set his coffee cup down on its saucer and leaned toward her across the small table in her sitting room. "Even in Cellaria, they will revere you as a saint when they find out. The girl who can birth stars," he said, his voice low.

The words sent a shiver of excitement or horror through her—she wasn't sure which—and they lingered with her for the rest of the day. Even now, as they climb the stairs toward Nigellus's laboratory together, Beatriz doesn't think she wants to be a saint. She wonders if the girl who can birth stars can do anything else.

Besides, saints die, don't they? It's an integral part of the role, and not one Beatriz is keen on.

More than anything, she wishes she could talk to Daphne. She knows she can't—not only because she doesn't know how Daphne managed to forge the connection between them in the first place and she isn't fool enough to put such words down on paper, but also because she doesn't trust Daphne. And judging by her sister's silence since Sophronia's death, Daphne doesn't trust her, either.

A shiver races down Beatriz's spine.

As they approach Nigellus's door, she pauses, looking back at Pasquale. "Thank you for coming with me. I don't . . ." She trails off, unable to give voice to the riot of emotions running through her, namely the fear. To admit fear is to admit weakness, she thinks. She doesn't know if her mother ever said those exact words, but she hears them in her voice all the same.

But Pasquale is not her mother. He offers her a small smile. "I won't leave your side," he promises her.

Beatriz nods and opens the door, stepping into Nigellus's laboratory to find him hunched over the telescope near the window. He must hear them come in, but he doesn't straighten up right away. As minutes pass, Beatriz clears her throat, but he doesn't move. Finally, he straightens and turns toward them, looking annoyed at their very presence.

"You're late," he says. His eyes flicker to Pasquale briefly, but he doesn't question his presence.

"If you don't expect that by now, you really only have yourself to blame," Beatriz tells him. "Pas is here in case I die."

Nigellus blinks, glancing at Pasquale again before looking back at Beatriz. "I don't see how his presence would help in that circumstance."

Beatriz clicks her tongue. "The correct answer, Nigellus, is *Of course you aren't going to die, Beatriz*," she tells him. "But his presence will help me to not die alone, at least, and he will witness what happens to me."

That causes Nigellus to raise his eyebrows. "Do you not trust me yet, Beatriz? Even after everything we've gone through?" It's difficult to tell with Nigellus, but she thinks he's being sarcastic.

"No," she says simply. "Shall we begin?"

Nigellus doesn't reply, instead gesturing her forward, toward the telescope.

"If I am going to die for this," Beatriz says, "or if my creating a new star or returning it to the sky doesn't work, I'd like my wish to count for something."

Nigellus's brow creases. "It sounds like you've decided what you'd like to wish for already, but I'd recommend caution if you're considering using the wish to hurt your mother. You can't, for example, wish a person dead."

Beatriz blinks. She's considered that, but there is no use wasting a wish on what poison could accomplish. Still, that is new information.

"You can't?" she asks.

Nigellus shakes his head. "One of a select few things a wish can't do. It also can't force love, bring anyone back from the dead. But tell me your wish and I'll tell you if it can be done."

"All right, then," Beatriz says, meeting Nigellus's gaze and lifting her chin. "I'm going to wish to heal someone."

Nigellus pauses, as if waiting for her to elaborate, but she doesn't. "Who?" he asks.

Beatriz smiles. "I'm not going to tell you that."

According to Violie, Nigellus was supposed to heal her mother's Vexis with stardust, but Ambrose has confirmed that the woman is still ill, and close to dying. Pasquale confirmed this afternoon that she is still hanging on to life, but only just. Beatriz isn't sure if her illness is because of Violie's betrayal of the empress or if there was never any intention of saving her in the first place, but she knows she can right that mistake now. She knows it's what Sophronia would do, in her position.

For a moment, Nigellus holds her gaze, as if debating whether or not to push her. His eyes narrow. "Is the person sick, or injured?" he asks.

"Does it make a difference?" Beatriz counters. "Healing is healing, and we're talking about pulling a star from the sky. I can't imagine it wouldn't be strong enough to accomplish this."

"And you won't tell me any more?" Nigellus asks.

Beatriz shakes her head.

Nigellus appears annoyed at that, but after a quick glance over his shoulder at the telescope, he sighs, shoulders sagging. "Very well, wish whatever you like. You know how to do it by now. The real mystery is what will happen after."

And just like that, the small victory she won by keeping a secret from Nigellus shrivels, overshadowed by her fear.

"Right," she says, struggling not to show it. "I'll just get on with it, then."

Pasquale gives Beatriz's hand a squeeze before she leaves his side, starting toward the telescope and waving Nigellus back to stand at the other side of the room. Aware of both Pasquale and Nigellus watching her, she leans over, placing her eye against the eyepiece and looking up at the magnified sky. She finds the Lost Voyager, the Clouded Sky, the Dancing Bear, but none of those constellations feel quite right for her wish. There's no sign of the Stinging Bee, either, but she looks for it all the same, wondering if the star she wished on the other night has reappeared yet. If Nigellus had seen it, he would have told her, she thinks. She moves the telescope toward the eastern edge of the sky, just as the Glittering Diamond edges into sight.

The Glittering Diamond signifies wealth, but also strength. Violie's mother can use all of the strength she can get, if she's going to heal.

Beatriz focuses on the constellation, twirling the gears on the side of the telescope until the stars making up the diamond come into focus. She should take a small star, one barely visible, like she has before, but she needs to be sure. Instead, she focuses on a large star toward the center of the diamond, making up the point of one of its facets.

There, she thinks. *That's my star.*

Beatriz closes her eyes, keeping the star in her mind, as she whispers her wish, knowing she will have to be as specific as she can be to ensure that it works.

"I wish Avalise Blanchette, at the Crimson Petal, were cured of Vexis." She thinks the words more than says them, though she gives them just enough breath that they are said aloud— not enough that they reach Nigellus's ears.

She feels the tug of magic go through her—a subtle thing, gentle as a summer breeze, but it leaves goose bumps in its wake. Though the room was quiet before, it's suddenly so quiet Beatriz can't hear anything at all—not her heartbeat, or her breathing, or the sound of Pasquale fidgeting behind her. All that exists is Beatriz herself, and the stars above. And then it is only the stars, and Beatriz ceases to exist altogether.

The first thing Beatriz is aware of is the cold stone floor beneath her and a pair of familiar arms around her shoulders.

Distantly, she hears someone calling her name—Pasquale, she thinks, but he's so far away.

"Beatriz," she hears again. He sounds frightened. "Open your eyes. Please."

Beatriz feels as if she could sooner lift the world onto her shoulders than open her eyes, but for Pasquale, she tries. It takes every bit of effort she can muster, but she manages to get her eyes open just enough to see the dim shadows of Nigellus's laboratory, Nigellus himself standing in front of her, and Pasquale's face looming over his, brow furrowed.

"Thank the stars," he mutters. "Are you all right?"

"No." It takes Beatriz a moment to realize she's spoken the word aloud. Her voice doesn't feel like her own—her body doesn't feel like her own, even. Part of her still feels as if she is somewhere above, floating among the stars. But already there is a dull ache working its way through her muscles, reminding her just how human she is.

Nigellus says nothing but holds toward her a vial full of shale-green liquid with an opalescent shimmer. Beatriz takes it but doesn't move to drink it, instead looking at Nigellus with what she hopes is a skeptical expression. She wants to raise an eyebrow, but even that small movement feels like too much work.

"An herbal blend, mixed with stardust," he explains, words crisp. He doesn't appear bothered by her current state, not like Pasquale, who is staring at her with panicked wide eyes. "It should dull the pain from using magic. I didn't realize you would take such a large star, but as you can see, the larger the star, the worse the aftereffects."

Her mother would surely call her a fool for taking a

potion when she doesn't know the exact contents, but Beatriz is desperate for relief. If her previous bouts of postmagic pain and fatigue are anything to go by, it will only get worse over the next few hours, and Beatriz doesn't know how she will survive that. She tosses the potion back, sputtering at its acrid taste, but she swallows it down.

"Did it work?" she asks, her voice coming out a croak. She forces herself to sit up, ignoring the pain slicing through her head. Pasquale helps her stay upright, keeping his arm braced around her shoulders.

"Difficult to say," Nigellus says, glancing behind him at the telescope a few feet away, and the pile of stardust gathered beside it, right where Beatriz was standing before she fainted. "You took the star down and you aren't dead, but that's all I can say at this moment. We'll have to wait for the Glittering Diamond to appear, and in the meantime, I'll need to take a sample of your blood before you go, and check your vitals."

Beatriz nods, moving to stand up, and Pasquale steadies her with an arm around her shoulders. As the world lurches beneath her feet, she is grateful that Pasquale is anchoring her, otherwise she would surely fall right back to the floor.

She coughs, and Nigellus passes her a handkerchief. The cough burns her throat and makes her chest ache, and she knows even before she lowers the handkerchief what she will find, but still it makes her stomach turn.

Spots of red against the stark white fabric—more blood even than before.

Beatriz awakes the morning after the experiment with a headache, though the potion Nigellus gave her seems to have helped somewhat. The curtains are drawn tight to block out the sunlight and servants instructed not to intrude unless the castle catches fire. By noon, though, the pain has passed and Beatriz manages to climb out of bed and ring for her maid to help her dress.

As the maid laces up the back of her gown, she clears her throat.

"Prince Pasquale asked to be alerted when you were feeling better, Your Highness," she says.

Beatriz nods, having expected as much, and she has plenty of questions for him, though she fears she won't like the answers. She must have passed out in Nigellus's laboratory. The last thing she remembers is coughing blood again, more than before. She's sure Pasquale is worried, but she hopes he has some answers from Nigellus as well.

"Have lunch brought to my sitting room, please," she says, affecting a weak smile. "I'm not feeling up for anything more than that, I'm afraid."

"Of course, Your Highness," the maid says, tying Beatriz's laces in a neat bow and dipping into a small curtsy before leaving the room.

Moments later, the door to Beatriz's room opens again and she turns, expecting Pasquale, but instead it's Nigellus standing in the doorway, dressed in his usual black cloak, his eyes somber as ever.

"How did you get in here?" she asks, stepping back in surprise.

"You aren't the only one who knows how to sneak around the palace," he says.

Beatriz lets out a long exhale. "Well?" she says. She assumes he's finished studying the blood he took from her last night after she passed out. "Am I dying?"

Nigellus doesn't answer right away, but just when Beatriz is about to snap at him to stop being so stars-cursed mysterious, he speaks, his voice surprisingly soft.

"Not today," he says.

"What is that supposed to mean?" Beatriz asks, struggling to keep her voice calm.

"Magic always has a cost, Princess," he says. "Yours doesn't kill stars, but it is killing you. Not immediately, though. I would have to run more tests to know the exact cost each wish takes from you, but—"

"But using my gift so many times would kill me all the quicker," Beatriz finishes, struggling to hold on to her composure, not to give in to the panic eating at her, the desperation for him to laugh, to tell her he's only joking, that of course magic isn't killing her. But she doubts Nigellus has ever made a joke in his life and he isn't going to start now.

Beatriz crosses her arms over her chest. "Is this the part where you tell me you told me so?"

"I don't believe I have to," he says. "But you know the truth now. I trust you won't be foolish enough to use magic again."

Beatriz opens her mouth to say of course she won't, but no words come out. She thinks about the things she's wished for so far—some of them downright foolish, certainly, but others weren't. If she could go back, knowing what she does now, she wouldn't waste wishes on Nicolo, or selfish emotions like homesickness. But she would make a wish to save her life and Pasquale's, like she did from the Sororia. And she would make the same wish she did last night, to heal Violie's mother—though in the future, she might try stardust first before resorting to such drastic measures.

"I'll certainly be more cautious in the future," she says finally.

Nigellus's dark eyebrows arch up. "You mean you would still use your magic, even knowing what it does?"

"It depends on the circumstances," she says. "But I'm glad to know what the cost is now, at least. Thank you for helping me discover it."

Nigellus only stares at her. "You've always been a reckless child," he says, shaking his head.

The words rankle. "Perhaps," she says. "But I'm going to die someday—sooner rather than later if my mother has her way. Pardon me if I don't see the value in hoarding scraps of a life I'm still lucky to have. I won't waste wishes on frivolous things, but if it means saving myself, or Pasquale, or Daphne—"

"No," Nigellus says, the word coming out harsh as a slap. "It's too dangerous."

"To me," Beatriz says. "And thanks to you, I fully understand just how dangerous it is."

"And if it isn't only to you?" he asks.

Beatriz blinks. "What do you mean by that?"

Nigellus shakes his head. "I've been consulting with other empyreas," he says after a moment.

"About me?" she asks, alarmed. "Nigellus, no one is

supposed to know about my magic. My mother has ears everywhere—"

"I'm aware," he interrupts. "But this is bigger than your mother."

The idea is laughable—nothing is bigger than Beatriz's mother.

"One replied," he says finally. "An empyrea with a gift for prophecies—she believes that your mother's wish and your gift are a sign from the stars, an omen of a fate she's seen coming for decades."

"And what fate is that?" she asks.

He holds her gaze, and while Beatriz doesn't think she's ever seen Nigellus anything but solemn, sullen, or frustrated, just now he can only be described as frightened. Despite herself, fear tugs at her as well.

"As the letter read: *the stars will turn dark*," he says.

Beatriz's stomach twists, but she struggles not to show how much the words unnerve her. "I don't see what that has to do with me or my magic."

"In this prophecy, Princess, you are the one who causes it."

Beatriz can't hold back a laugh. "Flattered as I am to have that sort of power, I believe your empyrea friend has perhaps been drinking too much."

"This isn't a joke," Nigellus snaps.

Beatriz knows that. The gravity of everything Nigellus has told her weighs heavily on her, an unbearable burden. If she thinks about it, she suspects it will break her, so she does what she's always done when someone has tried to lay problems on her shoulders—she shrugs.

"You're giving me abstract, long-term problems," she

tells him. "And at the moment, I have far too many concrete ones before me."

Nigellus's pale face reddens and she braces herself for shouting, but instead a knock at the door sounds and Pasquale enters, his gaze darting between Beatriz and Nigellus.

"Is everything all right?" he asks.

No, Beatriz thinks. *Magic is destroying me, and if some empyrea is correct, I'm going to destroy it right back. Nothing is all right.*

"Fine," she says, offering him a bright smile that feels hollow. "Nigellus was just leaving."

Nigellus holds her gaze, his eyes furious. "Your lessons are done," he tells her. "But we aren't."

Beatriz doesn't respond, watching Nigellus brush past Pasquale and out the door, closing it firmly behind him. When he's gone, Pasquale looks back to her, his face creased in worry.

"I take it that wasn't good news," he says.

Beatriz swallows, quickly deciding just how much she should tell him.

"Magic is having a negative effect on me," she says carefully. "Nigellus suspects it will get worse the more I use it and so I shouldn't use it at all. I believe it's best saved for emergencies."

Pasquale's eyes widen. "I'm inclined to agree with Nigellus," he says. "If your life is on the line—"

"If I hadn't used magic to get us out of Cellaria, we'd be good as dead by now," she points out. "And if I hadn't used magic yesterday, Violie's mother . . ." She trails off. "How is she?"

"The Crimson Petal was celebrating when I arrived," he says. "Avalise's recovery from her deathbed to the picture of health is being heralded as no less than a miracle."

Beatriz lets out a long breath. A woman will live because she willed it. The power of that floods through her veins, chased with something else, something warm and lovely. She realizes it's the first time she's used her power unselfishly, to benefit another person, and a stranger at that. It might be killing her, but it's given life to someone else.

And if Nigellus is right? a voice in her head whispers. *If there is a far higher cost to pay?*

She ignores it. The prophecy he shared was ridiculous, and Beatriz won't give it any more consideration than it deserves.

"Beatriz," Pasquale says. "What Nigellus told you—"

Beatriz interrupts him with a smile, coming toward him to take his hands in hers. "I promise, Pasquale. I won't use magic again unless it is truly an emergency and there is no other way through it."

Pasquale looks like he wants to argue that point, but they're interrupted by another knock at the door before a parade of servants enters, laying the small table with six covered plates and two glasses of lemonade.

"We'll have water instead," Beatriz tells the servant who sets down the glasses of lemonade. She nods and hurries off to replace them with fresh glasses and a ceramic pitcher. When Beatriz and Pasquale take their seats and the servants leave them alone, Pasquale speaks again.

"Not a fan of lemonade?" he asks.

"Oh, I adore lemonade," she says, reaching for the pitcher

to pour water into their glasses. "But the tartness can hide more poisons than I can count."

Pasquale, who has lifted his water glass to his lips, freezes and sets it back down again, looking unnerved. "Is that . . . a concern?" he asks warily.

Beatriz is tempted to lie to him, but she doesn't. "My mother always seems to be one step ahead of me," she says instead. "What with our plans to poison her, I can't help but fear that she's already decided to do the same to me. Logically, though, I know it wouldn't serve her goals. She needs us dead on Cellarian soil, by Cellarian hands."

Pasquale nods, considering this as he takes a small sip of water.

"You're more alike than I think you want to admit," he says finally. Before Beatriz can protest, he speaks again. "I don't mean it as an insult, Triz. But from what I've seen of your mother, you are both stubborn, both conniving, both ruthless. They aren't bad traits on their own, it's how they're used."

Beatriz still wants to protest. She hates the idea of being anything like her mother, of sharing any more than blood, but she knows she is stubborn, and conniving, and ruthless, and she knows where those traits come from.

"I hate her," she says after a moment. She can't remember a time she liked her mother—even as a child, she would rebel against everything the empress said—but it has been a long journey from childhood rebellion to outright hate.

Or not so long, perhaps. As long as it took the guillotine to fall on Sophronia's neck. There is no coming back from that, Beatriz knows. No maternal love to redeem them, no blood to bind them. Just hate, and yes, a few shared traits, for better or worse.

"But if your mother were in your position," Pasquale says when she stays silent, his voice gentle, "if she could save a stranger at the risk of hurting herself? When there is nothing in it for her but lingering pain and another step toward death? I don't know her well, but I don't believe she would consider that for a moment. You aren't like her in the ways that matter."

Beatriz nods, pressing her lips together. She doesn't want to talk about this, doesn't want to think about her mother or her magic or her death. She takes another sip of water to hide her unease. "What did they say, when Prince Pasquale of Cellaria arrived at a brothel, inquiring after the health of one of its workers?" she asks, changing the subject.

Pasquale's cheeks flush red. "No one tried to seduce me, if that's what you're asking," he says. "Apparently Ambrose had told Avalise and a few of her friends as much as he dared and they pieced together the rest when they heard word of his arrest."

Beatriz frowns, reaching across the table for one of the delicate tea sandwiches arranged in a tower—too many of them for her and Pasquale to possibly eat themselves.

"Is it safe, to have so many people know so much?" she asks.

Pasquale considers his next words carefully. "Ambrose is good at reading people," he says after a moment. "And it was my impression that Violie was very much loved by all of the women there. Most of them had known her since she was born, had a hand in raising her. Last they heard of her, she was in Temarin, so they were grateful when Ambrose assured them that she was safe and well. And now that you've healed Violie's mother—"

"They don't know I did that, though," Beatriz says.

Pasquale looks at her for a moment. "They don't know how you healed her," he corrects. "But my showing up hours after the woman's miraculous recovery, asking after her—"

"It could have been you," Beatriz points out.

"I'm Cellarian," he says, shrugging. "And so is Ambrose. But they know of our association, and when I left today, the madam took me aside. Her exact words were 'Tell Princess Beatriz that the Crimson Petal is hers.'"

Beatriz frowns, trying to wrap her mind around that.

"I know it's nothing," Pasquale says, misinterpreting Beatriz's silence. "Though they won't turn on us, I'm sure of it."

"No, I don't believe they will," Beatriz says, shaking her head as if to clear it. "But you're wrong—it isn't nothing."

Pasquale frowns. "How? A handful of women—"

"A handful of courtesans," Beatriz clarifies. "And the Crimson Petal is frequented by powerful patrons. It isn't nothing at all. It's a tool; we just need to figure out how to use it."

That night, Beatriz dreams of stars turning dark, the sky around them lightening until they shift into droplets of blood splattered against a white handkerchief, and Beatriz wakes up coughing. This time, though, blood doesn't accompany it, and when her cough stops, she looks toward the clock in the corner. It's nearly three in the morning, but she suspects she won't be able to find sleep again anytime soon, so she slips out of her bed, bundles herself up in her servant's cloak, and tiptoes out of her rooms and down to the dungeon once more, her feet knowing the way to Gisella's cell. This time, Gisella is waiting for her.

"Etheldaisy root powder," Gisella says with no preamble, her dark brown eyes almost glowing in the dim light.

"Pardon?" Beatriz asks.

"Etheldaisy," Gisella repeats. "It's native to the Alder Mountains, but I believe they're available elsewhere—"

"I know what etheldaisies are," Beatriz interrupts. "And yes, I can get it dried. I wasn't aware it was poisonous."

"It isn't," Gisella says, stretching out her legs in front of her before standing up from her cot. "But I've heard that when mixed with stardust, it can be poisonous if it reaches the bloodstream. I've never used it myself, obviously, but I assume you can access stardust easily enough."

"Stardust, yes. It's the bloodstream that will be the issue." Beatriz isn't sure she's ever seen her mother bleed. If Beatriz were to stab her, she half expects the blade would bend before it dared pierce the empress's skin. "I told you it needed to be absorbed through touch."

"What you asked was impossible. But that ring I borrowed when we helped Lord Savelle escape—the one with the well of poison and the needle. You could use something like that," she offers.

Beatriz snorts at Gisella taking any credit at all for helping rescue Lord Savelle. "The second the needle pierced the victim's skin, they would know," she says. "Besides, if I were going to use the poison ring, I could fill it with a far more common poison and be done with it. Which is why I asked for something transmissible through touch."

Gisella purses her lips. "If they inhale enough of it, it could reach their bloodstream," she says. "The death won't be instant, but it wouldn't take as long as King Cesare's did if they inhale it daily. Might this person, for example, use face powder?"

Beatriz doesn't answer, but she considers it, a plan beginning to take shape. It means she won't see her mother die, but Beatriz isn't sure whether that's a good or bad thing.

"You'll be ready to go when it's time," she says instead of admitting that.

Gisella raises her eyebrows. "It isn't as though I have other plans," she says. "Though I'm assuming you won't tell me anything more specific?"

Rather than answer, Beatriz turns and walks away from Gisella and out of the dungeon.

Beatriz

Beatriz doesn't dare raise any suspicions by asking a servant for dried etheldaisies. Instead, she goes into town herself, with Pasquale at her side and four guards for protection. Beatriz is sure they will report her actions to her mother—sure too that there are more than just the four she sees—but she's determined that she and Pasquale will show them nothing more remarkable than an idle royal couple spending the day shopping.

Beatriz keeps her arm linked through Pasquale's as they walk down Hapantoile's main street, lined with immaculate shopfronts selling everything from chocolates to perfumes to elaborate hats. Though it is a busy day, the other shoppers give them a wide berth, pausing to bow or curtsy as Beatriz and Pasquale pass. Beatriz is careful to keep a smile on her face and nods at each person, but she would much rather be doing this in disguise, sneaking out of the palace after dark like she has so many times before.

But the only people who sneak out are those with something to hide, and Beatriz suspects that she couldn't leave the palace without being followed, no matter how careful she tried to be. Better, then, to hide in plain sight.

"Oh, Pas, you must try Renauld's Chocolates," she says, giving him a beaming smile as she pulls him into the small shop, its large windows displaying elegant dark green boxes filled with an assortment of different-shaped and -colored chocolates that are nearly too pretty to eat. The shop is small enough that the guards are forced to wait outside, but Beatriz suspects she and Pasquale are still being watched, their lips perhaps read through the window. She wonders if, as soon as they're gone, someone will be in to question poor Renauld about what they purchased and what they said.

"Hello, Renauld," she says, smiling at the man who has owned this shop since Beatriz was a small child. He's portly, with close-cropped ginger hair and kind eyes.

"Your Highness," he says, bowing low before straightening up and frowning. "Or is it Your Majesty now?" he asks, eyes darting to Pasquale.

Truthfully, Beatriz isn't sure herself. People have called her both since she and Pasquale arrived. They were never properly made King and Queen of Cellaria, but since they are meant to be claiming that throne, that seems a moot point.

Rather than answering, she flashes Renauld a bright grin. "I've told you time and time again to call me Beatriz," she says, knowing he won't.

"Whatever title you might have, I'm glad to have you back in my shop," he says before his smile flickers. "And I was very sorry to hear about your sister," he adds.

Beatriz's chest tightens. No matter how many times she has heard those words over the last weeks, they always feel like a bucket of cold water being tossed over her head, a sharp reminder that Sophronia is dead.

"Thank you," she manages before hurrying to change the subject. "My husband adores chocolate," she says, squeezing Pasquale's arm. "I told him he simply must try yours. And, of course, I'm selfish enough to want my own box. The largest sizes, filled with whatever you recommend," she adds.

"Of course, Your Majesty," Renauld says, apparently deciding to err on the side of caution.

As he bustles to fill the boxes, Beatriz feigns interest in a shelf stocked with bottles of chocolate powder, angling her body so that her face isn't visible to the guards standing outside the window.

"Don't speak," she murmurs to Pasquale. "And don't look at me. Keep your face toward the window, so they don't think we're conversing."

Out of the corner of her eye, she sees Pasquale do as she says, despite the small furrow in his brow.

"Don't frown like that, either, or they'll know something is wrong," she adds. "Nothing *is* wrong. Apart from the obvious. But I'm fairly certain they are watching us. Reading lips, perhaps."

Pasquale doesn't say anything, but Beatriz feels his confusion. "It's a useful skill, though not one I ever had the patience for, admittedly. Daphne's quite good at it, though."

Pasquale still doesn't speak, and Beatriz takes a breath. "I can't explain it, but I feel they're watching closely—watching me closely. They might not think anything of our jaunt to the florist, but they might. However, if I distract them, there's nothing stopping you from getting the dried etheldaisy on your own."

"On my . . . ," Pasquale starts before remembering he isn't supposed to talk. He turns the words into a cough, bringing his hand up to cover his mouth.

"It'll be a simple thing—the flower shop is just two doors down. Tell them you want a bouquet of Princess Beatriz's favorites—they'll know what you mean. Then ask to add dried etheldaisy. Tell them I grew fond of etheldaisies in Cellaria."

Pasquale is still silent, and though she isn't sure what is going through his mind, she continues.

"There is little risk," she says. "My mother underestimates you, Pas. And no one will think there is anything strange about your buying your wife flowers. The guards won't be paying attention to you always—I'll make sure of it."

Beatriz and Pasquale leave the chocolatier, Pasquale carrying two emerald-green boxes tied with gold ribbons, which he passes to a waiting guard. Beatriz casts a look each way down the street, endeavoring to look as suspicious as possible. She turns back to Pasquale with a bright smile.

"Oh, darling, I forgot I have one other quick errand to run," she says, injecting her voice with a touch too much breeziness. "I wanted to stop by the milliner to buy a hat to send to Daphne."

"The milliner," Pasquale says, uncertain but trying to play along. "Which way is that?"

Beatriz laughs, shaking her head. "There's really no need for you to come with me—I'll only be a moment and it will be frightfully boring."

"I don't mind coming along," Pasquale says, and for a

second Beatriz worries she wasn't clear enough in the chocolatier and he doesn't understand their last-minute change of plans, but then she notes the glint in his eyes and she realizes he knows exactly what he's doing—making her look even more suspicious.

"No!" she says, a little too forcefully, before making a show of softening her tone with a smile. "No, that isn't necessary, Pas. I'll meet you back at the palace as soon as I'm through." Without waiting for his answer, she looks at the guards.

"You should stay with my husband," she says, looking toward the four guards. "It's quite possible King Nicolo sent assassins, now that he knows we are holding his sister hostage."

She knows there is no possibility the guards will let her go alone, but asking will only make her look like she's up to something.

"We're under strict orders to watch you both," the head guard, Alban, says, his eyes solely on Beatriz. She's happy to see a healthy dose of wariness there.

Beatriz pretends annoyance at that. "Fine," she says after a moment. "Though I don't see who could possibly be lying in wait at the milliner. Two of you with me, two of you with my husband, then."

Alban opens his mouth to argue, but Beatriz doesn't let him get that far, cutting in with her most flirtatious smile. "Come now, Alban—you and your men seem plenty capable— surely we can handle a trip to the milliner with only two guards, and Pas is only going back to the palace. Unless you think it's outside your abilities—"

"It isn't," Alban says, a little too quickly. He pauses, eyes darting between Beatriz and Pasquale, and Beatriz can almost see the wheels of his mind turning. "Torrence—you escort Prince Pasquale back to the palace, the rest of us will go with Princess Beatriz." When Beatriz raises her eyebrows at him, he shakes his head.

"The prince is not as easily recognized as you are in Hapantoile," he says. It's true enough, but Beatriz has never had any issue with security, even when she's slipped away from her guards altogether. But the fact that Alban sees her as a threat makes Beatriz feel a bit proud. Still, she makes a show of looking annoyed.

"Is that really necessary?" she asks.

Alban nods. "Unless you'd rather we all accompany you to the milliner—"

"No," Beatriz interrupts. "Three of you is more than enough." She turns back to Pasquale and reaches up to kiss his cheek, taking the opportunity to give his hand a reassuring squeeze. "I'll see you back at the palace."

He looks a bit green around the gills but nods, offering a small smile before they go their separate ways.

Beatriz enjoys taking the guards on a journey—first, at the milliner, she decides that Daphne won't want a hat after all, since most of the fashionable ones would be quite impractical in notoriously blustery Friv, though she buys three for herself, insisting to the owner, Madame Privé, that there is no need to deliver them to the palace when her guards can carry them. She leads the guards to a bookshop next, taking her time roaming its shelves and flirting shamelessly with the stock boy, ultimately buying a stack of books for Pasquale that the guards add to their piles. Then it's on to the perfumery, where the perfumer allows her to mix a custom fragrance for Daphne.

As the perfumer shows her around the store, letting her sample different scents, an idea occurs to Beatriz. One of the codes she and her sisters learned was flowers, and how different blooms could convey different messages. In a perfume, the difference between a rose that is pink for happiness and one that is dark red for mourning will be lost, but there are other flowers that might serve to get a rudimentary message to Daphne.

As she wanders the shop, she considers exactly what she wants to say to her sister and feels at a loss.

After a moment, she selects a small bottle of marigold, for grief, and sets it on the perfumer's counter.

She chooses rhododendron next, to signify danger, though she doubts Daphne will heed this warning more than any other she's given.

Finally, after much deliberation, she picks up a bottle of yarrow, setting it down beside the other two. The perfumer frowns.

"Are you certain, Your Highness?" she asks. "I am not certain those scents are often blended. Perhaps nettle with the yarrow? Or vanilla with the rhododendron? Marigold with citrus might be a more balanced combination?"

Beatriz pretends to consider it. "No," she says after a moment. "I believe my sister deserves a perfume like no one else has ever had—a perfume as unique as she is."

The perfumer hesitates a second longer but finally nods, taking the bottles. Beatriz follows her to her workbench, watching as she adds a few drops of each scent to an amber-colored crystal bottle. She screws on the top with its attached coral-pink atomizer.

"Would you like to sample it before I wrap it up?" she asks.

Beatriz nods and the woman squeezes the atomizer, emitting a cloud of perfume. Beatriz leans in and inhales.

It is not a scent she herself would wear, and she knows Daphne prefers more subtle perfumes, but the smell is inoffensive. Certainly not odd enough to merit suspicion.

"It's perfect—Daphne will love it," she tells the woman. "I'm sure it will bring to mind all of the wonderful days we spent wandering Mama's garden. Could I trouble you to have it sent directly to Friv?"

After the perfumery, Beatriz finally returns to the palace, sensing her guards' confusion all the way back. When she reaches her rooms and closes the door firmly behind her, Pasquale is already waiting, sitting on the overstuffed sofa with a bouquet of flowers resting on his knee. When he sees her, he bolts to stand.

"Any trouble?" she asks.

He shakes his head, holding the flowers out to her. It's her usual assortment of hydrangeas, orchids, and hellebores, but she sees five stalks of dried etheldaisies mixed in.

"I actually found it fun," he admits, somewhat sheepishly. "All the deception and sneaking about."

Beatriz laughs and takes one of the etheldaisies out. She examines it closely before glancing at Pasquale.

"Have you ever heard that etheldaisies are poisonous?" she asks, suddenly wary. After everything that's transpired between them, she would be a fool to take Gisella at her word.

Pasquale shakes his head. "But I asked the florist—not in any way that would raise suspicions," he adds quickly when Beatriz gives him a horrified look. "I simply told her that there was an old Cellarian wives' tale about etheldaisies and I didn't want to accidentally give my wife flowers that might hurt her."

Beatriz relaxes slightly. "And what did she say?" she asks.

"She said not to worry—the only way they would be toxic is if they found their way into your bloodstream in unfathomably great quantities. Which would be impossible."

"But Gisella is right: stardust would amplify the poison, making it more potent," Beatriz says. She turns the stem of the etheldaisy in her hands. She has the poison, now all she has to do is grind it and mix it in with her mother's face powder. The thought of that makes her feel ill, if only fleetingly. She doesn't think she will shed a tear for the empress, not after learning she had Sophronia killed, yet the woman is still her mother.

It needs to be done, she thinks. And since no one else will do it, it's up to her.

Daphne

When Daphne and the others arrive back at Eldevale Castle, they find it in chaos.

"Someone tried to murder Lady Eunice last night," the stable master explains to her as he and a handful of stable-boys take charge of the horses. Daphne's mind sticks on *tried to* and she struggles to hide a grimace. Clearly, she's over-estimated Violie's talents. She's so engrossed in thinking about how she can do the deed properly that she nearly misses the stable master's next words. "The villain has been caught, luckily, and Lady Eunice is expected to recover, though her maid wasn't so lucky. It has put everyone in quite a state today."

"Understandably so," Daphne manages to get out. She thinks she's hiding the maelstrom of her emotions well enough, but as soon as the stable master leaves, Bairre takes hold of her elbow, leading her away from the others.

"Daphne, what did you do?" he asks, and despite the tone of his voice, she's almost glad that he's speaking to her at all. He hasn't said so much as a word in her direction since their talk at the inn the night before.

"Nothing," Daphne says, which is true enough. She didn't

do anything, apart from pointing Violie in Eugenia's direction. Before she can explain further, Leopold approaches.

"Someone tried to kill my mother?" he says, not sounding remotely upset.

Daphne glances between them. "I . . . used stardust to communicate with Violie. I mentioned that if she felt confident your brothers would be safe in Rufus's care, it might be beneficial for her to take care of Eugenia herself."

"You what?" Bairre asks.

Daphne exhales. "I know I have plenty of sins to atone for, Bairre, but arranging Eugenia's assassination isn't one of them. Tell him, Leopold."

Leopold looks at Bairre. "She isn't wrong about that," he says. "The stars won't darken when my mother's life ends. But you can't let Violie pay the price for it."

Dread pools in Daphne's stomach and she knows Leopold is right. Daphne should have handled matters herself, even if it upset her mother, even if it revealed Daphne's new allegiances. *We need you to be brave now too, Daphne,* Sophronia's voice echoes in her mind.

"No, of course I won't," Daphne says to Leopold. "But we need to think this through carefully—the reason I sent Violie to do it without me was so my mother would be unaware that my loyalties have shifted. If she knows they have, we'd best be braced for war."

Her gaze lingers on Bairre. In an ideal world, she would have given him time to sort out his feelings and his alliances, to process everything she's told him, but time is a luxury they no longer have.

Bairre holds her gaze for a moment and eventually gives a short jerk of a nod.

"Do what needs to be done," he says, the words stilted.

It isn't the understanding or forgiveness Daphne hoped for, but it's enough, for now.

Daphne finds King Bartholomew in his study with two advisors she recognizes—Cliona's father, Lord Panlington, and Lord Yates—the three of them deep in what looks to be a very serious conversation. When she enters the room the three men look up at her in surprise before the king rises to his feet, his two advisors following a beat later and all three offering deep bows.

"Daphne," Bartholomew says, surprised. "I didn't know you'd returned."

"We've only just," Daphne says with a smile she hopes is bright enough to hide her fear. "But Bairre and I wanted you to be the first to hear the good news."

King Bartholomew raises his eyebrows. "Good news?"

Daphne glances sideways at Panlington and Yates, both of whom are watching her with unmasked curiosity. She returns her gaze to King Bartholomew and lowers her voice. "It might be best if we spoke in private?"

"Of course," King Bartholomew says, waving a hand to dismiss his advisors. When they are gone and King Bartholomew and Daphne are alone in the study, she smiles.

"We were able to locate Gideon and Reid," she says. "They are alive and safe."

"That, at least, *is* good news," King Bartholomew says,

running a hand through his short-cropped graying hair. "Where are they now?"

"On their way somewhere safe," Daphne says. At King Bartholomew's confused look, she continues. "It did not seem the castle was a very safe place for them—I'm sure their mother will agree. We were able to locate an ally of their family's willing to shelter them. Eugenia is welcome to join them as well," she adds, a lie, but what she hopes is a believable one. That Gideon and Reid are on their way to an ally of their family's is the only information Daphne could get from Leopold, and she hopes it's enough for the king.

King Bartholomew lets out a sigh and sinks back down into his chair. "While I do wish I'd been consulted on the matter, I believe the two of you made the right decision," he says. "I don't believe those boys or their mother are safe under my roof."

Daphne feigns confusion before letting understanding dawn on her face. "I heard word on my arrival that someone had been poisoned," she says slowly. "Tell me it wasn't Eugenia."

"I'm afraid so," King Bartholomew says.

"Is she . . . ?" Daphne asks, letting the words trail off. She knows Eugenia isn't dead, but she needs to know how severely she's been injured. The poison she told Violie to use is a potent one if used at close range, but even in smaller doses it can cause long-lasting complications—muscular paralysis, bleeding in the brain, seizures.

"The physician says she'll live," Bartholomew says. "But she'll have quite a long recovery ahead of her. Her maid wasn't so lucky."

Daphne bites her lip and glances away, letting her brow furrow. "I just don't understand why someone would do something like this," she says.

"The assassin herself was poisoned with the powder she intended to use on Eugenia. But as soon as she wakes, I'll make sure I get that answer," he says.

Daphne pauses. At least Violie is alive, though if she was poisoned, she might face the same long-term effects as Eugenia. And on top of that, Daphne knows the Frivians have no qualms about torture—it was used against those who arranged her own assassination attempts. King Bartholomew must misread the worry on her face.

"We have no reason to believe the girl was working with anyone else," he says. "I can assure you the castle is quite safe."

"Oh, that is a relief," Daphne says before pausing. "How sure are you that she was responsible and working on her own? I'm having difficulty imagining a girl capable of assassinating a queen all by herself. Perhaps it was someone else and she was merely in the wrong place at the wrong time?"

It's a long shot, but Daphne has made convincing arguments out of less.

King Bartholomew frowns. "I find that difficult to believe, given the circumstances," he says. "But, of course, she will be given a trial to defend herself and we will consider all evidence carefully before reaching a decision."

"Of course," Daphne says. "And when will that take place?"

"That depends largely on her recovery," he says. "But I would like this matter dealt with as soon as possible."

"I'm sure we all would," Daphne says. She decides to

press her luck further. "Perhaps I should speak with the assassin. It's possible this is the same one who targeted me, is it not? If so, I would like the chance to interrogate her myself. It's likely my doing so would unnerve her and give us our best chance of getting answers."

King Bartholomew shakes his head. "Much as I admire your courage, I can't allow it. The assassin might be a girl close to your own age, but she has proven herself dangerous, and it would be a mistake to underestimate what she's capable of."

Daphne wants to argue but forces herself to bite her tongue. She dips into a shallow curtsy. "Of course, Your Majesty. Please do keep me informed, both about Eugenia's recovery and the assassin's trial."

"Of course, Daphne," King Bartholomew says, inclining his head toward her. "Try to get some rest in the meantime, I'm sure your journey was very tiring."

Daphne knows there's little rest in her near future, but she nods and starts toward the door. When she reaches it, she pauses, looking back at King Bartholomew.

"It was a lovely ceremony, for Cillian," she tells him. "Bairre gave a wonderful speech, and the northern lights were a sight to behold."

King Bartholomew looks up at her again and offers a tight smile. "I'm glad to hear it," he says. "I was sorry I couldn't be there myself, but I hope he felt me there nonetheless."

Daphne gives him one final nod before leaving him alone in his study.

Daphne has just barely finished her bath and is pulling her dressing gown on when there is a knock at her door.

"Come in," she calls, tying the sash around her waist. She assumes it will be her maid, but when the door opens she turns to find Bairre in the doorway. "Oh," she says, surprised, crossing her arms over her chest. She's fully covered, she reminds herself, and he's seen her in a nightgown, which showed significantly more skin. But still, he blushes as he closes the door behind him.

"I'm sorry," he says, not quite looking at her. "But it's urgent."

Bairre, she notes, did not take the time to bathe, though he at least appears to have washed his face and changed out of his riding clothes.

"You confirmed it's Violie under arrest?" she asks, her stomach sinking even before he answers.

"It's her," Bairre says. "What did my father say?"

Daphne fills him in on the conversation she had with the king and Bairre nods, brow furrowed in thought.

"That fits with what I learned myself," he admits. "Eugenia's scream seems to have alerted her maid, who entered the room, surprising Violie into dropping the powder. Eugenia and Violie got smaller doses, but the maid died almost instantly."

Daphne wonders if she should make an effort to summon guilt over the unknown woman, but there's no time for that.

"Is that all the evidence?" she asks instead.

Bairre nods. "She was discovered in Eugenia's bedchamber

after a scream was heard. Three women were found inside: Violie, Eugenia, and the dead maid," he explains. "That's all the evidence, but it's more than enough."

"Only if Eugenia is in a state to identify her," Daphne points out.

"Even if she isn't," Bairre says. "Immediately after guards arrived, Eugenia pointed Violie out. By then she couldn't speak, but the guards believed her meaning was clear."

Daphne's mind spins. "Have they set a date for the trial?" she asks.

"The day after tomorrow," he says. "The physician says that if Violie hasn't woken by then, she never will."

Daphne doesn't let her mind linger on that thought. "Violie can say the maid did it," she says instead. "That she happened to be walking by when she heard Eugenia's scream."

Bairre winces.

"What?" Daphne asks, dread pooling in her belly.

"There is another witness," he says. "The cook, who Violie was working for, claims Violie—or Vera as she's been calling herself—was fixated on Eugenia. She said something about a threatening cake?"

Daphne blinks, trying and failing to wrap her mind around what, exactly, a threatening cake is.

Bairre continues. "The story making its way around is that she was an angry Temarinian rebel who followed Eugenia here and has been plotting revenge for weeks."

"Not the truth, but not so far from it either," Daphne says, sinking down onto her bed. "I have to speak with her. Violie, I mean."

"There's more," Bairre says slowly. "They're saying she's responsible for the attacks on you and on our wedding."

"Who is saying that?" Daphne asks, frowning.

Bairre doesn't answer right away. "I traced the rumor back to Lord Panlington," he says.

Daphne stares at him. "The rebels are using her as a scapegoat too," she says.

"It seems they . . . underestimated the negative effects of the bomb," he says slowly.

Daphne can't help but snort. "What, killing Fergal?" she asks. "I didn't realize he was so popular."

"He wasn't," Bairre says. "You, however, are."

It takes Daphne a moment to understand what he's saying. "Me," she says.

"The story has spread throughout Friv now, carried by the common people and the lairds who came for the Wedding That Wasn't, as it's come to be called. Apparently everyone is talking about the foreign princess who was supposed to crumple at the first gale winds, but instead survived three assassination attempts—four if you include the wedding, which most do—and never cowered, a strong horsewoman and excellent archer who puts many Frivians to shame, and that was before you insisted on trekking across Friv in the dead of winter to partake in the funeral rites of the betrothed you never got to meet. Even in the few hours since I've been back I've heard outlandish tales of stags in the woods bowing to you as their queen, of how on our journey to Lake Olveen, you and your horse left a trail of daffodils in your wake, how when you made your crossing through the river into Friv, you did so nude so that nothing would come between you and your country."

Daphne can't help but laugh. "Well, that one you know is a lie," she says, remembering how cold and miserable she was that day. If anything, she'd wished for *more* clothes. Bairre, however, doesn't laugh.

"It isn't a lie, not really. It's a myth," he says.

A myth they're building around me, Daphne thinks, trying and failing to understand that.

When she doesn't speak, Bairre continues.

"If the rebellion had set off a bomb at our wedding days after you'd arrived, they could have taken credit and people would have celebrated, Daphne. Maybe more so if you'd been killed as well. No one wanted you here—you knew that as well as anyone. But now . . ." He trails off.

"Now, I'm a folk heroine come to life, and the rebels have made themselves the villains of the story," Daphne finishes for him.

"It isn't the image they want to portray," he admits.

"No, I'm sure it's not," she says. She glances at the clock in her room—it's late, nearly midnight. "Nothing can be done tonight, Bairre," she tells him. "But tomorrow, I think it's long past time I spoke to Lord Panlington myself."

Bairre doesn't like that idea—she notices the way his frown deepens, his silver eyes narrow. Finally, though, he nods. "I'll arrange it," he says.

"Thank you," she says before hesitating. "Really, Bairre. I'm sure the last thing you want to be doing is helping me clean up my mess."

For a moment, he doesn't answer, but finally he lets out a long exhale. "The thing about your messes, Daphne, is that they tend to drag the rest of us into them by force."

He turns to go, but by the time he reaches the door, Daphne's anger catches up to her. "That's very rich, coming from someone who let a bomb knock me unconscious," she snaps.

Bairre freezes, and even though his back is to her, she knows her words hit their mark.

"I've told you the truth, Bairre, about everything, and there may be a lot that I've done that you might view as unforgivable, but we both know that goes both ways. The only difference is that I've told you my secrets; you're still keeping plenty of yours."

For just an instant, Daphne thinks he might turn back toward her, and she wishes he would—even if only to fight. But instead, he walks out of her room and closes the door firmly behind him.

Violie

Violie's head feels like it's crammed full of smoke and raw wool, but at least she isn't dead. She remembers enough about what happened in Eugenia's bedchamber to know that the fact that she is alive is little more than pure luck.

She also isn't in a dungeon—at least not the kind she might have imagined. It's a small room, with a door and a window, though the window is too small for a person to climb through and she knows without trying that the door is locked from the outside. But even if it isn't, it might as well be. Violie can barely move her limbs, let alone stand up. Her entire body feels like it is weighed down with sandbags.

So much for a quick and peaceful death. She wonders if she succeeded in killing Eugenia, or if the dowager queen is somewhere else, just as miserable as Violie.

The door opens and Violie lifts her head off the thin pillow, opening her eyes just wide enough to see one figure slip inside while a second lingers in the doorway. She blinks and they come into focus—Leopold and Bairre.

"The guards change in five minutes, so be quick," Bairre tells Leopold before closing the door again.

Leopold glances at the closed door before coming toward her.

"Violie, can you hear me?" he asks.

"A little too well," she says, managing to shift in bed just enough to sit up a little. "I'm not deaf, I can assure you."

Relief floods his face. "Thank the stars," he murmurs.

Thinking about the series of calamities that brought Violie here, she doesn't feel as if she owes the stars much gratitude at all, but Leopold is right—she is alive.

"Daphne . . . ," she starts.

"She told me everything," he says. "She shouldn't have asked this of you."

Violie laughs, the movement painful. "She didn't tell you everything, then," she says. "Daphne didn't *ask* anything of me. She suggested it, yes, but it was my decision."

Leopold frowns. "Why?"

"Daphne pointed out that if Eugenia died while Daphne was nearby, the empress would suspect her loyalties had shifted and it's better for the time being that she believes Daphne is loyal to her," Violie says.

"I understand that, but there were plenty of other ways," he says. "You should have talked to me about it, Violie. She's my mother."

"Exactly," Violie replies. When his frown deepens, she sighs. "You've said plenty of times now that you hate her for what she did to Sophie, that you'd kill her yourself."

"You think I didn't mean that?" he asks, shaking his head. "That I have any compassion left for her?"

"I do," Violie says. Leopold opens his mouth, but before he can argue, Violie continues. "I think that if we'd discussed it, you would have insisted on being the one to kill her, that you would have seen it as your responsibility. And you never would have forgiven yourself for it."

"You think I'm that weak?" he asks, taking a step back. "I know you see me as a sheltered, spoiled boy, Violie, and over the last few weeks, I've proven that time and again—"

"I don't see you as sheltered or spoiled," Violie interrupts. "Well, maybe sheltered, but in the same way you see me as being some kind of bloodthirsty murderess."

He pauses. "I don't see you like that, either," he says.

Violie bites her lip. "If I'd waited for you, discussed it with you, let you be the one to take her life, you would have done it without question, Leopold. But you aren't a murderer. And I didn't want to make you one."

Leopold doesn't answer, so Violie continues. "And beyond that, she is your mother. She's Gideon and Reid's mother. Would you have been able to look them in the eye and tell them what you'd done?"

He winces.

"Sophronia made me promise to protect you, and I don't think she was only talking about keeping you alive, Leopold."

Violie watches as Leopold's throat works.

"Daphne said that Sophie released you from that promise," he says finally.

Violie shrugs, even that small movement sending another bolt of pain through her. "She did," she says. "But maybe I don't want to see you become a murderer either, Leo."

For a moment, Leopold falls silent. "Thank you, Vi," he says quietly.

"Don't thank me," she says. "Your mother's still alive and I'll hang for attempted murder." She pauses. "Do they hang murderers in Friv? I know they burn them in Cellaria, but I'm not sure—"

"You aren't going to hang or burn," Leopold says. "I promise you that. Do you trust me?"

Violie looks at him, so different from the boy who appeared out of thin air in the cave nearly a month ago, fragile and wounded. Then, she couldn't even trust him to follow simple directions like stay quiet or don't go running back to Kavelle, where everyone wants you dead. Now, though?

"I trust you," she tells him.

Daphne

Daphne wakes to news that Violie—or rather, Vera— has regained consciousness, and that her trial will take place tomorrow night, which gives Daphne little time to execute her plan. Or, rather, the half plan she's managed to formulate while tossing and turning all night. Now, she's groggy and exhausted as her maid bustles around her room, relaying gossip about who she believes Vera to be, but Daphne is no closer to figuring out how to save Violie's life without implicating herself.

Though there are other matters she needs to take care of first, and she hopes a plan for the rest will occur to her before it's too late.

Breakfast with Lord Panlington has been set up in the conservatory, and Daphne is the last to arrive. When she passes the guards standing at the entrance and steps into the glass-walled space full of an assortment of flowers and trees, she sees Bairre and Cliona seated at a round table that overlooks the now-frozen garden below. Lord Panlington sits with his back to her, staying seated even when Bairre gets to his feet to pull out Daphne's chair for her.

"Good morning," she says, flashing her brightest smile at each of them, finally settling on Lord Panlington. "I hope I didn't keep you long?"

"This entire thing is a waste of my time, Princess," Lord Panlington says, sipping his coffee. "What little more you chose to waste so that you could make an entrance is negligible."

Daphne holds fast to her smile. "I'll make a deal with you, then, my lord—*I* won't waste your time with pleasantries if *you* don't waste my time pretending you don't need me more than I need you right now."

Cliona snorts into her teacup, earning a glare from her father. She straightens up and sets the teacup down, placing her hands on her lap. "This morning, my maid asked me if it was true that Princess Daphne bled stardust," she says conversationally. "Of course I told her that was ridiculous, but I don't think she believed me."

"I'll be sure to be extra mindful of people approaching me with sharp objects," Daphne says.

"I heard someone call her Saint Daphne," Bairre adds.

Lord Panlington shoots him a glare. "There's an easy enough way to put an end to *that*. After everything the two of you have told me, it would be prudent to simply have her killed."

"Clearly, you don't know much about saints," Daphne tells him. "But let me assure you, killing me is the last thing you want to do."

Lord Panlington sits back in his chair, folding his hands

over his belly. "Enlighten me, then," he says. "What should I do with a scheming foreign princess who has admitted she's done everything she can to destroy my country?"

Daphne smiles. "You should thank the stars every day that I've had a change of heart, or you would be bowing to my mother before the year is out."

Lord Panlington's mouth twists into a scowl. "How dare you," he says.

"How dare I?" she asks, laughing. "Which of us arranged the kidnapping of two innocent boys?" She doesn't add that she herself contemplated killing them, but her words find their mark, not just on Lord Panlington but on Cliona as well. Her flinch is small but visible as she waits for confirmation. She doesn't look surprised when he doesn't deny it.

"I have always done what is best for Friv," Lord Panlington says, his face turning red.

"Then I have no choice but to question your judgment, my lord," Daphne says. "Because I fail to see what good your rebellion has done for Friv since my arrival, apart from killing an empyrea. You think this is merely about Friv, isolated and alone and separate from the squabbles of the rest of the continent? You are a child who has been playing with toy soldiers, and war—real war—is about to start battering down your door."

"Don't speak to me about war, girl," Lord Panlington growls, sitting up and leaning toward Daphne, eyes blazing. "I know more about war than you could ever hope to know."

Bairre reaches up instinctively, shoving Lord Panlington back into his seat and away from Daphne. His eyes find hers, asking a question. *Are you all right?* She nods, refocusing on Lord Panlington.

"I can assure you, Lord Panlington, when my mother and her armies arrive in Friv, you'll yearn for the days of the Clan Wars. They'll seem like nothing more than friendly skirmishes compared to the nightmare of bloodshed she'll leave in her wake. And the only advantage you have against her right now is that she doesn't know that you have me."

Lord Panlington stares at Daphne across the table, fury still simmering in his eyes. Daphne holds his gaze, unflinching. For a long moment, neither speaks, and even Cliona and Bairre seem to be holding their breath.

Finally, Lord Panlington exhales a low chuckle, reaching for his teacup. In his large hand, the fragile painted cup looks ridiculous.

"I understand it now," he says, nodding slowly. "The rumors. I don't believe you're a saint by any means, if even half of what my daughter has told me is true, but I understand the myth." He looks at Bairre. "If we'd had a woman like her around in the Clan Wars, your father wouldn't be the one on the throne, I can tell you that much."

Bairre doesn't answer right away. "If you can see that, surely you understand what a threat her mother poses," he says finally.

Lord Panlington's mouth twists again and he lets out a noncommittal sound. "If your mother wants a war with Friv, she'll get one," he tells Daphne. "And if she thinks we'll be easy to conquer, we'll remind her why no enemy forces have dared to cross our border in three centuries."

Daphne wants to tell him that he's underestimating the empress, that he has no idea what she's capable of, but that will be a problem for another day. Right now, she has a more pressing one.

"The girl who tried to murder Queen Eugenia," she says. "The one you're trying to pin the bomb at my would-be wedding on. I need her to go free."

That causes Lord Panlington's eyebrows to arch high. "You ask too much."

"You know she had nothing to do with my wedding—you did."

"Yes," Lord Panlington says slowly. "But she'll hang for the assassination attempt on the queen alone; I don't see what harm it does to throw an extra charge at her."

"And if she didn't do that, either?" Daphne asks.

Lord Panlington laughs. "I find that difficult to believe, all things considered."

Daphne swallows. "Still," she says, "you have the king's ear. You could sway him to mercy, if you wished to."

Lord Panlington swallows the last of his tea. He gets to his feet and shakes his head. "If you manage to convince anyone that girl is innocent, I might believe you truly are a saint," he says. "We'll be in touch, Princess."

Daphne expects Cliona to follow her father out, but instead she reaches across the table to pour herself more tea.

"Well, that went about as well as anyone could have hoped for," she says lightly.

Daphne stares at her. "Violie is still due to go on trial, making her execution imminent. How well, exactly, did you hope for it to go?"

Cliona shrugs. "Well, there was little chance of avoiding a trial, wasn't there? Even if you could persuade him to put a good word in with the king, Bartholomew has his mind made up. The girl's fate is sealed, Daphne. Go on, tell her I'm right, Bairre."

Daphne looks to him and for a moment he doesn't speak. "She's right," he manages finally.

She hears what he doesn't say: *Her blood is on your hands.* Daphne has plenty of blood on her hands as it is, a few drops more shouldn't trouble her so much, but they do. She doesn't care what they say, she's going to find a way to save Violie.

"Then what exactly do I need your father's help for?" she snaps at Cliona. "If he can't stand up to Bartholomew, I can assure you he'll stand no chance against my mother."

"All the same," Bairre says, "the more friends on our side the better."

Our side. Daphne is so caught on those two words that she almost misses Cliona's reply.

"Let's not be hasty," she says, sipping her tea. "The enemy of my enemy might be my friend, but it isn't a friendship built to last."

The next morning, Daphne pays a visit to Eugenia on her sickbed, bringing a vase filled with carefully selected flowers gathered from the conservatory—marigold, yarrow, and rhododendrons. If she had more time, she would have tried to reclaim her poison ring from among Violie's things, but with the trial scheduled for tonight and the fact that Violie's room has likely already been searched, Daphne decides to take a different approach. Luckily, a gift from Beatriz arrived this morning—a bottle of perfume that Daphne supposes was meant to send a message rather than smell like perfume. As it is, though, the concentrated scent of the perfume is strong enough to mask the smell of the noxious poison she's added to the water in the vase. Even carrying the vase from her room to Eugenia's is enough to make her feel light-headed, but an hour of breathing in the fumes will be enough to finish what Violie started.

The guards let her past with little fuss after she explains that she wants to offer comfort to Lady Eunice. Given the powder Violie used on Eugenia, she expects to find the dowager queen looking as frail as she does, with sallow skin and half-closed eyes. But she doesn't expect to find King Bartholomew already at her bedside.

"Your Majesty," Daphne says, dipping into a curtsy.

King Bartholomew turns toward her, surprise showing on his face.

"Daphne," he says, offering her a tired smile. His eyes go to the flowers she carries. "It was very kind of you to bring those—I'm sure she'll appreciate them. Isn't that right, Eugenia?"

Eugenia tries to smile, but she can't quite manage it. Weak as she appears, Daphne suspects that if she'd inhaled just a bit more of the poison powder, she never would have woken.

Daphne moves to set the vase on Eugenia's bedside table.

"They smelled so lovely while I was having breakfast this morning," Daphne tells him.

"The scent is strong," Bartholomew agrees. "Odd for this time of year."

"I thought so as well," Daphne agrees. "But perhaps it will help to reinvigorate her senses and get her back to her usual self."

"Very thoughtful," Bartholomew agrees. "I was just leaving, but I wanted to let Eugenia know about you and Bairre locating her sons, that they are safe. And, of course, that the assassin we apprehended would be facing trial tonight."

Eugenia opens her mouth, trying to speak, but nothing comes out except a hoarse whisper that sounds to Daphne like "Violie." Bartholomew merely shakes his head.

"No, don't try to speak," he says, reaching for her hand. "It isn't worth straining yourself by voicing such unpleasantness—you must save your strength for getting better."

"I'll stay with her for a moment," Daphne offers. "I'm sure you have to prepare for the trial."

"You are truly sent from the stars, Daphne," he says, giving her shoulder a pat as he passes by.

Daphne gives a demure smile, but as soon as he leaves the room, it slides from her face and she turns to Eugenia, crossing to the side of her bed far from the vase of flowers and sitting down gingerly on the mattress beside her.

"My mother has a habit of making promises she has no intention of keeping," she tells Eugenia, her tone conversational. Eugenia struggles to move away from her, and since that only serves to put her closer to the noxious flowers, Daphne allows it. "I don't have to tell you that, I'm sure."

Eugenia watches Daphne with wary eyes. She asks something, though the words come out too hoarse to translate. Daphne assumes she's asking about her sons.

"They're safe," Daphne says. "Safe from her and you. Leopold was very relieved to see them again, I must say. Their reunion was truly heartwarming."

This time, Daphne hears her echo Leopold's name.

"Yes, he's alive and well too," Daphne tells her, allowing a smile to curl over her lips. "You are very lucky indeed—all of your lost children not so lost after all, and you narrowly avoiding death yourself! One might think you were blessed by the stars."

The look on Eugenia's face tells Daphne that she doesn't feel very blessed at all, but Daphne carries on.

"He had some stories to share, though," Daphne tells her, watching as Eugenia's already sallow skin turns a shade paler. "Outlandish stories that paint you as the one responsible for the mob that tried to kill him and succeeded in killing Sophie."

Eugenia shakes her head, opening her mouth, but now no words come out. She breaks off into a cough.

"As I said, outlandish stories. But stories that make *sense* the more one thinks about them," Daphne says, watching the shock and horror overtake Eugenia. "It's a shame you'll never see the northern lights, Eugenia. It was quite a transformative experience. They let me have one final conversation with my sister, a conversation I won't soon forget."

Eugenia coughs again, this cough louder, more wheezing.

"Your mother," she manages to rasp.

"You don't have to tell me anything about my mother," Daphne snaps. "As I said, she makes promises with no intention of keeping them—to you, to me, to Sophronia. But I am not my mother, and when I promise you that the next hour will be excruciating for you, that you will suffer in silence for every minute before you finally die, I mean it."

Now Eugenia tries to sit up, to call for help, but she is too weak, her throat too raw from Violie's poison. Not a sound comes out.

"The irony is," Daphne says, getting to her feet and smoothing her hands over her skirt, "if Sophronia were here, she would urge mercy. She would tell me to be compassionate, to understand what drove you to do what you've done, and I would likely listen to her. Sophronia made me a kinder person, but you had her killed and now you're left with the consequences."

With that said, Daphne turns her back on Eugenia, just as she breaks off into another cough. Daphne doesn't look back as she exits the bedroom, closing the door behind her and walking through the empty sitting room to the main door. When she passes the guards, she thanks them for allowing her in with a bright smile.

"The poor dear was utterly exhausted," she tells them. "But she needs her sleep if she's going to heal, so she is not to be disturbed for the next few hours at least, is that understood?" she asks.

Both guards bow their heads and assure her it is.

Daphne returns to her room to find Bairre waiting for her, pacing, but as soon as she enters he stops short, looking up at her with solemn eyes.

"Is it done?" he asks.

"Yes," Daphne says simply. She knows, on some level, that she should feel guilty about what she's done, that she should feel some small amount of remorse, but those emotions don't find her. In her mind, she hears Beatriz's voice, calling her a cold, ruthless bitch. Perhaps that has never been more true than it is now, but any remorse Daphne has in her is reserved for Violie.

"Are you all right?" Bairre asks her, lowering his voice though there is no one else in the room with them.

Daphne lets out a heavy sigh, removing her leather gloves and setting them on her desk before turning to face him. "What would you like me to say, Bairre?" she asks. "That I'm shaken up, horrified by what I had to do? I'm not. The truth is that I feel perfectly fine. After today, I will never think about that woman again. It's the truth, but it isn't what you want to hear, is it?"

For a moment, Bairre only stares at her. "Of course that's what I want to hear," he says finally. "What do you think? That I want you to suffer?"

"I think that you think I'm a monster, that I terrify you." The words burst forth, but it isn't until Daphne says them that she realizes they're the truth. And now that she's started, she can't stop. "And you're right to think that, truly, but I just can't stand you looking at me the way you are, especially when I still don't know what I can do to help Violie, who I do truly feel guilty over, whether you believe me or not. So if all you've come to do is judge me, please, please leave."

Bairre shakes his head, raking his hand through his hair and letting out a short, strained laugh. "Daphne, I have always been very honest about the fact that you terrify me," he points out. "But you aren't a monster. She was."

"I think that depends entirely on who you ask," Daphne mutters.

Bairre closes the distance between them in two long strides. "But you asked me," he says. "And I didn't have an answer for you at the inn because you gave me a lot to think about—I'm still thinking about it—but in case it hasn't been made abundantly clear by now: I am on your side. If you're a monster, fine. I'll be a monster too. We'll be monsters together."

Daphne swallows, looking up at him with uncertain eyes. Words leave her, so instead of speaking she rolls up onto the tips of her toes and kisses him. She feels his initial shock before he softens, his arms coming around to anchor her to him. After a too-brief moment, he pulls away.

"Not that I object, but I'm not sure there's time for that," he says, somewhat sheepishly. "Violie's trial is this evening. You don't have to attend."

"Of course I do," she says.

"No, Daphne, you don't," he says firmly. "You didn't force her to do anything—you gave her permission to do what she wanted. She chose."

On some level, Daphne knows Bairre is right. Violie is where she is because of her choices. Some part of Daphne

adds that she is where she is because of her own failure—
a part that has the voice of the empress. But Daphne knows
too that she used Sophronia's words to manipulate Violie,
to get what she wanted. Maybe that in and of itself isn't
wrong, but she knows Sophronia would be angry at her for
it nonetheless.

"You've done everything you can to help her, Daphne,"
Bairre adds when she doesn't speak. "But contrary to what
half of Friv believes, you can't actually perform miracles."

Daphne stares at him for a moment, that last word echoing in her mind. A slow smile spreads across her face.

"Maybe I can," she says. Her eyes dart to the grandfather
clock in the corner—ticking ever closer to the evening, when
Violie's trial is scheduled to start. "I need to speak with Leopold. Now."

Beatriz

Two days after her shopping expedition with Pasquale,
Beatriz gives him another mission—to attend a dinner her mother is throwing that night and pass on a
lie about Beatriz feeling indisposed, and to ensure that her
mother doesn't leave the ball that will follow the dinner early.
The latter part worries him, but Beatriz tells him he needn't
worry—her mother has never once left a party before midnight, and if necessary, he can waylay her for a few minutes
by asking her to dance. The prospect of dancing with the
empress doesn't put Pasquale any more at ease.

"Make sure to say I'm indisposed," she tells him as they
both get ready in her suite: he in a formal suit for the ball,
she in a servant's gown she's stolen from the laundry. "My
mother will take it to mean that I had too much to drink and
she'll be too busy being annoyed with me to be suspicious."

"And Nigellus?" Pasquale asks. He tries to hide his nerves
as she knots his burgundy silk cravat. "Do I tell him you're
indisposed too?"

Beatriz snorts. "No, that will take on a whole other meaning for him, I'm afraid," she says, remembering how insistent
he was that she never use her powers again. "I doubt he'll

ask about my whereabouts at all. Usually at these events, he just stands in the corner, looking miserable and glaring at everyone. I never understood why my mother insisted he attend, though tonight I'm glad of it. The last thing I want is another argument about what I can do with my magic."

"And if he leaves early?" Pasquale asks.

"Unlike my mother, I'm afraid Nigellus would reject your offer of a dance. I'm not sure I've ever seen him dance. He'll likely leave as quickly as my mother will allow," Beatriz says. "But it will be a quick thing, grinding up the etheldaisies and adding stardust. I'll be gone long before then."

"And you need to mix the poison in his laboratory?" Pasquale asks.

Beatriz nods. "It's the grinding of the dried flowers—I don't exactly keep a mortar and pestle on my vanity. They'll have one in the kitchen and the palace apothecary, but those places are far busier and the risk of getting caught is much higher. Besides, Nigellus keeps a large store of stardust in his laboratory, and I'd wager it's stronger stuff than what I could buy at the market."

"You never do things by halves, Triz," Pasquale says. "Not even regicide." He pauses, considering it. "Matricide, too."

Beatriz nods, finishing the cravat knot and dropping her hands, but Pasquale catches them.

"That wasn't judgment," he says quickly. "I'm with you, you know that, don't you?"

"I know," she says. Pasquale is with her. She doesn't know if there is a place she could go that he would not follow, carrying a torch to light their way. She would do the same for him, but still, it is a strange thing, this bond between them.

Not for the first time, she thinks how lucky she is that their paths converged. He is not the husband she wanted, but he's the friend she needed.

For all of that, though, this is something she has to do alone. There is no reason for both of them to leave Bessemia with bloodied hands.

She gives his hands a brief squeeze before releasing them. "We should go—the sooner I get to Nigellus's laboratory, the quicker I can leave."

Beatriz feels strange being in Nigellus's laboratory without Nigellus—like she's in a sea without fish or an aviary without birds. As she walks past his worktable, she can't help but examine it, noting the neat collection of beakers and tubes, organized by size and ready for use. His desk is as messy as it was the last time Beatriz was here, with six books opened and stacked on top of one another, like nesting dolls.

There is a pile of correspondence next to the books— much of it unopened, though a few letters appear to have been opened, read, and shoved aside.

She's tempted to snoop, but she told Pasquale she would hurry, so instead she finds a mortar and pestle among the organized equipment, along with a vial of stardust from the dozens Nigellus keeps in a cabinet beside his desk.

Setting up at the worktable, Beatriz withdraws the stalks of dried etheldaisy. She places the stalks in the mortar, the leaves and petals breaking off into flakes the more she handles them. Then she takes the pestle in hand and begins to grind them into a fine powder. When she's satisfied, she opens the vial of stardust and pours it into the mortar as well, mixing the powders as she makes her wish.

"I wish the effects of this poison are as lethal as possible," she says.

Nothing happens, and Beatriz isn't sure it worked. Nigellus himself said she doesn't have the same gifts other empyreas have with stardust, but she used it plenty of times before she knew she was an empyrea, so she hopes it works at least well enough.

She funnels the blended powder back into the now-empty stardust vial and reseals it, dropping it into her pocket. It feels odd to her, the poison strangely heavy, if not physically, then emotionally.

Beatriz is going to use it to murder her mother. She is going to sneak into the empress's bedchamber and mix the poison into her face powder before she, Pasquale, Ambrose, and Gisella leave the castle through the tunnel Sister Heloise told her about. No matter how many times she thinks through that plan, or even says it out loud to Pasquale, she can't quite wrap her mind around it.

She pushes the thought aside, carrying the mortar and pestle to the washbasin in the corner and pouring the jug of water over them to rinse away the poison, scrubbing a bit with a rag hanging beside the basin and washing her hands thoroughly afterward. She finds a clean rag to dry the mortar and pestle with, then returns them to their place on the equipment table.

Beatriz casts a final look around the laboratory to ensure everything is just as she found it and realizes she left the door to the stardust cupboard ajar. She shakes her head, chiding herself for her near slipup, as she crosses the room to close it.

As she does, her eyes fall on Nigellus's desk, noticing a letter that has been shoved to the far corner near the cabinet. A word catches her attention, in an unfamiliar plain script: *Daphne.* Without thinking twice, Beatriz snatches the letter off the desk, but before she can begin to read, footsteps sound outside the laboratory door. She shoves the letter into her cloak pocket with the poison and whirls to face the door just as it opens.

Nigellus stands in the doorway in the same formal suit she's seen him in at every previous ball she can remember, his eyes fixed on her. He doesn't look angry to find her here, which is a relief, but he is certainly confused.

"Princess Beatriz," he says, stepping into the room and closing the door behind him. "I'd heard you were ill."

Beatriz thinks quickly. "And it took you longer to get away from the ball than I expected—don't I have a lesson tonight?"

"I told you, your lessons are done," Nigellus says, frowning.

"But the Glittering Diamond," she says. "Has it reappeared?"

For a moment, Nigellus doesn't speak, he just looks at her in a way that makes her skin itch.

"It has, yes," he says slowly. "So has the Stinging Bee—that is the constellation you pulled a star from before, wasn't it?"

"Yes." Beatriz blinks, surprised. She asked the question as a way to explain her presence, but she'd assumed that if he had seen those constellations, he actually would have sent for her. After all, he might have put a stop to teaching her, but he'd said himself there was more for them to discuss. Why would he keep that to himself? But as soon as she thinks it, she understands why: because he wouldn't tell her anything that would encourage her to use her gift. The gift he believes is a curse.

"That's good to know," she says. Part of her wants to confront him over keeping that from her, to resurrect their argument from a couple of days ago—not because she expects that either of them will change their minds, but because arguing feels so natural to her. A voice in her head cautions her to be pragmatic, to focus on the task at hand instead of getting distracted by her emotions.

Ironically, the voice sounds like it belongs to her mother.

Beatriz clears her throat and continues. "I will, of course, exercise the utmost caution in regard to my power. I take it you still have no intention of teaching me any more."

"I don't think it would be wise to," he says, stepping farther into the room, but rather than waving her out, he closes the door, shutting them both inside. The sound of the door closing raises the hair on the back of Beatriz's neck—an outrageous response, she thinks. She's been alone with Nigellus before, and all of their previous lessons have taken place with the door closed. But as he said, there will be no more lessons.

"In that case, there's no cause for me to pester you further," Beatriz says, pasting a bright smile onto her face and moving toward the door, but Nigellus makes no move to step out of her way.

"Need I remind you what is at stake should you continue to use magic?" he asks.

"Oh, I know," Beatriz says. "My life, the fate of the world, stars turning dark. We've covered it."

She moves to step around him, but he continues to block her way.

"Have you ever taken anything seriously in your entire life, Beatriz?" he snaps. The anger is back in his voice, still so strange after a lifetime of seeing him nothing but detached. But rather than feeling frightened, Beatriz revels in his anger. She knows how to handle that, after all. She's had a lot of practice.

"I can assure you," she says, keeping her voice level, "I take many things seriously—my mother, for instance, and the threat she poses to me and the people I love. A few ominous words spoken by a stranger that may or may not have anything to do with me? That, I'm afraid, I can't summon the same level of somberness for."

Nigellus holds her gaze for a breath and Beatriz prepares herself for more of a fight, but instead he steps away, allowing her access to the door. She reaches for the doorknob before his voice stops her.

"Then you leave me no choice," he says softly.

Beatriz knows she shouldn't turn around. She should walk out that door and forget about Nigellus and his choices. She should follow through on the plan she and Pasquale hatched— use a wish to get Ambrose and Gisella out of prison, poison her mother's face powder, and escape through the tunnel in her bedroom. There is no room for deviation.

Still, she can't help turning back.

"No choice but what?" she asks.

Nigellus doesn't pay her any mind, though. He begins to pace the laboratory, hands twisting in front of him and face drawn. Watching him, Beatriz wonders when the last time he slept was. There is something haggard in his expression, a jerkiness to his movements, that she's never seen before.

"The stars will forgive me—they must," he says, though

Beatriz gets the feeling he isn't speaking to her but to himself. "Surely it is a necessary thing."

Dread pools in Beatriz's belly. She doesn't know what he's talking about, but she knows it's about her, and it doesn't sound good.

He crosses to the telescope and Beatriz follows, keeping a safe distance.

"What are you doing?" she asks as he fiddles with the dials, searching the skies for something.

"It has to be a large star," he says, still not acknowledging her. "To accomplish this, it has to be."

"What are you going to wish?" Beatriz asks, her voice louder this time, though she suspects she has at least an idea of the answer. He can't kill her—a wish can't accomplish that, he said it himself—but there are plenty of other ways he can hurt her. If she lets him.

He straightens up and spins toward her. "If you won't control your gift, you shouldn't be in possession of it. You'll thank me when it's done—it'll be a weight off your shoulders. A curse reversed."

But Beatriz doesn't see her magic as a curse. Yes, it's killing her, but it's also the best weapon she has against her mother—the only weapon she has.

Nigellus turns back toward the telescope. "Ah, the Empyrea's Staff—appropriate, I suppose," he mutters to himself. "I wish—"

Before Beatriz knows what she's doing she's lunging at him, knocking him away from the telescope and to the hard stone floor, then toppling after him. She scrambles to her feet and his hand closes around her ankle.

His voice comes out hoarse. "I wish . . . ," he says again, eyes turned up toward the stars shining down through the glass ceiling.

Beatriz grabs a beaker off the worktable and brings it down against his temple, shattering it in the process. His eyes flutter, but he recovers quickly, pushing himself to sit up.

"You can't stop me, Princess," he tells her, his eyes level on hers even as blood trickles down his face. "You can't stop me forever. And you will thank me one day, when this is all over."

Beatriz swallows, her mind whirling as her hand digs into the pocket of her skirt, pulling out the poison and keeping it closed tight in her fist. She can stop him, but she doesn't want to—not that way, at least. Not with poison intended for her mother.

"Please," she says softly. "Don't. This is my gift. You created me, remember? And the stars blessed me—blessed *us*."

"The stars cursed you with a power you will never be strong enough or wise enough to handle," he says, and Beatriz flinches at the words.

She hates them, hates him for saying them, but she also wonders if he's right. But he *can't* be right.

"This isn't about me, wielding power I can't control," she says through gritted teeth. "This is about you, not being able to do the same."

There is a flicker of something behind his silver eyes—something that tells Beatriz she's hit close to the truth of it. But just as quickly as it appeared, it's gone.

"I'm an empyrea," he tells her. "You are an abomination. And if you won't restrain yourself, I'll have to do it for you." He turns his face away from her, back to the stars above where the Empyrea's Staff is almost out of sight. It doesn't matter if his wish is granted—he's right. He'll keep trying, on another star, on another night. And Beatriz won't be able to stop him forever. He'll take her magic, take the only weapon she has, and there is only one thing she can do about it.

In a single motion, Beatriz smashes the glass vial of poison against the same temple she injured earlier, smearing the gray powder over the cut with her hand. His scream is instant and he recoils, his hands shoving at her, but it's too late. In a second, his scream stops. A few more pass before his eyes close, though his body continues convulsing.

Gisella did say the poison would work quickly if it reached the bloodstream. Beatriz swallows, looking down at Nigellus's twitching body. She nudges him with the toe of her boot, but he stays still. She crouches beside him, feeling for a pulse she doesn't find.

She doesn't find regret, either, or any other feeling as she looks into his empty eyes. She knows she should feel guilt, or at least horror over what she did, but those are missing as well. This is what she was raised to do, after all, and her mother trained her too well for her to fall apart now.

"Triz?" a voice says, and she whirls to find Pasquale in the doorway, taking in the scene with wide eyes. His eyes go to the blood on her hands from where she touched Nigellus's wound.

"It's not mine," she assures him quickly.

"I can't believe he attacked you," he says, closing the door behind him and coming toward her. "Are you all right? Is he . . ."

Beatriz knows she should correct him—Nigellus didn't

attack her. Not physically, at least. This wasn't an act of self-defense. She killed him for selfish purposes, to keep her power. She should correct him, but she doesn't.

"He's dead," she says instead. "I had to."

And even if that isn't the full truth, it feels true enough to Beatriz.

"I used the poison," she says, shaking her head. "There are no more etheldaisies to make another batch—"

"We don't have time for that," Pasquale says, shaking his head. "We have to leave tonight, before his body is found."

Beatriz wants to protest—she can't leave without striking against her mother, without killing her. Doing so, she knows, would be a grave mistake. Every day her mother continues to draw breath is a sword hanging over her head—over Daphne's and Pasquale's and so many others. But Pasquale is right—taking more time is too risky.

The logical side of Beatriz's mind takes over as she crosses to the basin in the corner, washing the blood from her hands.

"Help me move the body to the cupboard," she adds, nodding toward the cupboard on the far wall. "We might be able to buy a few hours at least."

Pasquale nods, the movement jerky.

"Pas, I . . . didn't have a choice," she says, and that, at least, is true. She needs him to understand it, that she isn't some sort of hard-hearted murderess, plotting to kill everyone around her—her mother first, now Nigellus. She might not feel guilt over killing him, but she does feel sad. He was no stranger, but someone she's known her entire life, someone who helped her, even saved her life. She's never trusted

Nigellus, that is true, but she still owes him a great deal and that is a debt that can never be repaid.

Pasquale looks at her, perplexed. "Of course you didn't," he says before understanding dawns in his eyes. "You didn't have a choice," he repeats.

Hearing him say those words helps, and she gives a quick nod.

"Come on," Pasquale says, placing a hand on her back in a way that feels like an anchor. "We've got a body to hide."

Beatriz sends Pasquale to the dungeon with three vials of star-dust from Nigellus's stash and specific instructions on how to use them, including the exact words he should say. One is to get past the guards, one to unlock Ambrose's cell, one to un-lock Gisella's—though Beatriz tells him whether he chooses to do so is entirely up to him, deal be damned. He also has a satchel full of servants' clothes for them to change into in order to reach Beatriz's mother's bedchamber undetected.

"Will stardust be enough for all that?" he asks when she explains the plan to him.

"Nigellus's stash is stronger than your average star-dust," she answers.

"But when you freed Lord Savelle, you needed your bracelet—stardust wouldn't have done that."

"The wish brought Lord Savelle to you and Ambrose. Unlocking a cell is smaller magic, and you'll have to do the work of getting them to me on your own," she tells him.

After he's gone, Beatriz finds a leather satchel hanging on a hook beside the door and fills it with the other vials of stardust in Nigellus's cabinet—more than enough to ensure that their journey to Friv is smooth. As she does, she can't help glancing at the cabinet in the corner where she and Pasquale stowed Nigellus's body.

Despite all of her training and lessons on how to kill a man, she has never actually done it before. It was somehow both easier and more difficult than she imagined, and now it's done. And despite the sick feeling that's taken up residence in her stomach, she knows that if she could go back, she wouldn't do anything differently.

Her mother taught her to eliminate threats, after all. And Nigellus was a threat.

That doesn't keep her fingers from shaking as she closes the leather satchel and slings the strap over her shoulder. She is about to leave the room when her hand brushes her skirt and the sound of crinkling paper reminds her of the letter she pocketed before Nigellus walked in—the one with Daphne's name on it.

She withdraws it as she makes her way down the spiral stairs, reading by the flickering light of the torches that line the walls.

Nigellus,

what you have told me about Beatriz is even more troubling than I feared, and makes me even more certain that her power will turn the stars dark and ruin the world at large.

I confess, I sensed there was something not quite right about Daphne, either, since the first time I met her, though if she had any kind of magic it would have manifested by now, and since Beatriz's power came from your foolishly creating her from the Empyrea's Staff, I must conclude there is something else the stars are trying to tell me. I've felt the stars and their anger these last sixteen years—at times I believed it was my own meddling that caused it, but now I am sure the blame rests at least mostly with you and the empress, though I can't even blame her for her folly—she didn't know better. You should have. Creating people by bringing down stars, Nigellus! It is blasphemous, far beyond anything that we have discussed previously.

I wrote before of the prophecy I've been hearing for months—the blood of stars and majesty spilled. I believed it once to be a warning, but I am beginning to believe it is a demand, of me and of us to fix the mistake you made sixteen years ago.

Aurelia

Beatriz finishes the letter just as her foot touches down on the last step of the stairway, her heart thudding in her chest. They're the words of a madwoman, but a madwoman who apparently has access to Daphne, and from the sound of it, a woman who means her sister harm.

It is more imperative than ever that she reach Daphne as soon as possible.

Violie

iolie is still feeling the aftereffects of the poison by the time the guards come to escort her to the trial that evening, so much so that they have to support her as she walks down the hall on shaky legs, hands bound behind her back with iron manacles. She is improving, though, which is a relief. A few more minutes breathing in the poison powder surely would have killed her. Of course, it would be much more of a relief if the hangman's noose weren't dangling before her—metaphorically, at least. She still has to go through a trial first.

As she slowly makes her way to the great hall where her trial will take place, she thanks the stars that there will be a trial at all. It occurs to her that if anyone even suspected she tried to kill royalty in Bessemia or Temarin—or even a lady, as Eugenia was pretending to be in Friv—she wouldn't have been afforded the same opportunity. But she *is* guilty, and she has no expectation of a different outcome.

When they reach the great hall, more guards are there to open the doors and Violie steps inside, the weight of hundreds of eyes on her. Glancing around the room, she feels her stomach drop—everyone in the castle must be here, gathered around a single chair set at the center of the room, servants and nobles alike, to see the girl who tried to assassinate a queen. And no matter what name she had given, most people seem to have known that's exactly what Eugenia is.

Violie's eyes scan the crowd, finding Leopold first, with a group of other servants watching from raised platforms along the room's back wall. He looks like he didn't sleep last night. She wishes she could tell him that it's all right, that as much as she does trust him, the mess she's created for herself is too much for him to ever clean up. She doesn't hold that against him.

Daphne and Bairre are standing behind King Bartholomew near the center of the room, just in front of the empty chair, but Daphne seems to be studiously avoiding looking at her. Instead, she is talking to Bairre, face turned away from Violie as the guards guide her to the chair.

At least Violie helped accomplish one thing in Friv, she thinks, her eyes lingering on Daphne. At least she was able to make Daphne see reason. At least the princess and Leopold will have each other for support now—they won't need her at all.

It's enough, she tells herself. Sophronia would be happy that she'd managed to accomplish that. And even with her execution on the horizon, Violie can't bring herself to regret anything that's led her here. Well, perhaps one thing—she wishes she'd succeeded in killing Eugenia.

Suddenly, Daphne turns toward her, eyes widening and mouth gaping open. She stares at Violie for a long moment as Violie is shoved toward the chair at the center of the room.

"Sophie!" Daphne cries out, and in an instant she is

pushing away from Bairre, past the king, and, ignoring the guards, she throws her arms around Violie's neck, holding her tight. "Oh, Sophie, you're alive!"

Violie freezes for just a moment, her mind struggling to catch up, but it's enough time for Daphne to whisper in her ear.

"Go along with it, it's the only way."

Violie's body moves before her mind can process, leaning into Daphne's embrace.

"Princess Daphne," King Bartholomew cuts in, as the guards pull Violie none too gently out of Daphne's resisting arms. "What is the meaning of this?"

Violie looks at Daphne, as eager for an explanation as anyone else present, though already she's beginning to understand Daphne's plan—Violie looks like Sophronia, a similarity Violie thought was the reason the empress chose her in the first place, a similarity that made Beatriz herself mistake Violie for her sister. And no one in Friv has ever seen Sophronia, no one except . . . Violie's eyes find Leopold's and he gives her a brief nod. He's in on this too, she realizes.

"I . . . I can't explain," Daphne says, shaking her head and clutching Violie's arm tightly. Tears are leaking down her cheeks now—a nice touch, Violie admits. She herself has always had trouble crying on cue, but Daphne is excellent at it. If Violie didn't know better, she'd swear the tears were genuine. "But it's my sister, it's Sophie—Queen Sophronia of Temarin. Everyone said she was dead, but she's here."

"That's impossible," King Bartholomew says, though his voice has softened. "Every report we heard—"

"I don't care about reports!" Daphne exclaims. "Do you think I don't know my own sister when she is right before my eyes? I'm telling you, this is Sophronia Fredericka Sol-uné, Princess of Bessemia and Queen of Temarin."

"It's true," Violie hears herself say. She's always been good at lying on her feet, and she allows that instinct to take over, crafting a story that fits in with the lie. "We arrived at the castle so I could seek my sister's aid, but before I could reach her, she was gone and I didn't know who else I could trust and . . ." She trails off, her eyes going back to Leopold as he pushes his way through the crowd. If she's meant to be Sophronia, that means Leopold can only be himself. "Leo!" she cries out.

"It is true," Leopold says, his own voice shaking as he comes to stand on Violie's other side.

"And who are you?" King Bartholomew demands.

Leopold holds his head high. "I'm Leopold Alexandre Bayard, King of Temarin," he says. "And this is my wife."

Chaos erupts in the great hall after Violie's and Leopold's proclamations, and King Bartholomew immediately orders the room cleared of everyone else apart from Violie, Bairre, Daphne, and one of his advisors. From her time working in the castle, Violie knows his name is Lord Panlington. Violie feels like everyone in the room is staring at her, staring at the woman they believe is Sophronia.

There is no going back from this, she realizes with a sinking stomach. From this moment forward, Violie will always be Sophronia. Reclaiming her true identity won't just mean losing her own life, but Daphne and Leopold have vouched for her identity. She can't reveal herself as a fraud without making frauds of them, too.

For the rest of her life, she will be Sophronia; Violie will be good as dead.

She wonders if that will ever not be strange to her: responding to Sophronia's name, stealing her sister, her husband, her very life—to say nothing of the fact that she is now pretending to be a queen of one country and a princess of another.

"You'd best start at the beginning," Bartholomew says now, looking between Violie and Leopold.

Violie knows she is a much better liar than Leopold, so she takes the reins. She clears her throat and lets her natural Bessemian accent come forth, with some minor adjustments to make her sound more like a princess than the daughter of a courtesan.

"When the Kavelle palace was attacked, Leopold and I found ourselves trapped and helpless. If not for the help of my maid, we would have been killed—as it was, she helped us escape and was killed in my place. We looked similar, you see: the same hair color, the same eyes, the same figure. Those who gathered to see the execution only ever saw me at a distance, it isn't surprising they believed she was me," Violie says. "Leopold and I, meanwhile, made our escape. We tried to go to Cellaria at first, since we both have family ties there, but we received word there had been a coup and his cousin and my sister had been exiled. It was unlikely we would have been welcome there, so we came here instead, on a boat. We arrived at the palace the night before Daphne and Prince Bairre left on Prince Cillian's starjourn."

Lord Panlington leans forward, but his eyes don't stay on her. Instead, they dart to Daphne and back several times—

perhaps searching for a resemblance—before settling back on Violie.

"Then why not reveal yourself then?" he asks. "You would have been reunited with your sister, and King Leopold's mother was here as well." When Bartholomew looks at him with a furrowed brow, Lord Panlington shakes his head. "Please, Bartholomew, it was the worst-kept secret in the castle."

"It was because of my mother that we kept ourselves hidden," Leopold says, jumping in with the part of the story Violie imagines he and Daphne worked out without her. "Much as it pains me to admit, she was involved with the riot in Temarin—she'd fueled it and financed it and arranged for the siege of the palace. She'd tried to kill Sophronia and me, and we were wary of making ourselves known to her. We were trying to figure out how to find Princess Daphne alone so Sophronia could speak with her privately, but then I heard about my brothers and I knew my mother was responsible for that as well."

King Bartholomew leans forward in his chair. "You believe your mother kidnapped your brothers."

Violie fights the urge to frown at him—Eugenia had nothing to do with kidnapping the princes. That was the rebels. But when she glances at Daphne, she catches something passing between Daphne and Lord Panlington. Lord Panlington leans back in his seat, mouth pursed.

"I know it," Leopold says, drawing Violie's attention back to him. "Gideon and Reid confessed it to me themselves, when we found them at Lake Olveen."

"They did," Bairre adds. "That was the true reason we thought it best to send them elsewhere instead of bringing them here. I'm sorry I couldn't tell you, Father, but it seemed wise to keep that quiet."

"They've been sent away from Vesteria, to stay with an ally of my family's," Leopold adds.

When his father turns to look at him, Bairre shrugs. "Leopold confessed his identity to us when we found the boys," he says, "and they recognized him at once. But we made the decision to withhold the information until we returned, to avoid rumors spreading faster than you could control them."

"You didn't tell me?" Daphne exclaims, managing to look truly surprised and hurt. "She's my sister and you knew she was alive?"

Bairre gives her a guilty look. "I thought it would be kinder to let you see her with your own eyes, instead of having to wait the whole journey back to know if it was the truth or not," he says, and Violie has to admit, it's a decent lie—not logical, admittedly, but the emotional motive is believable.

"I don't know if I would have believed you anyway," Daphne admits, squeezing Violie's arm tighter in her grip.

"And you?" Bartholomew asks, eyes returning to Violie. "Queen you may be, but you still stand accused of attempted murder."

"I didn't do it," Violie says. She feels Daphne's eyes on her, wary, and Violie can't blame her for her worry. But luckily, Violie can spin a story just as well as she can. "I did sneak into Eugenia's room, yes, but I only wished to speak with her. To understand why she'd tried to have Leo and me killed. What kind of mother could try to kill her own child?" She shakes her head. "I suppose I did want to scare her, that much is true, but I didn't try to kill her. That was Genevieve."

"Her maid?" Bartholomew asks, frowning.

Violie nods. "She was there when I snuck into the room, holding a strange container near Eugenia's face. When I entered, she startled and came toward me and we struggled, waking Eugenia up, but then Genevieve dropped the container and there was powder everywhere. I suspected it must be poisonous and tried to cover my mouth but . . . well, that's the last thing I remember."

"But why would her maid try to kill her?" Bartholomew asks.

Violie shrugs. "I expect the only person who can answer that question is Genevieve, and it's my understanding she didn't survive."

Bartholomew mulls this over for a long moment before shaking his head. "There will be no keeping your identities quiet now," he says finally. "The whole country will know before the end of the week, I'd wager. And they'll be none too happy that Friv is hosting a foreign king."

Lord Panlington makes a sound in the back of his throat and King Bartholomew turns to him.

"You disagree?" he asks.

"At least partly," Lord Panlington says, his eyes lingering on Daphne a moment longer before he turns fully to King Bartholomew. "The country will be upset if they believe they should be. This image of Friv as an independent country, one that needs no one and helps no one—it isn't sustainable. Even now, it's an illusion. We trade with the rest of the continent easily enough, don't we?"

Violie glances sideways at Daphne to see a small smile on her lips. Those are her words, she realizes.

"Perhaps," Lord Panlington continues, "it is time to show Friv just how strong we can be if we support and are supported by our allies."

"I agree with Lord Panlington," Bairre says.

"As do I," Daphne says before muttering "obviously."

King Bartholomew considers this for a long moment. "Very well," he says. "I'm not about to send you back to a country that tried to take your heads," he adds to Violie and Leopold. "But we will have to approach this carefully."

"If I may, Your Majesty," Daphne says, stepping forward. "I believe the best way to approach this is with the truth—it is a remarkable story, isn't it? Full of romance and adventure and hidden royalty—it almost sounds like a children's bedtime story. It will be difficult for anyone not to support them—support *us,*" she adds, looking at Violie again with such tenderness that Violie has to remind herself it isn't real. "Long-lost sisters, reunited."

"Well put, Princess," Lord Panlington says. "In fact, Bartholomew, I think you should capitalize on this, and the . . . fervor currently surrounding Princess Daphne. It won't do to be overshadowed by another royal love story under your own roof—Prince Bairre and Princess Daphne have waited so long already. Why not marry them as soon as possible?"

Beside Violie, Daphne goes suddenly still. Bairre, too, looks confused, though he tries to hide it. This, it seems, was not part of her plan.

"An excellent idea," Bartholomew says. "It is long overdue, and if we arrange a quick wedding, there is less chance for the rebels to interfere again. You'll marry tonight, at midnight, when the stars are at their brightest."

Beatriz

The empress will still be at the ball, but the guards stationed outside her bedchamber are a permanent fixture, though one Beatriz anticipates. She expected two, but as she approaches, she realizes there are four, which gives her a half second's pause before she pushes on with her plan. When the guards see her, she offers them a wide smile.

"Your Highness," the guards say, speaking at the same time with cursory bows.

"Hello," she says brightly. "I have a favor to ask of you—I want to buy my mother a bottle of perfume before my husband and I depart for Cellaria, to thank her for all of her help, but . . . oh, it's so silly—I'm worried I won't get her the right one. Might I pop in to see what scents she likes so I can shop accordingly? It will only take a moment."

The guards exchange a perplexed look before one clears his throat.

"Let me inquire whether she's receiving visitors, Your Highness," he says before ducking into the room.

Beatriz struggles to hold on to her sunny expression, even as her mind whirls in panic. What is her mother doing here? She should still be at the ball. This could ruin everything.

The guard reappears a few seconds later. "She'll see you," he tells Beatriz before ushering her into her mother's chambers.

Beatriz makes her way through the parlor and into the bedroom to find her mother standing beside the bed while a maid laces her into a ball gown, which deepens Beatriz's confusion.

"Darling," the empress says to Beatriz, with a smile that doesn't quite reach her eyes. "Your husband said you were indisposed."

"Oh, I'm feeling a bit better now, though I fear any dancing might upset my stomach, so I didn't think it wise for me to attend the ball—and speaking of which, why aren't you there?"

The empress snorts. "The oafish Baron of Gleen spilled red wine all over me when he bowed," she says. "I was forced to come and change into something clean."

The maid ties the empress's laces in a neat bow and Margaraux dismisses her with a nod. The maid slips out of the room, leaving Beatriz alone with her mother.

"So," the empress says. "You fed the guards some lie about buying me perfume?"

Beatriz is a good liar, she knows this, but lying to her mother requires expert skills, and a single wrong step could doom not only her but Pasquale and Ambrose as well. Beatriz affects a guilty smile.

"Well, I doubt they would have let even me examine your jewels, but it seemed a safe bet that your guards knew little about purchasing perfume."

"And you hoped they would simply let you in to snoop?" the empress asks.

The key to lying, Beatriz knows, is showing the target of your lies exactly what they wish to see, and the empress has always seen Beatriz as a thorn in her side. It's an easy enough role for Beatriz to play.

"Oh, with enough charm and the right amount of flirtation, we both know they would have," Beatriz tells her. "All my training would have been put to use, I assure you."

The empress narrows her eyes. "And what were you looking for?"

The empress believes Beatriz to be a rash and impulsive girl ruled by her emotions and prone to foolishness. She can use that against her now.

Beatriz bites her lip and glances away. "I was hoping to find the real letter King Nicolo sent you," she says. In truth, whatever Nicolo said to her mother is low on her list of things to worry about, but she hopes it will be a believable lie.

The empress says nothing, doesn't even deny that the letter she gave Beatriz was false. "How did you figure it out?"

Beatriz can't tell her mother the truth, so she shrugs again. "Unfortunately, I know Nicolo too well for that."

"You thought he would wax poetic about how in love he is with you?" the empress asks, her voice mocking.

"No," Beatriz says with a laugh. "But his lack of concern over his sister gave it away, if you must know."

The empress seems to accept that. "And what makes you think I would keep it here, rather than in my office?"

"What makes you think I didn't look there first?" Beatriz counters.

A flicker of doubt crosses her mother's face, but it's gone before Beatriz is certain it was ever there at all. "Why must you be so difficult, Beatriz?" the empress asks, all pretense of friendliness disappearing and leaving only exhaustion behind. How many times has Beatriz's mother called her difficult? There were times when it felt like a failing on Beatriz's part, but now she understands just what is difficult about her. She's difficult to handle, difficult to control, difficult to manipulate. If Beatriz hadn't been so difficult when she decided to rescue Lord Savelle, her mother's plan would have succeeded and she'd be dead.

Being difficult is what's kept Beatriz alive.

"Your sisters know better than to fight me every step of the way," the empress continues.

Some part of Beatriz wonders if her mother is trying to goad her, to make her snap. But the larger part of her doesn't care. After everything that's happened today, she doesn't have it in her to resist her mother's bait.

"Yes, that worked out awfully well for Sophronia, didn't it?" she says.

But perhaps it isn't bait at all, because if the empress was hoping to make Beatriz snap, she wouldn't look like Beatriz just slapped her.

"How dare you," the empress says, her voice dangerously low as she closes the distance between her and Beatriz with small, measured steps. "The lengths I went to in order to bring you and your sisters into this world, the education and training I instilled in you, the upbringing any girl in the world would kill for, and you are so ungrateful that you would blame me because Sophronia was a fool?"

"Sophie wasn't a fool," Beatriz says, holding her ground.

"She was, and so are you. If you weren't, you would be on

Cellaria's throne right now instead of skulking around my bedchamber like a common thief," the empress says. She holds Beatriz's gaze a second longer before turning away and walking toward the cabinet beside her bed. She takes a key from a chain around her neck and opens the lock, rifling through the contents of the drawer before pulling out a piece of paper. "You want to know what Nicolo's letter truly says?" she asks.

Suddenly, Beatriz thinks that's the last thing she wants to know. Whatever it is, it won't be good. It doesn't matter, she tells herself. She'll be gone tonight, headed to Friv, and none of it will matter. Before she can answer, her mother continues.

"He did express concern over his sister, even offered quite a sum for her safe return, but I found it far more interesting to read what he had to say to *you* about a certain offer he made the last time you spoke. An offer you didn't mention to me."

Beatriz lifts her chin. She has nothing to lose now. If her mother has known that for the last week and hasn't had Pasquale killed, that won't change in the next hour. After that, it will be too late.

"He wanted to marry me," she says, shrugging. "It seemed a moot point, given that I have a husband."

"But accidents do happen," the empress says. "Especially to disgraced heirs living in exile."

Beatriz's stomach twists at the threat against Pasquale, but she's careful not to show her mother that reaction. "And yet my husband seems immune to them."

"Of course he is, under my roof," the empress says. "It would be quite mortifying if I couldn't ensure the protection of my guests, wouldn't it? But you and your husband will be leaving for Cellaria tomorrow, if I have to have you dragged out of this palace by an army. Am I clear?"

Beatriz stares at her mother—not quite shocked, but horrified all the same. It doesn't matter that her mother's plan will never happen. Knowing this was what she intended, knowing how much of a threat she poses to Pasquale, hearing how coldly her mother can discuss this plot, makes her feel ill. Did she discuss Sophronia's death the same way?

"I hate you," Beatriz says.

The empress only laughs. "Find a new refrain, Beatriz," she says, tossing Nicolo's letter into the fireplace and crossing toward the door. "You've been singing that one practically since you learned how to speak and it's growing tiresome."

She starts toward the door, stopping abruptly in front of Beatriz. "You have two minutes to pull yourself together, Beatriz. It won't do for the guards to see you so worked up, but if you take any longer they'll drag you back to your room and make sure you stay there. Besides, I'd recommend you get some beauty sleep, my dove. You'll want to look your best when you're reunited with King Nicolo." She reaches up to give Beatriz a pat on the cheek that Beatriz struggles not to flinch away from and then she's gone, leaving Beatriz alone.

Beatriz doesn't doubt that her mother is serious about the guards removing her by force in two minutes' time, so she hurries with the rest of her plan, her hands shaking as she searches her mother's vanity, opening drawers and searching for anything out of the ordinary, but all of the cosmetics appear to be just that. Next, she searches the armoire, and when she finds the loose board at the bottom, she smiles, lifting it up and reaching inside. She withdraws a small enamel box painted blue and gold. Inside, she finds several unlabeled vials of various liquids and powders and one ring she recognizes right away—the same one the empress gave Beatriz and her sisters for their fifteenth birthday. One fitted with a hidden needle and a hollowed-out emerald filled with poison designed to knock a person unconscious.

Beatriz slips the ring onto her finger. She glances at the tall clock in the corner and hurries to her feet—her two minutes are nearly up.

Moving through her mother's sitting room, Beatriz reaches the door and opens it, facing the guards with her bright smile back in place. Only two guards remain, one on either side of the door. The other two must have accompanied her mother back to the ball.

"Ah, there you are, Your Highness," one says. "Her Majesty instructed me to escort you back to your room."

"I'm sure she did," she says, laying her hand on his arm just long enough that the needle of the poison ring pierces his skin.

"What—" he starts, but Beatriz gives him no time to finish, spinning away from him and grabbing the other guard's arm, catching him by surprise. In just seconds, both slump to the floor, their swords clattering on the marble.

A moment later, quiet footsteps sound down the hallway, growing louder. Beatriz recognizes Pasquale's steps before she sees him—the quiet rhythm she didn't even know she had memorized—along with two others. When he comes into sight, Ambrose and Gisella just behind him, all three dressed in servants' clothes, Beatriz tilts her head.

"Pasquale is more noble than I am," she tells Gisella as she ushers them inside the room. "I'd have let you rot."

Gisella looks unruffled by the comment, but Pasquale gives her a beseeching look.

"She's family," Pasquale says, glancing at the guards as he passes them. "Are they . . ."

"Unconscious," Beatriz assures him. "Come on, it's only a matter of time before someone notices two prisoners missing. You had no trouble using the stardust?"

"None," Pasquale tells her. "Just as you said—two wishes to open their cells, a third to assist us in getting past the guards without detection."

Beatriz nods, leading the three of them to the tall clock in the corner and following the instructions Sister Heloise gave her. She opens the glass covering the clock face and turns the minute hand three times counterclockwise, then the hour hand twice in the same direction, and the second hand eight times the other way. A click sounds in the otherwise silent room and the front panel of the clock's body pops open, creating a passage just large enough for a person to fit through. "Candles," she says over her shoulder, and Ambrose and Gisella take the candles from her mother's bedside tables, lighting them in the low-burning fireplace. Ambrose hands one to Beatriz, who leads the way into the passage.

"It's going to be a long walk," she says as she steps into the passage.

Daphne

Daphne stands in her bedroom, dressed in a wedding gown—this one much plainer than the two she's had before, sent over just minutes ago by Mrs. Nattermore, the dressmaker. Although the style may be plain, done in velvet so dark green it's nearly black, with a wide neck that shows her shoulders and no other embroidery or adornment, Daphne finds that it suits her. The bodice is fitted to her hips before belling out, though without any petticoats or cages, the skirt, too, hews close to her figure. Her last two wedding gowns were a blend of Frivian and Bessemian styles, but this one is purely Frivian.

Daphne should hate that, but she doesn't. As she looks in the mirror, twisting her body back and forth to see every angle, she decides she likes it. Not that it matters—she can't quite bring herself to believe that this wedding will get any further than the last. Lord Panlington will have something up his sleeve, some reason for moving the wedding to tonight. Perhaps he intends it to be a distraction, or there is someone else he needs to remove. Whatever his motives are, Daphne knows this will be another Wedding That Wasn't. At least she'll look good during it.

Or perhaps there is no distraction. Perhaps Lord Panlington took what Daphne said earlier to heart, and he intends to use her newfound popularity in Friv to his advantage. Perhaps this wedding actually will go through after all.

Daphne can't decide if that prospect thrills her or terrifies her. Marrying Bairre is one thing, but playing into what her mother wants is another matter entirely.

She dismissed her maids after they finished dressing her hair, piling her black waves on her head in a simple style and settling an emerald tiara on top. Now she's alone, staring at her reflection and thinking about who she was when she first set foot in Friv, ready to marry another prince, or even who she was the last time she stood in this room in a wedding gown, prepared to do her duty even as news of Sophronia's death gnawed at her. The girl in the mirror now is a stranger to those past versions of herself.

A knock interrupts her thoughts and she calls for whoever is there to come in, mildly surprised when the door opens and Violie steps into the room, closing the door behind her.

Now that she's out of the plain wool dresses she wore while masquerading as a servant, she looks all the more like Sophronia. The elegant pale blue ermine-trimmed gown even looks like something Sophronia might have picked out herself.

Daphne knows she should greet her by that name now, in case the guards waiting on the other side of the door overhear, but it tastes foul in her mouth. She feels Violie watching her as she opens her mouth, then closes it again.

"My mother and aunts used to call me Ace when I was younger," she says, her voice barely louder than a whisper.

"Perhaps we could say that it's a nickname you and Beatriz called her. That way, it's easier for you, and I don't need to learn to respond to yet another name."

Daphne nods slowly. This was her idea, and it worked, but it still twists her stomach that this near stranger has assumed her sister's identity. But she knows that if Sophronia were here, she would have allowed it. Stars, she would have insisted upon it.

"Ace, then," she says. "Shouldn't you be with everyone else in the chapel?"

If Violie is hurt by the dismissal, she doesn't show it. Instead, she reaches into the pocket of her gown and pulls out a vial of stardust. "I stole it from the lining of your cloak, along with all the other poisons," she says.

Daphne laughs. "If I'd made my mind up about killing Leopold—"

"I'm sure you would have found a way," Violie says. "But I didn't want to make it any easier for you." She steps forward, pressing the stardust into Daphne's hands. "I thought you might like to speak to Beatriz."

It isn't that Daphne hasn't considered reaching out to her sister before. Even earlier today, she considered asking Bairre for stardust, or even Cliona, but the truth is she doesn't know what to say to Beatriz, and she's more than a little afraid of what Beatriz might have to say back to her. She's afraid it will be no less than she deserves.

When Daphne doesn't close her hand around the stardust, Violie frowns, her eyes searching Daphne's.

"Someone needs to inform her about everything happening here, and I'm not keen on risking your mother intercepting a letter. I can try to reach out to her myself if you tell me what I need to do—"

"No," Daphne interrupts, finally taking hold of the stardust. "No, I'll do it myself."

Sophronia told her to be brave, after all, and that bravery isn't needed only in dealing with the empress but in dealing with Beatriz as well.

"You should go down to the chapel and tell everyone I'll be along soon."

Violie nods. For a moment, she seems to waver as to whether or not she should curtsy, but finally she just turns and walks out the door. Daphne can hear the low murmur of her speaking with the guards before the sound of her footsteps fades away.

Daphne sits down on the edge of her bed and stares at the vial in her hands. She can't take long—they're waiting for her to begin the wedding—so she doesn't let herself think too much before opening the vial and spreading the stardust over the back of her hand.

"I wish I could speak to Princess Beatriz Soluné."

By now, Daphne has done this enough that she knows what to expect, but she can't resist the deep exhale she lets out as soon as she feels Beatriz's presence in her mind.

"Daphne?" Beatriz says. "Is that you? I don't think anyone else in the world sighs like that."

"What does *that* mean?" Daphne responds, irritation and relief going to war inside her. "I sigh like a normal person."

For a moment, there is only silence, then Beatriz laughs and Daphne can't help but join in.

"You're safe?" Beatriz asks.

"Yes. You?"

"Yes." She pauses. "On my way out of Bessemia now."

Daphne processes this even as she hears what her sister is and isn't saying. What she herself is holding back. "On Mother's orders?" she asks.

Another pause. Even like this, Daphne can hear Beatriz weighing whether or not she can trust her. Daphne understands the hesitation, but it stings all the same.

"No," Beatriz says finally. "Decidedly *not* on Mother's orders, Daphne. She wanted to send me back to Cellaria."

"They'll kill you if you go back there," Daphne says without thinking. When Beatriz is silent in response, Daphne takes a breath. "But then, that's the point, isn't it?"

Beatriz lets out a shaky laugh. "Yes, that's the point. We're on our way to you instead."

"Thank the stars for that," Daphne says. Soon, she'll see her sister in person again, she'll get to hold Beatriz in her arms and hear their hearts beat together as one. It won't be the same, without Sophronia, but it will be as close as they can get now.

"You've had a change of heart," Beatriz says. "Did Violie get through to you?"

"Violie," Daphne confirms. "And Leopold. And Sophronia. I'll tell you more about that when you're here, but you should have been enough, Beatriz. You and Sophie before. It should have been enough and I'm sorry it wasn't."

Beatriz doesn't speak for a moment and Daphne fears the connection has broken, but then she hears Beatriz again.

"I don't think I'd have believed you, either," she says finally.

"There's one thing you should know before you arrive,"

Daphne says before quickly explaining the ordeal with Violie, now pretending to be Sophronia.

"Mother won't like that," Beatriz says with a laugh.

"No, I don't imagine she will," Daphne says. "I don't love it myself, if I'm being honest."

"Sophie would have, though," Beatriz says, and Daphne knows she's right. "Where are you now?"

Daphne glances in the mirror, at the image of herself in her wedding gown sitting on her bed.

"About to attend my wedding," she tells Beatriz, leaving out the details of the failed wedding before, her lingering doubt that this one will go any better.

But what will the rebels have to gain by setting it up now, only to halt it once more?

Daphne doesn't have an answer to that.

"Well, that should make Mother happy," Beatriz says.

"Perhaps, but only for a moment," Daphne replies. Only until she discovers that Daphne has aligned herself with the rebellion against her.

"I look forward to hearing more about that," Beatriz says. "We'll be in Friv in a few days."

There is so much more to say, but Daphne knows the connection between them is already fading.

"I'll see you soon, then," Daphne tells her. "I love you all the way to the stars, Triz."

"I love you all the way to the stars, Daph."

Daphne has spent her entire life imagining her wedding—it is, after all, what she has been raised for above all else. But she never imagined it happening like this: near midnight, in an undecorated castle chapel with a scant fifty people gathered, in a plain Frivian gown.

Of course, the wedding still might not actually happen, she reminds herself, but she can't think of a compelling reason for Lord Panlington to insist on setting it up tonight if he means to ruin it again.

Perhaps it's to do with Aurelia, she thinks as she eyes the empyrea standing at the front of the chapel with Bairre. Perhaps Cliona was right and Aurelia wasn't kidnapping the princes on his orders after all. Perhaps she'll prove to be the shortest-serving royal empyrea in history. Daphne hopes not—she might not trust Aurelia, but she is Bairre's mother, and Daphne doesn't want to see him lose anyone else.

Her eyes move to Violie and Leopold where they sit together in one of the pews, not touching but shoulder to shoulder. Though Daphne knows Lord Panlington has no reason to kill them, she still can't forget the bomb going off at her last wedding, Fergal's dead body so close to her, his lifeless eyes. She can't quell the fear that it will happen again now.

Daphne reaches Bairre and they join hands. When she meets his gaze, he gives her a small smile that she tries to return, but her stomach is tied in knots. What if something happens? What if nothing does?

"Prince Bairre, what do you ask of the stars?" Aurelia says, interrupting Daphne's thoughts.

Bairre clears his throat. "I ask the stars to grant us wisdom," he says.

"And Princess Daphne, what do you ask of the stars?" she says.

Daphne had given up hope that they would ever get here, and she finds herself fumbling. She settles on the wish her mother told her to make what feels like a lifetime ago.

"I wish the stars to grant us prosperity," she says, the words not quite feeling like her own.

Still, nothing happens, and Daphne is even more unnerved. She barely feels Aurelia take hold of her and Bairre's joined hands, lifting them up toward the glass ceiling that lets the stars shine down on them.

"Stars, bless this couple—Princess Daphne Therese Soluné and Prince Bairre Deasún—with wisdom and prosperity. In your name, I hereby pronounce them husband and wife, until you choose to call them home."

Daphne barely hears the cheers of the guests, barely notices Aurelia's eyes lingering on her with some unnameable emotion. Dimly, she feels Bairre's hand squeezing hers, hears him saying her name softly. Nothing went wrong, she thinks, no disaster struck, there was no ulterior motive for the ceremony after all.

She and Bairre are actually truly married.

Beatriz

Beatriz, Pasquale, Ambrose, and Gisella reach the safe house nearly four hours later, emerging into a damp, dark cellar. From there, they make their way up the stairs and through the house, finding the basket of fresh clothes—simpler than Beatriz and Pasquale's attire and far less distinctive than the palace servants' uniforms Gisella and Ambrose are wearing—and bundles of bread and cheese that Violie's mother and her friends at the Crimson Petal arranged to leave for them when Pasquale sent them word. They left four horses as well, and Beatriz and the others waste no time changing into the new clothes and leaving the safe house.

The empress will expect them to head north, and will no doubt set up a patrol along the Frivian border, so instead Beatriz leads them west, toward Lake Asteria. Once they reach the coast, they'll be able to book passage on ships—Beatriz, Pasquale, and Ambrose to Friv, and Gisella to Cellaria.

They don't stop until noon the following day, when all of them are so exhausted they're nearly falling off their horses. After finding an inn near the southern edge of Lake Asteria, they pay for two rooms. Pasquale and Ambrose take one, while Beatriz and Gisella take the other. Gisella isn't Beatriz's first choice of bedmate, but Pasquale and Ambrose deserve some time alone and someone has to keep an eye on Gisella, at least until they go their separate ways when they reach the harbor. They take turns bathing behind a screen, and while Gisella is doing so, Beatriz takes the liberty of drugging one of the bowls of soup the innkeeper brought them for lunch with a sleeping draught strong enough to keep Gisella unconscious for the rest of the day and night.

When Gisella emerges from behind the screen in her shift, her blond hair wet and braided, hanging over her shoulder, her eyes go straight to the bowl of soup Beatriz left on the table beside the bed.

"I take it that's for me," she says. It's the most she's said since they left the castle, and her voice comes out raspy from disuse. "Please tell me you don't think I'm stupid enough to eat it."

Beatriz sighs, holding up the poison ring on her finger. "Your choice, Gisella," she says, spinning it around her finger so Gisella can see the needle. "I've kept my end of the bargain, but that doesn't mean I trust you enough to sleep beside you unless I know you're out too."

Gisella's lips purse, her eyes on the ring. "What is your plan, then?" she asks.

Beatriz shrugs. "I don't trust you on your own in Bessemia, so we'll stay together until we reach the harbor and you can book passage on a ship to Cellaria."

"And where will you go?" Gisella asks. "Friv? Or farther?"

Beatriz only smiles. "You can't honestly believe I'd tell you that."

Gisella's jaw clenches, but after a moment, she nods and picks up the drugged bowl of soup from the table, lifting it to her lips and drinking several mouthfuls. It's only then that Beatriz realizes that she was all but starving in the dungeons. The pang of sympathy that goes through her is irritating— Gisella doesn't deserve sympathy.

"You can finish it," Beatriz tells her. "I didn't use *too* much of a sleeping draught in it—just enough to keep you asleep until after sunrise."

"Forgive me if I don't trust your expertise in poison," Gisella says, though after a moment, she takes another sip, then another. "You did need my help, after all." She pauses, finishing off the soup. "Did it work?"

Beatriz glances away, thinking of Nigellus as the life left his eyes. "Yes," she says. "Though not against my intended target. Plans change, we adapt. I'll get another chance." As she says the words, she wonders if they're true. She'll make them true.

They get ready for bed quickly and in silence, each sliding beneath the covers on opposite sides of the large bed. Tired as she is, Beatriz forces herself to stay awake. She won't sleep until she knows Gisella is unconscious.

Just when Beatriz is about to roll over and check if Gisella is truly asleep, she speaks.

"For what it's worth, I am sorry," she says.

It's the last thing Beatriz hears before she feels the press of a needle against the back of her neck and darkness swallows her whole.

Margaraux

E mpress Margaraux smells the body as soon as she steps into Nigellus's laboratory.

It's been two days since she saw Nigellus at the ball—the same night she last saw Beatriz—and she assumed he'd become engrossed in one of his experiments, but she couldn't wait another moment before apprising him of her new plans. Now, the smell of rotting flesh surrounding her, Margaraux finds herself unnerved.

The flies lead her to the body, their incessant buzzing drawing her to the cupboard. When she opens it, Nigellus's body spills out, his torso falling across her feet. With a cry of disgust, Margaraux steps back.

It's a shame, she thinks, looking down at him. Her shoes are brand-new, and now they are ruined—not by blood, admittedly, but still. The thought of a dead body touching them is not one that will ever leave her.

"Your Majesty," a guard says, coming into the room behind her. He stops short when he sees Nigellus's body.

"He's quite dead," Margaraux tells him when he simply stares at the body, agog. "Arrange for the body to be removed and disposed of. Respectfully, of course, Nigellus has been a friend and advisor for nearly two decades."

"Of . . . of course, Your Majesty," he says, bowing. "Should I arrange for an investigation as well?"

There seems to be little point—Margaraux knows Beatriz is responsible, though the how and why are a mystery. But as she thinks about it, she would wager that the how is tied to Gisella. Margaraux instructed her to give Beatriz a fake poison recipe, but the girl apparently saw fit to hedge her bets. Rather than be annoyed, Margaraux feels a grudging respect for her.

"Yes, an investigation will be needed," Margaraux says, returning to the present. She doesn't share her theory about Beatriz. As far as most of Bessemia knows, her daughters are the devoted, dutiful girls she raised them to be. That makes her think of Daphne, the daughter she believed would never betray her. But when she had her spies search Beatriz's room after she fled, they returned with a sealed letter found beneath her pillow—a letter Beatriz never received, apparently delivered after she had left.

In Sophie's last letter to me, she said that if the three of us went against Mama together, we could stand a chance of outsmarting her. I'm sorry that we'll never know if there was truth to that, but I am by your side now, and the stars themselves couldn't move me.

Daphne's betrayal stings far more than Beatriz's did, but it will make no difference in the end. In less than a month, they will both be dead, and Margaraux will have everything she ever wanted.

"Very well, Your Majesty," the guard says.

"Any sightings of Prince Pasquale?" she asks, just barely masking the annoyance that uttering his name raises in her. Gisella's job was to kill Pasquale before sending word to Margaraux so she could arrange a small escort to bring them to Cellaria, ideally framing his companion for the murder, but when Margaraux's men arrived, the entire house was empty.

Margaraux knows that Prince Pasquale would have stood little chance against Gisella—from what she could tell, he was a softhearted boy who wouldn't even see her betrayal coming. Perhaps she underestimated him, but Margaraux thinks it's far more likely that Gisella went back on that aspect of their arrangement, unable to kill her cousin.

Of course, Margaraux can't prove that, and Gisella accomplished the most important bit. By the end of the week, all of Bessemia and Cellaria will be talking about how romantic it is, Beatriz and King Nicolo, star-crossed lovers, torn apart by fate and Beatriz's jealous husband, but reunited when Beatriz ran away to be with him.

"I'm afraid not, Your Majesty," the guard says. "He seems to have disappeared into thin air."

"Well, he was last seen with a known criminal, so it's far more likely he's in a ditch somewhere, stripped of all his valuables," Empress Margaraux says.

If Pasquale doesn't turn up dead on his own soon enough, she's sure she won't have trouble finding a look-alike to use as a corpse. And as soon as Beatriz and Nicolo wed—by force, if necessary—their love story will have its tragic end and Cellaria will be hers. Then she'll have to turn her attention to Friv.

"I've also received word that a messenger from Friv has arrived," the guard adds, as if reading her mind.

"Excellent," Margaraux says, her gaze lingering a moment longer on Nigellus's waxy face, noting the gash on his temple and his open, empty eyes. Without him, no one would be calling her Your Majesty, but he's fulfilled his purpose. Still, she thinks she might miss him.

She turns her back on his lifeless body and strides out of the laboratory, the guard at her heels. A servant waits for her outside the door, and Margaraux snaps her fingers at the girl.

"Fetch another pair of shoes for me right away," she says. "Have them brought to the throne room—I expect them there before I arrive."

The maid bobs a quick curtsy before running ahead of Margaraux, down the stairs and out of sight.

The servant girl meets Margaraux at the entrance to the throne room, presenting a new pair of slippers for her to change into and taking her old ones away.

"Burn them," Margaraux tells the girl, who gives a nod.

Then she gestures for the guards to open the doors to the throne room and steps inside. A single messenger awaits her, dressed in Frivian colors and looking—and smelling—as if he came straight to the throne room from his horse.

It must be urgent, she thinks as she takes her throne. Perhaps Daphne is already dead, one of those incompetent assassins finally succeeding at what she hired them to do.

But the messenger bows low and says the last thing Margaraux expects.

"Your Majesty, I bring joyous news—Queen Sophronia is alive and safe in Friv, with her sister," he says.

For a long moment, Margaraux stares at him blankly, trying to make sense of the words he's spoken. Then she throws her head back and laughs.

Acknowledgments

I've said it before and I'm sure I'll say it again: getting a story from a fragment of an idea to the fully realized book you hold in your hands is a team effort, and I am so incredibly grateful for my team.

Thank you to my amazing editor, Krista Marino, whose insightful questions and suggestions made this a better book than I could have on my own, and to Lydia Gregovic, who helped make this book stronger as well. Thank you to my incredible agent, John Cusick, for his support and encouragement.

Thank you to everyone at Delacorte Press—Beverly Horowitz in particular—and to everyone at Random House Children's Books—the phenomenal Barbara Marcus; my incredible publicist, Jillian Vandall; Lili Feinberg; Jenn Inzetta; Emma Benshoff; Jen Valero; Tricia Previte; Shameiza Ally; Colleen Fellingham; and Tamar Schwartz.

Thank you to Lillian Liu for her stunning art and to Alison Impey for turning it into a beautiful cover. And thank you to Amanda Lovelace, whose poem "women are some kind of magic" provided a spark of inspiration for the title.

Thank you to my amazing family: my dad and my

stepmom, for their unwavering love and support, and my brother, Jerry, and sister-in-law, Jill. And thank you to my New York City family, Deborah Brown, Jefrey Pollock, and Jesse and Isaac.

Thank you to the friends who have been there for highs and lows and all the fun times in between: Cara and Alex Schaeffer, Alwyn Hamilton, Katherine Webber Tsang and Kevin Tsang, Samantha Shannon, Catherine Chan, Sasha Alsberg, Elizabeth Eulberg, and Julie Scheurl.

A little bonus thank-you to my two dogs, Neville and Circe, who always keep me grounded while I'm creating and exploring fantasy worlds. Please know that without fail, while I was writing every nail-biting part of this book, at least one of them had to go outside.

And last but certainly not least, thank you to my readers. I literally could not do this without you.

About the Author

Laura Sebastian grew up in South Florida and attended Savannah College of Art and Design. She now lives and writes in London, England, with her two dogs, Neville and Circe. Laura is the author of the *New York Times* bestselling Ash Princess series: *Ash Princess, Lady Smoke,* and *Ember Queen,* as well as *Castles in Their Bones* and its sequel, *Stardust in Their Veins; Half Sick of Shadows,* her first novel for adults; and *Into the Glades,* for middle-grade readers.

laurasebastianwrites.com
Twitter: @sebastian_lk
Instagram: @lauraksebastian
TikTok: @lauraksebastian